Praise for Jennifer Moore

'A really good psychological thriller . . . I couldn't put it down'
Reader review

'An enjoyable book which kept me on the edge of my seat'
Reader review

'Such a good read . . . It left me on the edge of my seat and
guessing the whole way through. I loved it' Reader review

'A gripping psychological thriller – well written and
very atmospheric' Reader review

'I absolutely loved this book' Reader review

'An ideal book for thriller lovers' Reader review

JENNIFER MOORE is a freelance writer, novelist and children's author. She was the first UK winner of the Commonwealth Short Story Prize and was previously shortlisted for the Greenhouse Funny Prize. Her short fiction and poetry have appeared in numerous publications on both sides of the Atlantic, including in the *Guardian*, *Mslexia*, *The First Line*, *Fiction Desk* and *Short Fiction*.

Also by Jennifer Moore

The Woman Before

The Wilderness Retreat

JENNIFER MOORE

ONE PLACE. MANY STORIES

HQ
An imprint of HarperCollins*Publishers* Ltd
1 London Bridge Street
London SE1 9GF

www.harpercollins.co.uk

HarperCollins*Publishers*
Macken House, 39/40 Mayor Street Upper,
Dublin 1 D01 C9W8
Ireland

This paperback edition 2023

1

First published in Great Britain by
HQ, an imprint of HarperCollins*Publishers* Ltd 2023

ISBN: 9780008535414

To Dafydd, Lucy and Dan, with love x

In the dark the windows look like eyes. Cold, unblinking eyes staring out into the wilderness, towards the silent trees of Dead Man's Forest and the icy depths of the lake beyond: the perfect place to hide a body.

That's when she hears it – when everything's at its quietest – the scratch, scratch, scratch of fingernails against bare wood. The same scratching noise she heard before, coming through her bedroom wall. Coming from the empty room nextdoor . . .

Chapter 1

Motherhood's all about tears – Bella knows that as well as anyone. She's done the long nights pacing the house with a red-faced bundle of rage, battling to see who can cry the hardest. She's served her time with colic drops and extra feeds, and pointless prayers offered up at hysterical o'clock in the morning: *Please stop screaming. Please go back to sleep. Please, please, please.* She's dealt with tearful tantrums and grazed knees, with broken limbs and a twice-broken heart, but nothing has quite prepared her for this.

'For goodness' sake, Mum, I'll be home again in twelve weeks.' Asher looks mortified and who can blame him? He's nervous enough about meeting the other students in his university flat as it is, without the added embarrassment of a blubbing mother in tow. 'This isn't a scene from your film,' he tells her. 'I'm not going to get poisoned, or stabbed, or clubbed over the head with a walking stick.'

The Screaming Hours isn't really Bella's film as such. She merely wrote the soundtrack. But the current image in her head, of Asher bleeding out on some dark, deserted pavement, is far scarier than any of the lurid, theatrical deaths in the film anyway. There's no need to build up the tension beforehand with the creepy *tap, tap, tap* of the muted woodblock. No need for moody minor cello

1

chords or skittering violins to bring the scene to life. It's terrifying enough as it is. But she pushes the image away and forces a smile, dabbing her eyes with her already sodden tissue.

'Don't let the killer hear you say that,' she tells him, trying to keep her voice light. Trying to joke her way out of the rising panic threatening to overwhelm her. 'It's not a walking stick, it's an orthopaedic cane. That's what he tells victim number two before he clobbers her over the head with it, anyway.' That bit was taken directly from the original novel. 'And no, I don't know what the difference is. Maybe it's like hamsters and hamstrings,' Bella adds, referring to the time two-year-old Asher came running out of playgroup in tears to tell her one of the helpers had injured her 'hamster' playing football.

But Asher isn't in the mood for tired old family reminiscences. The effort of shunting an entire carful of boxes up three flights of stairs has left him sticky with annoyance. He merely grunts, dumping a plastic tub of saucepans on the kitchen table as a passing girl with pink-streaked hair shoots him a half-wave through the open doorway. The famous Rosy he's been messaging all week on their flat group chat, perhaps? Or it could be Tilly from Newcastle . . . or Jess from North Wales. Not that Bella's committed all their details to memory or anything . . . Not that she's been casually drilling her son for information on exactly whom he'll be living with for the next nine months. Whom he'll be replacing her with. There are supposed to be two other boys moving in as well, but Asher only talks about the girls. He's blushing now as he waves back, but whoever she is – Rosy, Tilly, Jess or the mysterious flatmate who's yet to reveal themselves on social media – she's already gone.

'You'll be fine, I know you will,' Bella tells him, fumbling in her pocket for another tissue as they trudge back down to the car together. She should have thought to bring more. An entire box of tissues. It was all so different when she went to university though – there wasn't any crying then. That came later. 'We'll *both* be fine. I'll be too busy getting in touch with my inner self on this wilderness retreat to worry about you,' she adds, with another lame attempt at a joke. Asher's still refusing to play though – not even a flicker of a smile. When did her carefree son get so anxious and intense? What if that's how he comes across to the others? What if he doesn't manage to make friends? It's not only hideous accidents and unprovoked attacks that haunt her when she thinks about leaving him. It's all the other stuff too: friendships, relationships, drunken mistakes . . . Bella knows first-hand how easy it is for a young life to unravel.

'I'm your mum – it's my job to worry. But I *am* excited for you, sweetheart,' she says, risking further embarrassment by slipping her arm round his waist. 'Seriously, Ash, I couldn't be happier *or* prouder,' she adds, hoping it's true. Hoping that deep down there really is an altruistic part of her brimming with maternal pride and joy while the selfish, fearful part sobs into her tissue.

Mothers are supposed to be happy for their children. It's in the job description, somewhere between loving them unconditionally and teaching them how to cook a proper omelette. At least she got *that* bit right. Asher's cheese-and-mushroom omelettes are a beauty to behold. A beauty to be wolfed down, hot out of the pan, with a side portion of buttered baguette and a joint attack on the Saturday crossword. Oh, but she's going to miss their Saturday brunches. She's going to miss the dirty pan he leaves in the sink for her afterwards, and the unwiped crumbs and ketchup drips on the kitchen table. She's going to miss the filthy football boots strewn across the hall and the wet towel on the bathroom floor. She's missing them already and they've not even made it to 'goodbye' yet. Or have they?

'You don't have to stay, you know,' Asher tells her, pulling away on the pretext of fetching the last of his things out of the boot. *Last bag. Last box. Last precious moments with her baby boy.* The only thing left in there now is Bella's suitcase. 'I can unpack my own stuff,' he says, looping his rucksack strap over his shoulder.

A woman and her daughter cross the car park towards them, laden down with cases and crates. The other mother looks exactly like Bella feels – all scooped out and empty beneath her pasted-on smile.

'I see. Trying to get rid of me already, eh?' Bella says. 'Don't want your weepy old mum cramping your style?'

'It's not that,' Asher mumbles, although they both know that's *exactly* what it is. 'It's just . . .' And then, with a quick glance around the car park to check no one's watching, he flings his arms around her, burying his stubbled chin in the wilting frizz of her hair. She can still smell his little boy smell through the stale musk of sweat and deodorant. 'I'm going to miss you,' he whispers.

Not as much as I'll miss you. 'Don't be silly,' Bella says, blinking back fresh tears as she breathes him in. 'You'll be too busy having fun. And you'll be home again in no time at all. Twelve weeks is nothing,' she says, knowing full well she'll be the one counting them down. Twelve weeks. Eighty-four days. 'Have a fantastic time, sweetheart. Work hard. And take care of yourself, won't you?' There's a long list of other things she wants to tell him. *Make sure you eat properly. Don't mix your drinks. Remember to use protection. Don't get into fights. Steer clear of drugs. Stay out of trouble. Stay safe. Please, please stay safe.* But she doesn't want to spoil their last precious moments with a lecture.

'You too,' says Asher, pulling away again. He straightens himself up, shifting awkwardly from one foot to the other. 'Have a nice time in Sweden – I hope the retreat is as good in real life as it looks in the pictures. You could do with a proper holiday . . . away from the paparazzi,' he adds with a grin, 'now that you're a big-shot TV star.' He's referring to Bella's thirty minutes of fame as a last-minute replacement panellist on the quiz show *Music Masters* a few weeks before. Thirty minutes she'd happily forget.

'Thanks, sweetheart,' she says, knowing he's right. Not about the paparazzi, obviously, but a holiday is *exactly* what Bella needs: a luxurious adventure to look forward to after all the tears and fears of their final goodbye. Something to launch her into the next stage of her life in style. A wilderness retreat in Sweden wouldn't necessarily have been her first choice – Bella's never been that big on yoga and meditation – but it was a birthday present from her sister, Rachel. An incredibly generous present, organised on the sly with help from Asher. The pair of them have been plotting it ever since he accepted his unconditional place way back in the spring, and Bella's determined to make the most of the opportunity. It *does* look pretty amazing in the photos, and Scandinavia is somewhere she's always wanted to go.

'I mean it, Mum,' says Asher. 'You deserve a break. You've been so busy lately, trying to juggle your new job with running round after me . . . a bit of time off will do you good. I worry about you sometimes,' he says, as if he's the parent and Bella's the child. 'Promise me you'll make the most of this holiday. No changing your mind and checking out halfway through, like you did on that London theatre trip last year.'

Ah yes, the ill-fated weekend away with the girls from the office. Bella had already been getting cold feet before they left – it had felt wrong leaving Asher home alone in the middle of his mocks – and a tearful phone call from him after a bad maths paper on the Friday had seen her on the first train back home again.

'Promise me,' he repeats. 'Swear on Aunty Rachel's bird tattoo.' Bella smiles at the old family joke. It's a slightly damp-eyed, sniffing kind of smile but it *is* a smile. Asher was obsessed with her sister's hummingbird ankle tattoo when he was little, imbuing it with all sorts of magical powers.

'I promise,' she says. 'I solemnly swear on Aunty Rachel's bird tattoo that I'll stay the full week and make the most of it.'

It's going to be great, Bella tells herself, picturing the beautiful forest setting and the sumptuous accommodation. Six whole days of luxurious peace and quiet to help her recover from the wrench of leaving him, to reconnect with herself and recharge her creative batteries, plus the chance to broaden her horizons and try out

5

some new things. What's not to like? And who knows, maybe she'll discover her secret inner yogi while she's 'getting her Zen on' as Asher likes to call it. Or maybe she'll just enjoy getting back to nature, with some delicious food and drink thrown in for good measure, and use the time to crack on with her composition. It's her first proper commission off the back of her film score – a 'noir symphony' for the Scandi film festival – and Bella's determined to make the most of the opportunity. What better place to find some Scandi inspiration than Scandinavia itself? Perhaps this is The Universe's way of putting her exactly where she needs to be. That's what Rachel, who goes in for all that New Age karmic stuff, keeps telling her. But right now, Bella's place is here in the busy car park, with her boy. *My precious boy.*

'Give me a ring when you get the chance,' she tells him, bracing herself for their final goodbye. 'Let me know how you're settling in.'

'Will do.' No more joking now. Asher picks up the last box and leans in for one final peck on the cheek. A quick peck and a manly pat on the back as if Bella's swallowed a marble.

'I love you,' Bella says. *I love you. I love you. I love you.*

But he's already gone, rucksack slung carelessly over one shoulder, long legs loping off towards his new life. Without her.

Bella watches him until he turns in through the doorway. She watches the empty air he leaves behind as if she might summon him back through sheer longing. And then finally, when the emptiness becomes too much to bear – when the memories of her own fateful few weeks at university come crowding in, uninvited, to fill the space – she turns back to the car to begin her life without him.

Next stop, Sweden and a new me, she tells herself firmly as she sits behind the wheel, checking and double-checking her passport and tickets. *Relaxation and self-discovery, here I come.*

*

This is it then, *thinks Izzy.* The big goodbye.

'I'll miss you so much,' says Nat.

'I'll miss you too,' Izzy tells him, trying not to let her excitement show. Twelve whole weeks of freedom, away from her mother's endless rules. If only Nat were coming with her – if only he were an August baby like her, rather than September – it would be perfect. It'll be another whole year until he's off to university.

'I'll write to you every single day,' he whispers into her hair.

Izzy laughs. 'Don't be silly. You won't have time for that with your A levels and your evening job.'

'I'll make time. And once I get my first pay packet, I'll buy you a phone and then I can call you every day too.'

Izzy pulls away, feeling oddly claustrophobic all of a sudden. 'Don't make promises you can't keep,' she says. 'It'll start to feel like a chore otherwise, and that's the last thing I want. I'll be busy too, remember, with uni work . . . with lectures and seminars and—'

'Him,' Nat cuts in, a new edge to his voice. 'You'll be too busy mooning over him, won't you?' His eyes narrow. 'Admit it.'

Izzy's cheeks flush. 'What? No, of course not. He's my lecturer. Now you're really being silly.'

'You said you've got every CD he ever made. You said you used to have pictures of him all over your wall.'

'So?' Izzy says. She's never seen this jealous side of him before. 'You've got posters of The Voodoo Dolls on your wall. It doesn't mean anything. Besides, he's old enough to be my father.'

Nat says nothing.

'Please,' Izzy says, taking his hand in hers and squeezing it tight. 'Don't be like this. Don't spoil our last afternoon together.'

'You're right, I'm sorry. I just . . . I'm worried you're going to forget about me. That you'll meet someone else – some fancy classical music guy . . .'

'Don't be silly,' Izzy says again as she reaches forward to kiss him. His breath smells of fresh oranges, his lips sticky-sweet against hers. 'How could I forget about you?'

Chapter 2

There are still a couple of hours to kill before Bella's flight. She sits in one of the airport coffee bars, nursing an overpriced cup of tea, but can't face the thought of food. The cocktail of emotions swirling round her head – sadness and nervous excitement mixed with nostalgia for previous holidays with Asher – is playing havoc with her appetite. Asher's the one who enjoys the airport cafés, holiday anticipation making him hungrier than ever. It doesn't matter where they're flying to, or what time of the day or night it is, he's always got room for a hot toasted sandwich and a cake. But it's going to take more than a cheese and tuna ciabatta and a blueberry muffin to fill the aching space inside Bella today.

She finds herself thinking about their first ever holiday abroad, just the two of them, on a cheap package deal to Spain. Three-year-old Asher had been filled with wide-eyed wonder from the moment they stepped through the automatic doors at Heathrow. It was all so new and exciting to him. So new, in fact, that he'd clambered up onto the luggage belt after their suitcase when they checked in, thinking that was their route onto the plane. She used to tease him about it every holiday after that, until now. There's no one here to tease today.

It feels strange, after all their trips together, being at an airport on her own again. Strange and wrong. There'll be other trips together though, Bella tells herself. He'll still want to come on holiday with her in the summer. Won't he?

'Excuse me, is this seat taken?'

She looks up to see a tall, wiry man in an unseasonably festive jumper, complete with mini reindeer and trees. His tray, with a coffee and a sandwich, is already hovering over the table, suggesting she doesn't have much choice in the matter.

Bella shuffles her papers out of the way to make room for him. 'Yes, of course. I mean, no, it's free,' she adds, feeling oddly flustered. 'Help yourself. I was just reading through some work notes.' By 'notes' she means her scribbled jottings from early this morning, her latest attempt to try and pinpoint what's missing from the completed first movement of her symphony, with suggestions as to why the orchestration still sounds flat and lifeless. But 'reading' is a slight exaggeration. The notes might as well be written in Swedish for how much Bella's actually taken in. She's been too busy reminiscing. Too busy torturing herself with mental images of Asher sitting alone in his unpacked room while his new flatmates swan off to some freshers' event without him.

'Sorry,' says the man. 'Don't let me disturb you. I seem to have picked a bit of a busy time – all the other tables are taken.'

Bella glances round the café. It's filled up since she arrived, looking surprisingly packed for a Sunday.

'Honestly, it's fine, it's too noisy to concentrate properly anyway,' she tells him, hoping he's not planning on chatting. She's really not in the mood for small talk with a stranger. Perhaps she should finish her tea and go, or would that look too rude?

'You'll have to excuse the Christmas jumper,' says the man, peeling back the wrapper on his sandwich to release an unwelcome smell of egg mayonnaise. Bella hates egg sandwiches with a vengeance. 'I know it's not very seasonal but it's the warmest one I've got. It kind of goes with the Scandi theme too.'

Scandi? Fingers crossed they won't be sitting together if he's on the same flight as her, seeing as he clearly *does* want to chat. So much for not disturbing her.

'I couldn't fit it in my suitcase,' he says, through a mouthful of sandwich. Bella flinches as a speck of half-chewed bread lands on the table beside her tea. 'Not with all the books I've packed. So now I'm stuck wearing it, which I'm regretting already. It's pretty hot in here, isn't it?'

Is it? Bella hasn't really noticed. She's been in such a daze since she left Asher, she hasn't paid much attention to her surroundings. 'It's always hard to know what to pack,' she agrees, to be polite. But not *too* polite. She doesn't want to encourage him. She pulls out her phone in an effort to draw the conversation to a close, making a show of checking her screen. There's nothing new to see, of course – Bella already knows that, having turned it up to full volume *and* vibrate in case Asher messages her – but she opens up yesterday's text from her sister and pretends to study it all the same: **Good luck for tomorrow. No crying, remember! Have a fantastic time in Sweden. (You'd better, or there'll be trouble!) Can't wait to hear all about it xx**

The ploy seems to have worked. The man gets out his own phone and stares at it as he eats. Bella can see him out the corner of her eye, scrolling down the screen with a freshly licked finger. But then she sees him look up again, turning his attention back to her. Staring at her, in fact. Oh no, he's not going to try and chat her up, is he? The last thing she needs is unwanted attention from some egg-chomping weirdo in a Christmas jumper. She can already feel her cheeks growing warm under his gaze.

Finish your tea and go, she thinks, reaching for her cup. Too late.

'Excuse me?' he says again. 'I hope you don't mind me asking, but are you Bella?'

She panics for a moment. What is this? How does he know her name? But then he reaches into his flight bag and pulls out July's copy of *Culture Vulture* – the one with the page-long interview with up-and-coming new film composer Bella Burnstone.

The publicity guy for *The Screaming Hours* had organised it all, as part of a longer feature on behind-the-scenes film industry roles, but Bella hadn't expected people to actually *read* it, outside of her immediate family and friends. She hadn't expected to be invited to take part in a music quiz show on TV off the back of it. And she definitely hadn't expected complete strangers to recognise her from her photo, months later, or to accost her by name in the airport.

'Oh,' she says, recovering her composure. 'Yes, that's me.'

'I was just reading about you on the train. I'm a bit behind with my subscription – I've got them all backing up at home. I *thought* it was you though. I'm very good with names and faces,' he adds proudly. The man spreads the magazine out on the table and turns to the interview. 'Yes, here we are. Bella Burnstone, thirty-eight, studied music and composition at the University of . . .'

Bella's breath catches in her throat. 'No,' she cuts in, before he can read out the whole thing. 'I didn't,' she said. 'I mean, I *started* my degree there but . . . well, let's just say things didn't quite work out as planned.' That's putting it mildly. 'A couple of things I said were taken slightly out of context . . .'

'That's journalists for you,' says the man.

'Maybe,' says Bella. 'Or maybe I was a little naïve. I've never really done that sort of thing before – interviews and what-have-you. It's all a bit new to me.' She might have handed her notice in at the office in order to focus on *The Screaming Hours*, but Bella still feels more like a part-time administrator than a full-time composer.

'But you must have a lot of contacts in the film world now? I'm hoping to get into that line of work myself,' says the man, without waiting for an answer.

'Really? You're a composer too?' What were the chances of that? Or maybe it's not such a coincidence after all. Maybe he'd already spotted her in the café before he sat down and their whole conversation has been leading up to this point . . .

the bit where he starts schmoozing her, looking for an 'in'. If so, he's going to be sorely disappointed. They don't come more new-kid-on-the-block than Bella. Not that she's a kid, of course – compared to the director of *The Screaming Hours*, she's positively ancient – but in terms of experience in the field, she's as fresh as they get. For the first time in her life, she just happened to be in the right place at the right time . . . or rather her brother-in-law happened to be in the right place. *He's* the one with the film contacts. He's the one (with a bit of encouragement from Rachel) who persuaded his new gym buddy in San Francisco to listen to Bella's demo, despite her lack of experience. And now here she is, one film score later, finally following her career ambitions.

But it's not her music contacts the man's hoping to muscle in on, as it turns out. 'No, I'm a writer. Unpublished as yet, but I think the novel I'm working on at the moment would make an excellent film,' he says, with extra emphasis on the word 'excellent'. 'If I could just get it in front of the right people . . . you know how it is.'

Yes, Bella knows. She still can't believe her own luck. This time last year she was scratching around for radio advert jobs, writing jingles for garden centres and local taxi firms. And now her first film score is already under her belt, with an exciting commission as a result. Her first magazine interview. First time on telly. It feels like she could wake up at any moment and find the whole thing's been a dream.

'I'm Oscar, by the way,' says the man, reaching across the table to shake Bella's hand, his palm warm and clammy against hers. 'Oscar Wildman. I guess I was always going to be a writer with a name like that, right?!'

It sounds like a well-rehearsed joke. Bella wonders how many times he's made it before. She pulls back her hand and wipes it discreetly on her jeans.

'My tastes are a little darker than Mr Wilde's though,' says Oscar.

'I'm more of a sinister-figures-creeping-through-the-shadows-and-unearthed-skeletons kind of guy. Like *The Screaming Hours* . . . the novel, I mean. I bought a copy last week, as it happens, ready to bring away, but I've already finished it. It's one of those books that gets under your skin, isn't it? Especially that soft knocking sound the killer makes with his gloved knuckles while he's stalking his next victim . . . the way it worms its way into their heads when they're trying to sleep.' He waggles his fingers either side of his head, as if to demonstrate the effect. 'I think you mentioned that in your interview, didn't you? The director must have had a field day with it too.'

'Hmm, yes.' Whereabouts are you off to?' Bella asks, trying to change the subject. Trying to steer him away from any potential requests for the director's email address. *Please let it be Norway. Please tell me you're waiting for the afternoon flight to Oslo.*

'Sweden,' says Oscar. 'A week's yoga retreat in the middle of nowhere. Not really my kind of thing at all,' he adds, as if he's worried that she'll get the wrong idea about his inner calm and flexibility. 'I'm just using it as a research trip for my book. I thought a retreat would be a great place for a series of murders, with everyone cut off from the outside world.'

'Gosh, I hope not,' says Bella. 'I'm on my way to a Swedish retreat too, although not a yoga one. They call it a wilderness retreat, up in Dödmansskogen . . . I think that's how you say it. All forest walks and log fires, judging by the brochure, with a bit of yoga and New Age stuff thrown in for good measure. Not really my usual sort of holiday,' she finds herself explaining. 'It was a birthday present from my sister.'

'Seriously?' asks Oscar.

'Yes. I couldn't believe it. I mean, it wasn't even a special birthday. I think she still feels bad about moving to America and abandoning me – especially with my son going off to university. The two of them had arranged the whole thing between them . . .'

That's not the bit of the story Oscar's interested in though.

'Me too!' he interrupts. 'That's the same retreat *I'm* going to. I've been calling it a yoga retreat but yes, it's all that other stuff too . . . tree bathing and star meditation . . . and proper food and drink, thank goodness,' he adds. 'None of this fasting nonsense or gluten-free vegan carrot sticks. According to the reviews I read, the wine is very good.'

'Yes, I saw that too,' says Bella, feeling slightly claustrophobic at the thought of being stuck with Oscar for the week. Wine could well be the way forward if the other guests are all as intense as him. Or maybe this is what counts as small talk these days. Maybe she's out of practice.

'Wow,' says Oscar, shaking his head at the wonder of it all. 'What were the chances of that, eh? The two of us sat here together, both of us in the same line of work – both creatives, I mean – and both heading to the exact same place?'

Wow indeed. 'Yes, quite the coincidence,' agrees Bella. She's been looking forward to this trip as a chance to get away from everything. A chance to *retreat* from her worries about Asher and refocus on herself. But until now she's given little thought as to who else might be there. She hasn't stopped to consider the complete strangers she'll be living with for an entire week. The idea of six days trapped in a house with Oscar doesn't exactly fill her with joy.

He leans forward conspiratorially and drops his voice, as if the other people in the café might be secretly listening in on their conversation. 'You know what it means, of course? *Dödmansskogen?*' Bella can smell the egg on his breath. Egg and stale coffee – quite the combo.

She shakes her head. 'No. What *does* it mean?'

'The dead man's forest,' says Oscar, looking pleased with himself. 'Talk about creepy! I'll certainly be using *that* in my book.'

Bella doesn't quite know what to say to that. It seems somewhat at odds with the picturesque woodland vistas in the brochure. But there's no need to say anything because Oscar's already moved on.

'And what about the special guest? Do you know who that is?' he asks. 'The surprise big name?'

Bella shakes her head again. 'No idea,' she says. She hasn't paid much attention to that part of the programme. She's been too focused on the luxurious-looking lodge, with its beautiful en suite rooms and impressive sauna. That's all she's had the headspace for, really, with getting Asher ready for university and trying to work on her symphony. 'Perhaps the mystery is part of the fun,' she says. *More fun than Dead Man's Forest, anyway.*

Oscar starts on his second sandwich half. 'My money's on that awful woman on telly with the green streak in her hair. The one who does the yoga slot on that new morning show . . . Gloria Daybright, is that her name? No, not Gloria, *Glory*, that's it. Glory Daybright. I can't stand her,' he says, pulling a face. 'Still, I can always use her as inspiration for one of my victims.' He smiles to himself, revealing a stray bit of cress stuck in his bottom front teeth. 'Yes, I'll take special pleasure in killing *her* off. What do you think, a slow painful death down an abandoned well in the forest, with a broken spine, or adding something to the rainwater tank for her post "stretch, sweat and glow" outdoor shower? Acid maybe . . .'

'Gosh. They both sound er . . .' *Psychotic?* '... pretty brutal,' finishes Bella. 'Should *I* be worried?'

Oscar grins. *Yep, the cress is still there.* 'Not as long as you stay on my good side.'

'I see. Thanks for the warning,' she says, playing along. Wondering what the best way to extricate herself from the conversation is, Bella reaches for her tea and swigs the rest of it down in a few short gulps. It's cold and over-brewed, and far too milky for her liking, but it's gone now, that's the main thing. And with any luck she won't be far behind. 'I'm sorry, you must excuse me, but I've got a bit of shopping to do before the flight. I promised my son I'd pick him up some aftershave in duty free.' That's a lie. Asher doesn't even wear aftershave. He's on pretty casual terms with his razor, most of the time. But she might pop down to WHSmith and pick up a book for the plane . . . just in case she finds herself sitting next to Oscar.

'It was lovely to meet you,' she says, tucking her phone into her bag without so much as a second thought. 'I'm looking forward to our week in Dead Man's Forest.' Lies, lies and more lies. It's not until Bella's halfway down the escalator towards the main shopping concourse that she realises what's happened, or rather what *hasn't* happened. Thanks to Oscar and his egg sandwich she's managed a whole ten minutes without worrying about Asher once. The retreat seems to be working its distraction magic already, and she's not even on the plane yet. That's got to be a good sign, Bella thinks.

Chapter 3

The book Bella chose for the flight – a Scandi noir novel to get her in the mood for her symphony – doesn't even make it out of her bag. She can't quite face a missing-child thriller after all. She's too busy missing her own child. He's been away plenty of times before, on scout camping trips and foreign exchange visits, not to mention last month's rain-sodden music festival with friends, but never for this long. At least the retreat means she's not going straight back to an empty house, to Asher's empty stool at the breakfast bar and his empty armchair in front of the telly. It gives her time to get her head round it all. Not that it will be empty forever, that's what she needs to remember, even if it feels like it now. He'll be back at the end of term, if not before, with a case full of dirty washing and a head full of new experiences.

It was the same when he first started school, albeit on a smaller, shorter scale. Bella had felt the same hollow pang inside as she watched him totter into class beneath the adult-sized Batman rucksack he'd insisted on. It had felt like the end of an era – an era of shared books and board games and bus rides to the library, of mini adventures for two – but once she knew he'd settled in and was happy, the pangs had disappeared again. Asher might have been off having his own fun without her, but she got to

17

share his adventures with him afterwards over hot chocolate and homemade flapjacks. And now? Now he's moved onto bigger and better things, with an even bigger rucksack, and Bella will just have to wait a bit longer to hear about them. The time will go a lot quicker if she throws herself into her own adventures in the meantime. This isn't the end of her role as a mother, she tells herself, so much as the start of a new chapter. A new, exciting chapter for both of them.

The maternal worries that have kept her awake at night for the last few weeks are still there, but Bella shuts her eyes and focuses on the week ahead instead, swapping images of brawls in bars and dangerously drunken walks along the canal for those of the luxury lodge in Dödmansskogen. Swapping student squalor for stylish Scandi-chic décor and jaw-dropping views out over the crystal-clear lake. For steaming saunas and refreshing lungfuls of cool forest air. For head-clearing peace and tranquillity.

'Would you like a drink, madame?'

Bella hasn't been paying attention. She glances at the trolley, trying to work out if alcoholic drinks are included, to help kick off her holiday in style. And then she spots Oscar, a few rows ahead of her on the other side of the plane, sporting a plastic beaker of red wine.

'I'll have a wine please.'

'Of course, madame. Red or white?'

'White please. And can I get some water with that too?'

Bella's gaze drifts back to Oscar as the air hostess hands her the drinks and moves off down the aisle. He's in animated conversation with the woman behind him – a colourfully dressed lady in her late sixties, Bella guesses, with greying braids held in place with a Seventies-style silk scarf. Perhaps she's going to the retreat too. Perhaps Oscar's filling her in on some more potential deaths for Glory Daybright at this very moment:

I'm thinking something with wild animals, she imagines him saying. *Breaking both her legs, maybe, and daubing her with fresh*

blood . . . then leaving her in the forest to be ripped apart by wolves.
Was it northern Sweden where they reintroduced wild wolves, or
is Bella thinking of somewhere else? Or perhaps it wasn't real life
at all. Perhaps it was in one of the grisly Netflix thrillers she's
been watching in the hope that some of the atmospheric darkness
will rub off on her music.

Then again, maybe it's not wolves and savaged TV celebrities
Oscar's talking about at all. Maybe he's talking about *her*. Even
as she sits there, watching him, Bella sees Oscar pointing her
out to the woman. *That's her there. The film composer from the
magazine.* And now the woman's twisting round in her seat too,
craning her neck for a better look.

Bella smiles, lifting her glass of wine to them in a silent toast.
The woman smiles back at her – a warm, genuine-looking smile,
with a matching wave to go with it – and Bella feels a twitch of
excitement in her chest at the thought of getting to know some
new people while she's away. Maybe even making new friends.
Her social life has been somewhat lacking since she gave up work
– since Rachel moved to California, in fact – and the other guests
won't *all* be like Oscar. And the more of her wine Bella drinks,
the more excited she feels. This week away could be exactly what
she needs.

*

Just landed now, Bella texts Asher, as soon as she's switched her
phone out of airplane mode. **How's the unpacking going?** No
kisses – she doesn't want to embarrass him in front of his new
friends. And no soppy 'I love you'. No 'Missing you already', even
though she is.

Bella watches the 'sent' status change to 'delivered' and waits
for it to update to 'read'. She's still waiting as people begin to
congregate in the aisle, tugging their compact wheeled cases
and rucksacks out of the overhead lockers. She's still waiting
as the plane doors open and the impatient line of passengers

shuffles towards the exit. The fact that Asher's too busy to read her messages is a good sign though, she tells herself. It would be more worrying if he'd responded straight away. It means he must be out there meeting people instead of sitting in his room, staring at his phone. It means he's getting on with his new life, which is what Bella's doing too, just as she promised. *Promise me you'll make the most of this holiday.*

It turns out all the other retreat participants were on the same flight, although it's a much smaller group than Bella expected. Exclusivity must be part of the luxury package. It's just her, Oscar, the lady he was talking to before, a shaven-headed man in his thirties and two more people still to join them – plus the special guest who's due the next day. Bella pictures Glory Daybright striding out into the arrivals hall in her Lycra leggings and clingy vest top, oblivious to the many deaths Oscar's got lined up for her.

Marie Hardy, the retreat organiser, is there to pick them up in person, holding a handwritten *DÖDMANSSKOGEN WILDERNESS RETREAT* sign. She's not at all how Bella had imagined her from the group welcome email she and her husband had sent out – or from the grovelling apologetic follow-up email, after they realised they'd mistakenly shared everyone's contact details. She's much older for a start – close to retirement age at a guess – and decidedly less formal and businesslike in appearance. Her hair is long and grey, with a wide, flowered headband to keep it back from her make-up-free face.

There's nothing formal about her outfit either: a leaf-patterned kaftan-style top and a flowing green skirt reaching all the way down to her sandalled feet. She reminds Bella of her A-level English teacher, a self-proclaimed ageing hippy who used to troop them outside to recite poetry under the trees. It's Marie's manner of speaking and body language that surprise Bella most of all though, from the palms-together bow she made when she first greeted them – like the woman on Rachel's old yoga DVD – to her mini welcome speech about how she hopes their visit to Sweden will be one of personal growth and spiritual enrichment. But maybe Bella's reaction says more about her own lack of retreat experience than anything else. Maybe Marie's New Age vibe is perfectly normal and Bella's the one who's out of place. The lady with the braids is beaming in response to Marie's words, while the shaven-headed man nods quietly to himself. As for Oscar, he's whipped his leatherbound notebook out of his flight bag and is furiously scribbling something down. Ideas for his novel, maybe?

'I hope you all had a relaxing and nourishing journey,' Marie tells them now, drawing her hands through the air as if she's opening up an invisible book, 'and are ready to embrace your time in the wilderness. We've got a wonderful and rewarding programme lined up for you. We're just waiting for Hamar and Lena,' she adds, tilting her head towards the customs exit, 'and then that's everybody here. Apologies in advance for the state of the minibus. The heating's broken and the garage can't look at it until tomorrow.' Bella's half expecting her next sentence to be something about spiritual flames or drawing on their own inner warmth but the reality is much more prosaic. 'I'm afraid it might be a hat and scarf job if you've got them,' Marie finishes, with an apologetic smile.

Oscar seems delighted though. 'Good job I'm wearing my jumper,' he tells the shaven-headed man, pausing in his note-taking. 'You'll have to excuse the festive design, but it's the warmest one I've got. I'm Oscar by the way. Oscar Wildman, novelist-in-waiting. I guess I was always going to be a writer with a name like that.' He pauses briefly, as if he's waiting for a round of laughter, then presses on when it doesn't materialise. 'And this is Krista,' he adds, indicating the lady next to him, 'and Bella.'

Bella bristles inwardly. She's quite capable of introducing herself, thank you very much, but she forces a smile and waits for the man to return the introduction, wondering if that's *his* deodorant she can smell. It's the same as Asher's.

'I'm T,' says the man. 'As in the letter. And before you ask, no, it's not short for anything. My parents weren't particularly conventional when it came to naming their children.'

'Nice to meet you, T,' says Bella. *You smell just like my son.* 'Is this your first time on one of these retreats or are you a regular?'

But Oscar cuts them off before T can answer. 'Do you mind if I borrow that for my book?' he asks, flicking open his notebook again. 'Not your actual name, I mean, but the letter idea.'

T shrugs. 'I guess. Yeah, why not?'

'Perfect, thank you. I've been looking for something a bit more edgy for my antagonist,' Oscar explains. 'You know, something a bit more serial-killerish. He was Donald for a while, but my brother-in-law's called Donald and I don't want him to think I've used him as the model for my baddy. I mean, in lots of ways the baddy *is* based on him – they're both overbearing Scots with bad breath and a penchant for Eighties sports jackets, and I'm pretty sure he has a blow torch too now I think about it – but he might be a bit offended if he knew that.'

Really? thinks Bella, trying not to smile. *Do you think?*

'A letter on its own though . . . yes, that would be perfect.' Oscar sucks the top of his pen. 'Maybe an M. No, wait, that's James Bond territory. S? What do you think? Does S sound like someone who might torture his victims with a blow torch?'

T doesn't look as offended as he might, under the circumstances. 'I guess,' he says again.

Krista – who's been doing battle with a scarf that seems to have snagged on something in her suitcase, a proper thick, woolly job, unlike the one holding back her braids – pauses in her struggle to join in the discussion. 'Wow, that's fascinating,' she says. 'I think the names we give our children have real power to shape their personality, don't you? I mean, if you want your daughter to grow up into a go-getting business mogul, you don't call her Petal. And if you want your son to be in touch with his sensitive side, you don't give him a name like Rock or Thor.' Krista gives the scarf another tug. 'But a single letter ... gosh, I've never met anyone who's just an initial before.'

'Hi there,' says a giant bear of a man with broad shoulders and a cropped blonde beard, coming to a halt beside them. 'I'm Hamar.' He drops his heavy-looking holdall onto the floor and offers his hand to each of them in turn. Cue a fresh round of introductions, with another awkward attempt at literary humour from Oscar and yet more discussion about the novelty of T's name.

Krista almost topples over backwards as she finally pulls her scarf free – a chunky home-knitted affair with a pompom at each end. 'That's better. Tell me,' she says, turning back to T. 'Have you got any brothers or sisters? Are they letters too?'

T nods. 'Afraid so. Like I said, my parents are a bit out there. My older sister's B and my other sister's K. They're not so bad though – at least they *sound* like proper names. T just sounds like a hot drink.'

Or a serial killer, apparently, thinks Bella.

'Or Mr T,' says Hamar. 'You know, from that Eighties American show. What was it called? *The A-Team*, yes, that's it.'

'I used to get called that all the time at school,' T tells him. 'Been there, done that. Got the T-shirt.' He unzips his jacket to show them. He really *has* got the T-shirt. But Bella's more focused on the hot body smell that comes wafting out of his open jacket. Yes, that's definitely Asher's deodorant he's wearing. For a moment she's back at his university halls, hugging him goodbye, but then she pushes the image away again, dragging her mind back to the here and now.

'If you can't beat 'em, join 'em,' T's telling the others with a wry grin. 'It could be worse. At least my surname's not Bone.'

'Or Shirt,' says Oscar helpfully. Everyone laughs.

'Or Time,' says Krista.

Or Light. Or Cup ... or Tray. This game could go on for hours ...

'Hi there, you must be Lena,' says Marie, cutting through the silliness as a petite, dark-haired lady in a caramel cashmere coat wheels her suitcase up to join them. Marie bows again, her palms pressed together as if in prayer. 'Welcome to our little group,' she says, launching into another rendition of her personal growth and spiritual enrichment speech, followed by an even more apologetic explanation of the broken heating in the minibus. 'I can assure you that we place the utmost importance on both the physical and spiritual wellbeing of our guests,' Marie insists, leading the assembled group towards the exit. 'Unfortunately the downside of our wilderness location is that we're rather cut off from the outside world in terms of amenities, including mechanics, but I brought some blankets in case anyone gets too cold.'

'How long will it take to get there?' asks Lena. Bella's surprised to see her pulling a notebook and pen out of her handbag as she speaks. Not another writer, surely?

'About two hours,' says Marie, 'assuming we haven't had any more loose branches come down. I had to get Stuart to help me clear the track again on the way out. It's been unseasonably windy these last few nights. But these things are all part of life's rich tapestry. We just have to go with the flow.'

'I'm sure we can shift a few branches between us,' says Hamar. 'Or any stray elk that happen to be blocking our path.' Bella doesn't doubt it for one moment. He looks like he could pick up an entire tree trunk, single-handedly.

Marie smiles a calm, reassuring sort of smile. 'I don't think we'll require any elk removals today, although, as I said, we are very much off the beaten track. That's what makes Dödmansskogen such a special place. A true retreat from the rest of the world. Trust me,' she tells them. 'You'll never want to leave.'

'It sounds heavenly,' says Krista. 'Exactly what I need.'

'Me too,' agrees T.

'I hope you'll *all* find what you need there,' Marie answers.

Bella's not sure *what* she needs exactly, beyond some rest and relaxation and a distraction from missing Asher, but she finds herself caught up in the excitement all the same. Standing there in the tiny arrivals hall with a group of semi-strangers, she feels like she's on the brink of something. Something novel and exciting, to help shake her out of her old life and propel her towards the next chapter.

'This way to a better you,' says Marie, gesturing to the exit.

A better me. Bella turns the phrase over in her mind. *Yes, I like the sound of that.*

The temperature outside the airport is considerably colder than in the UK. Considerably colder than the forecast Bella looked at when she was deciding what clothes to pack. She almost envies Oscar his Christmas jumper as she sits shivering in the back of the minibus under one of Marie's blankets. Almost. He's busy chatting to Lena about his plans for his novel, having already treated her to his 'always going to be a writer with a name like that' line. Bella wonders whether his parents realised what they were unleashing when they chose it – whether they subscribed to Krista's views on child-naming. Perhaps Mr and Mrs Wildman really *did* think he'd grow up to be a writer with a name like that. Perhaps they were hoping he'd turn out witty and successful like his almost-namesake.

It took Bella a good month to settle on a name for Asher. According to her sister's baby book, the name meant 'joy', which was exactly what was missing from Bella's life back then. And joy is precisely what he brought her – so much joy – and he still does. She smiles to herself, remembering how he struggled to say his own name when he was first learning to speak. 'Asser' was as close as he could get for a while. She can still hear his little voice now, squeaking with excitement at the promise of a trip to the swings, or to feed his favourite duck – an albino mallard – at the local park. 'Asser's soos,' he'd squeal, toddling into the hall to fetch his tiny blue Velcro shoes. 'Me get Asser's soos.'

Little Asher would have loved this too, Bella thinks, as the minibus negotiates the rutted mud ridges and potholes of the forest track they've turned onto. The rougher and jerkier the journey the better as far as he was concerned, although bumpy pushchair rides on the cobbled streets near her sister's old house were his favourite. He'd be humming away and giggling to himself, enjoying the accompanying bounce in his voice as much as the bounce in his body. He was the same with fairground rides as he got older, revelling in the sort of stomach-lurching drops and roller-coaster loops that made Bella feel nauseous just looking at them. He certainly didn't get his daredevil side from her.

No one's ever accused Bella of being a daredevil. Choosing a university two hundred miles from home was probably the most daring thing she ever did as a kid, and look how that turned out . . .

'It's beautiful, isn't it?' says Krista, pointing out the window as she turns round in her seat to face Bella.

'What? Oh yes, lovely.' Bella brings her attention back to the late afternoon sun dappling the green curtain of trees on either side of them. Krista's right, it *is* beautiful. 'I've been looking forward to getting back to nature this week, and I can't wait to see the lodge itself. It looks amazing in the photos.'

'It certainly does,' enthuses Krista. 'Nothing but trees for miles and miles. It's going to be incredible. And the lake of course. The water looks so clear and inviting. I'll be in there the first chance I get. How about you? Do you like wild swimming too?'

'No, I'm more of a pool girl,' Bella says. 'My son always laughs at me on holiday for being such a wimp. Two minutes in the sea is more than enough for me, whereas he can't get enough of it. He's always loved the water though, ever since our first baby swim class. I used to call him my baby seal.'

'A boy after my own heart,' says Krista with a grin. 'How old is he now?'

'Eighteen. Just off to university – today, in fact. He's hoping to try out for a place on the water polo team, apparently. I'd never even *heard* of water polo when I was his age.'

Krista laughs. 'Me neither.' And then her expression changes, as if she's read something more in Bella's face. 'Don't worry,' she adds. 'He's going to be fine. Better than fine. He's probably having the time of his life already.'

'I know,' says Bella, nodding. 'It's just . . .' For a moment she's back there in the accommodation car park again, watching him walk away, the feel of his arms around her already nothing more than a memory. But then she blinks herself back to the present and smiles. 'You're right,' she says firmly. 'He'll be fine.'

'And so will you,' Krista tells her. 'It can be hard letting them go at first, I know that. I was the same when mine left home, but you'll be amazed how quickly you adjust. A bit of rest and relaxation will work wonders too, I'm sure. A week in the Swedish wilderness and you'll barely recognise yourself.'

'I hope so,' Bella says.

'I *know* so,' replies Krista, reaching back and squeezing her hand.

*

Izzy's stomach is a twisting tangle of nerves and excitement as she dumps the last of the boxes down on the narrow single bed. The room's small and cramped, with a dubious-looking stain on the rug and discoloured patches on the walls from other people's posters. It's also damp and draughty and smells of stale cigarette smoke. But as far as Izzy's concerned, it's perfect.

Her mother rubs at a coffee ring on the rickety-looking desk, still reeling from their run-in with the beer-drinking boys downstairs, and the discovery of the illicit corkscrew and bottle opener Izzy had snuck into the box of kitchen equipment.

'It'll be fine, Mum, I promise,' Izzy assures her, anxious to get to the goodbye stage. 'I'll be fine.' The sooner they get the final lectures out of the way – the long list of all the things she mustn't do, mustn't think, mustn't be – the sooner she can start her new life. Twelve whole weeks of blissful freedom.

Chapter 4

At last. The endless trees finally open out into a broad clearing and there it is, emerging from the forest like something out of a dream: Bella's home for the next six days.

Wow.

The lodge is even more impressive in real life than it looked in the photos, although Bella's not sure the term 'lodge' quite does it justice. This is no glorified cabin in the woods. It's huge, for starters, and achingly modern, with a stunning curved roof like something out of an architectural design show, beautiful stained-wood cladding and enormous picture windows suffused with a warm, yellowy light.

'What do you think?' asks Lena as Bella follows her out of the minibus. Her breath clouds in the cold air as she speaks. 'First impressions?'

'Amazing,' says Bella, pleased to be able to stretch out her legs again. 'Even better than I was expecting.' It's brighter than she was expecting too, for half past six in the evening – the sun's only just starting to set. The dark, northern winter beloved of Scandi crime writers has yet to arrive.

'Hmm, yes.' Lena nods to herself, as if she's still weighing up her own response to the place. 'It's certainly got the wow factor,

I'll give it that. Do you mind me asking what drew you to this particular retreat? Was it the location or the activity programme? I'm writing a review for a travel magazine,' she adds. 'Sorry, I probably should have mentioned that up front.'

'Oh I see. That's exciting,' says Bella. That explains the notebook, then. Not another novelist after all. 'It was actually a present from my sister, so the decision was already made for me.' But before she can elaborate, the huge front door of the lodge opens and a tall, bald man in a collarless white shirt steps out onto the gravel clutching a gong. Not exactly the greeting Bella was expecting at the end of a two-hour minibus ride, but there's a first time for everything.

BONG. The noise, when he strikes it with his beater, reverberates around the clearing, sending birds squawking up out of the trees. Bella can feel it reverberating inside her own chest too. *BONG.*

'*Välkommen till ert hem för veckan,*' the man announces to the assembled group with a theatrical flourish of his beater. '*Varmt välkommen till er alla.*'

Krista bursts into spontaneous applause and everyone else follows suit. 'I love it!' she enthuses. 'Talk about an impressive entrance! What does it mean?' she asks, turning to Marie.

'Welcome to the house of doom,' Hamar cuts in before Marie can reply, his voice low and dramatic like something out of a film trailer. 'Only kidding,' he adds with a grin, seeing Krista's shocked expression. 'It means a warm welcome to you all. My mother's Swedish,' he explains. 'I still understand the odd phrase although I'm a bit rusty these days.'

'*Underbar,*' says Marie softly, placing her palms together. 'Wonderful. This will be like a homecoming for you then.'

'*Underbar,*' echoes Krista, repeating it under her breath as if she's trying to commit it to memory. '*Underbar . . . underbar . . .* And what was the other one again? *Velkommen till . . .* no, it's no good, I've forgotten already! Perhaps you can teach me some more over dinner?'

'I'm still learning myself,' says Marie, modestly. 'Life's all about learning, don't you think? And here comes *my* teacher,' she adds, as the man with the gong heads over to join them. Not that he's holding the gong any more. 'I'd like you to meet my husband and fellow host, Stuart. When I first came here as a guest myself, just over five years ago, I was in a dark place emotionally, but with Stuart's help and guidance, and the transforming spiritual energy of nature in this wonderful place, I managed to turn things around again.'

Krista beams. 'And then you married him! Aw, that's so lovely. Good on you, Stuart.'

'Thank you,' says Stuart, smiling back at her. His voice is low and soothing. 'Welcome one and all. I'd just like to reassure you, before we go any further, that marrying me is not a compulsory part of the Dödmansskogen experience!'

Hamar lets out a loud guffaw of laughter. 'Phew! Pleased to hear it. No offence, Stu, you're not really my type though!'

'But I hope the beautiful setting and our carefully thought-out programme of events will work their magic on you all the same over the course of our time together,' Stuart finishes.

'You're *both* fully trained therapists though, right?' interrupts Lena, looking to Marie for confirmation.

'Yes, of course,' says Marie. 'I'd be very happy to show you my certification.'

'No, no, that's fine. Just checking.'

'Marie's also a qualified doctor,' says Stuart, with obvious pride. 'Although I'm pleased to report that we've not had any need of her medical expertise yet, beyond the odd insect bite. But perhaps we can carry on our introductions inside? You must all be cold and thirsty after your trial by broken minibus and we've got a nice log fire and some Swedish glögg waiting for you in our main reception room.'

'Glögg? That's like mulled wine, isn't it?' says Krista, shouting to make herself heard over the clatter of suitcase wheels on gravel.

'Very similar, yes,' replies Stuart, 'but with raisins and blanched almonds. You'll have to ask our resident chef, Saga, for the precise recipe. All I know is it's absolutely delicious.'

'I shall make a point of doing just that,' says Hamar. 'I've always wanted my own resident chef. Do I get to keep her at the end of the week?'

Everyone laughs. It feels like people are starting to relax into one another's company a little bit now, the initial awkwardness at the airport easing into something more companionable. Perhaps by the end of the week they'll feel like proper friends.

Bella follows the others through the impressive doorway into a bright, welcoming entrance area, with built-in shoe racks and a row of wall-mounted coat pegs shaped like wooden reindeer antlers. *Mmm, something smells good*, she thinks hungrily: a sweet, spiced cinnamon and cardamom sort of smell – that must be the famous glögg Stuart was telling them about – and a richer, darker scent of something savoury and meaty bubbling away underneath it. *Dinner, hopefully.* Her Sunday morning breakfast of homemade lemon and poppy seed muffins, forced down in the service station car park with Asher after their ridiculously early start, feels like half a lifetime ago now. No wonder her stomach's starting to rumble.

She's been looking forward to trying out some Scandinavian cuisine while she's here and broadening her culinary horizons. Her current knowledge of Swedish food is pretty much limited to what they serve in the IKEA café. Meatballs are Asher's favourite – he insists on buying a bag for the freezer every time they go, along with those packets of powdered sauce and the lingonberry jam. And a Daim bar cake, of course. Bella smiles to herself, recalling their last visit to the store: the official pre-university trip. Asher had such set ideas about what he wanted, much to her surprise, from the colour of his mugs to the size of his frying pan. 'I've got to be able to cook omelettes *and* pancakes in it,' he'd explained, as if they were the only kinds of food he planned on cooking.

But he must have guessed what she was thinking – he's always been good at reading her, at second-guessing what she's going to say – because he'd grinned his dimple-cheeked grin and told her not to worry. 'I'll be eating other stuff too,' he said, 'like takeaways and chocolate.'

The chic Scandi-style main reception room is also impressive, with its natural oak flooring and crisp white walls featuring arty-looking prints and floating shelves filled with trailing houseplants and a row of red Dala horses. But it's the warm glow of the fire that draws Bella's attention, and the smiling blonde girl with the tray of steaming mugs, standing beside it. The scene is a welcome contrast to the coldness of the forest outside – a coldness that seems to have crept into Bella's bones during the long minibus ride through the endless, endless trees.

'Hello,' says the girl. 'Welcome to Dödmansskogen. I'm Rosel. Please help yourself to a warming drink and make yourself at home.'

'That sounds heavenly, thank you,' says Krista. She parks her case in the corner of the room and takes a mug, closing her eyes as she inhales the fragrant steam coming off it, her face a picture of pure contentment. 'I've been looking forward to this for so long. Coming here, I mean,' she adds, 'not just the glögg!'

'Me too,' agrees T, joining her by the fire. 'It's been a seriously crap eighteen months. I'm talking splitting up with my partner of six years and being told I've got cancer level of crap. As for work . . . well, let's just say this trip couldn't have come at a better time.'

'Oh T, I'm so sorry,' says Krista, laying her hand on his arm. 'I hope you find what you're looking for here.'

'I hope you *all* find what you need to move forward on your personal healing journey,' says Marie.

It sounds a bit full-on to Bella's ears – the sort of New Age speak her mother would have dismissed as heathen nonsense. But then her mother was nothing if not blinkered in her views,

32

and Bella's in no hurry to take after her. Besides, she promised Asher she'd make the most of her time here, which means keeping an open mind. So she smiles and nods along with the others, trying to ignore the embarrassing growling noise coming from her stomach.

'I've already got what *I* need,' jokes Hamar, reaching for a mug of glögg and holding it up in the air like a trophy, before passing it on to Oscar, who's been surprisingly quiet since they arrived. 'Here,' he says, 'you look like you could do with one of these too. Been a long day, has it?'

'Me? No, no, I'm fine, thank you,' Oscar tells him. 'Never better. I was just pondering what poison would go best with mulled wine . . .'

But Hamar's already moved on, taking the entire tray from Rosel this time and dishing out the remaining drinks himself.

'Oh,' says Rosel, looking flustered. 'I could have done that but thank you.'

'Here's to us *all* finding what we're looking for,' Hamar booms. 'Cheers, everyone! *Skål!*'

'Cheers,' Bella echoes, holding her own mug aloft. *To an open mind and a new chapter,* she promises herself, taking a tentative sip of the still-steaming glögg. It's hot and sweet, but not too sweet, with just the right balance of spice and a nice alcoholic kick. *Delicious.*

She drinks to Asher, hoping he's settled in with his new flatmates. Praying that he's doing okay. She drinks to her new companions: to kind-hearted Krista and larger-than-life Hamar; to poor, beleaguered T, who smells just like her son; and to Dödmansskogen's resident scribes, Lena and Oscar. She drinks to her half-finished symphony and the next exciting stage in her career, the heady combination of hot wine – and brandy too perhaps, is that what she can taste? – and an empty stomach making her warm and woozy. *Cheers.*

Bella's still trying to coax the blanched almonds and raisins out from the bottom of her mug when Marie and Stuart start dishing out room keys.

'And last but not least, here's yours,' says Marie, handing Bella a silver Yale key. 'Number thirteen. Last room on the left,' she adds, pointing down one of the corridors leading off the main room. 'As your booking was a birthday present, you'll be in one of our superior suites.'

'Wow, thank you,' says Bella. 'I thought you'd be saving that for Lena if she's writing a review of the place?'

Marie smiles. 'That's what Stuart suggested too, but I think it's more important she gets an authentic experience. As Ralph Waldo Emerson said, "To be yourself in a world that is constantly trying to make you something else is the greatest accomplishment." Which means that until our special celebrity guest arrives, you'll have the whole wing to yourself.'

'I feel honoured,' Bella jokes. 'And when will we find out who this special guest is?'

'Not just yet, I'm afraid. It's hard keeping it a secret as I know you're going to love them, but some things are worth waiting for. Don't you think?' An answer, it would seem, *isn't* one of the things worth waiting for however. Marie's already moved on to offers of spare towels and toiletries along with details of the map, torch and itinerary Bella will find on her desk. 'We've got a great programme lined up for you.'

'I'm looking forward to it.'

'Wonderful,' says Marie. 'I'm looking forward to sharing in your growth and learning journey with you. Dinner's at eight. I hope you're hungry.'

*

'Hungry' is putting it mildly. Now that she's finally here, with all the stresses of the long day behind her and the enticing smell of dinner drifting down the corridor, Bella finds herself consumed with hunger. Her stomach is rumbling louder than ever as she sits down on the bed – the exquisitely comfortable king-sized bed, with a complimentary eye mask and organic lavender sleep balm waiting on her pillow – and gazes round at her opulent living quarters. The spacious room is chic and modern, with a designer-looking oak desk and chair, a smart curved sofa upholstered in a bright, flowered Marimekko-style fabric, one of those fancy coffee machines with the pods that come in their own presentation box, and an enormous window, with breathtaking views out to the trees beyond. *As if there was anything else to see,* Bella thinks, with a wry smile. The photographic feature wall behind her is filled with trees too – they're everywhere!

She checks her phone again – still no reply from Asher and no signal either by the looks of it – before making herself a cup of tea and polishing off an entire plate of complimentary *pepparkaka*. She recognises them from IKEA too, although these ones taste homemade – the lodge's private chef has clearly been busy. And then, once the *pepparkaka* have all gone, she starts on the emergency muesli bars from the bottom of her suitcase. Taking her own food on holiday stems from travels with Asher when he was little. When he was fussier and more prone to whining, and a well-timed snack could make all the difference between a nice afternoon out and a miserable one. Old habits die hard though and even now Bella never goes anywhere without an emergency cereal bar or a zip bag of nuts and raisins. It's a good job too, under the circumstances. The sugar hit is exactly what she needs.

She glances through the week's itinerary as she eats, wondering what 'shinrin-yoku' is. Something Japanese maybe? And what about 'guilt-purging'? It makes her think of coffee enemas, for some reason. 'Lake swimming' is less of a mystery, although she might leave that one to Krista. It sounds a little chilly for Bella's liking. She was hoping for a proper heated indoor pool – a luxury one with special lights and relaxing music like at that day spa she went to with Rachel for her thirtieth birthday – but there's no mention of that on the information sheet. There's the sauna, down in the basement, but no pool. Bella shrugs off her disappointment, conscious of how much thought (and money) her sister has put into getting her here. The last thing she wants to be is ungrateful.

She reads on, licking at a stray crumb of muesli bar on her bottom lip. Wednesday's 'aromatherapy tapping' sounds more like her cup of tea. She loved the essential oils candle Asher gave her for Christmas, and the fresh scent really did help focus her mind when she was working on her score. Bella's not quite sure what the tapping part is but she'll find out when she gets there . . . after she's finished her gong bathing, whatever that is.

Her phone buzzes in her pocket, pushing aside all thoughts of gongs and saunas. *Asher!*

But it's not Asher. It's not anyone. It's an automated message from her phone provider welcoming her to Sweden. The reception can't be very good out here full stop, if the text has taken all this time to arrive. And as for the 4G signal – well, there *is* no signal. Bella tries fiddling with the data roaming settings, turning her phone off and on again, but there's still nothing. What if Asher's been trying to reach her and can't get through? She didn't see anything on the information sheet about a Wi-Fi code for guests, but there must be one, surely? She'll have to remember to ask Marie at dinner.

Bella changes her top and cleans her teeth, dragging her fingers through the mess of her hair as she surveys her weary-looking reflection in the bathroom mirror. Too many sleepless nights in the run-up to Asher leaving have clearly taken their toll. Her skin looks dry and dull, and the bags under her eyes are a fetching shade of charcoal. But that's okay. It's what she's here for, after all – to recharge. To reset.

Tomorrow will be better. That's what she tells Asher when he's having a rough time of it. When he's disappointed with a test result, or his latest crush starts going out with someone else.

Gone are the days when Bella could magic it all better with a mere kiss, or turn hot tears of frustration into shrieks of laughter with a well-timed tickle, but she does her best. *Tomorrow will be better*, she tells her reflection. *You'll see.* And maybe it's the glögg and the sugary food talking, or perhaps the retreat is starting to work its magic already, because her reflection smiles right back at her, tired eyes lifting up at the corners. 'Tomorrow's going to be great,' she says out loud.

*

Izzy drinks in the throbbing buzz of noise in the lecture theatre as everyone takes their seats, grinning to herself through the fog of her first proper hangover. She's finally free. Free to go to parties and drink dubious amounts of cheap alcohol. Free to stay out as late as she wants. Free to spend time with her boyfriend without having to lie about it. Not that she'll be spending much time with Nat now, of course, with two hundred miles separating them. She hasn't even had time to answer his last letter . . . or the one before that . . .

Izzy feels a brief pang of guilt as she pictures him rushing down the stairs to check the post. Imagining his disappointed expression when she realises she still hasn't replied. But then the babble of voices in the lecture theatre suddenly goes quiet, and Izzy forgets all about Nat. She forgets about everything, save for the tall, dark-haired man striding across the front of the theatre towards the lectern, with the confident hip swagger of a rock star.

It's him, her old teenage crush, Ludwell Storm, with an emphasis on 'old'. Much too old for her. Not that she's interested anyway. She's got Nat now. But the heart Izzy's doodling across the top of her file pad tells another story, as does the peculiar somersaulting feeling in her stomach.

That face, she thinks, admiring the dark eyes and chiselled jawline.

Those hands, she thinks, remembering the way his fingers used to dart across the strings during his virtuoso days. Remembering the sheer power of his vibrato.

That voice, *she thinks as he welcomes his spellbound students to their first lecture, his smooth, rich tones resonating round the hall. Oh, that voice.*

Chapter 5

The candlelit dinner is every bit as tasty as it smells: a rich beef stew called *kalops*, served with potatoes and pickled beetroot, for everyone except Lena, who doesn't eat red meat. Her vegetable stew looks anaemic by comparison, but she pronounces it delicious all the same.

Stuart looks pleased, and possibly a little relieved? It must add a certain pressure, knowing one of his guests will be sharing their experience of the retreat – good or bad – with their entire readership. But then again, perhaps it comes with the territory, along with Tripadvisor reviews. Everyone's a critic these days, after all. Or perhaps he and Marie are too busy living in the present to concern themselves with trivial future concerns.

It's hard to believe, watching her, that Marie's only been working here a year. Now that Bella's got over her initial surprise, she can see how perfectly Marie fits the retreat host role, from her long, loose hair, hippy-style clothes and jangling silver charm bracelet, to the peculiar grace she had them all recite before dinner: *Let us give thanks to the bounty of the universe for bringing us sustenance and togetherness.* It was all Bella could do to stop herself from saying 'Amen' at the end.

'So,' Stuart says now, addressing the assembled guests, 'what brings you to Dödmansskogen?'

There's a slight pause, as if they're all expecting someone else to answer first. Or perhaps some reasons are too personal to share. But then Oscar breaks the awkwardness with an unashamed, 'Murder.'

Rosel, who's refilling Hamar's empty wineglass for him, lets out an audible gasp, dark wine spilling onto the crisp white tablecloth. 'Oh! Oh no, I'm so sorry,' she says, her face already red with embarrassment.

Hamar simply laughs, placing his bear-like hand over the back of hers and telling her not to worry. Telling her he'll protect her from Oscar's murderous impulses.

'No harm done,' adds Krista, swooping in with her own glass of white wine and tipping some onto the offending stain before dabbing it with her napkin. 'These things happen. And don't take any notice of Oscar, he's only here to *write* about murder, not commit it.'

'Yes, sorry,' says Oscar. 'I should have explained. I'm writing a thriller set in a remote retreat in the woods. I only kill with my words though.'

Hamar puts on his deep film trailer voice again: 'Some men kill with guns and knives,' he booms. 'Some kill with their bare hands. But Oscar Wildman does it with words.'

'Oh,' says Rosel, her blush deepening. 'I see. Sorry,' she says again, although Bella's not sure if the apology is aimed at Oscar or Hamar as she pulls her hand away from his.

'Well, I'm here thanks to a surprise present from my sister,' Bella announces, trying to change the subject and spare the girl any more embarrassment, 'with a little behind-the-scenes help from my scheming son. It turns out the two of them have been plotting together for months.'

'Ah, how lovely,' says Krista. 'And what a fantastic present!'

Bella nods. 'It's not something I'd ever think of booking myself either, which makes it even more special in a way.'

Marie's nodding too. 'The universe has a way of putting us exactly where we need to be,' she says. 'Even if we don't always recognise it at the time.'

'Do you mind if I jot that down?' asks Lena, pulling out her notebook. 'For anyone who doesn't already know, I'm here in a professional capacity, writing a feature review for my magazine. But I'm also here as a fellow guest, so please do let me know if anything I'm doing makes you at all uncomfortable. I wouldn't want anyone feeling like they're under observation,' she adds, with a sideways glance at T. 'That's not what this is about.'

Marie makes a flowing gesture with her hands, her charm bracelet jingling as she turns her palms up to the ceiling. 'Thank you for your honesty and openness, Lena. We're delighted to have you. I hope you find everything you're looking for, and more, here at Dödmansskogen.'

'Well I'm here for the food and drink,' says Hamar, through a mouthful of *kalops*. 'For a week with your wonderful chef. And the more of this delicious wine the universe provides me with, the better. A toast to our gracious hosts,' he adds, lifting his glass. 'To Stuart and Marie.'

'To Stuart and Marie!' Bella takes another swig of her wine along with everyone else.

'To Rosel and Saga!' adds Hamar. '*Skål!*'

'To Rosel and Saga!'

Hamar's on a roll now. 'And to the universe for bringing us all together,' he calls. Bella can't decide if he's being serious or not, but she drinks again all the same.

'As I said, me and the universe haven't been getting on too well lately,' pipes up T. 'But I'm glad it's brought me here. A bit of time out from all the shit that's been going on in my life – excuse my language – and the chance to reset. That's what I'm hoping for.'

'Time out from our troubles,' says Krista softly. 'Yes, I like the sound of that. The chance to escape our demons.' It's hard to imagine such a seemingly open, cheerful lady battling any inner demons, but she doesn't elaborate. And then the conversation moves on, or rather Oscar hijacks it by asking everyone where they think the best place to hide a body would be at a place like this. The suggestions start sensibly enough – a shallow grave in the woods; weighted down with stones at the bottom of the lake – but grow ever more elaborate and ridiculous as the group's wineglasses are drained and refilled. Every time Bella turns round it seems Rosel is back with another top-up, and by the time the plates are cleared away, she feels decidedly tipsy. A glance around the table tells her she's not the only one either. But it feels nice – it feels like everyone's starting to bond, albeit over dead bodies and their favourite scenes from horror films and thrillers, which is where the conversation seems to have drifted to. *Perfect inspiration for my Scandi noir symphony*, Bella thinks, smiling to herself as she reaches for her refilled glass.

It's dark outside now – proper Scandi crime drama dark, with the blackness of the night and Dead Man's Forest framed by the huge picture windows. But here inside the lodge, with the under-floor heating and the warm crackle of the log fire, the remote forest setting feels exactly that – remote. Remote and removed from the cheerful chatter around the table and the promise of an exciting week to come.

'That was absolutely delicious,' announces Hamar, dabbing his top lip with his napkin but missing the dried gravy stain on his chin. 'My compliments to the chef.'

'Hear, hear,' says Oscar, as Bella and the others murmur in agreement. 'I enjoyed every single mouthful.'

Stuart couldn't look more pleased if he tried. 'I'm so glad you enjoyed it. Saga's already left for the night, I think. She and her wife live all the way over on the other side of the lake, but I'll be sure to let her know.'

Hamar's face falls for a moment, but then the lazy grin is back again. 'Oh dear,' he says. 'Does that mean there's no pudding? I was looking forward to some *risgrynsgröt*, or a nice slice of *kardemummakaka*.'

Stuart laughs. 'It seems we have a Swedish dessert connoisseur in our midst! Fear not, Hamar. We might not have any authentic local delicacies for you tonight, but Saga's rustled up a rather tasty-looking wild raspberry tart for us all. Or there's fruit or yoghurt if anyone would rather have that.'

'Raspberry tart was Albo's favourite,' says T, to no one in particular. 'That's my partner. *Ex*-partner, I mean. I used to make it for him every year on our anniversary.'

'Albo?' echoes Lena. 'That's an unusual name. Is it short for something?'

'Alberto,' says T. 'He's Spanish.'

'Ah yes, of course.'

'You're better off without him,' says Krista, kindly. 'Here's to fresh starts and happier times ahead.'

'To fresh starts!' booms Hamar, wine sloshing over the side of his glass as he thrusts it in the air again. It must be his fourth or fifth, and he seems to have got a little louder with each one. They *all* have. Bella probably has too, although the voice in her head – the one that was telling her to slow down on the wine and switch to water instead – has fallen completely silent now.

'To fresh starts,' everyone echoes, as glasses are clinked up and down the table.

'Oh,' cries Marie suddenly, jumping out of her seat as if she's been stung, almost knocking Stuart's glass out of his hand in the process.

'Steady now. Anyone would think you'd been drinking,' says Hamar with a wink, although Marie's probably the only sober one there. She hasn't touched a drop of wine all night.

Perhaps the universe is telling her to stick to filtered water, thinks Bella, swallowing down a giggle. *Unless that's neat vodka she's been drinking.*

Marie takes no notice. 'I almost forgot,' she says, coming back to the table with a padlocked wooden box. 'A proper retreat should

43

be just that. A retreat from everything else that's going on out there . . .' She gestures towards the window and the blackness of the encroaching forest beyond. 'We call it a wilderness retreat for obvious reasons,' she tells them, 'but we like to think of it as much more than that. More of a *well*derness retreat.'

'That's so clever,' Krista gushes. 'I love it!'

'A place where you can find healing through and with nature . . . a place to let go of the past by embracing the true present. But to fully concentrate on what's going on in here,' Marie says, touching her hand to her forehead, 'and here,' she adds, moving it down to her heart, 'it's important to block out any unnecessary distractions. And that means switching off from the outside world.' Marie unlocks the box and places it in the centre of the table, as if it's part of a secret ceremony.

Bella shifts uneasily in her seat, hoping this doesn't mean what she *thinks* it means. She's out of luck though.

'If you could all place your phones inside, I'll return them to you at the end of the week,' says Marie. Her silver charm bracelet twinkles in the candlelight as she taps the top of the box. 'Not that we get any real reception out here anyway, which is part of what makes Dödmansskogen so perfect. The symbolism is important though, I think. Don't you?'

No, thinks Bella. Forget about symbolism. What about teenage sons leaving home for the first time? What about secretly stalking his Instagram account in the hope of seeing what he's up to, and making sure he's okay? She's not planning on being one of those embarrassing clingy mums who texts their children every five minutes, but the thought of not being able to text him if she needed to – not having her phone to hand in case he needs to text *her* – is enough to send her scrambling for her phone to message him while she still can. There'll be no WhatsApping or Instagram-checking after this. Not if her phone is locked up in Marie's black box. So much for remembering to ask for the Wi-Fi code.

'I'm officially declaring this a no-phone week,' Marie says, as everyone else switches off their mobiles. 'And perhaps you'd like to verbally state your intention as you place it in the box: *I release myself from the shackles of the outside world and embrace the wilderness within.*'

The shackles of the outside world? thinks Bella. *Since when did anyone refer to their phone as that?* It sounds slightly cultish to her. She glances round the table at the others, while she waits for her phone to pick up some reception, to see if they're as uncomfortable with this turn of events as she is. No one else looks particularly surprised though. Perhaps it was mentioned in one of the welcome emails and Bella missed it. Her head's been all over the place these last few weeks.

Krista's already placing her purple leather-cased phone in the box with exaggerated care, a solemn, serious look on her face as she recites Marie's strange chant: 'I release myself from the shackles of the outside world and embrace the wilderness within.'

What does 'the wilderness within' even mean?

T's up next, handing over his expensive-looking iPhone and repeating the mantra with gusto, as if he can't wait to embrace his inner wilderness. 'Being cut off from the rest of the world sounds good to me right now,' he adds, under his breath.

Oscar looks pretty pleased with himself – smug almost – as he places his inside too, but *he* seems incapable of releasing himself from the shackles of his own notebook. Bella spots him jotting down Marie's mantra in his tight, slanting handwriting even as he's saying the words out loud.

She doesn't see Hamar or Lena putting their phones in the box though. She doesn't hear them chanting. She's too busy texting Asher, despite her phone still claiming not to have any reception, tapping away on the screen as quickly as she can, which isn't very fast at all. Asher always says she types like a granny.

Hi sweetheart. Hope you're having a good night. I'm supposed to surrender my phone for the week and there's no

internet here, so don't worry if you don't hear from me. You've got the landline number in case of emergencies though.

He *has* got the landline number, hasn't he? For a moment she can't think.

Wait, yes, of course he has. Bella remembers now. She remembers looking up the international dialling code for Sweden. She remembers writing it down on the front of the envelope with his arrival instructions in it.

Take care and have fun. Love you lots xx

She presses the 'send' arrow but the message isn't going anywhere. Still no signal. *What now?*

Bella looks up to find everyone's gaze fixed on her. 'Any chance I could give mine in tomorrow, instead? Another night won't hurt, surely?'

'Wait, I didn't realise it was *optional*,' says Hamar. 'Can I have mine back too in that case?'

'And mine,' adds Lena.

Oh no, Bella thinks. *What have I started?*

Stuart shakes his head, looking genuinely upset. 'It really would be better for the group dynamic if *everyone* participates,' he says. 'It's not meant to be a punishment, it's about cutting out unnecessary distractions and interference. It's about being present in the moment. But if you'd rather not join in, then that's fine. It's not our intention to make anyone feel uncomfortable.'

But Bella *does* feel uncomfortable. She feels like she's letting the others down by not playing the game. She feels as if she's letting Rachel down too, by clinging on to her worries about Asher instead of embracing the programme. She glances back down at the stubborn phone screen one last time, willing the message to send. *Come on, damn you.*

'It's . . . it's fine,' she says at last, admitting defeat, forcing a smile as she leans across the table and places her mobile into the box with the others. 'It's not fair to have one rule for me and another for everyone else. I mean, it's only symbolic, isn't it? I can always get it out again if I need it. If it's urgent . . .'

Stuart smiles at her. 'Absolutely. Although as Marie says, most mobiles are next to useless out here anyway.'

'One of the many hidden blessings of this place,' his wife adds, with a matching smile of her own.

Maybe it's a good thing, Bella tells herself. Maybe it will force her to focus on herself this week. That's what she's here for, after all. 'It was only because of my son,' she says out loud, explaining her reluctance to join in. She pushes away the image of Asher, all alone in his room, trying to reach her. Chances are, he'll be too busy having fun with his new friends to give her a second thought. 'He's just started at university. I'm sure he'll be fine though.'

'Of course he will,' says Krista, reaching over and squeezing her hand, just as she'd done in the minibus earlier. 'And so will you.'

'I know,' says Bella, wishing she shared the older woman's confidence. 'To new beginnings,' she adds, picking up her near-empty wineglass and toasting the others, trying to smooth over the awkwardness. At least she's been spared the whole escaping-the-shackles-of-the-outside-world-and-releasing-the-wilderness-within part of the ceremony. Everyone else seems to have forgotten and Bella's in no hurry to remind them.

'Wait,' says Hamar. 'You can't toast like that.' He refills Bella's wineglass for her, topping up his own while he's at it. 'That's better. To new beginnings,' he says. 'To fresh starts and raspberry tarts. Speaking of which, where's Rosel? I need my pudding.'

47

Chapter 6

'SURPRISE!'

Oh yes, it's a surprise all right. Izzy's already fuelled up on cheap vodka, ready for a night out, when the doorbell rings.

'Nat!'

She's pleased to see him, of course she is, only . . . only she's still finding her feet with this new life of drunken late nights and random parties in random people's flats, and the effort of fitting in is taking up every ounce of her energy at the moment. She doesn't want to be 'that girl' any more: the square classical music nerd with the obsessively overprotective mother. And she doesn't want to be the girl who stays in her bedroom pining for her boyfriend back home and missing all the fun. But one look at Nat's puppy-dog face and big, hopeful brown eyes, at the rumpled state of his blue sweatshirt with the lizard logo after so many hours in the car, and she knows there's no way she's going to that party now. No way she's going anywhere this weekend.

It's not until afterwards, as they lie tangled and sticky with sweat in the narrow confines of her single bed that those hopeful brown eyes narrow. That the questions about Ludwell start, along with an unwanted sense of déjà vu on her part.

'What? Don't be silly. He's my lecturer. We've been through all this.'

'That was before,' Nat says. 'Before you stopped answering my letters. Before you were too busy with your new life for me.'

'That's not true,' Izzy protests, pushing down a fresh wave of guilt. 'I was going to write back to you tomorrow. Please, Nat, don't be like this.'

'I'm not being like anything,' he says, sullenly. 'I'm not the one who's changed.'

*

Bella shouldn't have had that fourth glass of wine at dinner. Or was it her fifth? She lost track with all the endless toasts. Her dreams that night are splintered, stuttering affairs – the same snatched images playing on a loop somewhere between sleep and wakefulness. She's trying to reach Asher on the phone but the buttons are moving under her fingers and she keeps typing the number in wrong. The more she tries the worse it gets, but Bella won't give up. She *can't* give up. She keeps on trying . . . and trying . . . rousing briefly to turn over, only to sink back into the same frustrating pattern, of nines where threes should be and fours instead of fives . . .

Bella wakes again in a sweat, unsure for a moment where she is. Sweden. The retreat. Yes, she remembers now. She remembers saying goodbye to Asher . . . she remembers locking her phone in Marie's black box . . .

The clock on her bedside table says 04:12, the red numbers glowing in the darkness of the room. Bella turns on the lamp, already missing her mobile – her lifeline to the outside world. The more immediate world outside her window is still black and foreboding when she pulls up the blind to check. *I'm sure it'll seem different in the morning*, she tells herself, heading to the bathroom for a glass of water. Her head feels stuffy and swirly at the same time. *Tomorrow will be better.* Except it's already tomorrow – already Monday – whether she likes it or not.

After an hour of tossing and turning and counting her breaths in a futile effort to clear her head, Bella gives up. She pulls a cardigan on over her pyjama top and makes herself a cup of coffee with the fancy coffee machine. Mmm, the smell alone is pure luxury. Perhaps she should have a look at her symphony while she's waiting for everyone else to wake up, and see if the Scandinavian landscape is working its magic yet. Even though she promised Rachel and Asher she'd use this time away for some proper rest and relaxation, a bit of longhand composition while it's quiet hardly counts as work. It's only work if it *feels* like work. That's what she told herself as she was packing her suitcase, sneaking in manuscript paper and a printout of her first and second movements – what little there is of the second movement so far, anyway. Yes, it's only an issue if it stops her from doing something better. But if it takes her mind off missing Asher – and her phone – then that's a positive, right? And if she can crack the recalcitrant opening section of the second movement while she's here that would be a real bonus. It feels too sparse and tepid at the moment. Too flat. The whole *score* feels a little on the flat side, come to that. It needs more tension. More atmosphere. More darkness.

Bella raises the blind again and sits down at the desk, peering out into the pre-dawn gloom of the trees beyond. There's something rustling in the undergrowth and a furtive scratching sound from somewhere close by, like sharpened claws or fingernails against bare wood, followed by a low, keening cry from somewhere further off, deeper into the forest. *Now that's atmosphere,* she thinks, pulling her cardigan tighter across her chest. *Perfect.* She takes a big gulp of coffee, scalding her mouth in the process, then gets to work – *re*work rather – on her opening section, trying to instil some of the brooding darkness of the landscape into her music.

The result feels different, somehow, to her usual style – more discordant, more raw – with sudden swooping glissandos over stabbing pizzicato tritones in the cellos. The devil's chord. She brings in an oboe, then changes her mind, swapping it for a cor anglais. Yes, that's better. In the end Bella probably takes out more notes than she adds, trimming and changing as she goes, but it's better than it was. A definite improvement.

Hunger is starting to get the better of her now though. Her stomach feels hollow and empty again, and it's still a good two hours until breakfast. It's a shame she ate all the *pepparkaka* and muesli bars last night. Maybe there'll be something laid out in the dining room for early risers. Some more biscuits perhaps, unless they're considered too unhealthy now that the retreat is in full swing, or a bit of fruit.

Bella slips her room key into her pyjama pocket and creeps out into the quiet of the corridor. There's a warm, yellowy light coming from under the laundry room door, suggesting someone else is already up and about – or maybe it was left on all night? – but no other signs of life. She closes her own door as softly as she can, forgetting for a moment that hers is the only occupied room in this part of the building, until the famous celebrity guest arrives.

The thin strip of illumination from the laundry room is enough to get her to the end of the corridor. Once she's through the door at the end it's a different story though. Bella runs her fingers along the wall, feeling for a light switch and missing her phone, with its built-in torch, all over again. Maybe she should retrace her steps and get the proper torch from her room . . . Ah no, wait, *that* feels like a switch there. Yes, that's better.

Her body stiffens at the sound of a door opening somewhere on the other side of the building, as if she's been caught doing something she shouldn't. As if she's back at her mum's house as a teenager, creeping in after her curfew . . . Bella's natural instinct is to turn tail and flee back to her bedroom before anyone sees her, but that's ridiculous. She's not doing anything wrong. *Get a grip*, she tells herself, shaking her head at her own jumpiness.

She waits for a moment to see who it is, bracing herself for awkward early morning small talk in her nightclothes. Her money's on Krista – up early for some pre-dawn meditation. Or Stuart or Marie, stealing an early start on the day ahead while it's nice and peaceful. But no one comes. The lodge falls quiet again. Bella heads on into the dining room, where the big wooden table stands empty, stripped of its tablecloth and place settings from the night before, along with anything edible. Even the locked black box of confiscated phones has gone. The sleek Scandi-style sideboard is similarly devoid of food, much to her stomach-growling disappointment.

Bella carries on to the kitchen beyond, bed-socked feet padding softly across the heated floor. The vast designer kitchen is every bit as impressive as the rest of the house, with gleaming white wooden units and a wraparound oak worktop that reaches right down to the stone-tiled floor at each end. The large island in the centre of the room sports its own built-in hob (in addition to the enormous stainless-steel range behind it) with an orderly line of bar stools tucked in tight along the other side. Everything is pleasingly neat and minimalist, lending the room an air of spotless organisation. A little *too* neat and minimalist for Bella's liking at that exact moment in time. A stray tin of *pepparkaka* would have been good, or a bowl of bananas. There must be *something* she can find to eat in a kitchen as big as this though.

The first few cupboards she tries are full of crockery – neatly matching white plates and bowls in an impressive array of sizes – but then she strikes lucky. The next cupboard along isn't a cupboard at all. It's the fridge, and a well-stocked one at that, with an entire pull-out drawer just for fruit. Just for apples, in fact. Bella glances over her shoulder to check that no one's watching before she takes one – it feels oddly like stealing. But Stuart did say they should make themselves at home while they were here (at least Bella *thinks* that's what he said, somewhere around the third or fourth glass of wine). And surely no one's going to mind if she takes an apple back to her room?

She pauses again in the doorway, listening. Are those footsteps she can hear? Footsteps and an odd scratching noise. Bella slips the apple into her pyjama pocket and scurries back to her room like a thief, turning the lights off again as she goes.

Made it, she thinks, pleased to be back in her own space. She fixes herself another fancy coffee and settles down at the desk with her composition and her illicit pre-breakfast snack, humming through the twisting melody as it passes from one instrument line to the other, above the echoing crunch of apple. It feels like she's finally starting to get somewhere with this movement. Finally making some headway.

It takes a few minutes of stop-starting, of adding in another few bars only to delete them, before she manages to pick up the creative thread again, but once she's finally back in the zone, there's no stopping her. She doesn't notice the sun creeping up behind the trees, or her apple core rolling off the desk onto the floor. She doesn't notice the undrunk coffee growing cold beside her. She doesn't even notice the folded slip of paper being pushed under the door. Not until the bedside alarm clock brings her rudely back to reality with a high-pitched series of beeps. It's only then, as Bella's rushing across the room to silence it, that she spots the note.

At first she thinks it must be an updated itinerary for the day, or some kind of health and safety form that needs filling out, but on closer inspection the paper looks like it's been torn out of a notebook – a good quality one with nice thick pages. Bella unfolds the note and stares in queasy shock at the short message written inside:

I KNOW WHAT YOU DID

Chapter 7

What on earth . . .?

I KNOW WHAT YOU DID. That's all it says. Five simple words handwritten in thick block capitals. It's like something out of a horror film. A cheesy Nineties horror film, admittedly, but the effect is no less chilling for that.

I know what you did.

After a stunned moment of disbelief, of staring at the letters and waiting for them to rearrange themselves into something less sinister, Bella opens her bedroom door and peers out. There's no one there though. Even the light from the laundry room has disappeared now.

There must be some mistake, she thinks, closing the door again and relocking it behind her. *It can't be for me. I haven't done anything. Unless . . . unless it's something to do with the apple.*

Maybe someone saw her taking it from the fridge and smuggling it back to her room? But that theory doesn't get her very far. Why would anyone write a threatening anonymous note about a missing piece of fruit?

Her second thought, on turning it over in her hands and rereading it for the umpteenth time, is that it's someone's idea of a joke. Yes, that makes more sense. Hamar, perhaps. *Everything* seems like a joke to him. Perhaps it was him she heard up and about earlier. Maybe he saw her taking the apple and this is his idea of fun. Or then again, it could be Oscar – he seems pretty obsessed with all things thriller-related . . . *and* he's got a note-book, Bella remembers. Maybe this is some twisted attempt at research on his part, at getting under the skin of his antagonist. Or maybe it's *her* skin, he wants to get under. Maybe he's using Bella to test out his victim's characterisation instead? She wouldn't put it past him.

Either way – joke or research – it's not on. They really had her going there for a moment. She can still feel her heart racing inside her chest, like the drum line in the accelerando passage she's just been working on, her breath loud and fast against the quietness of the room. But if they're hoping for a *public* rise out of her then they're going to be out of luck. Bella fully intends to make the most of today – the first full day of her holiday and her new self – and she's not going to let some silly note ruin it before it's even begun. She screws the offending bit of paper up into a tight ball and throws it into the copper wastepaper bin under her desk. *There, that's what I think of you,* she murmurs under her breath.

*

A long, trestle-style table has appeared in the dining room since Bella's early morning wanderings. It groans beneath an impressive breakfast spread of fresh fruit salad and homemade granola, of open sandwiches with cheese or cod roe spread, of cold boiled eggs and warm croissants, of tiny apple pastries and delicious-smelling cinnamon buns, fresh from the oven. Everyone except T is there to enjoy it, already comparing notes on their first night's sleep and plans for the day ahead.

'I slept surprisingly well,' says Krista. 'It must be all this fresh forest air. It's so beautiful out there.'

'You say beautiful, I say creepy and atmospheric. *Exactly* what I was hoping for,' Oscar replies with a wide, uncovered yawn. Bella can see bits of half-chewed boiled egg clinging to his molars. 'I was awake stupidly early this morning,' he continues, 'to make notes on the setting for my first murder . . . which is why I'm on my third cup of writer's fuel already.' He gestures towards the half-empty coffee mug in front of him, but Bella's more interested in the notebook tucked away beside his plate. More interested in the idea that he was prowling round the house before everyone else was up.

I knew it, she thinks. *It was you I heard when I went to the kitchen, wasn't it? And you're the one who put that stupid note under my door.*

'It really is a dream location,' Oscar goes on. 'Don't you think? The perfect place for a series of murderous mind games and grisly killings. I'm so glad I came.'

Bella busies herself with her own coffee, refusing to make eye contact. Refusing to take the bait. If it's a reaction Oscar's after, for his precious book, then he's out of luck. But on the other hand, if she doesn't mention the note at all, he might think she's too scared to bring it up . . .

'Don't say that,' Krista tells him. 'It's not creepy, it's beautiful. I was up early this morning too – I usually am. I took a walk through the woods to the lake, just as the sun was coming up. Oh my, you should have seen the reflection in the water. And the little birds . . . Beautiful,' she repeats, smiling to herself at the memory.

'That sounds lovely,' Bella says. 'If I'd known you were up and about, I might have joined you. I only went as far as the kitchen for something to eat.' She casts a quick glance over at Oscar, but he's busy peeling another boiled egg. 'And when I got back . . . no, it was later than that . . . it was when I finished the work I was doing, I found a note under my door.' Oscar's still fully focused on his egg, piling up the little fragments of shell on the side of his plate.

'What sort of note?' asks Lena. Bella hadn't realised she was listening.

'Clearly someone's idea of a joke,' Bella says, dismissively. 'It just said *I know what you did*.'

There's a sharp intake of breath from Krista. 'Now *that's* creepy,' she says.

'So what *have* you done?' asks Lena. 'Is there something you'd like to confess?' It's hard to tell if she's joking or not. Her deadpan expression is giving nothing away.

Bella laughs. 'Of course not. I haven't done anything ... unless you count taking an apple from the fridge this morning. I hardly think *that* warrants an anonymous note under my door.'

'Perhaps it was Hamar,' suggests Krista, lowering her voice to a whisper. 'He strikes me as a bit of a joker.' A joker with surprisingly good hearing it would seem. He stops on his way back from the buffet table, putting his hand on the back of Bella's chair.

'What's all this?' he asks. 'What are you ladies saying about me?'

'Bella stole an apple from the kitchen this morning,' says Oscar with a wink. 'And now someone's left her an anonymous note, saying they know what she's done. Krista thought it might be you.'

Krista blushes, mumbling something incoherent under her breath, but Hamar doesn't seem the slightest bit offended.

'Nothing to do with me,' he says, with an easy shrug. 'Maybe it was Saga. Perhaps she was saving that particular apple to make some *äppelkakan* for our *fika* this morning.'

Oscar laughs. 'All very mysterious if you ask me, but perfect material for my novel.' And with that he opens up his notebook and begins to write.

There's nothing mysterious about it at all, thinks Bella, changing the subject by asking if anyone's seen T yet this morning. *It was you. I know it was.* And there's the evidence right there, the ragged slither of paper along the spine where a page has been torn out. But when she gets back to her room after breakfast and goes to retrieve the balled-up note, just in case word gets back to Stuart or Marie and they ask to see it, she discovers it's already gone. The bin's empty.

Oh well, never mind. She's got better things to think about right now. Like the guided wilderness walk with Stuart – her first session of the day. Bella tidies her composition away into her desk drawer, feeling another tiny thrill of excitement at the thought of how much better it's going to sound with these new changes, and unpacks her walking boots. *Swedish wilderness, here I come.*

*

Izzy already knew, even before Nat left, that it was over. She'd known it when the weight of him, pressing against her in the night, felt like a weight – a hot, suffocating weight – rather than a comfort. When she told him how much she missed him and realised it wasn't true. Not any more. But she didn't want him driving all the way home, alone and upset, so she took the coward's way out and said nothing, hating herself for how quickly her own feelings had changed. How quickly they'd been eclipsed by the rush and novelty of her new life.

He deserves better than her. Better than the break-up letter currently waiting in the postbox at the end of the road, even as Izzy waits at the crowded bar of The Black Swan for a round of drinks. Her flatmates seem to think a change of venue for the drowning of her Nat-shaped sorrows is all Izzy needs, as if she can outrun – outdrink – her guilt by swapping cheap wine from the local off-licence for expensive spirits from the local pub. But the more she drinks, the guiltier Izzy feels. It's going to take more than alcohol to make her forget her troubles tonight. It's going to take—

Ludwell? *She peers through the jostling sea of student bodies towards the tall, dark-haired man a few barstools up, wearing a red R.E.M. T-shirt and nursing what looks like a double whisky. She didn't have Ludwell Storm pegged as an R.E.M. fan, but it's definitely him. She'd know that face anywhere. The face of a thousand cheesy teenage fantasies . . .*

Chapter 8

'Sorry I'm late,' says T, who's the last to arrive. Everyone else is already waiting outside, coated and booted, breathing in the heady pine scent and shuffling their feet up and down on the gravel to keep warm. 'I forgot to set the alarm last night,' he explains as he attempts to do up his jacket zip with one hand. He's clutching a reusable cup of something in the other – coffee, by the smell of it, with a hint of something sweet in there too. Cinnamon perhaps. Bella can't smell Asher's deodorant scent on him today though. Maybe he was in such a rush he forgot to put any on. He's looking decidedly dishevelled, with his shirt untucked and his bootlaces undone, and a full chin of stubble. 'I'm so used to relying on my phone to wake me up, it didn't occur to me, which is how I managed to sleep right through breakfast. Completely dead to the world, I was. Luckily Rosel was able to sort me out with some coffee and cake. I think my early start yesterday morning must have caught up with me.'

Yesterday morning. For a moment or two, Bella can't think what she was doing then. And then it hits her. Asher! Of course! It's hard to believe that was only yesterday. It feels like days since they were driving up the M5 with all his stuff. A lifetime ago. She's pretty sure he won't have made it out of bed yet either. That's if he's even *gone* to bed. His freshers' week programme of parties and clubs sounded pretty full-on.

'Not to worry,' says Stuart. 'We've been enjoying the beautiful fresh air, but now that everyone's here I think we might get started. Nothing too ambitious this morning – just an easy stroll down to the lake so that everyone can get their bearings, with a short breathing and body scan meditation while we're enjoying the peace and tranquillity of the setting, then an optional extra loop along one of the forest paths for anyone who's feeling more energetic. And I'll also be giving you an impromptu guide to some of the local flora and fauna, at Oscar's request.'

Typical, thinks Bella. He probably wants to know about poisonous berries for his precious book.

'We're hoping to run foraging workshops in the future,' says Stuart, 'which we're very excited about, but I'm afraid we're not quite set up for them yet. You'll all have to come back again next year,' he jokes.

'How many times can we come back before we have to marry you?' asks Hamar and everyone laughs.

'Marriage isn't compulsory I can assure you,' chuckles Stuart, 'but return guests are always very welcome. It feels like old friends returning to the fold . . . and it shows we must be doing something right when people come back for more. It proves that they appreciate the beauty and serenity of Dödmansskogen as much as we do.'

Bella's secretly relieved to have missed out on the foraging. She's never enjoyed those survival programmes on TV where people live off grubs and unappetising bits of vegetation, and wouldn't trust herself to tell the difference between an edible mushroom and a poisonous toadstool. Oscar's all ears though. He's already quizzing Stuart on the defining character traits of a typical retreat guest, notebook at the ready, before they've even left the parking area. He's already pumping him for information on suspected poisonings and wild animal attacks, and the likelihood of a winter guest dying of hypothermia if they got locked out overnight. Whereas Lena, on the other hand, seems surprisingly *un*interested in anything Stuart has to say. She's too busy trying to engage T in conversation about some dating app that one of her friends had recommended.

'A beautiful day, isn't it?' says Krista, falling into step beside Bella as they head off down the path.

'Yes,' Bella agrees. Cold but beautiful. And green. *Everything* looks green in the chilly light of day, from the dark, scented greens of the pine trees – or are they spruces? – to the multi-toned carpet covering the forest floor. A rich carpet of lichens and moss, beneath a covering of dropped needles, of elegant feathery ferns and small shrubby plants that Stuart might be able to identify for her if he wasn't so busy being grilled by Oscar.

'I'm sure it's nothing to worry about,' Krista adds.

'Sorry?' Bella looks at her new friend in surprise. Has she missed something?

'The note,' Krista says. 'I'm sure it really is just someone's idea of a joke.' She lowers her voice. 'I still think it's Hamar. I caught him skulking around the house when I went out for my walk this morning. He seemed very on edge when I stopped to say hello, too. He almost jumped out of his skin.'

It seems like everyone was up early this morning, with the obvious exception of T. 'Hmm, maybe,' says Bella, although her money's still on Oscar. 'I'm fine though, really. It's not worth getting upset about. Just someone's silly idea of a joke, as you say.'

'I'm glad to hear it,' says Krista. 'You've got enough on your plate with your son. I'm sorry you didn't get to speak to him before you had to give your phone in last night.'

Bella shrugs. 'It's probably a good thing really. Saves me checking it every five minutes to see if he's messaged me yet. It's only ever been the two of us, you see,' she adds by way of explanation, not wanting Krista to think she's some kind of neurotic helicopter parent. 'I just need to get used to being on my own, I guess.'

'Ah yes, the dreaded empty nest. As I said yesterday, you *do* adjust though. Once you know they're all settled in, you'll start to relax and enjoy a bit more time and space for yourself. No more late-night taxi service back from parties. No more festering piles of dirty dishes in their bedroom, or dirty socks on the bathroom floor. There'll be some things you don't miss at all!'

Bella knows all that, and yet . . . What if he *doesn't* settle in? What if the closeness of their relationship has left Asher poorly equipped for life on his own? What if she's been *over*-parenting him all this time, overcompensating for how unprepared she was for motherhood at the start? For his lack of a father? There's more to independent living than knowing how to cook an omelette.

'How old are *your* children?' she asks out loud, hoping to distract herself from pointless worries with a change of subject. 'How many do you have?'

'Thirty-three,' says Krista. 'I mean, that's how old they are. Not how many children I've got.' She lets out a snort of laughter. 'Oh my, thirty-three children! Can you imagine? That would be a *lot* of dirty socks on the bathroom floor. No, just the two for me, thank goodness. Twins. And twin grandchildren on the way. My daughter's due at the end of November.'

Bella can hear the excitement in her voice, and maybe a bit of fear mixed in there too. 'Oh wow, congratulations. So I guess you're squeezing your holiday in while you can, before you start your grandmother duties? It'll be all hands on deck with twins, I imagine.'

'Exactly,' says Krista. 'Although I usually try and get away somewhere at this time of year anyway. Somewhere nice and quiet, for a bit of peace and reflection.' The excitement in her voice has gone again. 'It's the anniversary of my husband's death on Wednesday,' she adds. 'He died in a hit-and-run accident five years ago.'

'I'm so sorry, I er . . . I don't know what to say.' It's true. Bella certainly wasn't expecting the conversation to take *that* turn. She doesn't even know where to look. How did they get from dirty socks on the floor to here?

Krista shrugs. 'What *can* you say? I still wake up every morning cursing the coward who robbed me of my soulmate. But cursing them won't bring him back, will it? So I try to focus on my blessings instead. On my children. And now my grandchildren.'

'You know who did it, then?' asks Bella, regretting it the moment the words have left her mouth. Whatever the appropriate response is, it's not *that*.

'No, I don't know anything,' says Krista, her expression darkening. 'There were no witnesses unfortunately and the police investigation was as good as useless.' She drops her voice, although everyone else is too far ahead now to hear. 'I even went to see a psychic last year, hoping *she* might be able to help. I don't know what I was hoping for exactly – a name? A description? But the most I got out of her was a suggestion that I look towards Scandinavia for the culprit . . . I mean, what kind of an answer is that?'

Bella shivers. 'I'm so sorry,' she says again, acutely conscious of the banality of her response. But Krista's right. What *can* you say to someone who's lost a loved one in such horrific circumstances? Who's still looking for answers all these years later? Krista might talk the talk about focusing on her blessings instead – perhaps that really *is* what she's doing out here in the northern wilds – but the hunger for answers, for justice, is still there, bubbling away under the surface. That much is clear, even from their short conversation. And her comment at dinner last night, about escaping her demons, makes much more sense now. Bella's own demons seem like small fry by comparison.

'Come on, you dawdlers,' says Hamar, dropping back from the rest of the group to join them. 'You're missing all the gossip.'

'Gossip?' repeats Krista, with a mischievous smile. 'What gossip?' It's like someone's pressed a secret switch behind her eyes and the old cheery Krista is back again. Bella can't help feeling relieved. Whatever Hamar's juicy titbit is, it's got to be easier to navigate than a dead husband whose killer was never found.

'The gossip about our mystery guest,' says Hamar, as if the answer is obvious. As if that's the only topic of conversation worth anyone's attention. Things must have moved on from poisonous berries and dating apps then. 'Stuart just let slip who he is.'

Who he *is*, Bella notes. There goes Oscar's theory about Glory Daybright.

'Well, I say Stuart let it slip, but Lena pretty much drummed it out of him in the end.' Hamar chuckles to himself. 'I suppose she needs all the info she can get on him for her travel piece . . . although it's a bit late to be googling him now unless she's got a secret phone stashed away somewhere.'

A second phone – Bella wishes she'd thought of that. Not that she knew she'd have to surrender her first one. Not that she's even *got* a second phone.

'So?' says Krista. 'Are you going to tell us or not? Who is it?'

'Ludwell Storm.'

Ludwell. Bella's heart stops. That's what it feels like, anyway, as if her heart's stopped and all the air's been sucked out of her lungs.

'Ludwell Storm . . .' Krista repeats as if she's trying to place the name. 'Oh wait, he's that music therapy guy, right? The one who wrote *Music at the Heart*? I *loved* that book. I've listened to a few of his podcasts too, now I think about it. They were really good as well.'

Ludwell. There's no way Bella could forget his name. It's carved into every cell of her body. His name, his face, his voice.

'Really? I'll have to give them a try when I get my phone back,' says Hamar. 'T was just saying how good they were too – how he used to listen to them when he was feeling rough from the chemotherapy. And I think Ludwell Storm used to be a big name in music in his own right; I remember seeing an interview with him on television a few years ago. He used to play the violin . . . or was it the viola?'

'It was the violin,' says Bella. Or maybe she only *thinks* it.

'Oscar's quite the fan too apparently. He said he was expecting it to be that Glory Daybright lady, so it's a result as far as he's concerned. The only person who didn't seem very impressed was Lena. It doesn't sound like she's much of a fan.'

Lena's not the only one who's disappointed, although 'disappointed' is putting it mildly. 'Gutted' would be closer to the mark. 'Terrified'. Ludwell Storm is the very last person Bella wants to be trapped with on a retreat in the middle of nowhere. Even the thought of him makes her feel sick inside. Her inner demons might have been small compared to Krista's, but they just got a whole lot bigger.

Chapter 9

The rest of the guided walk, and the lakeside meditation, passes in something of a blur. The rest of the *day* is pretty much a blur, come to that. Bella mumbles and stumbles her way through her one-to-one welcome session with Marie, before excusing herself and heading back outside for some fresh air. The tranquil setting does nothing to calm the thoughts swirling round inside her head though. *Why Ludwell? Why here? Why now?* Maybe he's got a new book to plug. She'd know that if she'd read the interview with him in the culture section of the Saturday paper the other month about the breakdown of his marriage: 'Ludwell on Loneliness – the Therapist's Approach'. But Bella couldn't even bring herself to look at his photo, throwing the entire supplement in the recycling bin, unread.

What if he recognises me? she thinks as she circles back towards the lodge.

He won't. Not after all these years. I'm not the same person any more.

But what if he does? What if I let something slip by mistake and he works it out?

This can't be happening.

It *is* happening though, whether Bella likes it or not. Ludwell's plane gets in this afternoon, at the same time as hers did yesterday, and short of begging Marie to take her back to the airport and hiding in the toilets until he's gone – how would she explain that to Rachel and Asher? – Bella can't see a viable way out of this. That's assuming she can even *get* another flight back to the UK at this notice. No, there's no escape from this. She's just going to have to brazen it out and hope for the best.

'Are you all right?' asks Marie, when they catch up again over their morning *fika*. 'You're looking a bit pale. And you were very quiet in our meeting earlier. I hope you're enjoying your time here at the retreat?'

'What? Erm . . . yes, sorry. I'm fine.' Bella's still thinking about Ludwell. She can't *stop* thinking about him. 'A bit tired, that's all,' she says. 'I was awake really early this morning . . . in fact I haven't been sleeping well for a while actually. My son . . .' The rest of the sentence tails away into silence.

My beautiful boy. Oh Asher.

'Ah yes, Asher,' Marie says. She doesn't seem to have noticed the tea spilling over the edge of her cup. It trickles down her floaty scarf onto the waxed wooden floor below. 'Eighteen years old and off on his big university adventure. It's hard to believe . . . you don't look old enough.'

Bella manages a weak smile. She certainly *feels* old enough. Well, one half of her does: the sleep-deprived, frazzled half. But thanks to the Ludwell Storm revelation, the other half feels more like a panicking teenager right now, counting down the hours – and minutes – until he gets here, still desperately trying to think of a way out. If a forged sick note would get her excused from the rest of the retreat, then Bella would be back in her room penning one at that very moment.

'Eighteen years old,' Marie repeats, a wistful edge to her voice. 'They think they're all grown up at that age, don't they? But they're still so easily hurt. So vulnerable. It doesn't take much to crush their vital spirit.'

Don't tell me that. Bella feels a sudden rush of longing for Asher; a need to wrap her arms around his skinny chest and breathe in the sour-edged tang of his deodorant; to bask in the sound of his laughter as he tries to squirm his way out of her unwanted embrace. 'How about you?' she asks out loud. 'Do you have any children?'

Marie fingers the silver heart charm on her bracelet. 'I had a son,' she says. 'But . . . but he's not with us any more. Not in this spiritual plane. He still lives in here though.' She touches her palm to her chest.

Bella can already feel the blood rushing to her cheeks. She won't be looking pale any more, that's for certain. 'Oh no, I'm so sorry.' *Me and my big mouth,* she thinks, even though there's no way she could have known. It feels like her conversation with Krista all over again, only worse. All the dead relatives seem to be coming out today . . . She puts her hand on Marie's arm in a gesture of sympathy but it's clearly the wrong move. The slight flinch gives it away, along with the tightening of the older woman's lips. Bella snatches her hand back and pretends to brush pastry crumbs off her jumper instead. Not that she's actually eaten any of the mid-morning pastries. Her yo-yo-ing appetite has well and truly disappeared again.

It's still absent without leave at lunchtime. The meal comes and goes in another blur of other people's conversations. A blur of untouched food. Bella's head is still full of Ludwell. And Asher. And Krista's dead husband and Marie's dead son. It's too full to think about the note under her door. Until the others are finishing off their apple cake dessert, that is. Until Marie and Stuart excuse themselves to catch up on some admin and Hamar fetches Saga out of the kitchen to meet everyone.

'Here she is,' he announces, pressing big, beefy fingers into the poor woman's arm as he presents her to the assembled diners. She looks tiny beside him, her blonde hair pulled back in a tight ponytail that accentuates the sharp contours of her cheeks. She looks decidedly uncomfortable too – as if she'd rather be back in the kitchen tidying up than paraded round the dining room – her gaze shifting nervously from one end of the table to the other. 'This is the lady who's keeping us so well fed. *Äppelkakan var utsökt*,' says Hamar, bringing his thumb and fingers to his lips, like a television chef tasting their own perfected sauce. 'That's about the limit of my Swedish there,' he adds with a wink in Krista's direction, 'before you get *too* impressed. I'm *very* rusty.'

'What does it mean?' asks Krista. 'No, wait, let me guess. The apple cake was . . .'

'Delicious,' Hamar finishes for her. '*Perfekt*.'

Krista grins. 'I think I can guess that last bit. And you're right, it was perfectly delicious. Thank you, Saga.'

There are more murmurs of appreciation from round the table. 'And don't worry, Bella,' Hamar adds with a wink. 'Saga's forgiven you for pinching her apple this morning. She says she'll leave some fruit and biscuits out in the dining room in case you're snooping around early again tomorrow.' He switches into a low, dramatic voice – what Bella now thinks of as his film trailer voice – saying, '*She knows what you did . . .*'

'I wasn't snooping,' Bella protests, as everyone turns to stare at her. 'I was just a bit hungry. I'm sorry,' she tells Saga, inwardly cursing Hamar for making a scene. She wishes she'd kept the business with the note to herself now. 'Hopefully I won't be awake quite so early tomorrow.' That's probably wishful thinking under the circumstances though. Bella will be lucky if she gets *any* sleep tonight. 'And hopefully no more notes,' she adds in an undertone.

Saga gives her a tight-lipped smile. 'If you'll excuse me, I must be getting back to the kitchen,' she says, extricating herself from Hamar's grip on her arm. Her English is perfect. 'I still have some bits to prepare for tomorrow. It was nice to meet you all. I'm glad you liked the apple cake.' And with that she's gone, much to Bella's embarrassed relief.

'She didn't seem very surprised when I told her about your

apple thieving,' Hamar observes, as the kitchen door shuts behind her. 'I think she could be your stalker, you know . . . your apple stalker!' He laughs out loud at his own pun, looking annoyingly pleased with himself.

Bella isn't laughing though. He and Oscar are as bad as each other.

'Relax,' says Hamar, seeing the look on her face. 'I'm only teasing.'

It's all one big joke to him, isn't it?

'What's this about a note?' asks T. 'Have I missed something?'

'No,' Bella assures him, before Hamar can answer. 'Nothing worth repeating, trust me.'

'Oh, okay then, fair enough.' T sounds peeved at being kept out of the loop. 'I only ask because someone put a note under my door this morning too, by mistake. It clearly wasn't meant for me.'

'*Another* note?' says Hamar. 'The plot thickens. Are you writing this down, Oscar? And what did your note say then T? "I know what you did too"?'

T shakes his head. 'No. Nothing like that. It said, "Sorry about yesterday. I'll explain everything. Meet me by the lake at midnight." That's how I knew I wasn't the intended recipient.'

'Ooh, intriguing,' says Krista. 'It sounds like something out of a romantic comedy.'

'Or a thriller,' pipes up Oscar on cue. 'It could be a trap to lure our unsuspecting hero down to the deserted lake in the middle of the night, and then BAM!' he cries, bringing his cake fork down on an imaginary victim's skull. 'Bam, bam, bam.' His death-by-cake-fork dramatisation bears little resemblance to any night-time murder scene Bella's ever watched. It's broad daylight for one thing, and his murder weapon weighs about as much as a toothbrush. But there's something about the expression on his face – the look in his eyes – that sends a shiver down her spine. She can almost hear the music from her film score playing over the top: a series of vicious stabbing chords and screaming violins.

But then Oscar lets out an over-dramatic, 'Die, damn you, why won't you die?' and the moment is broken.

'Gee, thanks for that,' says T. 'No after-dinner stroll down to the lake for *me* tonight then. Not unless I want to be brutally savaged with a cake fork.'

'It might look like a cake fork to the uninitiated,' says Oscar. 'But I think you'll find it's really a crowbar. You can do a surprising amount of damage to a person's skull with one of those, you know. Let alone their face . . .'

'Hey, cut that out, will you?' says Lena. 'Some of us are still trying to eat.'

'Sorry.' Krista's the one apologising though. Oscar looks unrepentant.

'I think we'll *all* be keeping away from the lake tonight after that delightful demonstration,' says Hamar. 'I don't know about you, but I'll be keeping a safe distance from Oscar too. And cake forks . . .'

Chapter 10

There's nothing scheduled for the second half of Monday afternoon, following Stuart's introduction to journaling session. 'Free time for relaxation' is all it says on Bella's itinerary. But Bella's never felt *less* relaxed. T's bagsied the sauna, which rules that out – the thought of making awkward conversation in her swimming costume is more than she can handle right now – and Krista and Lena are off to swim in the lake with Hamar. Bella didn't have Lena pegged as a wild swimmer, but then she doesn't really know much about her, does she? Except for her job, and the fact that she doesn't think Ludwell is a very good celebrity guest. That's *one* thing they have in common at least. As for Oscar, he disappeared off after lunch to work on a new idea for his book, which just leaves Bella and the crazy cacophony of thoughts whirring round inside her brain. For a second she's almost tempted to grab her swimming costume and join the lake party, but only for a second. She thinks about the breathless cold of the water against her skin, and the dark, unknown depths waiting under the sun-dazzled surface – the perfect place for a corpse according to someone last night, although she can't recall who – and decides on another walk instead.

She explores the network of paths running from the back of

the lodge, heading ever deeper into the forest, away from the lake, but the trees don't have the calming effect she was hoping for. They feel like they're closing in on her, threatening to swallow the path and Bella herself. She's not a hundred per cent sure her map skills will be up to navigating her way back if she gets herself lost, either. Locking up everyone's phones in a box for the week to block out unnecessary distractions is all well and good, but what if she needs Google Maps to take her back to the lodge? What if she needs to call for help?

Bella retraces her steps and heads back to her room. Maybe she'll have more luck distracting herself with that book she picked up at the airport, although she can't even remember what it's about. Perhaps reading will help take her mind off Ludwell, or sleep. Yes, sleep would be even better. If only she could set her alarm for the end of the week and skip through all the awkward Ludwell days in the middle.

It's no good. Bella might be tired, but she's not sleepy. Quite the opposite, in fact. She feels jumpy and exposed, her nerves on edge as she reaches for her airport book instead. That's a non-starter too though. A quick refresher glance at the blurb on the back is enough to convince her of that:

DI Marion Tucker has seen her fair share of violent killings in the city. But the sleepy island village she once called 'home' has always been a welcome respite from the darkness of her job. Until now. What begins as a straightforward missing-child case – a young boy, last seen heading for the woods behind his house – soon escalates into something much darker, dragging her into a complex web of intrigue and violence and long-forgotten secrets. This might not be Marion's case to investigate, but it's her past, and she's involved whether she likes it or not. Bodies can stay buried, but secrets can't.

No, that's not what Bella needs right now. Secrets *can* stay buried. That's the message she's after. Secrets can stay buried and pasts can be forgotten.

That's that then. Walks are out. Sleep's out. Reading's out.

And there's no minibar in her room so it looks like drinking's out too, which is a shame. Bella's not much of a drinker usually – a couple of glasses of wine at the weekend and that's about it – but she could murder a vodka and Coke right now. Make that a double, in fact. The dish of fancy-looking organic camomile teabags on the tray by the kettle, with a helpful 'organic camomile teabags' label, doesn't have quite the same allure somehow.

Bella fixes herself a luxury decaf coffee instead and sits at her desk, staring out of the window and pretending to work. Whatever brief burst of inspiration she may have felt that morning has well and truly upped and gone. Gone to the airport with Marie to wait for Ludwell, most likely. *Maybe his flight will be delayed,* she thinks, looking at the clear blue sky for a glimpse of approaching storm clouds. No such luck. *Maybe something will crop up and he'll have to cancel the trip at the last minute. Some kind of family emergency . . . his mum, perhaps.* And then Bella catches herself, ashamed to be wishing a medical crisis on a complete stranger. It's no good anyway. Ludwell's coming, whether she likes it or not. She can already picture him sauntering through customs with that long-legged hip swagger of his. Can already hear his polished laugh as Marie tells him about the broken heating in the minibus. '*Ah, don't worry,*' he'll say, charming her with his fake smile. '*I had my fair share of bad transfers when I was on tour.*'

Bella's roused from her imaginings by a knock at the door. It's Saga. 'I'm sorry to disturb you,' she says in her crisp English, with only the slightest hint of an accent. 'I just wanted to apologise for before. For what Hamar said. He's a bit of a stirrer, I think. Is that the right word? Someone who likes to stir up trouble.'

'Yes.' That's the perfect word for Hamar. He's a stirrer, all right.

'I don't know anything about that note,' Saga continues, 'and I've got better things to worry about than missing apples. But I'll be sure to leave some fruit and biscuits out in future, as I said before. I'm sorry I forgot to do it last night. I had a lot on my mind.'

Haven't we all? Perhaps a place like this naturally attracts people with problems, Bella thinks. People looking to escape from something, whether that's grief, poor health, a failed relationship, or an empty nest . . . although the emptiness of her nest is the least of her worries after the Ludwell Storm bombshell. Only twenty minutes now until his plane's due in. Another thirty minutes or so to see him through passport control and luggage reclaim – it doesn't take long at such a small airport – and then a couple of hours back to the lodge. And then . . .

'No need to apologise,' she tells Saga, dragging her mind back to the present. 'And don't you worry about Hamar. I've got his number.'

'What do you mean?'

'Oh, it's just an expression,' says Bella. Maybe the colloquialism doesn't translate well into Swedish. 'It means I know what he's like. A stirrer,' she adds, seeing the worried look on the other woman's face.

Saga's expression eases. 'Ah yes, I see. Okay, good. Thank you for being so understanding. I'd better get back to the kitchen, I suppose. Two more hungry mouths to feed tonight.'

Two? puzzles Bella. *Why, who else is coming?* But it's too late to ask. Saga's already gone.

*

There he is. At least, there's the minibus, pulling up outside the lodge. Bella can hear it from her room. She didn't *mean* to walk over to the window – it wasn't a conscious choice on her part – but that's where she finds herself now, craning her neck in an attempt to see the parking area. It's just outside her line of vision though. All she can do is press her ear against the cold glass and listen. She listens to the sound of the minibus door sliding open and a man's voice – *his* voice – saying what a perfect spot this is for a retreat. How he's sorry again to have missed all the fun of the first day, but his wife couldn't get her meeting rearranged.

His wife? No, she must have misheard. He and his wife split up, didn't they? Bella assumed that's what the interview in the Saturday supplement, 'Ludwell on Loneliness – the Therapist's Approach', was all about. But maybe she got the wrong end of the stick from the cover tagline. Maybe she *should* have read the article after all. And now Marie's saying something about dinner, and someone's laughing. Who's that? The minibus door slams shut and Bella can hear a suitcase being pulled across the gravel. Or is it two suitcases? Then everything goes quiet again until the sound of wheels and voices reappears in the corridor, heading (presumably) for room eleven or twelve. *Why does his room have to be so close to mine?* She hears the sound of a door opening. A door shutting. And then nothing.

That's that then – he's finally here. No escape now. Even if Bella cries off dinner, even if she feigns illness and keeps to her bed for the next twenty-four hours, she'll still have to face him eventually. She'll still have to face what happened that night. The thought makes her feel genuinely ill, sending a sudden wave of nausea gushing into her chest. Bella rushes to the bathroom and pulls up the toilet seat, dry-heaving into the waiting pan. But the sickness isn't in her stomach, it's in her head. It's been in her head all these years, biding its time and waiting.

She wipes a thin line of drool from her lips and leans back against the cool tiled wall, trying to calm the racing in her chest. Deep breath in. Deep breath out.

It's just nerves, Isabella, she hears her mother's voice saying. *A few deep breaths and you'll be fine. Head up, shoulders back and show them what you're made of.* But this isn't a music festival, with a ten-minute piece in front of a middle-aged adjudicator and a room full of parents. It's not an audition or an exam. This is Ludwell Storm. This is the biggest, most important performance of her life. Bella pulls her head up and forces her shoulders back, like her mum always told her to, pushing out from her diaphragm as she takes another long breath in. Channelling the air through the narrow funnel of her lips as she breathes it out again, letting the tension go. *In and out. In and out.* She can't let him see the terrified teenager still hiding inside. She can't risk him recognising her.

But the very idea of Ludwell sitting across the table from her at dinner is enough to turn the clock back all those years. The mere thought of those cold blue eyes staring back at her across the laden plates is enough to strip away the protective shield Bella's spent the last two decades building round the scared young girl within. So much for her relaxing break at the retreat, she thinks, closing her eyes against the injustice of it all. She'd never have agreed to come this week, no matter how awkward it made things with Rachel, if she'd known who the celebrity guest was. *Why him? Why here? Why now?*

She turns her mind to Asher instead. *Breathing in . . . and out.* She thinks about the tight grip of his chubby baby fingers on hers. *In . . . and out.* She thinks about his warm peppermint breath on her cheek when he came crawling into her bed after a nightmare. *In . . . and out, in and out.* She thinks about the sullen teenage scowl erupting into sudden laughter over a rude joke on a comedy show, and the awkward preciousness of his whispered words in the car park the previous day: 'I'm going to miss you.'

'Not as much as I'm going to miss you,' she whispers back to the empty bathroom.

The deep breathing seems to be helping. The wild beating in her chest is starting to ease now, the wave of nausea retreating. Bella pulls herself up off the floor and switches on the shower, twisting the dials as hot and hard as they'll go, hoping to wash away the last of her panic. She's not the same scared girl she was back then, she tells herself, discarding her clothes in an Asher-like heap on the floor. She's a woman now. A mother. She's a successful composer at the start of an exciting new chapter in her career.

And maybe he's not the same man either, she realises with a jolt, as she steps into the hot rush of water and pulls the door shut behind her. Maybe Ludwell has changed too.

*

It starts as a drunken dare from one of her flatmates – 'I think you should go over there and offer to buy him a drink. Best cure for a broken heart and all that. Go on, I dare you' – and ends as something else altogether. Izzy doesn't even remember agreeing, but she must have done, because one minute she's sitting at the table with her friends, pointing out the object of her teenage crush across the crowded pub, and the next she's up at the bar with Ludwell, talking gushingly about how many of his concerts she's been to and how many hundreds of times she's listened to his CDs . . . And then, after a few more drinks, Ludwell's inviting her back to his house to see his priceless violin. Izzy's not sure if that's a euphemism, a come-on. Is he flirting with her – it feels like flirting – or does he really just want to show her his instrument?

Her legs object the moment she leaves the swaying safety of the bar stool, refusing to walk in a straight line. But he's there to steady her – Ludwell Storm is there to steady her – catching her in his strong arms as she lurches unsteadily towards the jutting corner of a nearby table. How many times has she fantasised about being held by those same arms? And then he's saying something about her dress, how it makes her look like someone she's never heard of – a film star? – and she's giggling back at him. He's definitely flirting now, she thinks, giggling and blushing and wishing the pub wasn't spinning quite so fast and then . . . and then they're outside in the cold evening air. In the dark. Together. And Izzy's not giggling any more.

A streetlight flickers at the end of the road and she sways again, teetering on the edge of the kerb, revelling in the steadying touch of his hands on her shoulders. Kiss me, *she thinks.*

Kiss me, *she thinks again when they pause outside a church a bit later. When he fixes his blue eyes on her and smiles.* This is it, *she thinks.* This is where he kisses me. *But instead he tells her about a concert he'd played there when he was a student himself. 'When I was your age,' he says, as if age matters. As if the years between them mean anything to Izzy.*

Something strange happens to the time after that. It could be minutes later or it could be half an hour when Izzy finds herself walking down a road of big, fancy-looking houses. Farringdon Mews. 'Is this where you live?' she asks him. Or maybe she only thinks it because the conversation seems to have moved on without her. Without a reply. He's staring down at her now, his blue eyes burning into hers, asking her if she's sure. 'Are you sure?'

'I'm sure,' she tells him, even though she can't remember what the question was. Or maybe that was the question? And now they're inside the hallway of one of the houses and he's finally kissing her. That's what she thinks to herself: Finally . . .

And then . . .

. . . and then nothing.

Chapter 11

There's a lump the size of a golf ball in Bella's throat as she walks into the dining room, some thirty minutes later, her towel-dried hair still damp against the back of her neck. It took her so long to choose her outfit (finally deciding on her favourite blue jumper – a present from Asher – for luck) that she hasn't had time to blow-dry her hair. Damp hair, no make-up and the beginnings of a spot on her chin – that's the look she's sporting for her grand reunion with Ludwell Storm. But he's not even here yet.

'Hi,' says Krista as Bella takes a seat between her and Hamar, opposite Lena and T. That's good. No chance of Ludwell ending up next to her. 'We missed you this afternoon. It was so beautiful down at the lake, you should have come.'

'Don't listen to her,' says Hamar. 'It was *horrible* down at the lake. Absolutely freezing. I thought I was going to die of hypothermia.'

'Such a wimp,' remarks Lena, with a rare smile. 'I thought you Swedes were made of sterner stuff than that. I thought you were *used* to the cold.'

'Ah yes, but I'm only half-Swedish,' says Hamar. 'And I've lived most of my life in the UK. Your British softness must have rubbed off on me.'

'So which half is it?' asks T.

'I'm sorry?'

'Which half of you is the Swedish half? Left or right?'

Hamar grins. 'The top half,' he says. 'That's why I didn't make it any deeper than waist level – because my wimpy British bottom couldn't cope. My hardy Viking blood is all up here,' he says, indicating his upper body. 'If I'd gone in headfirst I'd have been fine.'

Lena laughs. The effect on her face is nothing short of transformative. She looks softer. Kinder. 'We'll hold you to that. Maybe Stuart can fix us up with a diving board before we go tomorrow.'

'Tomorrow? You think I'm going anywhere near that ice bath again tomorrow?' Hamar shakes his head. 'No, tomorrow I'll be in the sauna. That's more my temperature.'

Bella lets their conversation wash over her, envying them their easy banter. That's as much of their chatter as she hears though. Because out of the corner of her eye she can see Stuart easing back his chair at the other end of the table. She can see him standing up to greet whoever it is who's just walked in. *Ludwell*, she thinks, twisting round in her own seat to see. But it isn't Ludwell. It's Marie – who's changed into another long, tasselled skirt for the occasion – and a woman with a crisp blonde bob in a peach-coloured dress. *Mrs* Storm.

Something tightens inside Bella's stomach, like an iron fist squeezing at her insides. She hadn't misheard after all then. She sinks down in her seat, pressing her spine into the back of her chair, as Marie clears her throat and introduces Ludwell's wife, Julia, to everyone. 'We're so pleased you could join us,' she gushes. 'Stuart, can you see where Rosel's got to with the wine?'

'Thank you,' says Julia, smiling round the table. 'I'm not very good with names, I'm afraid, so you'll have to bear with me if I forget who everyone is. But it's lovely to be here. Ludwell won't be long,' she adds apologetically. 'He's just outside making a quick call before he hands his mobile in, assuming he can get enough reception. I'm looking forward to some time away from

81

my phone. It's so hard to switch off otherwise, isn't it? There's always another email to reply to . . . Ah, here he is now.'

Yes. Here he is, looking exactly like Bella remembers. The same hip swagger. The same fake smile and polished laugh: 'Sorry about that, everyone. Awfully rude of me, I know.' Same blue eyes. Same long violinist's fingers on his right hand, pushing back a stray lock of hair from his face with the same easy charm. He hasn't even had the good grace to go grey. Or if he has, he's done a good job of hiding it, like his damaged left hand tucked away in his pocket.

He hasn't changed at all, Bella thinks, the lump in her throat growing bigger than ever, the iron fist in her stomach tightening its hold. *But I have,* she reminds herself as Ludwell takes his seat next to Julia and shakes Oscar's hand. *I'm not the same person I was back then.*

Rosel comes hurrying out of the kitchen with bottles of wine and mineral water on a tray as Oscar begins his familiar introduction: 'Oscar Wildman,' Bella hears him saying. 'I guess I was always going to be a writer with a name like that.'

'Indeed,' says Ludwell. 'I love Oscar Wilde. Especially his *Salome*. And the Strauss version too, of course.'

'Red or white?' asks Hamar, jumping up and taking charge of wine Rosel has deposited at their end of the table, while she works her way round the other end, filling people's glasses.

Whichever's strongest, thinks Bella.

*

Bella's appetite is still non-existent. The food is delicious apparently – everyone says so – but her taste buds seem to have packed up and gone for the night and the lump in her throat is refusing to budge, which makes swallowing feel like hard work. Conversations ebb and flow around her but Bella's head is too full of Ludwell to take much else in. Correction, too full of Ludwell *and Julia*. And now it's full of wine too. Krista only had the one small glass of white tonight, but Bella's making up for her friend's abstinence by downing one glass after another. It's a bad idea, she knows that. It's a terrible idea, under the circumstances. But right now, it's the only one she's got.

The room's already starting to spin when the moment she's been dreading all evening – all day – finally arrives.

'Hi there,' says Ludwell, who's doing an after-dinner tour of the table like the celebrity he is, winning the other guests over one by one with his smooth talking and air of genuine engagement. Everyone except Lena, that is, who's already excused herself to go and work on her article. Bella would have done the same if she hadn't been frozen with nerves. *Should* have done the same. Too late now though. To leave now would only draw *more* attention to herself.

The others are lapping up Ludwell's charm offensive – lapping *him* up. Hamar is all smiles and hearty backslaps when the great man gets to him, and Krista is practically purring. And then it's Bella's turn. There's no backing out now. No escape. He's already crouching down beside her, leaning in with his fancy aftershave smell and air of natural confidence. He's close enough that she can see the tiny brown mole above his left eyebrow and a telltale half centimetre of grey hair at the roots of his parting. Close enough to see the stubs of his fingers as he reaches his left hand to the back of her chair to steady himself.

It's going to be all right though. He doesn't recognise her. Or if he does, he's doing a good job of hiding it . . . out of considera-tion for his wife, no doubt, sitting at the other end of the table. The lovely Julia. Then again, Bella thinks, perhaps it's not simply a case of Ludwell not *recognising* her. Perhaps he doesn't even remember her. Maybe the single most important event of her life meant nothing to him. The idea fills her with a sudden rush of anger. Stupid, irrational, wine-fuelled anger – the last thing she wants is for him to make the connection between them – but anger all the same.

'Hi,' she replies, relieved to find that her voice still works. It's too early to tell if she's slurring her words yet, but her tongue feels fat in her mouth. She takes an extra swig of wine for courage. 'Nice to meet you,' she adds, by which she means, *I'd hoped I'd never see you again.* 'I'm Bella.'

'Bella's a musician too,' says Krista. 'A composer.'

No, no, don't tell him that.

'Really? I used to teach a bit of composition myself, back in the day,' says Ludwell. 'Whereabouts did you study?'

Bella lowers her voice. At least she tries to. It still sounds loud and echoing inside her head. 'Oh no, I didn't go down the university route,' she tells him, hoping that Oscar isn't listening. Hoping he's not about to jump in and correct her: *But when we were talking about your interview in* Culture Vulture *you said . . .* A quick glance along the table is enough to reassure her though. Oscar is deep in conversation with Julia. He's probably mining her for information on the best way to kill someone with a dentist's drill – apparently she's head of the dentistry school at one of the London universities – or the perfect place to hide the body afterwards.

No, it's not Oscar she needs to worry about. It's Krista. Oscar must have filled her in on Bella's career in some detail during the flight, unless she secretly researched all the other guests before she got here.

'She's very talented though,' Krista tells Ludwell, as if she's worried Bella might be selling herself short. 'She's written the soundtrack to *The Screaming Hours.*'

No, don't tell him that either. He might go and look me up after dinner and put two and two together . . . Except he won't. Of course he won't. Because he won't have his phone on him. *Yes! Hooray for Marie's black box!*

'I presume you're not in academe any more though?' says Bella, feigning ignorance as she tries to steer the conversation away from her again. 'Or do you still teach alongside all the media stuff?' *How was that? Too much? Or not enough?* It's hard to tell through the veil of alcohol. What was she thinking, drinking all that wine? And yet somehow she finds herself reaching out for her glass again. Finds herself gulping down another large mouthful.

Ludwell smiles. 'No, something had to give,' he says. 'It's not quite how I expected my career to pan out, but then life never turns out exactly how you think it will, does it?'

'No,' Bella agrees. 'It doesn't.' She remembers how thrilled she was when she got her university offer. Remembers ripping open the envelope and letting out a genuine squeal of excitement at the thought of studying with the great Ludwell Storm. She can still remember the look of disappointment on her mum's face when she told her that's where she'd be going. Not to the Royal College where she'd spent so many Saturdays as a junior exhibitioner. Not to any of the conservatoires. She remembers the look on her boyfriend's face, too . . . Poor, sweet Nat. It's been a long time since Bella's thought of him. Nathanial Stocker. How different would her life have been if she'd stayed with him?

Ludwell shakes his head. 'If someone had told me twenty years ago that I'd be a visiting speaker at a wilderness retreat in Sweden I'd have laughed. I'm not sure I'd even *heard* of music therapy back then. And yet here I am. And here *you* are. It's lovely to meet you, Belle. I look forward to hearing more about your film work. Such an interesting field of composition. But you'll have to excuse me,' he says, dismissing her with another phoney smile as he pulls himself back up to his full height. 'I can see my wife signalling to me. I'd better go and see what she wants.'

It's Bella, you bastard.

Ludwell turns back to face her. 'Sorry, what was that?'

Oh crap, I didn't say that out loud, did I?

'Oh, n-nothing. I just er . . . Bella,' she stammers, her hand already reaching back for her wineglass. 'My name's not Belle, it's Bella.'

'Yes, of course, sorry. Short for Isabella, I presume? But Bella rather than Izzy. Got it.'

Izzy. Her name still sounds the same on his lips all these years later. The slightest of lisps on the 'z' lending it a more languorous, sensuous edge.

'No,' she lies. 'It's not short for anything. Just plain Bella on its own.'

And that should have been it. First meeting done and dusted. But the short delay over her name is long enough for his wife to give up waiting for him. For her to get up out of her seat and fetch him in person.

'Ah Julia,' says Ludwell. 'I'd like you to meet Bella. Bella with an "a",' he adds with a wink. 'Not Belle. Definitely not Belle. Bella's a fellow musician, darling – a composer.'

'Oh really? How nice.' Julia gives a cursory nod in Bella's direction. 'I'm sorry to interrupt your music chat, but I think I'm getting one of my headaches,' she tells Ludwell. 'I'm going to take a couple of tablets and turn in for the night . . . see if I can nip it in the bud.'

'Of course, darling. I hope that does the trick. I could do with an earlyish night myself to be honest. I didn't sleep very well yesterday.'

Tell me about it, thinks Bella, feeling nauseous at the sight of Ludwell's good hand on his wife's back. The easy intimacy of the gesture – the way he's stroking up and down her lower spine with his fingers – makes her feel quite sick. Or maybe it's the tone of his voice – the oiliness of that '*darling*'. Or it could be the smoked sausage stroganoff sloshing round in a churning sea of wine inside Bella's stomach.

'Right, I'll love you and leave you then,' says Julia. 'Nice to meet you, Bella with an "a".'

'You too,' Bella replies, trying to ignore the swirling in her stomach. *No more wine*, she tells herself queasily. *That last glass was a bad idea.* 'I hope you're feeling better soon.'

And that should have been *that*. First meeting with the wife done and dusted too. But for some reason Julia's still there. Still staring at her with an unsettling air of scrutiny. 'You look very familiar actually, now I come to think about it,' she's saying. 'I can't quite put my finger on it though . . . Have we met before?'

'No, I don't think so,' says Bella, thirty-eight-year-old mother of one. *Drunken* thirty-eight-year-old mother of one. The room's really starting to spin now.

Yes, shouts nineteen-year-old Izzy. *That was me on your doorstep that day. Don't you remember?* Why would she though? Why would Ludwell Storm's beautiful, poised wife remember *her*?

'Oh,' Bella gasps, as a sudden gush of nausea comes rushing up from her stomach. No, something more than nausea. *This can't be happening.*

But it is.

'I'm sorry,' she cries. 'I have to go. I think I'm going to be—'

Too late.

Bella watches in detached horror as half a plate of smoked sausage stroganoff and goodness knows how many glasses of wine make an unwelcome reappearance all down her jumper. All down the hem of Julia's pretty peach dress to the floor, splashing back up onto her elegant cream shoes.

There's a collective gasp of shock from the others round the table. An even louder gasp from Julia herself.

'I . . . I'm so sorry,' Bella stammers, clutching at the table for support as the room lurches ever more wildly around her, knocking her wineglass onto the floor as she does so.

You'll remember me now, she thinks, closing her eyes against the gory paprika-orange horror of it all. *There'll be no forgetting this.*

*

Where am I?

Izzy panics as she stares around the unfamiliar bedroom, her head dizzy and pounding, her stomach cramped with pain. The sharp beam of light coming through the gap in the thick jacquard curtains – a painful, blinding light that drills right through her half-closed eyelids to the throbbing ache inside her skull – does nothing to illuminate the situation. She's still in the dark as to where she is or how she got there.

The bed she finds herself in, wearing just her bra and knickers, is large and comfortable, with crisp, white bed linen and soft pillows . . . like a hotel bed. But there are too many personal touches for this to be a hotel room: the quirky bedside clock, shaped like a violin; the pile of clothes on the plush upholstered chair in the corner; the cluttered dressing table under the window, with expensive-looking lipsticks and bottles of nail varnish scattered across the polished surface like coloured jewels. And there, on the floor, her own discarded dress from last night.

What have I done?

Izzy closes her eyes again, her stomach clenching at the scent of burnt toast that comes snaking through the darkness to find her. Burnt toast and coffee, that's what it smells like . . . and something else . . . a tangy citrus smell with a touch of musk, like a man's aftershave, that nudges at the edges of her barely conscious brain like a reminder of something important . . . no, not something, someone . . .

But then the someone is right there in the room with her – Ludwell! She remembers now! – shaking her roughly by the shoulder and telling her to wake up. Telling her his wife is on her way back and Izzy needs to hurry up and go.

His wife? No, this can't be happening. But it is. It already has. Izzy still can't recall how she got from the hallway last night to here, semi-naked in her lecturer's bed, but there's no time to puzzle it out now, as a sudden burst of nausea – of sour alcohol and guilt – comes rushing up her throat. She staggers across the room to the fancy-looking en suite, with its walk-in shower and glitzy gold tiles, prostrating herself before the toilet as the noxious mixture of vodka, whisky and beer, of tequila and shame, churning around inside her stomach, takes its natural course. Just in time.

Chapter 12

In her dream, Bella's back at the Storms' house, ringing the doorbell over and over again until Julia finally comes to let her in. But as soon as Bella steps inside, she finds herself back in the lodge kitchen instead, with a row of apples lined up along the work surface. The other retreat guests are there too, crowding round an enormous silver fridge, trying to stop Bella from reaching the baby she can hear crying inside. *Asher!*

He must be cold in there – cold and scared. She needs to get him out. But the others keep pushing her back again.

'Not after what you did to me,' says Julia.

'Not until you bring back Saga's apple,' booms Hamar, his face contorted with laughter.

'You're not going anywhere,' Krista joins in. 'Not until I find my husband's killer. I need answers.'

'And I need another body for my book,' says Oscar.

'Asher!' Bella screams, desperate to reach him before it's too late. 'ASHER!'

She can still feel his name echoing in her head when she opens her eyes, roused by a noise: a soft scratching sound coming from the other side of the wall. From the empty room nextdoor. Or maybe the noise was in her dream. Maybe it was Asher trying to get out, grinding his heels against the fridge door ... Bella's heart is thumping with residual panic as she lies there in the darkness, listening, but the noise has gone again now.

Her duvet feels heavy and oppressive against her body, her pillow too hot under her head. A glass of water, that's what she needs. A cold glass of water to soothe the raw soreness of her throat and ease the dizzy throbbing in her head. Bella reaches for the bedside light and switches it on. *Woah, that's bright.* Shielding her eyes against the dazzling glare, she pulls herself up into a sitting position and immediately regrets it. The throbbing in her head while she was horizontal was nothing compared to the thumping blare of pain that hits her as she draws vertical. How much did she drink last night?

Last night. It's all starting to come back to her now. Snatches of it, anyway. Wine and stroganoff ... More wine ... Ludwell ... What was it he'd said to her? Bella can't quite recall the details. But then Julia was there too ... and then ... The mere memory is enough to send her running back to the bathroom to empty her stomach all over again. Not that there's much left in it *to* empty. No, because it's all over Julia Storm's shoes.

Bella clings to the toilet bowl in an effort to make the floor tiles stay still, groaning at the full horror of her humiliation. It's just as well Asher can't see her now, after all her lectures about sensible drinking. *I'm not saying you can't have fun,* she'd told him, *but don't go crazy, that's all. Don't get so drunk that you don't know what you're doing.* She forgot to add in the bit about not throwing up at the dining table in front of a room full of relative strangers. About the perils of vomiting smoked sausage onto someone's shoes when you're trying to keep a low profile.

The bit *after* the shoe incident is a complete blank though. Someone must have helped Bella back to her room and got her cleaned up. Did they help her get undressed too? The idea makes her feel decidedly uncomfortable. And what about her jumper? What happened to that? She doesn't remember seeing it on her dash from her bed to the bathroom, but she had other, more pressing worries on her mind at the time. Bella drags herself back up off the floor and fills the toothbrush glass by the sink with water, taking a gulp and swilling it round before spitting it back out into the sink. Orange spit. Yuck.

The feel of water on her tongue seems to have awakened her thirst though – a sudden, desperate thirst. *Slow sips now*, she tells herself, resisting the urge to down the entire glass in one. That never ends well on a queasy stomach. But the water tastes good. It tastes cold and clean. She finishes off the first glass and runs herself another. And when that's all gone, she splashes some cold water on her face, wincing at the sudden shock of it against her skin, then drags a toothbrush round her mouth. There, that's better. A *bit* better anyway. The room is still spinning but not quite so fast any more. She rummages through her travel toiletries bag for some paracetamol and swallows them down before heading back to the bedroom to look for her missing jumper. It's a special one – a birthday present from Asher when he was fourteen, in her favourite shade of blue – and it probably needs to go into soak if it's not already too late for that.

She finds her jeans and T-shirt from the night before, folded up in a neat pile on the sofa, but there's no sign of the jumper. It's not on the desk chair either, or the desk itself, although it looks like someone's cleared away Bella's dirty cup from the day before. The same someone, presumably, who tidied her pencils and eraser back into her pencil case, now sitting neatly alongside her manuscript paper and her trusty block of Post-it notes. And what's that, by the window? An apple? How on earth did that get there?

Bella goes to pick it up and cries out in disgust, dropping it straight back down onto the desk with a muffled thump. There's a hole around the stalk, where the skin and flesh should be, a wiggling, writhing hole of tiny white maggots. The sight of them makes her retch all over again. She grabs the copper bin from

91

under her desk and rolls the offending fruit inside, then opens the window, letting a blast of cold air into the room.

Bella leans out into the night, tipping up the bin and listening for the soft thud of the apple on the ground below. Listening in the darkness and trying not to think of the shiny white bodies still writhing around inside its hollowed-out flesh. But the bin, when she pulls it back inside and examines it, is empty, thank goodness. No extra guests shimmying up the copper wall. She shuts the window, checks the bin one last time and staggers back towards her bed, exhausted by her efforts. And then, as a fresh wave of nausea comes for her, Bella closes her eyes and lies back down in the hope of riding it out, pulling up the duvet for warmth. That's better.

She almost drops off to sleep again but then the full enormity of what's happened catches up with her. The full horror. What if there are more of them still wriggling around her room? What if some had already escaped out of the apple onto her desk? They could be hiding under her pencil case even now, or burrowing away inside it, into the hidden corners and crevices. Bella drags herself up out of bed a second time and switches on the overhead light, then checks each object on her desk in turn. Nothing under her pencil case. Nothing *inside* it either. The book of manuscript paper seems clear of any unwanted extras too, and there's nothing on the Post-it notes except for her own scrawled memos: *more depth needed in bars 30-45? Bassoon line too prominent in bars 50-60? Try muting the violas?* But then something rustles as she reaches for the Dödmansskogen map and she pulls back in fear. Ridiculous fear, Bella knows that – a tiny grub is no match for a fully grown woman – but fear all the same.

This calls for reinforcements. She grabs a cardigan from the built-in wardrobe, checking it carefully before she puts it on, in case any strays have magically managed to wriggle across the room and bury themselves in her clothes. And then, armed with the torch from beside her bed, she sets off unsteadily for the kitchen in search of some bug spray. Something strong enough to disinfect her desk and kill any lurkers.

Bella's head still throbs but the worst of the dizziness seems to have passed now – the shock must have sobered her up. The queasy swirling in her stomach seems to have eased too, replaced by a crawling sensation up her arms and legs, like tiny creatures wriggling and burrowing under her skin. Why would someone leave a maggot-infested apple in her room? Where would they even find one in the first place? And how long has it been there? Was it there when she went to bed? If only Bella could remember how she got to bed in the first place. The idea of someone sneaking around inside her room while she was asleep is almost as disturbing as the apple itself.

Her window was definitely locked. She remembers sliding the catch across to open it when she tipped out the bin, so whoever the perpetrator was, they didn't get in that way. And her door was locked too – it locks automatically on closing – which means Bella's at just as much of a loss to know *how* someone got in to leave such a horrible gift on her desk as to why they'd want to in the first place. Is it the same person who left the note under her door? Oscar, testing out another storyline for his precious novel? Hamar? Could this be another one of his 'jokes'? Or maybe it's Julia, paying her back for the humiliating episode at dinner? It seems unlikely, but once the thought's in her head, wriggling and burrowing into her brain like a little white maggot, it's hard to shake it out again. *Maybe she knows . . . knows who I am. Knows what I did . . .*

'Hello? Who's that?'

Bella's reaching for the dining room light switch when a voice calls out to her.

She swings round in surprise, the beam of her torch picking out a ghostly white figure at the other end of the room. It's not a ghost though, it's Marie, dressed in an old-fashioned long white nightdress – the sort of thing Bella's mother used to wear.

'Goodness,' says Bella. 'You made me jump. Oh, sorry,' she adds, pointing the torch down to the floor, away from Marie's eyes. 'I didn't mean to dazzle you.'

She reaches for the light switch a second time. *There, that's better,* she thinks as the dining room transforms back from a dark, creepy horror film set to something out of a glossy home-decorating magazine. 'Sorry,' she says again. 'Did I wake you?'

'No, I've been up and down half the night. It was the wind that disturbed me the first time – it sounded pretty wild out there – and then later . . .' Marie pauses for a moment, shivering in her nightie. 'I thought I heard a noise outside – like someone walking across the gravel – but I couldn't see anything when I went to check. I've been wide awake ever since. Not even my trusty sleep meditation is working for me tonight. My mind feels too crowded with thoughts of the past to fully surrender to the present.'

Your son, Bella thinks with a pang, her own emergency temporarily forgotten.

'So I was just coming to make myself some hot milk,' Marie finishes. 'Sometimes we have to take care of the body to help take care of the mind. And how about you? How are you feeling now?'

'What?' It takes Bella's alcohol-fuddled brain an extra second or two to process the question. She's still thinking about Marie's son. About how she'd manage if anything ever happened to Asher. 'Oh yes, thank you. Much better. I'm so sorry about dinner . . . about, well you know. It's mortifying. I er . . .' She tries to think of an excuse for what happened. Something to make it less embarrassing. But there *is* no excuse. She drank herself silly and then threw up on Julia Storm's shoes. End of story.

'Don't worry,' says Marie kindly. 'These things happen, especially in times of emotional imbalance. Or perhaps you ate something that didn't agree with you at the airport. Food poisoning can sometimes take a couple of days to work through your system. As long as you're all right – that's all that matters.'

Nothing to do with all that wine I drank. No, definitely not. 'Yes, perhaps it *was* a touch of food poisoning,' says Bella, grateful for the lie, even as her headache continues to pound away behind her eyes, waiting for the paracetamol to take effect. 'Maybe that's why I was off my food earlier in the day.' *Nothing to do with the imminent arrival of Ludwell Storm.* 'Thank you for sorting me out afterwards . . . helping me back to my room, I mean.' She can hardly admit that the rest of the night is a complete blank. Not if it was supposed to be food poisoning.

'Oh no, that wasn't me,' says Marie. 'That was Krista, bless her. She was very worried about you.'

'Yes, of course it was. I remember now,' Bella lies. Her only memory of Krista from after dinner is from her dream . . . She can still see her now, snarling into her face, demanding answers. *Not until I find my husband's killer* . . . Bella blinks, forcing the image away again. 'And she was the only one in my room? Oscar didn't offer to help at all?' *Or Hamar? Or Julia?* Or maybe the apple culprit is the same mysterious someone whom Marie heard creeping around outside . . .

'Oscar?' Marie looks puzzled. 'No. He left not long after you did. Said he wanted to finish off the chapter he was working on. Apparently the ideas are coming thick and fast since he got here. Maybe we should think about branching out into running writers' retreats too!'

'So just Krista then?' Bella's conscious of how odd her questions must sound but she needs to get this straight. She needs to know. 'She's definitely the only one who was in my room last night?'

'As far as I'm aware, yes. I lent her my key as she couldn't find yours – I don't think she felt very comfortable going through your pockets – but she brought it straight back afterwards. I hope that's okay? You weren't really in any state to ask, what with the er . . . with the food poisoning.' Marie's expression darkens. 'Why? Is something wrong? Is there something missing from your room?'

'No,' says Bella. 'The opposite. Someone left an apple on my desk.'

'Oh, that's all right then. You had me worried there for a moment.'

'No,' says Bella again. 'It's not all right. It was full of maggots.'

Marie pulls a face. 'That's horrible. Are you sure? Is it still there now?'

Bella shakes her head. 'I threw it out the window, but I was worried there might be more of them. More maggots, I mean.' She squirms inwardly at the thought. At the feel of the word on her tongue. 'I think I heard them crawling round inside the map. I was on my way to the kitchen to look for some bug spray.' It sounds kind of crazy when she says it out loud. *She* sounds kind of crazy.

'We don't keep that sort of thing in the kitchen for health and safety reasons,' says Marie. 'It's not good for the body or the mind to be around such unnatural, toxic substances.' And then her language and her expression soften a little. 'I imagine it'll be in the cleaning cupboard if we've got any, but I'm not sure it's the sort of thing you want to be spraying around before you go to sleep anyway. Why don't I make you a nice cup of camomile tea to take back to bed, while I heat up my milk, and then I'll come and check your room over for you? Just to put your mind at rest. Sometimes the brain plays tricks on us when we're unwell. I remember when my first husband was running a fever one Christmas – he was convinced there were beetles running across his pillow. I came up to bed to find him shaking it over the carpet, trying to flick them off with his fingers. He didn't even remember it the next day.'

You don't believe me, do you? You think I imagined the whole thing. But they were there. I know they were. Bella can still see them now in her mind's eye, squirming over each other like blind white worms. But then again, what if she *did* imagine it? She runs her tongue around her mouth, trying to decide if it tastes of toothpaste or not. What if the alcohol was playing tricks on her brain and she dreamt the whole thing, from drinking the water in the bathroom to the apple on her desk? Just like she dreamt about the crying coming from the fridge?

'Don't worry about the tea, I can fix myself a cup back in my room,' she tells Marie as she follows her into the kitchen, not wanting to put her out. 'I'll just sit quietly while you get your milk. The change of scene will do me good. Thank you,' she adds, in case she sounds ungrateful.

Bella takes a seat on one of the breakfast bar stools while Marie bustles around the kitchen. She's still thinking about her dream. It was all so real: Hamar's laugh; the look on Krista's face; Asher's crying cutting through her like a physical pain. Just like the apple seemed real at the time . . . *could* that have been a dream too? She's starting to doubt the whole thing now. There *had* been a lot of talk about apples at breakfast. And then Saga had come to her room to talk about leaving some fruit out for her. She'll have to have a look in the morning, when it's light. If the maggoty apple *was* real, it'll still be there, won't it? And if it's not . . . well, that's a good thing. Bella hopes she *did* dream the whole thing.

'Biscuit?' Marie offers her the tin. 'I think Saga meant to leave them in the dining room – she said something about putting some snacks out for early risers – but she must have forgotten. She seems a bit distracted this week. Not her usual organised self.'

'Thank you,' says Bella. It might be a good idea to get some food inside her if she can stomach it. A biscuit should be okay. No apples though – the very thought makes her shudder. It'll be a long time until she can manage one of those again.

'There we go,' says Marie, as she pours the freshly heated milk into a mug. 'Now for a quick check round your room – make sure everything's as it should be – and then we can both get back to bed.'

'That would be great.'

Bella's room smells unpleasantly sour when she opens the door again. The quick blast of air from the open window earlier has done nothing to clear the fug of alcoholic sweat and stale vomit.

That's if she *did* open the window. Or was that part of the dream too? 'Sorry,' she says. 'Let me get a bit of fresh air in here.'

Marie brushes the suggestion aside with a wave of her hand. 'No, no, that's fine. You need to keep yourself nice and warm if you're under the weather. Now then, where's that rustling map of yours? Ah yes, here we go.'

Bella keeps her distance as Marie opens the map out and checks it for unwanted visitors.

Nothing.

She turns it over and checks the other side, giving it a shake for good measure.

Nothing there either.

'Perhaps it was something outside the window you heard,' Marie suggests. 'The wind in the trees. As I say, it was pretty wild earlier. Or a bird. I used to hear all sorts of strange sounds in the middle of the night when I first started coming here. Strange scratchings coming from the walls. I don't really notice them any more though. Apart from tonight,' she adds with a wry laugh. 'I suspect my mysterious gravel-tramping trespasser was probably just an animal too though. A deer most likely, unnerved by the storm – we get a few of them out here. Stuart's even spotted the odd elk in the summer months. No bears as yet though, I'm relieved to say. We must count our blessings wherever we find them.'

Marie crouches down and runs her hand along the underside of the desk, her bra line pressing through the thin fabric of her nightie. Bella turns away, embarrassed, as if she's prying on a secret part of the older woman's life. Her mother used to sleep in one too but it seems at odds, somehow, with Marie's relaxed, hippy-style of dressing during the day.

'All clear,' she announces, suppressing a yawn as she straightens up again. 'Nothing for you to worry about here. I'll let you get back to sleep, shall I?'

'Thank you,' Bella says. 'I'm sorry to have kept you up for

nothing. And sorry again for last night. I'm going to have some serious grovelling to do when I see Julia tomorrow.'

'I'm sure she won't hold it against you,' Marie tells her. 'And you mustn't hold it against yourself either. Forgiveness begins with forgiving yourself. With self-acceptance. Just get yourself back to sleep and with any luck you'll be right as rain tomorrow.'

Tomorrow will be better, Bella tells herself as Marie closes the door softly behind her. *Except it* won't *be, will it?* Ludwell and Julia will still be here tomorrow. Everyone else will still be here too, with the gory details of Bella's impromptu after-dinner entertainment still fresh in their minds. The best she can say about tomorrow is that it's one day closer to leaving. One day closer to seeing Asher again.

She crosses over to the window and peers out into the darkness. It's eerily quiet out there now. Eerily still. Bella must have slept right through the storm, but there's no sleep left in her now. Maybe a camomile tea isn't such a bad idea, after all, if she can stomach it. She fills the kettle and switches it on, wondering whether Asher's back from his night of clubbing yet – *every* night seems to be club night in freshers' week – or if he's still going strong. Wondering if he's treated his new friends to his famous chicken dance yet – the one he always does to cheer her up, knowing it'll make her laugh – or if he's too busy playing it cool. What wouldn't she give to see him doing his chicken dance right now?

Bella jumps. *What was that?* A knock at the door – quiet enough to keep from waking up her next-door-but-one neighbours, but loud enough to startle her.

'Who's there?' she calls back in a stage whisper, pressing her ear against the wood.

'It's Stuart,' comes the muted reply. 'Marie said you were having a bad night, so I thought I'd bring you some of my special sleep tea. I'll leave it outside for you, shall I?'

'No, no, it's fine, I'm decent,' Bella says, opening the door to him. Stuart looks vaguely monkish, standing there in his brown

99

dressing gown, holding out a metal tea strainer and a small bag of something resembling potpourri, like an offering.

'Thank you,' she says, taking them. 'That's really thoughtful. Perfect timing, too. The kettle's just boiling now.'

'A couple of spoonfuls should be enough to do the trick,' he tells her. 'Let it steep for a few minutes and then you're good to go. I swear by it myself, although Marie still prefers her hot milk.'

'Thank you,' Bella says again, genuinely touched by the gesture.

Stuart smiles. 'My pleasure. That's what I'm here for. Sleep well.'

Chapter 13

Tuesday morning. Four whole days still to go, and a pounding hangover to try and shake off. Hopefully the fresh air will help. It's cold outside, with a touch of something damp in the air. It must have rained properly during the early hours though. The gravel is shiny wet beneath Bella's feet as she skirts around the side of the lodge, head throbbing and stomach churning, in search of the apple she may or may not have thrown out the window the night before. The whole episode feels more dreamlike than ever now after another few hours' sleep, courtesy of Stuart's special tea and the residual alcohol still sloshing through Bella's veins. That's if the fevered, duvet-tangled snatches of unconsciousness can really be classed as sleep.

Yes, she concludes as she picks her way towards the bedrooms and the encroaching line of trees, as the gravel gives way to soft, mossy soil, *the apple seems more like a dream than anything now, just like the baby in the fridge*. But what about the strange scratching noise she heard coming from the room nextdoor – the *empty* room – when she woke up in a cold sweat an hour or so later? The memory seems even creepier somehow, in the cold light of day, than it did at the time. Did Bella dream that too or was there really something there in the walls? *Or someone*, she thinks, imagining fingernails scratching painted plaster. Picturing someone on the other side of the wall, breathing into the darkness a few feet away from her bed. Like the killer in *The Screaming Hours*, tapping his gloved hands against the wall in the hotel scene, while his next victim lies sleeping nextdoor. The image, coupled with the chilly morning air playing around her neck, makes her shiver.

She shouldn't have drunk so much at dinner. Her brain clearly can't cope with it any more. *No more wine for me tonight,* Bella vows. No more acting like a silly, boozy teenager and embarrassing herself. That's assuming she's still here by tonight . . . Maybe she should talk to Marie and Stuart after breakfast and find out when the next flight home is, just in case. Rachel would understand, wouldn't she? And Asher . . . Bella hasn't forgotten her promise to him to stay and make the most of this week. She knows how invested he is in this trip on her behalf, even arranging his accommodation moving-in slot to tie in with her flight so she could go straight on to the airport afterwards. But he wouldn't want her to be miserable, any more than her sister would. They wouldn't want her to feel scared. It's supposed to be a holiday, after all, not a punishment. And right now, traipsing through the cold, looking for a maggot-infested piece of fruit and worrying about creepy scratching noises in the night don't seem like Bella's idea of fun. And neither does the prospect of another day under the same roof as Ludwell.

The blind is down in the first room Bella comes to – that must be number eleven, Ludwell and Julia's room. They're clearly awake though . . . already up and arguing by the sounds of it.

'How was I to know?' Ludwell's voice – Bella would know it anywhere. 'You're the one who wanted to come with me. And I agreed because I thought it would be good for us. I thought it would be good for *you.*'

'Good for me? Well, you got that wrong, didn't you?' Julia snaps back at him. 'I didn't expect to have your sordid past thrown back in my face. It's humiliating.'

Bella's breath catches in her throat. Wait, are they talking about her? Is *she* the sordid past being thrown back (or should that be throwing *up*) in Julia's face? *No¸* she tells herself, clinging on to the flimsy hope that she's misunderstood. They could have been talking about anyone. Or any*thing*. Who knows what sordid secrets a man like Ludwell might be harbouring?

'I'm sorry, darling,' he says. 'If I'd known for one minute she'd be here, I'd never have agreed to it in the first place. I'd never have come.'

Bella's heart sinks. There's no explaining *that* away as a misunderstanding.

They know, she thinks. *They know who I am. They must have recognised me after all. What if they put two and two together and . . .?* Bella feels hot suddenly, despite the chilly air, a fluttery panic beating inside her chest.

'Don't you *darling* me,' she hears Julia say, her voice low and growly with anger. But then the panic takes full hold of Bella, blood pounding in her ears and echoing round her skull, and it's all she can do to keep from falling as the dizziness of the night makes an unwelcome return.

They know.

Time stays still as she stands there, swaying, the ground spinning under her feet. She should never have come. This was a mistake. This whole stupid trip has been one big mistake from start to finish.

They know. The same two words pulse inside her head, over and over again, as she stretches out a steadying hand to the wall. *They know.* And for a moment, a seemingly endless moment, that's all Bella can think. But then the giddiness eases a little and the first flush of panic retreats, leaving more balanced thoughts in its wake. *Even if they* did *recognise me, that doesn't mean they know the full story.*

The pulsing in Bella's head is easing now, too. She can hear Julia's voice again. 'You told me things would be different this time. You *promised*.'

'They *are* different,' Ludwell insists. '*I'm* different. I felt just as sick as you when I saw her. I feel sick when I think about her now.'

But not as sick as me, thinks Bella darkly. *You didn't vomit all over your wife's shoes, did you?*

'I didn't know she'd be here,' Ludwell says again. 'I swear.'

'*You* feel sick,' screams Julia. 'What about me? Just the *thought* of the two of you together . . . My head feels like it's going to explode.'

'You do look pale. Shall I let some fresh air in?' Ludwell offers.

But Bella doesn't hang around to hear Julia's reply. She hurries on past the Storms' window before anyone spots her, to the empty room beyond, where she heard the weird scratching sound coming from last night. Where she *thought* she heard it coming from, rather. But the blind in room twelve is firmly down too, and no amount of staring at her own ghostly reflection, peering back at her from the dark glass, is going to tell Bella whether she dreamt it or not.

Focus on the apple, she tells herself instead, forcing herself to keep walking. Trying to keep her confused barrage of thoughts in check. *One crisis at a time*. But there *is* no apple. It's not underneath her window and it's not caught in the low-lying shrubs beyond. Of course it's possible an animal has made off with it in the meantime: a passing deer – do deer eat apples? – or a crow, maybe. She remembers reading an article about crows burying bits of meat under the earth to attract egg-laying flies in order to harvest the hatching maggots at a later date. Maybe a crow spotted his readymade breakfast wriggling around inside the apple and made off with the whole thing. But it's much more likely that the apple wasn't there in the first place. That she really did dream the whole thing . . . like the baby in the fridge and the scratching fingernails . . . Perhaps it was *all* a dream.

Bella's still waiting for the feeling of relief to kick in. But if it was all a dream, what are those marks, almost like footprints, doing under her window? She didn't notice them at first – her brain was too focused on the apple – but now that she steps back and examines them, that's exactly what they look like: a churned-up, muddied muddle of prints. They can't *all* be hers . . . can they? She picks up her booted right foot and surveys the soft soil clinging to the sole, as if that might shed some light on the matter. But there's no matching to be done. The imprints under her window aren't distinct enough for that. She can't even tell what size feet might have made them. Or when. It could have been someone cleaning the windows at the weekend for all Bella knows. There's nothing to indicate how fresh the marks are. Nothing but a nasty, nagging feeling in the pit of her stomach to add to her general unease, and a new line of worry to add to all the others.

But then she remembers the rustling sound she heard in the night, that she thought was coming from the map. What if it *was* someone outside, watching her through the thin blind? Watching her backlit shadow moving about the room? Listening in? It could be the same someone Marie heard last night, walking across the gravel. The thought sends a fresh wave of shivers down Bella's neck as the rank of imagined night-time stalkers grows: someone outside her window in the darkness; someone scratching their nails down the other side of the wall; someone right there *inside* her room, leaving maggot-infested gifts on her desk . . . If one of them's real – if these semi-footprints in the soil really *do* belong to someone else – does that mean they all are?

Breakfast is already underway by the time Bella's taken off her muddy shoes and dropped her coat back to her room; by the time she's plucked up the courage to face everybody after the humiliating spectacle she made of herself at dinner last night. By the time she's plucked up the courage to face Ludwell and Julia, after the row she's just overheard. *They know!* But neither of them said anything last night (at least nothing that Bella remembers, which isn't necessarily the same thing), so maybe they plan on keeping it to themselves to avoid further embarrassment. And if not . . . well, hiding in her room is only putting off the inevitable, Bella tells herself. She'll have to see them eventually, unless she wants to go hungry, and the sooner she gets her apologies out of the way and some solid food inside her stomach, the better. Once she's seen off the worst of her hangover, she can think about working out her exit strategy. Knocking the rest of the retreat on the head and getting out of here is looking like an increasingly attractive option.

A few days ago, the thought of returning home to an empty house would have filled Bella with dread but it's surprisingly appealing now. Yes, it'll be strange and sad without Asher there, but Ludwell and Julia won't be there either, which is a definite plus point. There's no sign of them in the dining room yet though – perhaps they're still rowing in their bedroom. Maybe if Bella's quick she can get through breakfast before they put in an appearance.

Lena is deep in conversation with T, an expression of intense concentration on her face. T, on the other hand, looks like he'd rather be back in bed than answering questions at this time of the morning. Or maybe he just wants to be left in peace to enjoy his morning shot of caffeine, like Krista a few seats along, nursing a mug of coffee between her cupped hands and staring into space. She looks tired today, Bella thinks with a pang. Tired and sad. And Oscar? Oscar's just Oscar, sitting there in his usual spot, peeling a boiled egg as he reads through his notebook, mouthing something under his breath. Plotting, no doubt. Stuart's already there too, mopping up a spill at the far end of the table, stopping briefly to greet Bella as she comes in, but there's no sign of Marie. Hamar's yet to put in an appearance either. Oh no, wait, here he comes now, emerging from the kitchen as Bella makes a surreptitious dash for the coffee machine, whistling tunelessly to himself.

'Beautiful day for it,' he announces to no one in particular. Rosel follows him out with a fresh platter of pastries, flinching visibly as he touches her on the shoulder. 'Here,' he says, 'let me take those for you.' He grabs hold of the platter before she can answer, and carries them over to the buffet table, dismissing her with an exaggerated wave of his free hand.

Bella takes a couple of pastries for herself – she's not sure she can face the cod roe this morning – and joins Krista at the table. 'Morning. Are you okay?'

Krista looks up in surprise. 'Oh, yes, I'm fine. Thank you. Just a bit of a rough night. I was dreaming about my husband—'

'No,' interrupts Oscar. 'That's all wrong,' he says, putting down his boiled egg and ripping the offending page out of his notebook. He screws it up into a tight ball and lets out a loud sigh of frustration. 'I really thought I'd got it that time, but all I've done is open up a bigger plot hole than before.'

Something snaps inside Bella as she sits there listening to him. Maybe it's the memory of that torn-out page she found pushed under her door. Maybe it's the alarming conversation she's just overheard outside the Storms' window still playing on her mind, coupled with guilt at the thought of Krista having to help her to bed the night before and deal with her drunken mess. Or maybe it's the sheer self-obsessed rudeness of the man, thinking the whole world revolves around him and his stupid book.

'Hey, where do you get off interrupting Krista like that?' she says, the words flying out of her mouth with surprising vehemence. 'What makes you think any of us want to hear about the size of your plot hole? I was asking Krista if she was all right – I *wasn't* asking you how your novel was going.'

It's hard to tell who's more shocked – Krista or Oscar, or Bella herself. She hasn't finished yet though. 'But while we *are* on the subject, I know it was you who put that ridiculous note under my door yesterday. I came here for a break – a chance to regather and move forward with my life – not to be a guinea pig for your book research. So in future I'll thank you to keep your stupid novel to yourself.' She stops to catch her breath, feeling the sudden tide of anger retreating again almost as quickly as it arrived.

Oscar's mouth hangs open as he stares back at her. 'What do

you mean? I didn't go near your door yesterday. I don't even know which room you're in.'

'It was a page from your notebook,' Bella insists, although she's less certain than she was a minute ago. Maybe it *wasn't* Oscar after all. Maybe it was just Hamar joking around, like Krista said. He seems to get off on winding people up. Or perhaps the note was meant for someone else. Perhaps there'd been a mix-up with the rooms, like with the message T found under *his* door. Oscar's got a point there – how *would* he know which bedroom was hers? Unless he'd been spying on her . . .

'I spotted it at breakfast yesterday,' Bella says, pointing to the notebook as she ploughs on regardless. No going back now. 'I saw the place where you'd torn the page out. I know what *you* did,' she tells him, quoting the message back at him. 'And I don't appreciate it.'

Oscar licks the top of his index finger and leafs through his notebook. 'You mean *here*?' he asks, pointing to the torn-out stub. 'That was at the airport café on Sunday, after you left to go to the duty free shop. I realised I'd got my main characters' opening scene all wrong and ripped the page out in frustration.' He carries on leafing through with his fingers but there are no more stubs to be found.

'Really?' says Bella. He could just be saying that to get himself out of trouble.

'Really,' Oscar insists. 'I'll prove it.' He gets up from the table, almost knocking over the chair as he does so, and hurries out of the dining room.

'What's all this?' asks Hamar, joining them. 'I hope you're not making a scene again. Some of us are still recovering from last night's performance. You don't know what you missed, Lena. You should have stayed for the grand finale.'

Bella resists the urge to kick him under the table and focuses her energies on blushing instead. Lena and T have broken off their conversation to listen in. *Everybody's* listening.

'You're not helping, Hamar,' says Krista, her usually bright singsong voice loaded with warning.

'I'm only teasing,' he says. 'You know me, that's just the way I roll. Ask T. I've been trying to get a rise out of him this morning, too, over his secret affair with Marie, but he's refusing to bite. Despite the fact that they were looking *very* cosy when I bumped into them coming out of the kitchen together late last night . . .' He winks in Stuart's direction. 'And I notice your lovely wife's conspicuous by her absence this morning, Stupot. Coincidence? You tell me.' But then his expression changes, his smile withering under the combined force of T's and Krista's glares. 'Relax, I'm just messing around. Stuart knows I don't mean any harm. Don't you? And so does Bella.'

'I . . . I'd rather forget about last night,' Bella stammers. 'I'm not sure I remember it all but the bits I *do* remember . . . I can only apologise to everyone. And thank you for taking care of me,' she adds, turning to Krista. 'I really appreciate it.' Now's probably not the time to ask about her missing jumper, even if it is her favourite. Even though Asher had taken over his friend's local paper round for a fortnight, while said friend was nursing a busted ankle, to help pay for it. No, now's not the time to demand it back. Now's the time for Bella to blush and grovel and wait for the ground to swallow her up.

But Krista must have read her mind. 'If you're wondering where your jumper is, I put it into soak in the laundry room last night. Rosel says she'll pop it in the machine when she does her next load later. It doesn't look like it's stained. And no need to apologise for anything,' she adds, squeezing Bella's hand. 'We're just glad to see you up and about. You had us worried there last night.'

'Thank you,' says Bella, returning the squeeze. 'Thank you both,' she adds, spotting Rosel topping up the jugs of juice at the buffet table.

'Good old Rosel,' says Hamar. 'Such a dependable girl.'

Rosel's blushing too now. It must be catching. Has something happened between her and Hamar? Did Bella miss *that* last night as well? But there's no time to dwell on it now, because here comes Oscar, clutching a crumpled sheet of paper.

'There you go,' he says, laying it down next to Bella's plate. 'It was still in my flight bag.'

Bella lets go of Krista's hand and stares at the page of notes in front of her, about a character called Saskia and her first meeting with someone called Jonas. There's a big diagonal line drawn across the page as if Oscar changed his mind about what he'd written, and the paper's clearly been scrumpled up into a ball at some stage too.

'Happy now?' demands Oscar. 'I was inspired after meeting you – after the coincidence of the two of us choosing the same table – and realised that's what my story needed too: coincidence. The bigger the better. I wanted my readers to wonder if Jonas having booked the seat opposite Saskia on the train was too convenient to be pure chance. I wanted to sow that little seed of doubt in their mind that he might have engineered the whole thing from the start.'

Bella doesn't know what to say – other than 'sorry'. 'I guess I jumped to conclusions. I should have stopped to ask before I started throwing accusations around. Sorry,' she says again, glancing back at Oscar's open notebook to see the words DEAD MAN and SCRATCHING FINGERNAILS written at the bottom of the page in capital letters, followed by an arrow pointing to something she can't make out at this distance. Her throat tightens. 'What's that?' she asks, pointing with her own chipped-polish fingernail.

'The story about the man in the coffin,' says Oscar, still sounding aggrieved. 'From last night.' He pauses, as if he's waiting for a response from Bella. For a nod of recognition, maybe.

But Bella just stares at him, still trying to process what he's telling her. *What story from last night?* she's thinking.

'The one Stuart was telling us,' Oscar adds. 'The one that gave Dödmansskogen its name . . . The Dead Man's Forest?'

Bella's got no memory of any story about a man though, dead or alive. 'Oh,' she says, embarrassed and disconcerted in equal measures. She's thinking about that peculiar scratching sound in the night, like fingernails down a wall . . . 'I must have missed that. What happened to him?'

'According to Stuart, he was a feared local bandit, known as "the coffin filler", who ambushed lone travellers in the forest, slitting their throats and stealing their possessions. He was finally caught by a group of vigilantes who sealed him up inside a crude wooden coffin and left him there amongst the trees to die. They say you can still hear his ghostly nails scraping against the wood at night, as he tries to claw his way out . . .'

A finger of ice – no finger*nails*, just ice – snakes its way down Bella's spine. 'That's horrible,' she murmurs with a shiver. It doesn't sound like the sort of thing she'd forget very easily but perhaps she *did* hear it after all. Maybe the scratching noise in the night was her brain's way of processing the story, turning it into another fevered alcohol-fuelled dream.

She's spared any further thoughts on the subject by the arrival of Marie, gliding into the dining room with an air of cheerful calmness that belies the dark shadows under her eyes. 'Good morning. I hope the new day finds you filled with fresh light and energy,' Marie says, gazing round at the assembled diners, 'and the beauty of our forest wilderness is working its healing magic on you all.'

'Never better,' replies Hamar. His gaze flicks back to the kitchen for the briefest of moments – an almost imperceptible flicker – and then he grins. 'The wilderness is certainly agreeing with *me*. Not sure the same can be said for Bella though.'

And there he goes again, *stirring*, Bella thinks, remembering her brief conversation with Saga the day before. The man's remorseless.

Marie frowns. 'Oh dear, I'm sorry to hear that.' She grabs one of the spare chairs from the other end of the table and drags it

111

across to where Bella's sitting, its metal legs scraping unpleasantly against the polished wood floor. 'Are you still feeling rough today?' she asks, before lowering her voice to a whisper. 'You haven't seen any more . . . er, *things* from last night?'

'No,' Bella whispers back, shaking her head. 'Nothing like that. Maybe I imagined the whole thing.' She didn't imagine the footprints under her window though, did she? And the scratching? What about that? She shivers again at the memory, real or not. 'I'm sorry for keeping you up last night. I hope you managed to get back to sleep okay, afterwards.' She pauses for a moment, stealing herself for what's coming. 'Please don't take this the wrong way, but I'm struggling a bit with the whole retreat. I feel terrible – I mean, it's an amazing place and I'm really lucky to be here, but . . .' This is harder than she thought. It's starting to sound like a break-up speech. *It's not you, it's me.* 'But I'm not in the best place right now,' Bella stammers, 'and I think . . . well, I'm not sure *this* is the best place either at the moment. Not for me. I wondered when the next flight back was . . .'

Marie's the one shaking her head now. 'Oh dear,' she says again, her voice still at whisper level. 'I'm sorry you're feeling like that.' She presses her hand to her chest as if the idea brings her physical discomfort. 'And I'm sorry to be the bearer of bad news, but I don't think you'll be going anywhere just yet. A couple of trees came down in the storm last night – two enormous ones, right across the road – which means nobody's coming in or out until we can get them shifted. They lost a lot of trees north of here too, and the man I spoke to this morning said they're prioritising the main roads. We'll be clear by the weekend though – he assured me of that – so there shouldn't be any problem getting you to your flight on Saturday. But in the meantime . . .'

. . . In the meantime, I'm stuck here whether I like it or not. That's what you're saying, isn't it?

'In the meantime, it looks as if the universe has other plans for you, I'm afraid,' Marie finishes. She touches a hand to Bella's arm but then snatches it back again as if she's worried she might have crossed a line. 'I'm so sorry,' she says again, looking pained. 'If you wouldn't mind keeping this to yourself for now though. I don't want to alarm the others unnecessarily.'

Bella nods. Why couldn't the trees have come down *before* Ludwell was due to arrive? Or before Bella's own flight, come to that? Yes, it would have been better for her if the whole week had been cancelled. If only the universe had thought to write *that* into its plans. 'It's fine,' she lies. 'I just wanted to see what my options were, that's all.'

And now I know. There are no options.

'Maybe it's a blessing in disguise,' Marie suggests. 'Maybe you'll feel differently by tomorrow, after a better night's sleep. I do hope so.'

'Yes, maybe,' says Bella. At least that solves the issue of how to break the news to Rachel and Asher about cutting her trip short. And maybe Marie's right. Maybe she *will* feel better by tomorrow. She remembers the holiday to Rome a few years ago, when she and Asher had their homeward flights cancelled after a fire at the airport. The twenty-four-hour delay had seemed like the biggest nuisance ever at first, but they'd decided to make the best of it. Twenty-four bonus hours spent on a train ride out to Ostia Antica, followed by a mellow evening back in the city, photographing cats amongst the ancient ruins, with another visit to their local gelateria. Asher had declared it his favourite day of the entire holiday. Things – also known as 'the universe' – do have a surprising way of working out sometimes, Bella reminds herself.

'But do come and find me if you've got any concerns you'd like to talk through in the meantime,' Marie says earnestly. 'Or if there's anything Stuart and I can do to make your stay here more emotionally rewarding. Anything at all. Even if you just fancy a cup of tea and a friendly chat,' she adds, bringing her hands together again, as if in prayer. 'I might be able to wrangle a slice of one of Saga's delicious cakes if we're lucky. How does that sound?'

'Thank you,' says Bella. What else *can* she say? 'That sounds good.' But no matter how hard she tries to look on the bright side, what she still feels is trapped. Trapped in the middle of nowhere with an obsessed writer and the class clown. With Ludwell Storm and his puked-on wife, and a messy barrage of memories she'd rather forget.

*

Izzy feels sick as she waits on the doorstep, listening to the ding of the bell echoing down the hall. But this isn't the familiar, queasy nausea of the last few weeks, which has her retching into her bedroom sink each morning. It's a nervous, breathless sensation that sets her stomach swirling and her legs trembling beneath her. A trembling that spreads through her whole body as the door swings open and a tall, slim woman with a smart blonde bob smiles back at her.

Izzy reaches for the right words to begin, for a simple 'hi' to get the ball rolling. But she can't even manage that. Her tongue's too big for her mouth, her throat too tight to talk.

'Can I help you?' The woman's smile is colder now.

'I . . . er . . .' It's not too late to change her mind. To pretend she's got the wrong house. Not too late to turn around and run. 'I'm looking for Ludwell.' Now it's too late. 'I mean Dr Storm. Mr Storm,' Izzy corrects herself. Ludwell doesn't actually have a PhD.

The woman looks her up and down. 'You're one of his students?'

Izzy nods.

'I'm not sure he's . . .' the woman begins, turning at the sound of someone coming down the hall behind her. Ludwell. 'Ah, there you are. One of your students is here to see you, darling,' She turns back to Izzy, her expression downright frosty now. 'I didn't catch your name.'

That's because I didn't *tell* you my name, *Izzy thinks. 'Izzy,'* she says out loud. 'Isabella Burnstone. I'm doing the orchestration module this term.'

Ludwell appears at his wife's side, the two of them framed together in the wide doorway like the perfect married couple. But then his wife excuses herself and Izzy and Ludwell are alone once more.

'I'm sorry to interrupt your weekend,' Izzy begins. Can his wife still hear them? 'But something important's come up . . .'

'How did you get my address?' asks Ludwell, as if it was someone else who invited her back here that night. As if it was another man entirely who leaned her up against the hall wall and kissed her . . . who threw her out of bed the next morning like a piece of trash.

'I . . . I . . .' She searches his face for a hint of recognition and finds nothing. It must be because of his wife, Izzy thinks. The wife she's spent the last seven weeks trying not to think about. In her head she thought it would be *him* who answered the door. She thought they'd be alone. 'I'm sorry,' she stammers. 'I . . . I shouldn't have come.'

'No,' agrees Ludwell. His eyes are cold and angry-looking. 'It really isn't appropriate for students to doorstep members of staff. If you've come about a coursework extension then you can take it up with the department office. Anything else will have to wait until my next office hour.'

'But . . .' It's not about coursework, it's about your baby, *she wants to tell him. Our baby.*

'There's a list of times outside my office door,' says Ludwell, his voice loaded with irritation. 'You can make an appointment to see me then, like any other student.' Then he shuts the door in Izzy's face.

Chapter 14

Bella almost makes it back from breakfast without having to face the Storms. Perhaps they're still rowing, she thinks, or maybe Julia's headache has put paid to their dining plans. But then the door to room eleven opens, just as she turns into the corridor, and there they are.

Oh crap, this is it. Bella's legs are already shaking as she steels herself for what's coming next – for the painful unravelling of the last nineteen years of her life. And here they are again, those same two words beating inside her head: *They know. They know. They know.*

'Good morning,' says Julia. It's a rather forced 'good morning' but at least it's civil. Not what Bella was expecting after the vitriolic exchange she'd overheard outside their window.

'Morning,' she replies, her voice little more than a croak. Ludwell settles for a curt smile and a nod.

'It's Bella, isn't it?' says Julia. 'How are you feeling? Better, I hope.' There's nothing forced about that though. She sounds genuinely kind and concerned.

Bella blinks in surprise. What happened to *I didn't expect to have your sordid past thrown back in my face?* 'Me? Oh, much better, thanks,' she says. 'How about you?' The question's out of her mouth before she realises her mistake. The only reason she knows Julia's feeling poorly is because she's been eavesdropping. She curses inwardly, but she needn't have worried. It's fine.

'My headache from last night, you mean?' asks Julia. 'Not so great to be honest. I'm still suffering.'

Of course! Bella had forgotten, in all the subsequent 'excitement', about the headache that had brought Julia down to her end of the table after dinner. 'I'm sorry to hear that,' she says. 'I'm so sorry about last night in general. I'll pay for any cleaning costs obviously, and a replacement pair of shoes if necessary. I don't know what else to say. It's mortifying.'

'Not to worry,' Julia tells her. 'These things happen. Between you and me, I don't even like that dress particularly. It was an anniversary present from Ludwell.'

Bella sneaks a glance at Ludwell's face but he's not giving anything away. If he *is* offended, he's keeping it to himself.

'And to be honest, I've got more pressing concerns right now than the state of my clothes,' says Julia, shooting her husband a withering look.

But Ludwell's gaze has turned to Bella. 'What university did you say you were at again?' he asks. 'I'm sure I know you from somewhere.'

What is this? Bella thinks, reeling from the sudden change of subject. Is this some kind of weird 'good cop, bad cop' thing they've got going to try and force a confession out of her? She swallows, her breakfast sour in the back of her throat as she looks from one to the other. 'I didn't,' she says at last. 'I never went to university. I get that a lot though,' she lies, as if it's still worth trying to hide the truth from them. 'I've just got one of those faces. Sorry, you'll have to excuse me. I need to use the bathroom.' And with that she flees back to her room like a frightened child.

*

Tuesday morning, session two: lake swimming. *Cold* lake swimming at that, which isn't Bella's idea of fun. Hamar didn't exactly sell the experience to her after his dip yesterday either. But here he is again, back for another try, despite his previous protestations to the contrary. And here's Bella, already shivering in her borrowed wetsuit before she's dipped so much as a toe in. It was that or stay back at the lodge with Ludwell and Julia, which was what swung it in the end. Ludwell has a heart condition, apparently, which is exacerbated by cold water. The fact that he's got a heart at all is news to Bella. She didn't quite catch what Julia's excuse was for skipping the group swim session, but Bella's grateful for it all the same.

They'd both joined in with the first session of the day – a guided 'self-kindness and forgiveness' meditation led by Stuart, in a small clearing a few hundred metres from the lodge. But it had been easy enough to keep out of their way. Easy enough for Bella to shut her eyes and let Stuart's warm, mellifluous voice carry her away from her growing troubles for a short, blissful while. An eyes-shut meditation with the whole group is one thing though, a cosy hour with just the three of them is quite another. As soon as Ludwell announced that he and Julia would be staying put rather than swimming, if anyone wanted to join them, Bella had resigned herself to an icy dip. And now here she is, watching in awe as Krista strides out to waist level without so much as a gasp, before dropping down into the water and kicking off into an elegant front crawl, her bright yellow swimming cap cutting through the water like a speeding rubber duck. Someone behind Bella starts to clap and whistle as Lena follows suit. Neither one of them have bothered with a wetsuit. They're clearly made of sterner stuff than the others.

'Come on in,' Krista calls back to the shore as she twists around to tread water. 'It's lovely.'

'It's beautiful once you're in,' agrees Lena, her petite, muscular body cutting through the water with impressive grace.

Bella doesn't have to join them to know it *isn't* lovely. And it *won't* be beautiful once she's in because she's not planning on doing any actual swimming. She can already feel the cold coming off the lake, despite Stuart's reassurance that it's a balmy eleven degrees today. Balmy by his standards maybe but not by hers. T and Oscar are edging their way in too now, putting her to shame, with Stuart close behind. And Hamar? She doesn't know what's happened to him.

'It's honestly not that cold,' Stuart says coaxingly. 'Some of our guests who are a bit reluctant initially say it's one of their favourite parts of the retreat once they give it a try. Not to put any pressure on though,' he adds with a smile. 'We just want to make sure you get the most out of your time here with us.' Perhaps Marie's filled him in on their conversation about getting an earlier flight home. 'It really is a magical place once you open your heart and your mind to it.'

Bella thinks again of how much thought and effort (and money) Rachel put into getting her here. She thinks of her promise to Asher to make the most of the opportunity, and her promise to herself to be open to new experiences. If she's going to be stuck at Dödmansskogen for the next few days perhaps she *should* make the effort – at least have a paddle now that she's here. She shuffles forward a few more steps until the water laps at her feet, to show willing, and then shuffles straight back out again. No, that's far too cold.

'You'll have to go in a bit further than that to get the benefits,' says Stuart, with a chuckle. 'You'll feel great afterwards, I promise.'

But Bella can't be persuaded. It's not the afterwards part she's worried about, it's the now. 'Sorry, I'm still feeling a bit delicate,' she tells him. 'I might just watch from the platform instead.' She picks her way back to the wooden landing stage, where Stuart's left out flasks of hot chocolate and a big pile of fluffy towels, wrapping one around her shoulders and settling herself down with her feet dangling over the water.

Ah yes, that's better. It really is. Out here, away from the lodge and the tangle of worries that come with it, Bella feels considerably calmer than she did at breakfast. The whole business with the apple and the run-in with Ludwell and Julia this morning feel like a world away as she sits watching the weak rays of the sun glinting on the water. Maybe there really is something therapeutic about being out in the wild.

Stuart's meditation session seemed to help too, although Bella's pretty sure she was doing it wrong. The more she tried to focus on sending healing light down through her body, the busier her mind seemed to get. But once she gave that up as a bad job and simply focused on breathing in and out – her regular relaxation technique in other words – she started to calm down again. And the part where Stuart asked everyone to think about something in their past they felt bad about and send it away into the wilderness with forgiveness, that was nice too. Bella found herself focusing on the time she told her mum she was staying at a friend's house – her studious parent-approved friend from youth orchestra – and spent the night at a party instead. It was only a little lie (although it seemed like a big deal at the time) and it wasn't as if she'd been labouring under a heavy burden of guilt ever since, but it was still nice to let it go. To imagine it carried away on the warmth of her out breath to become one with the trees and the cold morning air.

That was the night she met Nat – a night of firsts. First illicit party. First proper drink. Her first proper kiss. Bella smiles to herself at the memory. She hasn't thought about Nat in forever – well, apart from yesterday when she was talking to Ludwell – but she can still picture that sweatshirt he always wore, even now: the blue one with the white lizard logo. That's how she knew it was love – when he let her borrow his precious lizard top. Except it wasn't really love, looking back. At least, not for her. Otherwise she'd have tried harder to make things work when she went to university. She wouldn't have sent him that letter after his first and only visit, telling him it was over. *It's not you, it's me.* She wouldn't have sent his subsequent letters back unopened in the hope that he'd finally get the message and move on. Poor Nat, he didn't deserve any of that.

Bella tries breathing out her long-buried guilt over him. She pictures his tear-stained face as he read those final words from her, and tries sending the image out towards the lake. *Say goodbye to your burden and watch it float away.* That's what Stuart said they had to do. But Nat isn't floating anywhere. Quite the opposite. Bella finds herself thinking about the ring he gave her on their third date – a mood ring from that funny New Age shop in the old town, with all the different flavours of incense sticks and the beautiful tarot cards in the window. He was quite the romantic really, looking back. Bella certainly can't imagine Asher buying a girl any kind of jewellery so soon into a relationship. But maybe the rules have changed since her day. Maybe that would come across as over-keen and intense rather than romantic. Nat *was* pretty intense, which was part of the problem. It must have been all that Gothic heartthrob music he used to listen to.

Of course, Nat would be in his late thirties too now – he was only a month younger than Bella, despite being a whole school year below her. Too old and jaded for all that heart-on-sleeve stuff most likely, for handpicked bouquets of wildflowers – buttercups and daisies and those little pink ones that used to grow along the side of the road – tied up with elastic bands. Too old for long, rambling poems about the weight of love, posted through her front door after a couple of days apart. Too old to copy out the lyrics to 'Voodoo Love Nurse' and 'Horns of a Doll-Emma' with a calligraphy pen, to go with the mix tape he'd spent all night making. He's probably married with 2.4 children now and working as an estate agent. Probably a little paunchier round the edges and a little thinner on top, if the men Bella's friends have tried fixing her up with lately are anything to go by. Tried and failed. *Maybe when Asher's left home* – that's always been her standard response to any awkward attempts at matchmaking. *Maybe when it's just me on my own I can think about dating.* And now it *is* just her on her own, but the idea of dating a paunchy divorcee with a receding hairline is still as unappealing as ever.

Perhaps if she'd stayed with Nat, if she'd given the whole long-distance relationship thing a proper go, Bella's life would have been different. Easier. But it's impossible to imagine a version of her life without Asher in it. She can't even bring herself to try.

Asher. It must be getting on for eleven o'clock and Bella's barely given a second thought to how he's settling in since she woke up today. Her mind's been so busy worrying about everything else, that she hasn't had the mental space to worry about him. To miss him. For a moment she feels guilty – guilt mixed with a sudden, irrational panic that *not* worrying about her son collapsing from dehydration or sleeping through a fire alarm somehow makes it more likely to happen – but then she pushes the feeling away again. That's nonsense. A bit of distance is a good thing. It's healthy . . . if you can call her worries about Ludwell and Julia, and mysterious goings-on in the middle of the night 'healthy'.

'Bella!' A sudden cry brings her back to the here and now with a jolt. She opens her eyes to see Lena calling to her from the lake. Krista's there too but the others are all the way over the side now. 'Look out!'

There's a split second of incomprehension – *what do you mean?* – and then something, or someone, barrels into her from behind, pushing her off the wooden platform towards the waiting water below. The towel slips from Bella's shoulders as she falls, arms flailing wildly, fingers clawing at the empty air. And then the lake rushes up to meet her like a solid sheet of ice.

Smash.

The cold splinters against her cheeks as she crashes into the water, snatching the breath from her lungs. *Hahhhh!* And then the water closes in over her head for a moment – a seemingly endless moment – filling her nose and mouth.

I'm drowning, she thinks, hands and legs floundering, striking out in blind, breathless terror, lungs burning inside her chest.

Help!

Fragmented images flash through Bella's panicked mind . . . Asher at his first baby swim session . . . Ludwell's cold blue eyes . . . fingers scratching against wood . . . a dark figure on the wooden platform forcing her into the water . . .

No, no, no!

Help!

Chapter 15

The lake is an icy, churning prison, closing in over her head.

Fear floods Bella's brain as she thrashes about, trying to get back to the surface. But then somehow she's up again, head out, coughing and spluttering and pawing at the water like a wild animal. It's not that her brain has forgotten how to swim, it's her limbs that seem to be having trouble remembering.

You need to stay calm.

You need to breathe.

That's better. Yes. Her arms are working now, pushing back against the water. Her legs find their rhythm too as her body rights itself, head and neck lifted clear of the surface.

Breathe.

Breathe.

But it's not over yet. A second wave of panic hits as Bella feels hands reaching for her, clawing at her wetsuit. She can see the blurred shape of her attacker out the corner of her eye.

'No!' she screams. 'Get off me!' At least, that's what she's screaming in her head. What comes out of her mouth is a spluttering gush of half-swallowed lake water followed by a terrified bout of coughing. She jerks away from her assailant, reeling sideways and kicking out with her legs. There's a high-pitched yelp as her foot makes contact with something soft and fleshy.

'Bella, it's all right. It's me. Krista. I was just trying to help. You looked like you were struggling.'

Bella stops kicking and twists round in the water to see. Yes. It's Krista. And Lena's there too, treading water beside them.

'I . . . I thought you were . . .' But Bella can't quite say *what* she thought. Only that someone wanted to hurt her. 'Somebody pushed me,' she gasps, still struggling to control her breath. That bit was real enough. Wasn't it?

'I know,' says Krista. 'Lena tried to warn you, but it was too late.'

Bella! Look out! Yes, that's right. She remembers now.

'He was too quick,' says Lena.

He. Who's he? Bella steers herself round in the water, turning back to face the wooden platform. To see Hamar grinning down at her.

You! 'That wasn't funny,' she calls, feeling a rush of anger. *Bastard.* 'I thought I was . . .' *I thought I was drowning. I thought someone was trying to kill me.* It sounds ridiculous now, even to her.

'Don't give him the satisfaction,' says Krista. 'Come on, forget about Hamar and let's concentrate on getting you out of here. On getting you warm and dry. You've had a nasty shock but you're going to be fine.' She hesitates. 'Are you okay to swim back on your own?'

'Yes,' says Bella, as anger gives way to embarrassment. 'Yes of course.' The water's not *that* cold. Not really. *Talk about an overreaction.* She kicks off towards the shore, wishing she'd never come. Never come swimming – even a cosy hour with Ludwell and Julia would have been better than this. Never come to Dödmansskogen. She should have stayed at home with her work and her sadness and waited for the Asher-shaped hole inside to mend of its own accord.

*

'There now,' Krista says. She'd insisted on walking Bella back to her room, once she'd finished laying into Hamar for his childish and irresponsible behaviour. 'You get yourself in the shower and warm up, and I'll make you some tea.'

Bella opens her mouth to protest – *There's no need, really, I'm fine* – but then closes it again. Who's she kidding? She's not fine at all. She's stuck in the arse-end of nowhere with Ludwell-effing-Storm and no phone. She hasn't heard from Asher in two days (although it feels more like two weeks – two lifetimes) and she's just been half-drowned in a freezing cold lake, thinking someone was trying to kill her. No, if there's one thing Bella *isn't* right now, it's fine. So she does as she's told, locking the bathroom door behind her and struggling out of her wetsuit, grateful for Krista's mothering. At least *someone's* on her side.

The shower feels like hot needles on her skin, but it does the trick. Bella can feel the chill of the lake and the icy fist of fear inside her chest melting away as she washes off the last traces of her ordeal with the complimentary body scrub and a generous helping of shampoo. Yes, that's better. By the time she's dried and body-lotioned, and cuddled up inside the fluffy white dressing gown Krista's thoughtfully hung up on the back of the door for her, Bella's almost back to her old self again. Not that she's quite sure *which* old self she's back to: the grown woman who waved her son off to university two days ago, or the teenage version still trapped in her own university nightmare.

'Here,' says Krista, as Bella emerges from the steamy bathroom. She hands her a mug of unpleasantly milky-looking tea. 'I put some sugar in it too, for shock.'

'Thank you.' Bella smiles, grateful for the gesture if not the actual tea, which she has no intention of drinking if she can help it. Overly milky tea turns her stomach at the best of times, let alone *sweet* milky tea. 'That's very kind. What about you though? You should go and get changed, you must be freezing in your wet costume,' she says, suddenly aware of how little Krista is wearing under her towel.

'I will in a minute,' Krista agrees, 'once I know you're okay.'

'I'm fine now,' Bella insists. 'Really. I've just had a lot going on this week and my nerves are all on edge. That's why I freaked out like that in the lake.'

'Ludwell, you mean? And Julia?'

Bella stares at her in surprise. 'No,' she says, immediately on the defensive. 'Why would you say that?' Her voice comes out sharper than she intended.

'No reason.' Krista looks embarrassed as if she realises she's touched a raw nerve. 'It was just something you mentioned last night, that's all.'

Oh crap. 'What? What did I say? Was this before I was sick or afterwards?' There are clearly gaps in her memory from before, including Stuart's Dead Man's Forest story, but *everything* after that point is still a blur.

'Afterwards,' says Krista, 'when I was helping you to bed. You were raving about him.'

'Raving? I don't think so.' Bella wasn't so far gone as all that, surely? 'I'm not really his biggest fan. Not any more.'

Krista shakes her head. 'No, I mean raving as in talking too fast . . . as in not making an awful lot of sense.'

'Oh. I see.' Bella doesn't like the sound of that very much. 'What *sort* of stuff was I saying about him?'

'Just what a smug bastard he was and how you'd never have come if you'd known he and his wife were going to be here. "His bitch wife" were your exact words, I think. And then something about Asher and how you'd only done it to protect him and how you couldn't bear the thought of him resenting you . . .' She shrugs. 'Like I say, you weren't making much sense.'

It all makes perfect sense to Bella though. She takes a sip of milky tea to cover her discomfort and almost gags as the sugar hits the back of her throat.

'The two of you have clearly got history,' says Krista. 'To be honest, I'd already guessed as much. I saw your face when Hamar first mentioned his name yesterday. I saw how pale and frightened you looked.'

Bella nods slowly. There's no point denying it.

'Would it help to talk about it? I'm a pretty good listener.'

Bella's still nodding. Maybe it *would* help. Better than trying to drink her way out of dealing with it, anyway, which seems to have been her approach so far. And maybe it's better if Krista hears it from her, the real story that is, rather than making up her own version of events based on last night's drunken ramblings. 'Not here though,' she says, remembering the row she'd overheard outside Ludwell and Julia's window that morning. 'I don't like the idea of anyone listening in.' The bedroom walls feel rather thin all of a sudden, and Bella still can't shake the memory of that scratching noise from nextdoor. 'Maybe we could go for a walk?'

'Sounds good to me,' says Krista. 'I found the perfect place when I was out this morning. How about if I pop back to my room and stick some clothes on, and meet you out the front in ten minutes, say?'

'Lovely,' Bella agrees, even though there's nothing lovely about any of this. The thought of opening up to someone she barely knows – of sharing the burden of her secret after all these years carrying it alone – fills her with fresh dread. Krista's been nothing but kind though and Bella's confident she can trust her. At least, she hopes she can.

'And don't forget your tea,' Krista adds. 'It'll do you good.'

'I won't,' Bella promises, tipping it down the sink the moment she's gone.

Chapter 16

'But this is the way to the lake,' says Bella as Krista leads her along the pine-scented track, fallen needles pressed beneath their feet. 'I don't want to go back there.' She can't face seeing the others again. Not yet.

'Don't worry,' Krista assures her. 'We're not going that far. There's another turning just down here.' She points to an unlikely-looking path, almost covered over with moss and ferns, and Bella starts to wonder if they should have brought the map with them. That's if the route's even marked on it. But a closer inspection reveals that someone's been here relatively recently, with a line of footprints pressed into what's left of the path. They're not Krista's though – they're too big. Huge, in fact.

'Ow!' Something sharp catches at Bella's hand as she brushes past.

'Oh yes, sorry,' says Krista. 'Watch out for those spiky things. I don't know what they are, but they're lethal. And mind how you go on those rocks – the mossy ones can be a bit slippery. It widens out again soon – it's only this first section that's tricky. It'll be worth it though, you'll see.'

Bella can feel her resolve weakening with every step. Why did she agree to this again? Why did she think tramping off into the middle of nowhere to talk about Ludwell was a good idea? *Nothing* about this feels like a good idea. But then her new friend's probably pieced most of the story together already, thanks to Bella's 'ravings' last night. She might as well hear the full version now. It's also possible, Bella thinks, that *Krista* could do with someone to talk to as well. She's clearly not over her husband's death, and the fact that she's chosen to spend the anniversary here in Sweden, after the psychic mentioned a Scandinavian connection to the killer, speaks volumes. Maybe she's here looking for clues, rather than closure . . .

For one horrible moment Bella wonders if Krista suspects *her*. Was there more to the psychic's revelation than Krista's letting on – something that brought her to this precise place on this precise week? She thinks of the note under her door: *I know what you did.* What if this whole heart-to-heart talk is nothing to do with *helping* Bella and everything to do with getting her all alone, in the middle of the forest . . .?

No. That's ridiculous. She feels bad for even *thinking* it after everything Krista's done for her, especially as Bella's the one who suggested they come somewhere more private to talk. It's this place, that's all. It's being cooped up in the middle of nowhere with her old fears and memories, with Hamar's pranks and Oscar's ridiculous thriller plots. It's too many sleepless nights playing into her growing sense of paranoia. *Get a grip*, she tells herself firmly, ducking her head to avoid a sharp, jutting branch, conveniently positioned at eye level. Eye-*gouging* level.

The path's wider here at least, and the conditions underfoot are definitely easier. But it feels like they're heading back towards the lake again. Bella can hear a bubble of sound coming through the trees – the sound of voices and water – and her mood grows even darker as she recalls the stupid grin on Hamar's face after he pushed her in. Everything's a game to him, isn't it? *I wish* you'd *drown*, she thinks, breaking off a twig and snapping it in half.

'There,' says Krista at last, pointing to a painted wooden bird hide, camouflaged against the matching green of the surrounding trees. 'I almost walked straight past it this morning. I don't think it's marked on the map, either, so I'm pretty sure we'll have it to ourselves.'

Bella used to enjoy watching the sparrows and blackbirds in the garden with Asher when he was little, before the new neighbours moved in with their killer cat. She remembers the laminated bird-spotting chart she made for him, with everything from blue tits and robins to starlings and magpies. But it was only ever sparrows who visited the bird table she set up near the window, and that big dopey wood pigeon he used to call Coo-Coo. *I'd forgotten all about Coo-Coo*, she thinks, smiling briefly at the memory.

'After you,' says Krista.

The air inside is cold and damp. It's gloomy too – the only light comes from the open door and the long, narrow viewing strip cut into the front wall, facing back towards the lake. It feels secret and secluded, which is probably why Krista chose it. Bella peers out of the viewing window for a moment or two, as if she really is here to look for wildlife – for Coo-Coo's Swedish cousins – and then takes a seat on the low wooden bench behind her.

'Thank you for this,' she says as Krista joins her. 'For everything, I mean. I'm not usually such a mess.'

'I never thought that,' says Krista kindly. 'You just seem a little . . .' she searches for the right word '. . . troubled.'

Yes. That sounds about right. 'It's everything at once,' Bella tells her. 'Leaving Asher . . . that business at the lake . . . and seeing Ludwell again.' She doesn't mention the apple though. That might render her more 'delusional' than 'troubled' and Bella's still unsure herself whether it was ever there or not. She doesn't mention the strange noise she heard in the night, either, which has been playing on her mind after that horrible story Oscar told her at breakfast.

'Seeing him again?' Krista says, trying to coax the story out of her. 'So I was right. You and Ludwell *do* have history?'

Bella nods. 'I was a big fan of his when I was younger. I played

131

the violin too back then, pretty seriously, and used to go up to London with my mum every Saturday for lessons at the Royal College of Music. Sometimes we'd stay on afterwards to see a concert, which is where I first saw him.' She feels her cheeks grow warm as she fills in some of the details of her teenage obsession: the CDs listened to on repeat, the pictures Blu-tacked to her bedroom wall and the initialled hearts scrawled all over her school pencil case. '… And then he had his accident – the one where he lost his fingers – and it felt like *my* world had ended too. That sounds a bit dramatic, I know, but for me it was like my favourite band splitting up. It was like a Beatles fan hearing about the shooting of John Lennon. I was completely devastated, knowing that I'd never hear him play again …'

Yes, Bella can still remember that terrible teenage anguish. 'I was a pretty geeky kid back then,' she says, by way of explanation. 'My mum was ridiculously strict' – *that's putting it mildly* – 'and I went to an all-girls' school on a music scholarship, so I didn't really get to meet many boys my own age. Classical violinists were as close to pin-ups as I got. Which is why it felt like the end of the world when Ludwell's career was cut short, putting paid to my fantasy of getting a place in one of the big London orchestras and our eyes meeting across a crowded stage …' It sounds excruciating saying it out loud, but there it is. If she's going to tell the story she might as well tell it properly. 'But then when I heard he'd been offered a job at the university, the dream was back again. Only this time our eyes would meet over a crowded lecture theatre …'

Krista smiles back at her encouragingly, as if to say, *Go on, I'm listening*. If she *is* judging her – and Bella wouldn't blame her, it's a pretty cringeworthy story – then she's doing a good job of hiding it.

'It sounds pathetic, I know,' says Bella. 'I'd be horrified if I thought Asher had chosen his university course because of a crush. It was a good course though, and by the time I applied I'd already decided I didn't want to be a performer. I didn't want to go down the conservatoire route – that was my mum's dream for me, not mine. And in fact, by the time I got my place I'd already met someone else anyway. Someone my own age.'

Bella scratches at a dry patch of skin on the back of her hand. 'I feel a bit bad, looking back,' she says, 'for how I treated him, but I'd never had a boyfriend before. I really *did* think he was the one, for a while. Nat, his name was. He was sweet enough but . . .' She loses her thread for a moment, wondering how she got onto Nat in the first place. Perhaps it was an attempt to prove to Krista – or to herself – that she'd grown out of her ridiculous Ludwell obsession by the time she went to university. Only she hadn't, had she? That was the problem.

'I'm guessing you broke his heart,' says Krista.

Bella nods. 'Yes, I guess I did. But long-distance relationships never really work, do they? At least, they didn't back then, before texting and FaceTime and what have you – it's probably different now. But yes, everything seemed different when I got to university and my life finally opened up. No more Mum monitoring my every move. No rigid practice timetables to keep to.'

'I felt exactly the same when I finally left home,' says Krista. 'That sense of liberation – I remember it well. It was my dad who was the strict one in our house, but my mum went along with all his rules and restrictions. I think I'd have married my husband even if I didn't love him, just to get out of there.' She smiles – a sad sort of smile that makes Bella feel even guiltier for her recent silly suspicions and brings home just how much grief Krista must still be carrying around. And here *she* is, burdening the poor woman with her own problems.

'But your mother approved of Nat?' says Krista, returning to the story. 'She didn't mind you seeing him?'

Bella's thrown for a second. What's that got to do with anything?

'My dad would have gone crazy if he thought I was dating

someone while I was still at school,' Krista clarifies. 'But your mum didn't mind you having a boyfriend?'

'Oh I see. No, she didn't even know about him. I used to tell her I was staying behind after school to do extra practice, during the week, and then sneak off to meet Nat at his house. His dad was really laid back, so that was fine. And then at weekends Nat used to go and stay with his mum in the city and I'd be busy doing music stuff with mine. It worked out pretty neatly. There's no way Mum would have given us her blessing if she *had* known though. She had me later in life – my sister Rachel was already in her teens when I was born – and my dad died not long afterwards. Mum was in a bit of a bad place back then, by all accounts, and if it hadn't been for Rachel, I don't know how we'd have managed. She was more like a parent to me than a sister for the first few years of my life. But Mum got herself together again eventually, and then when Rachel left home she kind of swung round the other way and went into mothering overdrive. Overcompensating, I guess. And she got heavily into this local church group too – not the nice normal church we used to go to when I was little, but a really strict organisation that seemed more keen on controlling people than spreading the Christian faith – which meant she no longer approved of alcohol, or lipstick, or boys.' *Or fun. Or love.*

Bella shakes her head. 'Anyway, I don't want to talk about her. We didn't exactly part on the best of terms and now . . .' *Now it's too late.* She doesn't need to finish the sentence though. Krista's already reaching for her arm as if she's guessed how that particular part of the story played out. Perhaps she recognises the loss and guilt – the weight of all those unsaid things. And the anger? Does she recognise that too?

'Sorry,' Bella says. 'This is turning into a bit of an epic, isn't it? I'll skip to the important part.' The part she's been dreading. Her throat feels sandpaper dry as she begins: 'I was out at a pub with some uni friends one weekend and . . .'

Her throat might be dry but her palms are wet with sweat as

she relives that night – that sordid, drunken night – from when she told her friends to go home without her, all the way to the hungover humiliation of the following morning and the discovery, weeks later, that she was pregnant. She breaks off suddenly, mid-sentence, cocking her head to one side. *What was that noise?*

'What is it?' asks Krista. 'What's wrong?'

'I thought . . . I thought heard someone,' says Bella. *I thought I heard them scratching against the wall.* Her skin prickles at the very idea but there's nothing to hear now. Nothing but the autumn breeze whispering through the trees.

Scratch, scratch, scratch. 'There it is again. Can't you hear it? That scratching noise?' *Like fingernails against bare wood.* Bella can't just hear it, she can *feel* it too, like a matching rhythmic itch under her own skin. *Scratch, scratch, scratch.* She can feel invisible eyes watching her as she sits there. Observing her. Boring into her. She jumps up, rushing to the open doorway to look, but there's no one there.

'Probably just the wind,' says Krista. 'Or an animal of some kind.'

Bella stares into the dense, claustrophobic green of the forest, watching for signs of movement. Searching for something to explain the tiny shivers running up and down her spine. There's nothing there to see though. 'Yes,' she says at last, admitting defeat as she comes back to her seat, feeling silly and paranoid. 'It must have been. Where was I?' She's lost the thread of her own story, her head too full of lurking eavesdroppers. Of phantom extras from an old ghost story.

'You discovered you were pregnant,' Krista says, her voice soft and gentle. 'That must have been a shock, especially at such a young age.' She doesn't *seem* particularly shocked though – she must have guessed where the story was headed. It was pretty obvious, to everyone except Bella's younger self, who'd been clinging to the hope that her missed period was down to too many late nights and stress over her first big essay deadline. So yes, somehow it *was* still a shock when her first test came up positive. And all the others she did afterwards, in the hope of getting a different answer.

'But it *was* consensual?' Krista asks.

'Yes,' says Bella. 'It must have been. At least I think so. I . . . I don't really remember anything about it. I don't think he *forced* me, or anything,' she adds quickly. 'That's not what this is about.'

'But he was in a position of authority and he took advantage of you.'

'I was old enough to know what I was doing,' Bella insists. Only she wasn't. She didn't. She was a repressed teenager with a stupid crush on a man almost twice her age. She was out of her depth and she was drunk. And then she was pregnant. 'I didn't know what to do when I found out,' she admits. 'I couldn't tell my mum. I couldn't tell anyone. Not at first.'

'Not even your boyfriend from home?'

Bella shakes her head. 'Nat and I weren't together by then. He didn't take the break-up very well, either. He kept writing to me, begging me to give him another chance. It was horrible. I never told Ludwell either,' she says, lowering her voice to whisper. 'I dropped out of university instead and moved in with my sister after Mum threw me out. Ludwell doesn't know about Asher, and Asher doesn't know about him – so please don't say anything. Promise me you won't.'

The thought of losing her son to Ludwell and Julia – to the wealthy, secure upbringing they'd be able to offer him – has been a constant source of fear to Bella over the years. Ever since she read that article on the department noticeboard, in fact. Even now, with Asher safely past the age of messy custody battles, the idea of losing him still terrifies her. She still wakes up in the middle of the night sometimes, drenched in sweat after a dream about Asher turning against her, blaming her for keeping his father from him all these years.

'My lips are sealed,' Krista assures her.

'Thank you,' Bella says. 'I know Asher's got a right to know. They *both* have but . . .' She can feel herself welling up as she talks. 'What if he resents me for keeping him to myself all these years? When he was little, I used to tell him that not having a dad made him extra special. I told him I didn't just love him twice as much as other mums, but three times as much. And he said he loved me three times as much as any other boy. I don't even know how it started but that used to be our running joke. As he's got older, I worry that he's missed out though. That *he* thinks he's missed out. I thought I was protecting him,' she insists, 'but now . . .'

'You did what you thought was best for your boy,' says Krista kindly. 'Like any mother would. But now you're worried that Ludwell might put two and two together, is that it? You're worried he might recognise you?'

'I . . . I think he already has,' Bella says, thinking of the row she overheard coming from the Storms' bedroom this morning. 'Already recognised me, I mean. He's acting like we've never met, like he's got no idea who I am, but I'm not buying it . . .' Ludwell knows who she is, Bella's sure of it. And so does Julia.

I didn't expect to have your sordid past thrown back in my face. It's humiliating.

I'm sorry, darling. If I'd known for one minute she'd be here, I'd never have agreed to it in the first place. I'd never have come.

No matter how many times she plays it back in her head, the result is still the same. *Who else could they have been talking about?*

Bella stiffens at a sound from outside. Not scratching this time though – more of a rustle. Like someone in the undergrowth shifting position. 'What was that?' She can feel her heart speeding up as she hurries back to the doorway and peers out a second time. 'Hello?' she calls. 'Who's there?'

Chapter 17

There's no answer.

'It's probably just birds or squirrels,' says Krista, joining her at the hide doorway.

But the panic is still there in Bella's chest, still thumping away – residual panic from her fright in the lake, most likely, coupled with that silly story Oscar was telling her over breakfast about how Dödmansskogen got its name. Just because it was silly doesn't mean it didn't get under her skin though. That it didn't put her on edge after the strange scratching noise in the night. Or maybe it was sharing her darkest secrets with Krista that's left her feeling nervous and exposed. What if it wasn't birds or squirrels? What if it was someone listening in on their conversation?

'Or a deer, even,' Krista adds. 'I'm guessing there's lots of wildlife round here if this is where people come to watch it.'

There's more rustling from a nearby clump of trees as Bella steps outside to investigate further, blinking in the dappled sunlight after the oppressive gloom of the hide. But by the time she reaches the trees, there's nothing there to see. *No one* there to see.

'Bella?' Krista follows her out, her face a picture of concern. 'Are you okay?'

'No,' Bella tells her. 'I'm not. It's this place. It's really got me on edge, jumping at shadows and chasing after phantoms.' *Phantom apples. Phantom eavesdroppers. Phantom nails scratching at the wall of an empty room.* 'It feels like—' *It feels like someone's out to get me,* that's what she was going to say. But it sounds too silly and alarmist to admit to out loud. 'It's kind of creepy,' she says instead. 'Don't you think? Especially at night.'

Krista shakes her head. 'I like it here. No traffic. No television. No phones. The rest of the world feels a long way away, which is exactly what I was after. Maybe you'll feel more relaxed too, after this afternoon's music therapy session?'

With Ludwell? Hah!

'Ah, maybe not,' says Krista, realising her mistake. 'Sorry, I forgot who's running it.'

'I might decide to have a headache this afternoon,' says Bella, stiffening in response to another rustle in the trees. But this one sounds different. This one really *does* sound like a bird. And there it is, a tiny light brown one with fluffy grey feathers on its belly and a black-and-white head. 'The less I see of Ludwell and his wife the better.'

'You might be worrying over nothing,' Krista tells her. 'Perhaps he really *doesn't* recognise you. It was all so long ago.'

'But I heard them arguing this morning,' Bella insists, still keeping her voice low. She can't shake the idea that there was someone there before. Someone listening in on her long-buried secrets. 'Ludwell said he wouldn't have agreed to come if he'd known for one minute I'd be here.'

'And he was definitely talking about you? He mentioned you by name?'

'No, but who else could it be?'

Krista looks uncomfortable, as if the question's hit a nerve. As if she knows something she shouldn't. 'All I'm saying is don't jump to conclusions. Maybe it's not as bad as you think.' She makes a big show of checking her watch. 'The others will be finished at the lake by now. Perhaps we should think about heading back to the lodge too.'

'Yes,' agrees Bella, sensing the sudden shift in the other woman's body language. She's not sure *what's* changed exactly, but Krista clearly doesn't want to be there any more. 'Thank you again for looking after me. For listening.'

'My pleasure. I hope it helped.'

'Definitely,' says Bella, which is only half a lie. It felt good to have someone tell her she was overreacting and the chances of Ludwell recognising her now were slim, although she's still not convinced. Why was he quizzing her about university again after breakfast? *I'm sure I know you from somewhere* – that's what he said. And there's no getting away from what Bella heard outside their window this morning, whatever Krista might think. As for the idea that someone might have been outside the hide just now, doing exactly the same thing – lurking in the undergrowth and listening in to *their* conversation – that's enough to send proper shivers down Bella's spine. But she forces a smile all the same.

'I'm always happy to return the favour,' she says, 'if *you* need a sympathetic ear. I know my problems must seem a bit pathetic compared to yours.'

'Thank you. I appreciate that, but I'm okay.' Krista's expression darkens. 'It's not sympathy I need, but answers. Answers and justice.'

*

Stuart's waiting for them at the lodge door. 'Oh Bella, there you are,' he says, eyebrows knotted with concern. 'I've been looking everywhere for you. I wanted to check you were okay after what happened at the lake. I'm so sorry – I didn't realise until it was too late. I should have stopped him.' He shakes his head. 'The truth is I shouldn't have been so far out in the first place. From where I was it just looked like a bit of fun, like harmless horseplay. I didn't realise what a fright he'd given you until Lena filled me in afterwards . . . She said you were in shock and Krista had taken you back to your room to recover.'

Bella's cheeks grow warm. 'It's not your fault,' she says. 'I overreacted.'

'No, you didn't,' Krista tells her firmly. 'There's nothing *fun* about pushing someone into cold water. Hamar acted like a jerk. *He's* the one who should be apologising.'

'I've already had a word with him,' says Stuart. 'A healthy group dynamic is very important to us here at the retreat, and we go to great efforts to help foster that with our programme of activities and convivial mealtimes. At least I *hope* our guests find them convivial. I've always thought food should be about sharing and enjoyment rather than diets and abstinence. Time spent with others can teach us a lot about ourselves . . . which is why I'm very disappointed and sorry about your experience this morning. I hope you're feeling okay now?'

Bella nods. 'I'm fine,' she says. What else *can* she say? He looks so worried that she hasn't got the heart to tell him the truth. How she can still feel the breathless, burning panic in her lungs even now, just thinking about it. How if it wasn't for the trees blocking the road, she'd be asking Marie to fire up the minibus right now, or asking Stuart for the number of the nearest taxi firm. Not that there are likely to be many of those all the way out here.

'And I sincerely hope you won't let it colour the rest of your stay,' Stuart adds with what seems like genuine concern, although he's probably got half an eye on her potential review afterwards as well. And Lena's piece – he must be worried about that too. Mention of a dangerous incident at the on-site lake wouldn't look very good, would it?

'I'll try not to,' says Bella, wishing it was that easy. Wishing she could recapture some of her earlier enthusiasm for the place. The initial holiday buzz has well and truly fizzled out now though. It feels more like a question of gritting her teeth and getting through it, without any other strange incidences, hopefully. She's not sure her nerves will cope with any more weirdness.

'And please let me know if there's anything at all Marie and I can do for you,' Stuart says. 'Our guests' welfare is our top priority.'

Hire a helicopter to take me to the airport? Lock Ludwell and Julia in their room for the rest of the week? Give me back my phone and magic up some mobile reception so that I can call my son? After congratulating herself on going a whole morning without worrying about Asher, Bella suddenly misses him so much it hurts.

'Any extra meditation sessions you'd like us to run for example, to help you relax. Any more sleep tea in case of another disturbed night.'

Disturbed, thinks Bella. *Yes, 'disturbed' is a good word for it.* She still feels pretty disturbed now, thinking about that apple with its wriggling inhabitants squirming around inside. And the footprints outside her window . . . 'Thank you,' she says. 'I might take you up on some more tea. It did help, I think. I managed a *few* hours' sleep afterwards which was more than I thought I would, given everything that had been going on.' Presumably Marie has already filled Stuart in on the apple episode. 'And that was *before* I found the footprints under my window,' she adds, half-hoping he'll jump in with an innocent explanation to set her mind at rest. *Ah yes, those would have been my prints you saw. I was out looking for mushrooms this morning as part of my foraging training . . .*

But there's no explanation forthcoming. 'Oh,' says Stuart, looking surprised. 'That's odd. I'll er . . . I'll have a check with Marie, see if she knows anything about it, and get back to you.'

'Thank you, that would be great,' Bella says, realising Krista's not the only one in need of answers.

*

Stuart's as good as his word. Ten minutes later there's a knock on Bella's door. She opens it to find Marie standing there, clutching a bowl of oranges and bananas.

'I brought you some fruit,' she says redundantly. That much was clear already. 'A sign of Nature's bounty and goodness. No apples though,' she adds quickly. 'Not after last night.'

Bella shudders at the memory. Even if she *did* imagine the whole thing, the mere thought of biting into an apple is enough to set her teeth on edge. 'Thank you.' She gets the feeling there's more to come though . . . that the fruit is simply an excuse. And she's right.

'I wanted to have a quiet word with you while I was here, too,' says Marie, edging herself into the room and closing the door softly behind her. 'Stuart mentioned you were worried about someone outside your window – something to do with some footprints?'

Bella nods. 'I was looking for the apple. To see if it was still there, or if I'd dreamt the whole thing, but there was no sign of it.' She presses on. 'It looked like someone else had been out there too though, where the wet soil was all scuffed up. It looked like footprints.'

Marie's the one nodding now. 'I see. That must have been worrying after the confused events of last night but I'm sure it's nothing to be concerned about. I'm sure there's a simple enough explanation.' She doesn't actually offer one though. 'Sometimes the mind has a way of looking for patterns where there aren't any,' she says instead, as if it's all in Bella's head. 'And you've clearly got a *lot* on your mind at the moment.'

'I suppose so.'

'Add in a lack of sleep and a touch of er . . . *food poisoning* . . . and it's no wonder you're feeling out of balance and on edge.'

'Yes, I guess you're right,' says Bella, although she still can't shake the idea of a stranger lurking outside her window in the middle of the night. 'While you're here, can I ask about the room nextdoor? It *is* empty, isn't it?'

Marie frowns. 'Yes, why?'

'No reason,' says Bella, deciding to keep the scratching sounds to herself for now, in case Marie thinks she imagined them too. Maybe she did. Maybe her brain *has* been looking for patterns that aren't really there, reading dark, hidden connections into otherwise random events: the footprints, the noises in the night, the apple that may or may not have been a dream . . . and not forgetting the anonymous note under her door, of course. Bella wonders if anyone's told Marie and Stuart about *that*. A note that had vanished when she went back to get it, just like the apple. But the note was definitely real. She was wide awake and sober when she found it. Bella can still remember the feel of the paper in her fingers. The precise thickness of the black-inked letters on the page: *I know what you did.*

'And who's in charge of emptying the guests' bins?' she asks, thinking out loud. The answer must be Rosel, surely, but how would she have had time to go round sorting out everyone's rubbish if she was on breakfast duty yesterday? *Was* she on breakfast duty yesterday? Bella can't quite recall now. So much has happened since then. But the beds didn't get made up until later – she remembers that much. She remembers coming back to a neatly made bed and replenished tea and coffee supplies after their morning walk. Remembers staring round the freshly serviced room in despair, at the thought of Ludwell Storm on his way to Dödmansskogen. Surely it would have made more sense to empty the bins at the same time?

'Rosel takes care of the day-to-day domestic tasks in general,' says Marie, looking puzzled, 'and Saga's in charge of the catering. But we all pitch in together if needs be. Why do you ask?'

'Oh, just wondering. It's nothing, really,' Bella assures her, still trying – and failing – to put the pieces together in a way that makes sense. Compared to the nastiness of the note itself and the mystery surrounding its anonymous author, the exact details of its disposal hardly feels important. And compared to everything that's happened subsequently, it's pretty insignificant. But it nags at her, even after Marie's gone, taking Bella's discarded wetsuit with her: the feeling that something's not right.

Chapter 18

That same nagging sensation, coupled with a growing need for answers, finds Bella in the kitchen a short while later. A deliciously rich smell of cooking meat, and something sweet and fruity, fills the air.

'Yesterday? I cleaned all the rooms while you were out on the guided wilderness walk,' says Rosel, who's helping Saga with the final lunch preparations. 'Why? Is there a problem?'

'And that's when you emptied the bins too?' Bella checks. 'You didn't do that earlier, while we were having breakfast?'

Rosel frowns. 'No. Why?' she asks again.

Suddenly the lunch doesn't smell quite so delicious after all. Who else has been in Bella's room, then? 'I threw something away yesterday morning,' she explains, 'and then changed my mind. But when I went back after breakfast to find it, the bin was empty, which seemed a bit strange.'

Rosel's frown deepens. 'Yes, that *is* strange. Whatever it was you threw away, it wasn't me who took it though.'

'Wait,' says Saga, her cheeks flushed with heat from the oven, as she twists round to face Bella. 'Is this the note you were all talking about at lunch yesterday? The one Hamar pretended *I* wrote?'

'Yes, that's the one,' Bella admits. Is it her imagination or does

Rosel flinch at the mention of Hamar's name? Just like she flinched this morning, when he touched her on the shoulder. 'I screwed it up in a ball and tossed it in the bin, but then I changed my mind later and went to get it back. Don't worry,' she tells Saga, 'I know it was nothing to do with you, despite Hamar's stirring.' She watches Rosel more carefully this time as she says his name. Watches the girl's gaze flick from Bella to Saga and then quickly down to the floor, wondering if there really *is* something going on between them. The idea makes Bella decidedly uncomfortable, but maybe she's reading too much into the situation because of her own experience with Ludwell. Maybe she's seeing things that aren't actually there. *Again*. 'It's not really the note itself I'm worried about,' she continues, 'so much as the thought of someone in my room. I don't even know how they'd have got in, if the door was locked . . . unless . . . unless I didn't shut it properly on my way out to breakfast . . .' It seems unlikely, but Bella can't be a hundred per cent certain at this distance. So much has happened since then. *Ludwell* has happened since then.

'Is everything okay?' Bella asks, as the two women exchange a glance. Rosel looks more uncomfortable than ever.

'We're just running a bit behind,' answers Saga, reaching into a nearby drawer for a spatula, 'which means we're not as relaxed as we might be. Lena's been in here half the morning asking questions about the other guests for her article.'

Rosel mutters something in Swedish under her breath. '*Nyfiken slyna.*'

Bella's no idea what that means but it doesn't sound very complimentary.

'Apart from that, everything's fine though,' says Saga, with another loaded glance at her colleague. But Rosel looks far from fine.

'What is it? What aren't you telling me? Is it something to with Hamar?' Bella asks, her fingers tightening into fists.

'No, *no*,' says Rosel quickly. *A little* too *quickly?* 'It's nothing to do with him, I swear. It . . . it's me,' she blurts. 'I'm missing some keys – I can't find them anywhere.'

'As in your work keys?' Bella's stomach lurches. 'The keys to all the guest rooms?' *Including mine.*

'It's the spare set that usually lives in the office,' Rosel says, her voice little more than a whisper. 'I lent them to the lady who comes in to help with the big weekend clean when we're running retreats two weeks in a row, and I forgot to put them back afterwards. I must have put them down somewhere, or perhaps they fell out of my pocket . . . I don't know. I can't remember. I was in such a rush to get everything ready in time. It was only this morning, when one of the guests locked themselves out of their room, that I realised I still hadn't returned them . . . and now . . .' She tugs at a bit of skin around her thumbnail. 'I've looked everywhere.'

Bella stares at her. 'So you're saying there's an entire set of keys that you can't account for, and you don't even know how long they've been missing?'

'It's not as bad as it sounds,' says Rosel. 'They're around here somewhere. They must be. Please don't say anything to Stuart and Marie,' she adds. 'I don't want them thinking I've caused some big security . . . er . . . what's the word?'

'Breach,' says Saga.

Rosel nods. 'Breach,' she repeats, like an echo.

'But they need to know,' Bella insists. '*Everyone* needs to know. From where I'm standing it *is* a security breach. How do you know someone else hasn't found them? They could be prowling round our bedrooms at night while we're asleep.'

Rosel looks horrified. 'No,' she says. 'If anyone here had found them, they'd have handed them in to the office.'

'Or kept them,' insists Bella. 'That explains my missing note, anyway. Whoever's got your keys must have used them to get into my room that first morning, while I was at breakfast, and steal the note out of my bin.' *And leave the apple on my desk the next night,* she thinks.

'Why?' asks Saga. 'Why would they have done that?'

'Because . . .' Bella can't answer that one. *Why* would *anyone have broken into her room to rifle through her rubbish?* A suspect needs motive as well as opportunity – she knows that from all those crime dramas she's been watching.

'Maybe the note was mislaid too?' Saga suggests. 'Just like the keys. Maybe you missed the bin when you threw the bit of paper away and it rolled out of sight under your desk? Rosel probably swept it up without noticing when she cleaned your room later on.'

It's *possible*, Bella concedes. But not very likely.

'Yes,' says Rosel. 'That must be what happened. Please,' she begs. 'I'm going to tell Stuart and Marie about the keys if I still can't find them, I promise. I just want to have one last search for them this afternoon, when it's quiet.' She looks on the verge of tears. 'I really need this job. My dad's sick and my mum's had to give up work to look after him and . . .' The rest of the sentence trails away. 'Please don't say anything,' she says again. 'They can't have gone far.'

Bella hesitates.

'There's nothing sinister about it,' Saga insists. 'They probably slipped out of her pocket, that's all.'

'Okay,' says Bella. 'I'll keep it to myself. For now.' What else *can* she say? Perhaps Saga's right. Perhaps there *is* an innocent explanation for it all. 'Let me know when you find them,' she adds, 'just to put my mind at rest. I'll keep an eye out for them too in the meantime.' Her eyes are already scanning the expensive tiled floor as she says it, searching for a telltale glint of silver, as if they might be lurking there in plain sight.

'Thank you,' says Rosel with a sigh of relief.

*

There's no sign of the keys in the dining room as Bella retraces her steps through the quiet lodge, wondering where everyone is. No sign of them in the main reception room – not on the polished oak floor or kicked under the Sixties-style sideboard. They haven't slipped down the back of the sofa, although they'd be in good company if they had, what with all the crumbs and coins and random bits of fluff Bella hooks out with her finger. It's been a while since anyone cleaned down there, she thinks, remembering the messy jumble of chocolate wrappers and toys she and Asher discovered behind the cushions of *their* old, inherited sofa when they finally upgraded to a new one. She can still hear his little voice now, exclaiming in wonder over each find: *My Lego knight! How did he get down there? My water squirter! My robot pencil!*

Those days feel a million miles away now though. *Asher* feels a million miles away. Bella hauls herself back up to window height with a sigh, to see two figures standing outside the lodge in animated conversation: Lena and T. Have they been there all along? Bella didn't have them pegged as obvious friends but she noticed they were sitting together at breakfast this morning too. Maybe Lena's been interviewing him for her travel article . . . or maybe they've got more in common than Bella realises.

For a moment, as they lean in towards each other, it looks as if they're about to embrace. But it's not love in the air. Bella can't hear what they're saying but she can read their body language. She can see T's angrily jabbing finger and Lena's raised palms. Can see her backing away as if she's refusing to be drawn in. It must be something in the air today, she thinks – an air of disagreement. First Ludwell and Julia, and now Lena and T. But what have *they* got to argue about?

Bella jumps at the sound of footsteps behind her, spinning round in red-cheeked embarrassment as if she's been caught spying.

'What are you doing?' asks Oscar, glancing from Bella to the window and back again.

'Nothing,' she answers with guilty speed. 'I just . . . I was just looking for . . .' She's about to say 'the keys' but then she remembers her promise to Rosel. 'For Stuart,' she says. 'I er . . .

I wanted to ask him more about that story – the one you were telling me this morning, with the scratching fingernails.' It's the first thing that comes into her head. 'He's not here though,' she says, redundantly.

'I've got a pamphlet of local legends he dug out for me last night, in my room,' says Oscar. 'All the details are in there. Some of the other stories are quite creepy, too – I'm trying to work out how I can weave them into my book.'

Of course you are, thinks Bella. The man's obsessed.

'I've finished making my notes though,' he adds, 'if you want to borrow it.'

'Thank you, yes, creepy sounds good,' says Bella, although she's pretty creeped out already after last night. 'It might give me some inspiration for the piece I'm working on at the moment.' In truth, she's barely thought about her symphony all day but maybe some spooky local legends will get the creative juices flowing again.

'No problem,' says Oscar. 'I'll fetch it for you now.'

Bella follows him back to his room, venturing into the other guest wing for the first time. No sign of any lost keys down here, either. 'This is me,' he says, stopping at the first door they come to and fishing his own key out of his pocket. 'Stay here, I won't be a sec.' It's the very opposite of an invitation but Bella catches hold of the door before it closes and follows him in all the same. It's too good an opportunity to miss, given that she still doesn't know for sure it was Hamar who put that note under her door rather than Oscar. Maybe he's got another notebook – a *second* notebook – lurking somewhere on his desk.

Oscar's room is smaller than hers, but the expensive finish is exactly the same. The designer desk and the coffee machine are identical. There's no second notebook to be seen though, just a framed photograph of a smiling older lady with red hair and sunglasses. He catches her looking at it and his face changes.

'My mother,' he says, reaching out a finger and touching the top of the frame. 'My *late* mother.'

'Oh, I'm so sorry.' *Not another one,* thinks Bella. Dödmansskogen is full of people with broken hearts. 'She looks lovely.'

'She is,' says Oscar, picking the photograph up and then putting it down again. 'She was. It's still a bit raw,' he says, as if to explain why he's now dabbing surreptitiously at his left eye.

'I'm sorry,' says Bella again. *I lost my mother too,* she thinks of telling him, but then doesn't. It's not the same thing at all. She can see that by the pained expression on his face. A pained expression which is now turning to embarrassment.

'Don't worry, I'm not some Norman Bates weirdo with a mother obsession,' he says as he turns away to look inside the desk drawer. 'But we *were* close. She's the reason I'm here, in fact. She made me promise to follow my dream . . . Here we are,' Oscar announces, before Bella can work out a suitable response. He thrusts an unprepossessing A5 pamphlet at her, with a black-and-white picture of a rabid-looking dog on the front. 'Stuart said one of their previous guests sent it to him. It's a bit of a homemade job but the stories are good.'

'Thank you. I er . . . Are you okay?' Bella blurts out.

Oscar nods, but his eyes are damp with tears. 'I will be,' he says.

*

A contrite Hamar joins Bella at lunch a while later, planting his heavy frame down in the free chair beside her and clapping his hand to her shoulder. 'I've come to apologise,' he says. 'I'm sorry. For the silliness at the lake,' he clarifies, as if there might be other apologies owing elsewhere. 'It was a childish stunt and I didn't think it through. I get a bit carried away sometimes.'

'Yes,' says Bella. 'So I gather.' She can't bring herself to tell him it's fine because it's not. It was frightening and humiliating and she's a long way from forgiving him. 'I've had enough of your jokes already, thank you, so if you're planning anything else . . . well, just don't, okay? I'd appreciate it if you left me alone from now on.' *And leave poor Rosel alone too,* she thinks.

'Okay.' Hamar looks hurt, as if he's the one who's been victimised. 'If that's what you want. I'm sorry,' he says again, retreating to the other end of the table to quiz Stuart and Marie on the delights of the lunch menu, leaving Bella to enjoy her pre-lunch glass of water in peace. It's a slightly strained peace though. She gets the distinct feeling that Lena and Krista, who join her shortly afterwards, are tiptoeing around her. Has Krista said something? Is that why Lena keeps looking at her oddly? Or did she spot Bella at the window when she and T were arguing? Or maybe it's neither – maybe Bella's just being paranoid.

With the arrival of Oscar and T, conversation turns to the weather and T's dog, Pookie, a tiny short-haired breed with an entire wardrobe of dog sweaters and coats for when the temperature drops. It all seems civil enough between T and Lena now, although Bella's only half-listening to what's actually being said. She's too busy looking at the empty seats at the other end of the table and wondering where the Storms are. That's two meals in a row they've missed.

'My partner wasn't a fan though,' says T, as Bella tunes back in again. They're still talking about dog clothes. 'My *ex*-partner. Nor was Pookie, come to that. I managed to keep the hat on her long enough to take the photo but that was it. I've still got it on my phone, I'll show you.' He reaches into his fleece pocket and then stops short. 'Ah, no phone. I keep forgetting.'

'Released from the shackles of the outside world to embrace the wilderness within,' murmurs Lena under her breath. 'How timely.'

T bites his lip but says nothing.

'It's disconcerting being without a phone, isn't it?' says Krista, who doesn't seem to have heard. 'I didn't realise quite how much time I spend checking mine until now. It's been a useful exercise from that point of view, although I'm sure I'll go back to my evil addicted ways as soon as I'm home.'

Bella's always telling Asher he spends too long on his phone, but she'd give anything to have hers back too now. To see if there are any messages from him. But then again, if he *has* messaged her and not got a reply yet, he might be worried. Especially if he didn't get her text from Sunday night . . .

'It's a pain, that's what it is.' Oscar sounds decidedly put out. 'Not being able to look things up on Google as I write is a complete nightmare.' Bella's glad to see him back to his usual self.

'I agree,' says Lena. 'You wouldn't believe how many times I've gone to double-check something online, forgetting that I'm stuck in the dark ages this week. I'll have an entire notebook of things to look up by the time I leave,' she adds, with a sly glance in T's direction, 'and goodness knows how many hours' worth of material to go through on the old Dictaphone I borrowed from my boss. I really miss my speech-to-text app too.'

'What makes it even more annoying is that I came prepared.' Oscar lowers his voice and leans in over his half-eaten *pitepalt*: pork-stuffed potato dumplings with butter and some kind of jam stuff. Lingonberry maybe? 'The phone I gave in is actually my old one – I kept my real one back for research purposes. But I might as well not have bothered. There's no signal out here anyway, which is doubly frustrating as the writing's going so well. This place is the *perfect* setting for my book, with the dark, encroaching forest and only one road out . . . not to mention all the strange noises at night. If I was a psycho looking for my next batch of victims, this is exactly the sort of place I'd choose.'

Krista shivers. 'Don't say that. That's horrible.'

'It's true though,' says T. 'We're pretty much trapped here, aren't we? It's not like we can call an Uber, is it?'

He looks like he's about to say something else but Bella jumps in first: 'What sort of noises?'

'Huh?' says T.

'Sorry, I was talking to Oscar. You said there were strange noises at night. Do you mean like footsteps? Like people creeping round in the dark? Or animal sounds?' *Scratching sounds . . .*

'Both,' says Oscar. 'It sounded like a fox or something, snuffling around out there this morning. But they were definitely human footsteps I heard while I was working on my latest chapter last night. And when I looked out my window a bit later – it must have been quarter to twelve – I saw a ghostly figure in white heading down the path as if they were going to the lake . . .'

Krista laughs nervously. 'Stop it. You had me going there.'

'I'm serious,' Oscar says. 'Okay, so they might not have been wearing white – I might have used a bit of artistic licence there – but it *was* pretty eerie. The way the light from their torch radiated out in the mist, or the rain, whatever it was. It looked like something out of a ghost film.'

'And this was last night, you said?' asks T.

Oscar nods. 'Yes. Why?'

'I'm just thinking about that note I found under my door yesterday morning. The one saying to meet by the lake at midnight. Whoever it was *really* meant for, I bet that's who you saw . . . on their way to their secret meeting.' He glances round the table as if he's watching their reactions. As if he's sizing them up as potential suspects.

'Not a ghost then,' says Oscar with a grin. 'Just a clandestine rendezvous. I wonder who it was? I almost wish I'd followed them now. It could have been the start of a good sub-plot.'

'I don't like the thought of *anyone* creeping round out there in the dark,' says Krista. 'Can we talk about something else?'

Oscar shrugs. 'Like what?'

'I don't know. Like more pets in silly outfits. Not that I'm saying Pookie's outfits sound silly,' she corrects herself. 'I meant cute. *Cute* outfits.'

'Or we could talk about what's going on with our fellow guests,' suggests Lena.

Bella glances instinctively at T, wondering again what it was the two of them were arguing about. His eyes are fixed on Lena, his cheeks even paler than usual.

'What do you mean?' asks Krista, picking up on the sudden tension. 'Am I missing something?'

'Hamar and Rosel,' says Lena, gesturing with a slight incline of her head.

Not T then. Is it Bella's imagination or is that a small sigh of relief from him?

'Do you think she has a crush on him?' Lena asks.

Bella turns her attention back to the other end of the table. To Rosel, who's handing Hamar a glass of beer, blushing furiously at something he's saying.

Or maybe it's the other way round, she thinks. *Maybe he's the one chasing her.* 'I hope not, for her sake,' she says out loud. 'I wouldn't trust Hamar as far as I could throw him.'

'I thought he was the one throwing you. Straight into the lake, wasn't it?' jokes T, a slight colour returning to his cheeks now. 'Sorry, that was insensitive.'

'Please, can we talk about something else?' Bella asks, echoing Krista's request. The thought of the lake still gives her shivers.

'Yes, of course, I'm sorry. How about Ludwell and Julia?' T asks, changing to an even *worse* subject. Bella's stomach clenches at the mere mention of their names. 'Where are they? What's happened to *them*, do you think?'

Lena's expression darkens. 'In their room, I assume,' she says, with a brief glance back towards their empty chairs. 'Julia's not well apparently.'

'Perhaps it's a touch of what Bella had last night,' T suggests. 'A twelve-hour bug, or something.'

'That was food poisoning,' Bella says, still playing along with Marie's story. 'From something I ate on the way out, most likely. It can take a while for symptoms to appear.'

'Eighteen to thirty-six hours for *Clostridium botulinum*,' agrees Oscar. 'That's the bacteria that causes botulism. And up to six days for salmonella. Listeria's even longer. That can be more like one to four weeks before you get any symptoms.

Botulism's the best though if you're looking to finish someone off.'

T laughs. 'Which you always seem to be. You do realise you'll be the prime suspect when the bodies start turning up?'

'Stop it,' scolds Krista. 'I don't know how we got from poodles to poison and dead bodies.'

And Ludwell, thinks Bella. For a while there, at the hide, it had felt good to tell Krista the truth. To have finally shared the secret of Asher's paternity. Bella had never even told her sister the full story, for fear she'd go in guns blazing, demanding Ludwell's resignation. But unburdening herself hasn't changed anything, has it? She's still stuck here with him and his wife and the fear that *they* somehow know too. Maggot-filled apples and strange scratchings in the wall are nothing compared to the thought of losing Asher. Nothing's as scary as the thought of him hating her for what she's done. For keeping him from his father all these years.

*

It takes Izzy three whole days to pluck up the courage to try again. But here she is, knocking on Ludwell's office door at the appointed hour, feeling even sicker than before.

'Come in.' His voice is brisk and businesslike.

Deep breath in, *Izzy tells herself, trying to still the wild trembling in her legs.* Deep breath out. You can do this.

'Come in,' he calls again, an edge of impatience creeping into his voice.

Deep breath . . . Here goes nothing.

Ludwell's blue eyes are cold and unwelcoming as he looks up from his desk. 'Oh,' he says, 'it's you.'

The trembling in Izzy's legs is a full-on shake now. It's hard to imagine he's the same man. The man who bought her drinks at the bar and listened to her stupid tales of teenage infatuation . . . who steadied her when she swayed on the pavement . . . the man who kissed her up against the wall . . .

'I was hoping you'd come,' he adds.

You were? *Izzy feels a sudden surge of optimism. Maybe it's going to be okay. She doesn't know what 'okay' means in this situation, exactly – she's not naïve enough to imagine that he'll leave his wife for her and the baby and the three of them can play happy families together . . . she's not even sure she wants the happy-families ending – but his response still gives her hope. Hope that she doesn't have to face this on her own any more.*

Ludwell isn't finished yet though. 'I wanted to talk to you . . . to tell you to keep away from my house. From my wife.'

'But . . . But that night . . .' *she begins.* 'The night we—'

'No,' *Ludwell cuts in firmly.* 'We didn't. Nothing happened.'

'But . . .' Come on, you can do this. Just tell him. Two words – I'm pregnant – how hard can it be?

'Nothing. Happened,' *Ludwell says again, as if he's stuck on repeat.*

Nothing happened . . . nothing happened . . . nothing happened.

Izzy's hands move instinctively to her stomach as the first tears trickle down her cheeks. But it did, *she thinks.* It's the biggest thing that's ever happened to her. It's still happening now, deep inside of her, even as she fumbles for the door handle, eyes misted with tears. Her son or daughter – Ludwell's son or daughter – is happening whether Izzy likes it or not.

Chapter 19

'I'm sorry,' Bella tells Marie on the way out of lunch, feigning a headache. 'I'm going to have to give Ludwell's music therapy session a miss. I think bed's the best place for me at the moment.'

Marie looks suitably sympathetic. 'You are pale. I hope it *is* just a headache.'

'I'll be fine after a bit of rest, I'm sure,' Bella tells her.

Maybe sleep really *will* do her some good after such a disturbed night, she decides when she gets back to her room, pulling down the blind and climbing into bed fully dressed. Maybe some proper rest will help get the whirl of thoughts in her head into perspective. Sleep will make the time go quicker too. How is it still only Tuesday? Four more days until Bella gets out of here. Four more days until she gets to speak to Asher. That'll be the first thing she does, as soon as she gets her phone back and manages to get some connection. Maybe she was wrong to keep his father from him all these years. But the thought of losing him – especially to a creep like Ludwell Storm – was too much. It still is.

Bella lies there for a good twenty minutes, listening to the ticking seconds on her watch and the eerie stillness of her room. No scratching sounds this time. No footsteps. There's scarcely any noise at all, save for the occasional tweeting bird outside and the cacophony of her own thoughts. Sleep might be exactly what her overwrought mind needs, but her brain steadfastly refuses to switch off. The old worries are back with a vengeance now, mixing with the new ones in a cocktail of unanswerable questions. *What if it all comes out and Ludwell decides to make contact with his son? What if Asher's been miserable at university all this time and hasn't been able to get hold of her? What if something's happened and no one knows how to reach her?* Bad things happen to people all the time . . . like Marie's son.

'*I* had a son,' Marie said, not '*we* had a son', which means she must have lost him before she married Stuart. But the grief was still raw – Bella could see it in her eyes. *Just like Krista. Just like Oscar.* It feels like she's surrounded by loss, as if the whole world is full of dead mothers, dead husbands, dead sons . . . Asher could be next. In fact, he could be lying in hospital, or worse, at that very moment and Bella wouldn't even know.

Stop it, she tells herself. What would Asher say if he were here now? He'd tell her she needs to get a grip, and he'd be right. *This isn't a scene from your film. I'm not going to get poisoned, or stabbed, or clubbed over the head with a walking stick.* Those were practically his last words to her on Sunday, along with *Promise you'll make the most of this holiday. No changing your mind and checking out halfway through, like you did on that London theatre trip last year.* And *I miss you.*

'I miss you too,' she whispers into the silence. *I miss you so much it hurts.* But a promise is a promise. She's supposed to be making the most of her time here, which means getting a grip on her spiralling fears and pulling herself together. Asher's got the emergency number for the lodge landline if he needs to get through to her. If he's at all worried about not being able to reach her on her mobile – if he never got her message from Sunday – then that's what he'll do. But chances are he'll be too busy enjoying freshers' week to even think about ringing his mum, which is exactly how it should be. *No news is good news*, Bella reminds herself.

She fetches some water from the bathroom and sits down at the desk to get started on some composition, with the pamphlet of local legends at the ready in case her own dark thoughts and fears aren't enough. But then she changes her mind, reaching for a blank sheet of manuscript paper instead, and a pen. The Writing Your Way Out of Worry workshop with Stuart isn't until Friday morning, but there's nothing to stop her giving it a try on her own now. Committing her ever-growing list of anxieties to paper might help her get a handle on them – and maybe even spark some potential solutions. It's time to get *pro*active, she decides, rather than *re*active.

The exercise feels stilted and awkward at first. Bella's never been one for committing her problems to diaries or pouring out her emotions in poems. Poetry was more Nat's style. But she perseveres all the same, trying to break her increasing sense of panic down into its constituent parts – working each separate thread of worry free from the overall tangle. It's all there: everything from not being able to contact Asher and potential confrontations with Ludwell and Julia, to Rosel's missing keys and the fact that until the fallen trees get moved, there's no way out. It feels genuinely therapeutic to write them down, as if she's emptying her head of her worries by committing them to paper. And, perhaps because the paper in question *is* manuscript paper, Bella finds a tune worming its way into her head of its own accord, as she rereads her list. The start of a tune anyway – a rich, resonant cello line, rising up out of the darkness above low chromatic shivers on the double bass. And a long, high single note on the clarinet – no, wait, an oboe – starting softly at first and then crescendo-ing, getting louder and louder until it breaks into a new, haunting melody, against the *scratch, scratch, scratch* of a guiro . . .

Her frayed nerves feel more like nervous excitement as she turns to a new sheet of manuscript paper and starts scribbling it down, desperate to capture it while it's still fresh in her head. Maybe her first instincts were right after all. Maybe this is an even better way of writing her way through her worries – not with words, but with music. Her own personal form of music therapy that has nothing, thankfully, to do with Ludwell's session. If Bella's going to be sitting in her room feeling scared, she might as well be *productively* scared. She might as well channel some of that fear and anxiety into her work. And who knows, this might be *it*. This might, finally, be the way into her second movement – the inspiration she's been waiting for.

It's a good call. Once Bella's started, she can't stop. It feels oddly primal and instinctive working like this again, without recourse to her computer and noise-cancelling headphones, but before long she's so deep in her work that any external sounds – the birds outside the window and the distant hum of a hoover – fade away into insignificance. She doesn't stop for a drink or a snack, or to use the toilet, her bodily needs forgotten in the rare rush of creative energy.

Bella can barely remember when she had such a productive afternoon. Yesterday morning's impromptu session was good, but this is even better. Worry and paranoia seem to be feeding her creativity rather than stymieing it, bringing a claustrophobic darkness and intensity to her work that's exactly what her second movement needs. And the longer into the afternoon she works, the better she feels. Her fears and worries are still there – after all, nothing's actually changed – but she's more in control of them now. She's *taking* control of them, channelling them into her music and making order out of her own mental chaos. By the time she finally breaks off to check the time – just after 6.45 p.m. – Bella's head feels clearer and calmer than it has since she arrived.

She leans back in her seat with a satisfied stretch and a wide, unchecked yawn. Her neck and shoulders are stiff from spending so long hunched over her desk but that's a small price to pay for such a good afternoon's work. It's a shame, too, that she missed the second session of the afternoon – she rather liked the sound

162

of Stuart's shinrin-yoku (forest-bathing), once she found out what it was – but the trees will still be there tomorrow. And although an afternoon of focused composition is unlikely to make it onto any retreat itineraries, it's been just as therapeutic in its way. Maybe she should forget about the rest of the organised activities altogether and keep to her room for the rest of her stay. She could feign a weeklong headache and treat it solely as a work retreat rather than a wilderness one. That would keep her nicely out of Ludwell's path too.

But no sooner has the thought crossed her mind than she hears a noise coming from over by the sofa. A scratching noise from the empty room nextdoor. It's softer and more muffled than the off-beat guiro line in her piece – designed to throw the audience rhythmically and set their teeth on edge – but it's loud enough, and clear enough, to catch her ear all the same. It sounds like . . . like there's something behind the wall, or *in* the wall. Something trying to claw its way out. And unlike the scratching noise she heard last night, there's no writing it off as a dream this time. Bella's wide awake. She's wide awake and trembling as she crosses the room and lays her palms flat against the wall.

Scrrrratch. Scrrrrratch. Scrrrrratch.

'Hello'?' she calls. 'Is there someone there?' It's too rhythmic and precise to be mice or rats. 'Can you hear me?'

There's no reply. Of course there isn't. Because that would be crazy. The room's empty – Marie already confirmed as much.

It's like Stuart's story, Bella thinks with a shiver. *With the ghostly fingernails . . .*

No, it's not, she tells herself. *It's nothing like that.*

She fetches the local legends pamphlet Oscar gave her, and settles down on the sofa, skimming through 'The Coffin Filler of Dödmansskogen' in the hope of *proving* that the story bears no relation to the noise coming from the wall. In the hope of being able to dismiss the whole thing as a load of superstitious nonsense . . . which is exactly what it turns out to be. Gruesome nonsense admittedly, especially the line about the bandit wearing his fingers down to bloodied stumps as he tries to claw his way out of the coffin, but nonsense all the same. And as for the part about the ghostly scratching being heard before someone dies . . . well, that's just pure campfire tale ghoulishness . . . isn't it?

Scrrrratch. Scrrrrratch. Scrrrrratch.

'Stop it!' Bella thumps the sides of her fists against the wall as if to ward off any further attempts to scare her. It must be rats after all. It *has* to be. Or some particularly noisy species of wood-boring insect, eating away at the wall from the inside. Something like a deathwatch beetle. They're supposed to be harbingers of death too . . .

'Stop it,' she says again, but to herself this time. 'Get a grip.' She needs to get a grip and she needs to hurry up and get ready for dinner. The thought of facing the Storms again holds little appeal, but the thought of staying in her room, alone, listening for creepy noises in the wall, doesn't appeal much either. Suddenly the solitude that was so welcome and productive this afternoon is the last thing she wants any more. *Safety in numbers,* that's what Bella's thinking now, as she tidies away her work and heads for the bathroom. Even if those numbers include Ludwell and Julia.

*

Ludwell and Julia Storm. There they are, gazing down at Izzy from the department noticeboard. It's an article from one of the weekend supplements – an article about Ludwell's generous work with the new children's orchestra he set up, with the equally generous support of his wife.

'Yes, of course we'd have loved a family of our own,' *Izzy reads, her breath catching in her throat,* **'but it never quite happened for us.'** *That's as far as she gets before the words start to blur. Before the image of Ludwell and Julia cuddling up in their fancy bedroom with* her *baby forces its way into Izzy's head.*

We'd have loved a family of our own.

No, *she thinks, her own confused feelings suddenly crystallising.* It's not your baby, *she tells the smug couple in the photograph, her hands slipping down to her stomach to protect the new life growing inside.* It's mine.

Chapter 20

Bella's brief enthusiasm for company retreats again the moment she walks into dinner. There he is, Ludwell, already sitting at the table, staring morosely into a glass of water as if he's disappointed it's not something stronger.

'Ah, hello there,' he says. 'I'm glad to see I'm not the only one in need of food. I was starting to wonder if I'd got the wrong time.' He pauses, eyeing her with an unwelcome scrutiny. 'I didn't see you at my session this afternoon.'

And, just like that, Bella's a tongue-tied teenager again.

'No,' she says. *Tries* to say. It takes her two goes to get the word out. She'd forgotten the stomach-dropping, stomach-churning effect the man had on her. *Has* on her, rather. Present tense. 'Sorry. I was feeling a bit under the weather. I missed Stuart's tree-bathing session too.'

'Perhaps there's something going round. Julia's been off form as well today, feeling washed out and spacey. "Drugged" is the word she used, in fact, but given her resistance to anything stronger than paracetamol, I think we can safely rule that one out!'

'I'm sorry to hear that. And sorry again about last night. That has to be one of the most embarrassing moments of my life.'

Ludwell waves her words away. 'These things happen. Julia and

I were sat next to a young mother and her little boy on a trip to Australia once. He spent the first half of the flight screaming and the second half projectile-vomiting. Thank goodness for the airport showers when we got to Hong Kong. We ended up buying new sets of clothes and binning our old ones before the second leg of our journey, much to the relief of the rest of the plane, I imagine.'

Bella forces a smile. She's spent so many years demonising the man – spent so long avoiding his books and articles and TV appearances – that it seems strange to be here making small talk with him. Or rather listening to *him* making small talk, while she plans her escape to the other end of the table and prays that the others arrive soon. But then Ludwell gestures to the empty chair to his left and invites her to take a seat. And even while every fibre of her body is crying out 'no' – the last person in the world she wants to be trapped next to for an entire evening is Ludwell Storm – Bella somehow hears the words 'thank you' coming out of her mouth. Finds herself sitting down beside him as he pours her a glass of water and asks if *she's* got any children.

Her immediate reaction is relief. *He doesn't know about Asher*, she thinks. *Thank goodness*. Perhaps Krista was right and the row she heard outside the Storms' bedroom this morning *wasn't* about her after all. Maybe Ludwell genuinely doesn't know who Bella is. Maybe he never gave her a second thought after he shut her down in his office that day, telling her that as far he was concerned nothing happened between them.

You're the one who missed out though. You're the one who never got to know your son. Never got to cuddle his chubby little arms and legs into your chest. Never got to see his first smile. First words. First steps. First everything.

'Ah,' Bella says, swivelling round in her seat at the sound of voices from behind. It's Stuart and T. 'Here come the others.' Perfect timing! 'I'm sorry,' she says as Stuart approaches. 'I think

I'm sitting in your seat.' She picks up her water and pushes back her chair, but Stuart puts his hand on her shoulder.

'No, no, you stay where you are,' he says. 'I was going to suggest we mix things up a bit tonight anyway. That's the problem with such a big table – it's not very good for the group dynamic. You never get to hear what people at the far end are talking about and vice versa.'

That's fine by me. Really. Or maybe you could send Ludwell down to the other end? That would work . . .

T takes the seat on the other side of her, trapping Bella in place.

'Hi there. We were just talking children,' Ludwell explains.

No, we weren't. We were desperately trying to avoid *talking about children.*

'Oh right, yes,' says T. 'That's why you didn't want to give your phone in the other night, wasn't it? Because of your son.'

Bella nods. 'It's no big deal though. I'm sure he's fine.'

'How old is he?' asks Ludwell.

'Oh, he's all grown up now,' says Bella, trying to keep her answer as vague as possible. Trying to avoid looking at Ludwell as she says it.

'Just started uni,' says T. 'That's right, isn't it?'

Bella swallows. 'Yes, well remembered.' *Come on, think of something else to say. Change the subject.*

'I guess that gives you more time to focus on your work,' says T.

No, not work, thinks Bella. *Another subject.* But her mind's gone blank and it's too late anyway. Ludwell's already picked up the conversational baton and he's running with it.

'What is it you do?' he asks.

Bella can feel her indignation rising. She might have been pretty wasted last night but she's sure she's already had this conversation with him. Except it turns out Ludwell's not talking to her. He's *looking* at her – an uncomfortable, piercing sort of look as if he's still trying to place where he's seen her before – but it's T he's addressing. 'Something in computing, is that right?'

It's T's turn to look uncomfortable now. 'App development mainly. All very tedious,' he says, his gaze flicking briefly to the other end of the table, towards Lena and Krista. 'To be honest, I've come here to *escape* work. I'd rather hear more about your son, Bella. What subject is he reading?'

'History,' Bella says, keeping her reply as short and uninteresting as possible. 'Oh look, here comes the wine.' And even though she was one hundred per cent committed to a dry night tonight, she finds herself agreeing to a glass of white all the same, in order to whisper to Rosel as she leans in to pour it: 'Any sign of the keys?'

The girl pauses, her eyes wide and frightened for a moment. But then her neat, business-like smile is back again. 'Everything's fine,' she says by way of an answer, filling Bella's glass almost to the brim. 'Enjoy your meal.'

So you have *found them?* Bella wants to ask. *Why didn't you let me know? Where were they?* But Rosel has already moved on – as has the conversation round the table. T is telling them a story about his own university days . . . something to do with a drunken party on a bridge, drinking some weird hallucinogenic spirit from Mexico. A party that ended in hospitalisation for three of his closest friends. 'Not that your son will be doing anything like that, of course,' he adds, remembering who his audience is. 'I'm sure he's much more sensible than I was at that age.'

Yes, Bella thinks. *Of course he is.* At least, she *hopes* he is. If only she knew how he was doing. How he was getting on.

'Is there any chance I can have my phone back after dinner?' she blurts out, shouting down the table towards Stuart on a sudden whim. 'And access to your Wi-Fi code?' she adds at a more reasonable volume, as everyone turns to stare. 'Sorry, I didn't mean to interrupt.'

Bella takes a big slug of wine in an effort to cool the heat flooding into her cheeks. Then another. The look on Stuart's face as he considers his response doesn't fill her with much hope though. Anyone would think she was asking for one of his kidneys. She keeps drinking.

'If Bella's getting her phone back, then I want mine back too,' pipes up Oscar. 'I need to find out whether it would be possible to garrotte someone with a standard fishing line, or whether it would snap.'

'It depends how much of a fight they put up,' says Hamar. 'I'm joking,' he adds, in response to something Bella can't see. A kick under the table from Krista, maybe?

'No one's getting their phone back to look up murder techniques,' says Marie firmly, from the far end of the table.

'What about you, Lena?' says Oscar. He's like a dog with a bone. 'You said you could do with access to the internet too.'

But Lena refuses to play. 'No, it's fine,' she says. 'I can wait until the end of the week. If those are the rules . . .'

That's when Bella loses her nerve. 'I'm sorry. Forget I said anything.' She takes another large gulp of wine. Water would have been better, but somehow it's the wineglass she finds herself reaching for. It seems to have emptied itself without her noticing.

'Here,' says Ludwell, picking up the half-full bottle Rosel left on the table. 'Let me top you up.'

No, I'm fine. That's what Bella *should* be saying. *I'm not really drinking tonight.* But what she *actually* says is 'thank you'.

Just one more, she promises herself as he pours, her face still burning. *Just the one.* And she really means it this time, until halfway through the soup starter when Ludwell leans in close – so close she can feel his breath on her cheek – and says, 'I'm still trying to think where I know you from.' That's the point when 'just the one' switches from just the one glass to just the one bottle.

And there it is: proof that Krista was right. The argument she overheard between him and Julia really *must* have been about someone else. That's what the rational part of Bella's brain is saying. But the emotional, alcohol-soaked part still isn't buying it. The idea that there could be two women from Ludwell's past on the same retreat feels like too much of a coincidence, and she can't shake the feeling that he's toying with her. That he knows exactly who she is, and this is some weird power game he's playing. Bella denies any knowledge of a prior meeting – of course she does – but she can feel his gaze lingering on her during the meal, taking her right back to that fateful night at the pub all those years before.

She's replayed her drunken, snapshot memories of that night – and the disastrously brief meetings she had with him all those weeks later – so many times in her head over the years, searching for a glimpse of Asher in her memories of his father. But Asher is every bit a Burnstone, thank goodness, apart from his nose. He has Bella's hazel eyes, Bella's wild brown hair, Bella's dimpled cheeks. He hasn't inherited the long, bony Burnstone beak – lucky boy – but his babyish button nose clearly doesn't come from Ludwell either. And nor does his sweet, caring personality and endearing awkwardness.

'Wait, I've got it. I know why you look so familiar,' Ludwell announces halfway through dessert. The touch of his hand on Bella's arm is like an electric shock, sending her reeling back in her seat. Or maybe it's the dread of what he's about to say that hits her like a bolt, making her heart pound inside her chest. She takes another gulp of wine and braces herself for the inevitable.

'… You were on *Music Masters* the other month, weren't you? With Albert Cawston and Ray Pruce? Ray's an old music chum of mine from our conservatoire days,' he explains. 'I'll have to see if I've still got it saved onto the box when I get back.'

'I wouldn't bother,' says Bella quickly. 'I only managed to answer two questions. But yes, that was me though,' she adds, giddy with relief. 'A late stand-in for a more impressive guest as I understand it.'

'I *knew* I recognised you from somewhere. It's been driving me crazy all evening. Since I got here, in fact. I can relax now though.'

You and me both, thinks Bella, the pounding in her chest already easing. Slowing.

But Ludwell hasn't finished yet. 'Well,' he adds, his expression darkening. 'Relax isn't *quite* the right word. I can't really relax with Julia poorly. And this business with the note hasn't exactly helped matters.'

The note? 'What do you mean?' asks Bella.

'Oh yes,' pipes up T. 'You'd have missed all this. It was very dramatic. Ludwell went to pull his notes out of his bag while we were getting ready for the session – the notes for his music therapy talk, I mean – and found an anonymous letter. Just like the one you got yesterday. It said . . .' He stops and looks at Ludwell. 'Sorry, you'd probably rather tell the story yourself.'

But Ludwell shakes his head. 'No, no, be my guest. It's no big deal, really. Someone's idea of a joke, that's all, like Marie said. It's got Julia shaken up though. That's what really makes *me* cross. I wish I'd never told her about it now.'

'So what *did* it say?' asks Bella, trying to steer the conversation back to the crucial part.

'I know what you did,' says Ludwell, fixing her with his cold blue eyes.

Bella stares back at him in shock. Two identical notes. That *can't* be a coincidence.

Julia, she thinks. *She knows what happened between us that night. Someone here must have told her.* But Krista wouldn't have betrayed her confidence like that, would she? Maybe Ludwell confided in someone too, then. Maybe he was up late drinking with Hamar last night, or Oscar or T, or Stuart, and the whole sorry story came pouring out. Or maybe there really *was* someone lurking outside the hide earlier, eavesdropping on Bella's conversation. It could be any one of them, she thinks, glancing round the table at the assembled guests and staff. Except the timing's are all wrong, she realises, aren't they? Whatever the notes are referring to, it can't be their one-night stand. Bella got *her* note before the Storms had even arrived. Before anyone here could have found out about their shared sordid past.

Maybe it's Hamar again then, rehashing the same joke. Or Oscar, hoping for a better reaction than he got from Bella. Or . . . or Krista, moving on to her next suspect . . . What was it she said this morning? *It's not sympathy I need, but answers. Answers and justice.* What if her touchy-feely friendship act is precisely that – an act?

No, Krista wouldn't hurt a fly. She's here to escape her own grief, not to play cruel mind games with someone she's only just met. A virtual stranger. But that's the problem, isn't it? They're *all* strangers. What possible motive would any one of them have for trying to scare her? To scare *them*, she corrects herself. It looks like she and Ludwell are in this together now – whatever 'this' is – whether Bella likes it or not.

'A bit of silliness, that's all,' says Ludwell, reaching for his wineglass. 'That's what I keep telling Julia.'

'Yes, I'm sure you're right,' Bella agrees, reaching for her own glass in an attempt to drown out the fresh whirl of worries spinning round her head. *Unless . . .* Unless there's something else going on here, she thinks. Something bigger and darker – something they're both missing.

Chapter 21

Bella's all set to make her excuses after dinner. A headache, she'll say, or tiredness. Both are true. Her body feels heavy and sluggish from too much wine and too little sleep. There's a starlit walk planned tonight, which Asher would have loved – he used to have his own mini telescope when he was younger, and glow-in-the-dark stars stuck all over his bedroom ceiling – but the only place Bella wants to be now is bed, with the door firmly locked behind her. Until she remembers the scratching sound coming from the room nextdoor, that is. Until she thinks of the footprints under her window. And now Ludwell's matching note . . . If it *is* just a joke, it's not a very funny one. Which is why she joins everyone else outside a short while later, freshly layered up and torch at the ready. Everyone except Ludwell, who's gone back to his room to be with Julia, and Lena, who's turned in early to work on her article.

The sky's like something out of a picture book: an inky black background studded with gold. It's beautiful.

'Wow,' breathes Krista, craning her head back. 'That's amazing.'

Bella nods. She was right: Asher would love this. She's glad she's not out here on her own though. The sky above might be beautiful but the dense forest stretching away in all directions is decidedly creepy in the dark.

174

'There's supposed to be a storm coming in later,' observes Stuart. 'So we'll have to make the most of the clear conditions while we can.'

Not another one, thinks Bella, praying that it doesn't bring any more trees down. She can't bear the thought of any further delay to her homeward plans.

Marie stretches out her arms, reaching her hands up towards the as yet cloudless, star-pricked sky. 'The perfect time to explore the bounty of the universe in her full beauty,' she croons.

'The bounty of the universe,' Krista echoes. 'Yes, I like that.'

Bounty of the universe? Bella rolls her eyes. She's not in the mood for that kind of stuff tonight. She and the universe aren't on the best of terms right now. But then Krista puts an arm round her waist, pulling her into a sideways hug – 'Are you okay?' – and Bella feels bad for being so mean-spirited.

'I'm fine,' she says. 'Sorry. I've got a lot on my mind tonight.'

Krista nods. 'Ah yes. You heard about Ludwell's note then, I take it? If you want to talk . . .'

'I'm fine,' Bella says again. 'Really. Thank you though,' she adds, pulling her hood up over her head and trying to pull herself together while she's at it. *Proactive not reactive, remember?*

She and Krista fall into step with T as the party sets off through Dead Man's Forest, down towards the lake, torches trained together on the path to light the way.

'It's so beautiful out here,' says Krista. 'It's a shame Lena couldn't join us. It might have been a nice thing to include in her article . . . her travel piece, I mean.'

'I'd say she's got more than enough for her article,' mutters T darkly.

'Really?' Krista sounds surprised. 'But it's only Tuesday. We've only been here two full days, although it feels like longer, don't you think?'

'Much longer,' agrees T.

Definitely. They've been the longest two days of Bella's life.

'She left early yesterday too, thinking about it now,' says Krista. 'She must be very committed.'

T grunts – the sort of grunt Bella gets from Asher when she asks him to empty the dishwasher. She'd give anything for one of those precious grunts now though. For a sigh, even. An eye roll.

It sounds like things are still tense between T and Lena. Perhaps it's something to do with Lena's work that's rubbed him up the wrong way, Bella thinks. Something to do with all the questions she's been asking. Saga and Rosel seemed pretty down on her too. 'Or maybe she's had enough of us,' she says out loud, trying to lighten the atmosphere.

'No, I'm sure it's not that,' says Krista, missing the joke. 'Nothing to do with you two, anyway.'

T responds with another Asher-style grunt. 'I'm not so sure about that.'

'Oh, really?' Krista sounds surprised. 'Have I missed something?'

'No. You haven't missed anything. Sorry, you'll have to excuse me, I just remembered I need to talk to Oscar,' says T, striding off down the path.

'Oh dear,' murmurs Krista. 'I don't know what that was about.'

'They had a bit of a run-in this afternoon, I think,' says Bella. 'Wait, who were *you* talking about then? Who else does Lena have a problem with?'

'Oh, nobody. At least not as far as I know.'

Bella can't see Krista's expression in the dark, but she can hear the nervousness in her voice. The nervousness of someone who realises they've said more than they should. Could it be something to do with what she'd said earlier, about Ludwell and Julia's row? *And he was definitely talking about you? He mentioned you by name?* Could *Lena* be the woman from Ludwell's 'sordid past' who'd got Julia so upset? If he was capable of cheating on his wife before – and Bella and Asher are living proof of that – it's not much of a stretch to imagine him cheating again.

It's the coincidence of it all that's the stretch, with Lena just

176

happening to end up on the same retreat as her former lover . . . as if it wasn't coincidence enough *Bella* being here with Ludwell. Unless . . . unless that's *not* a coincidence, Bella thinks with a jolt. She remembers the Einstein quote from the back of that sci-fi kid's novel Asher used to like – the one he used to reread on holiday every year: 'Coincidence is God's way of remaining anonymous.' Could Rachel have planned the whole thing? Did she somehow know that Ludwell was going to be the celebrity guest this week? Maybe she sweet-talked Stuart into giving her the list of all the visiting speakers before stumping up the deposit – she wouldn't put it past her – then arranged for Bella to be here at the same time, remembering her teenage obsession with the man. Maybe it's the timing of the trip to coincide with Asher going away that's the *real* coincidence, in fact.

If that's the case, if Rachel somehow knew Ludwell was going to be here, then it stands to reason that Lena – a trained journalist – could have found that out too. Perhaps she knew all along who the special celebrity guest was going to be, and her disappointed reaction to the big reveal yesterday morning was just a cover. That would explain why she's here this precise week, writing her travel piece . . . because she's hoping to rekindle their past affair . . . And maybe . . . yes, maybe *that's* why she and Ludwell have both cried off tonight's walk.

The idea gives Bella a perverse sense of hope. If she's right, then Ludwell's got far more pressing concerns than the teenager he had a one-night stand with all those years before. He's got better things to think about than why that same teenager dropped out of university a week later and whether she might have been pregnant at the time.

Her mood darkens again as they draw near to the lake though, her thoughts turning back to her unwelcome morning plunge into the water. She can still feel that blind, breathless sense of panic in her chest even now, hours later, mixed in with the humiliation of it all. The embarrassment of her own overreaction. It wouldn't seem like an overreaction now though, not with the water looking so black and foreboding. Out here in the darkness it really *does* seem like the sort of place to dispose of a dead body, just like someone suggested for Oscar's book on their first night.

'Would anyone like me to lead a short moon meditation while we're here?' asks Stuart, as they stand looking out over the water. Or trying to *avoid* looking out over the water in Bella's case. Trying to avoid even thinking about the water, and the dark, icy depths waiting beneath the surface.

'Oh yes, please,' says Krista, predictably. 'That sounds wonderful.'

It's not wonderful though. Stuart's warm, comforting voice isn't working for Bella tonight. She doesn't feel relaxed or at one with nature as the group breathes in healing starlight and breathes out the dark thoughts within. *Her* dark thoughts aren't going anywhere. They're gathering strength – like the storm that's heading towards Dödmansskogen – getting bigger and darker with every breath. And the more she tries to focus on Stuart's voice, the more her mind turns to long-drowned corpses at the bottom of the lake. To maggots wriggling and squirming through cold, white apple flesh. To scratching fingernails down walls . . .

Scratch. Scratch. Scratch.

Bella's eyes flick open in fright.

There it is again, louder and faster than before.

'Did you hear that?' she asks, interrupting Stuart mid-meditation. 'That scratching noise.'

Scratch, scratch, scratch.

'Yes, I can hear it too,' says Krista. 'Oh, that's really creepy.'

'Watch out,' Hamar hisses. 'It's coming from that tree behind you.'

Bella lets out an involuntary yelp as she flings herself forward. Away from the trees. Away from the noise.

'Hey, steady now,' says Stuart, catching her in his arms. 'We don't want you ending up in the lake again.'

Someone laughs. A deep belly laugh.

'And Hamar, if you could refrain from scaring our guests, I'd appreciate it,' Stuart adds, with an air of weariness, as he releases Bella again.

More laughter. 'I should have known it was you,' says Krista, but she's laughing too.

'What?' Hamar holds up his hands in a gesture of mock innocence, sending the beam of his torch arcing off through the trees. 'It's not like anyone believes that old story about the ghost in the forest. Apart from Bella, maybe . . .'

They're all laughing now. That's what it feels like, anyway. Bella clenches her free hand into a fist, fear turning seamlessly to anger. Or maybe it's still fear that's driving her anger even now. Maybe the sudden rush of loathing she feels for every one of them is only because she's scared. She hates their smug laughing faces and she hates the fact that she's trapped here in the middle of nowhere with them in the first place.

I wish I'd never come, she thinks, fighting back hot, angry tears.

I wish Rachel had never found this stupid place.

*

Her dreams that night are dark and fractured: snatches of the day's real events mixed with the usual dreamlike nonsense. One moment Bella's in the lake, thrashing under the water, and the next thing she's back at the lodge, on her hands and knees, searching for Rosel's missing keys. Asher's there too – baby Asher – crawling off across the dining-room floor towards the sideboard with the sliding panelled doors. And then, before Bella can get to him – before she can stop him – he's pulling himself up on his feet. He's pulling back the sliding door and crawling inside, closing the door behind him. But then somehow the door's locked and Bella can't get it open again – not without the lost keys – and Asher's scratching his soft little nails against the wood and sobbing.

'Mummy's here,' she tells him. 'It's okay. I'm going to get you out.' But it's not okay, because the keys are at the bottom of the lake. Of course, she remembers now . . .

She dreams that Asher – all grown up again – is staying in the nextdoor room, but there's no scratching noise this time, just a low sobbing coming through the wall. And when she calls to him through the wall, trying to comfort him, he screams at her to leave him alone. Bella's not giving up that easily though. She goes outside and knocks on the window instead. 'I know what you did,' he yells, his face contorted with anger. 'You took away my dad. I hate you!'

Somewhere around 2 a.m. Bella wakes, heart already thumping, to the sound of thunder. To the sound of the wind howling wolf-like round the lodge, whipping the trees into a whispered frenzy. Stuart was right about the storm then. She thinks of Asher running into her bedroom when he was little, torn between fear and fascination. Fear of the thunder, that had him burying his head into her chest for protection, and fascination with the 'lighterning' that followed. 'Was that it?' he'd say, jerking his head back up like a meerkat as the bedroom flashed with brightness. 'Was that the lighterning?' But for Bella there's nothing but fear tonight. Even when the storm moves on, when the thunder dies to a distant rumble and the wind and the rain ease away again – when there's nothing but the sound of scratching nails from somewhere behind the wall – the fear is as strong as ever. It seeps back into her dreams . . . dreams of Hamar nailing her into a coffin in the middle of the woods, her fingers clawing at the lid as he hammers it into place. 'Let me go! Please. Let me go!'

If only it was *all* a dream, Bella thinks as she wakes again, drenched in sweat. As her breathing slowly returns to normal and she opens her eyes. If only she was waking up back in her own bed at home to find that the whole wilderness retreat and everyone here had just been one bad dream from start to finish. But there's no escape from the nightmare of her week at Dödmansskogen.

Wednesday morning, she thinks miserably. Three more nights to go and counting.

It's not even six o'clock yet but Bella's throat is too dry to get back to sleep. She drags herself out of bed and picks up her empty water glass, heading for the bathroom. And that's when she sees it: another note. There's no mistaking it for a daily itinerary or a health and safety form this time. There's no naïve assumption that it must be something to do with the retreat. Her heart is already thumping in her chest as she reaches down to pick up the folded piece of paper – torn from a different notebook this time by the looks of it – and opens it up:

> *I found something I think you should see. Meet me in the studio before breakfast. I'll be there from 7.00 a.m.*
> *Lena*

The studio. She must mean the big room at the back of the lodge where they have their indoor activity sessions. No great mystery there. The rest of the message is nothing *but* mystery though. What can Lena possibly have found that necessitates a secret meeting? Something to do with T? Is this what they were arguing about yesterday? But Bella barely knows T. Something to with Ludwell then? It must be. Something to do with *Bella* and Ludwell. Does she know about their past? And what about Asher? Does Lena know about *him*? She stares at the note until her eyes sting, trying to make sense of what she's seeing. Trying to second-guess the other woman's motives. Pity? Altruism? Jealousy? Is she trying to help Bella or blackmail her?

Chapter 22

It's one of the longest hours of Bella's life. Longer than that last endless hour of labour, even, with Rachel squeezing her hand and telling her she was doing brilliantly, that it would soon be over. If only Rachel were here now, to hold her hand and tell her everything's going to be okay. If only Asher were here. But Rachel's on the other side of the world and Asher might as well be.

Bella showers and dresses, turning Lena's note over and over in her mind. Does that mean she was behind the first note too? And Ludwell's? It *could* be the same handwriting. But then why make those two notes anonymous and then sign her name on this one? No amount of scalding hot coffee or pacing up and down the room makes the answers any clearer though. No amount of picking things up off her desk – her manuscript book, the pamphlet from Oscar, the trashy thriller from the airport – only to put them down again, can cast any light on the situation. She pulls up the blind and resumes her nervous pacing until it's finally, *finally* time to go. Close enough, anyway.

The studio is little more than a fancy glass box built onto the back of the lodge, although there's nothing 'little' about it. There's nothing little about the views either – the vast window panels framing the endless forest beyond. But Bella's not here for the views, she's here for answers.

There's no sign of Lena though. Not at 6.55 a.m. when Bella arrives and resumes her nervous pacing. Not at 7 a.m. when Lena's note said she'd be here. Not at 7.05 a.m. when Bella opens the door to stare pointlessly down the corridor. Not at 7.10 a.m. when she pulls the crumpled note out of her pocket to reread it for the fifth time, in case she got the time wrong, even though she knows perfectly well that she hasn't. Every single word of the message is too firmly ingrained in her memory to allow any room for mistakes. So where is she? Why isn't Lena here?

There's still no sign of her by 7.25 a.m. when Bella admits defeat and sets off for the dining room, a clashing cocktail of emotions fighting for her attention: jittery nerves and impatience . . . and anger. She feels stood up and silly and unsure of her next move. Should she say something to Lena when she sees her at breakfast – *Where were you? What did you want to show me?* – or act as if nothing's happened? But there's no rush to decide. She's not there yet. Nobody's there yet, except for Ludwell, loading up his plate at the buffet table. For a moment Bella thinks about turning round and going again, but it's too late. He's already seen her.

'Ah, Bella. Good morning,' he says. The brightness in his voice sounds hollow though, Bella notices, as she joins him at the buffet, trying to decide which of the delicious-looking foods on offer – if any – she can actually stomach. He looks slightly more dishevelled this morning too, with his stubble the wrong side of designer and bags under his eyes. She could have sworn he was wearing that same shirt yesterday too. Maybe he's starting to take after his son on that score . . . Bella's chest tightens at the thought of their shared genes. At the idea that the man beside her could be Asher in forty years' time.

'Morning,' she says, helping herself to rye bread and cheese she has no intention of eating. Pouring herself another cup of coffee. 'Are you on your own again? Is Julia still poorly?' *Are you having an affair with Lena?* That's what she really wants to ask. *Do you know why she wants to see me? And where she is now? Why didn't she turn up?*

Ludwell nods. 'She's still out of sorts, yes.' He lets out a sigh and lowers his voice to a near-whisper. 'The thing is, we had a bit of trouble a few years ago with some er . . . some unwanted attention, and this week's brought it all back again. Between you and me, I wish I'd never come. I *wouldn't* have come if I'd known a certain someone was going to be here too . . . and I definitely wouldn't have persuaded Marie to let Julia join me.'

'Someone?'

Ludwell sighs again. 'It's a long, sordid story, I'm afraid. Certainly not my finest hour. It's all water under the bridge now though . . . at least it was.'

'Who do you mean?' Bella tries again, less subtly this time. He can't be referring to *her*, otherwise he'd have said, surely? And the timings are all wrong too – this was a few years ago, not the best part of two decades. Krista and Marie don't seem very likely candidates either. It's Lena. It has to be. But that still doesn't explain why she wanted to meet with Bella this morning, or the change of heart. If there is a connection, Bella can't see it.

'I'd rather not name any names if you don't mind,' says Ludwell. 'The less people here who know, the better, and I don't want to make things even harder for Julia. Especially with that horrible note yesterday, on top of everything else.'

'Do you still think it's a joke?' Bella presses on without waiting for an answer. 'Has anyone else had one do you think, or just us? And if so, why . . . why us?' She breaks off again as the dining room door opens. *Lena?*

It's Hamar. 'Good morning,' he says, as cheerful as ever. 'What are you two looking so cloak and dagger about?'

Bella answers without thinking, automatically on the defensive. 'Nothing.'

'Hmm, a likely story,' he teases. 'If I didn't know you better, I'd say you were plotting.'

You don't know me at all, thinks Bella, trying – and failing – to think of a clever answer. 'Was it you?' she asks instead. 'Were you the one who put that note under my door on Sunday morning? And the matching one in Ludwell's bag yesterday? No more messing around, Hamar, we need to know.' *Bella* needs to know, anyway. It feels different now that Ludwell's got one too. It feels like the two of them are being targeted by someone.

Hamar's grin fades. 'No,' he says, looking hurt. 'Of course not. I know I joke around a bit but there's no harm in it. At least, I don't *mean* any harm. I'm not always the best in new social situations so I tend to overcompensate. Like at the lake yesterday. Stuart's already chewed me off about that and I don't blame him.'

When are we talking about? Bella thinks. *Yesterday morning when you pushed me, or last night when you made a laughing stock of me?*

'I've got some stuff of my own going on at the moment too, which is no excuse I know, but I'm . . .' Hamar shakes his head. 'Look, I'm sorry again, Bella,' he says. 'I really took it too far yesterday morning, I know that. I feel terrible. But I didn't write that note and I didn't put it under your door.'

He seems pretty genuine, but Bella's not sure that's good news. She *wants* it to have been Hamar messing around, she realises, trying to get a rise out of her. Or Oscar testing out a plot line for his book. Yes, she'd happily settle for Oscar over someone who really *does* think she did something. *I know what you did.* Someone like Lena? *Where on earth is she?*

Breakfast is soon underway in earnest, but there's still no sign of Lena, and none of the other guests can shed any light on her absence. Not that they seem particularly bothered. They're more interested in Stuart's apologetic announcement that they're running low on milk and cheese. 'We were due a delivery first thing this morning,' he explains, sheepishly, 'but the road's blocked at the moment. Don't worry though,' he adds. 'We've been onto the appropriate authorities who've assured us that they'll have them cleared by Saturday, so there should be no trouble getting you back to the airport.'

'I wouldn't mind being trapped here for another week,' says Oscar. 'The ideas are coming thick and fast now. And so are the bodies!'

Bella's in no mood for his corpse jokes today. Whatever the universe is trying to tell her, she doesn't like it. The news about the blocked road isn't exactly new to her but somehow she feels even more trapped than before. Trapped in the middle of nowhere with this sorry lot. And now Lena's done a disappearing trick and none of them even seem to care. She must be here somewhere though. After all, there's no way out, is there?

Bella's mind swings back to the notes and their anonymous author. If Hamar and Oscar are telling the truth, then that rules both of them out. *If* they're telling the truth. Which leaves Lena, wherever she is, and the other people sitting round this table – not forgetting Rosel and Saga, in the kitchen, of course. But what do any of them have against her and Ludwell? *What is it they think we've done?* Unless it's *not* just her and Ludwell . . . What if there are more matching notes out there but the recipients are too scared to say anything? Like when the killer leaves that appointment card for his third victim in *The Screaming Hours* and she's too scared to show the policemen making door-to-door enquiries because she's worried he's watching the house . . .

This isn't a scene from your film, she hears Asher's voice telling her.

No, she thinks. *It's not. But it's starting to feel like it.*

Bella picks up her rye bread and cheese without thinking, absent-mindedly nibbling at it as she watches the others for any signs of suspicious behaviour. Absent-mindedly washing it down with another cup of coffee. But either she's not very good at this, or there's nothing there to spot. No sly glances. No

186

veiled references. Just a group of semi-strangers eating breakfast together, all keeping their secrets firmly to themselves. Maybe she should excuse herself and go and look for Lena. Perhaps she's the key to all of this. *I found something I think you should see.* But it's too late. *Bella's* too late.

'Right,' announces Marie, before Bella can make her excuses. 'I know there's nothing marked on your itinerary until ten today, but Stuart and I thought it might be nice to squeeze in a group session on affirmations. Time away from the pressures of modern life is always rewarding, as I hope you're all discovering for yourselves by now, but it can also be confronting. We're so used to our social media feeds and twenty-four-hour news channels telling us what to think and feel, that too much space with our own unfiltered thoughts can leave us feeling a little lost or anxious.'

Lost and anxious? thinks Bella. *And the rest.*

There are a few nods of recognition around the table. Oscar even seems to be making notes, unless he's just jotting down new ways for his poor characters to die . . . force-feeding them poisoned boiled eggs, maybe, or disembowelling them with a grapefruit spoon.

'So we thought a session on how to focus that spare mental energy in a positive direction might be useful,' says Marie. 'And hopefully create some new habits that you can incorporate into your everyday life when you get back home.'

Home. Bella's never been one for homesickness – apart from a miserable youth orchestra tour to Italy where she came down with gastric flu – but she's certainly feeling homesick now. Homesick. Asher-sick. Phone-sick. Being-anywhere-but-here-sick. 'I can't wait to get back to everyday life,' she tells Krista, under her breath.

'Maybe you need to give things here a proper try then,' says Krista. 'Stop hiding out in your room and join in a bit more. I know you've got issues,' she adds, 'but so's everyone. We've all got our own baggage. Our own demons.'

Woah. Where did that come from?

'I'm sorry,' says Krista, as if she realises she's gone too far. 'I didn't mean . . . Sorry,' she says again. 'It's the actual anniversary today and it's hitting me even harder than usual. He'd have been so excited about becoming a grandad.'

'Oh gosh, yes, of course, I'm the one who should be sorry.' Bella remembers Krista telling her now. Five years on Wednesday, that's what she'd said on their walk together that first morning. Five years since a stranger – a stranger with a Scandinavian connection, if her so-called psychic's to be believed – mowed down the love of her life and carried on driving. 'If there's anything I can do . . .' she says, realising how stupid it sounds the minute the words leave her mouth. What can she possibly do to make it better?

'You can pass me another of those apple pastry things, for starters,' replies Krista, with a smile. It's not a very convincing one but it *is* a smile. Maybe that means Bella's forgiven. 'And perhaps you can keep me company today? I thought getting away from it all would help – it usually does – but today . . . I don't know. Maybe it's like Marie says. Maybe it's too much space with my own unfiltered thoughts.'

'Of course,' says Bella, as she reaches across for the plate of pastries: an overspill from the laden buffet table. Her search for Lena – her search for answers – will just have to wait.

Chapter 23

There's no sign of Lena down at the lake, where Bella chants affirmations at her own reflection, feeling every bit as awkward and silly as she imagined she would:

'I am present.

'I am calm and content.

'I am focused on the possibilities of a new day, filled with fresh opportunities to grow.'

One of the younger girls from her old office used to wax lyrical about the benefits of daily affirmations but they're not really Bella's style. Besides which, they're all lies. Every single word coming out of her mouth is an out-and-out lie, and her brain isn't fooled for one moment. Right now, Bella's the very opposite of present – she's too busy flitting between thoughts of Ludwell, and Asher and Lena, and memories of yesterday's ill-fated dip, to focus on the current moment. She can still feel the water stinging at the back of her throat, a day later, and the cold taste of it in her mouth – the taste of rotting vegetation. Bella's not calm or content either, far from it, and out here, at Dödmansskogen, the possibilities of the new day are enough to fill her with dread. What's this place going to throw at her next?

But she chants along with the others all the same, conscious of her promise to keep Krista company today and her promise to Asher to see this thing out. What choice does she have? There's no leaving early now.

'I am present.

'I am calm and content.

'I am focused on the possibilities of a new day, filled with fresh opportunities to grow.'

It's even harder to stay focused when Marie asks everyone to move on from the generic starter affirmations and come up with their own. Bella finds herself listening to what everyone else is saying instead, subconsciously trying to pick out individual voices amongst the general melee:

'I find justice through perseverance . . .'

'I am a talented writer, worthy of every success coming my way . . .'

'I rise above accusations. The only person I need to answer to is myself . . .'

'I am all that she wants and needs. I am able to turn back the clock and find happiness . . .'

As for Bella herself, she hardly knows where to start. What *does* she want, apart from getting out of here? She wants Asher to be happy and she wants to find a way to be happy without him. She wants her film score to be a success and she wants to see where this new orchestral piece leads her. She wants to let go of the past, to let go of her guilt over her mother's death and forgive herself for not being there at the end. For not even knowing it *was* the end. She wants to tell Asher the truth about his father and let him decide what he wants to do with that information. Yes, Bella realises with an audible 'oh' of surprise, that really *is* what she wants. What she should have done a long time ago for both their sakes. When Asher gets back home at Christmas, she's going to sit him down and tell him everything.

'I am honest with myself and the people I love,' she says, trying it out for size. But only very quietly. She doesn't feel any less ridiculous talking to her own reflection in public than she did before.

'I am strong,' she adds in a half-whisper. A bit of added grit wouldn't go amiss either to help her through the next few days.

'I rise above silly jokes and mind games.

'I am brave.

'I am determined.'

Her reflection stares back at her, a slight ripple crossing its brow, as if to say, *Really?*

By the time the session's over Bella *does* feel more determined though. Determined to find Lena and get to the bottom of what it is she's discovered. Determined to work out who's behind the first note and what it is they think they know. But not yet. That will have to wait until later because she's equally determined to repay Krista's kindness by being there for her today. Even if that means enduring a so-called gong bath in the middle of a chilly Swedish forest while nursing the stubborn remains of a hangover . . . which is exactly where Bella finds herself an hour later. At least there's no actual bathing this time though, no plunging into cold lakes. All that's required of her for this activity is relaxing on her mat while Stuart bangs his big brass gongs, which should be easy enough. And if the vibrations really *do* take her to the promised meditative state, healing and revitalising her body while relaxing her mind, then so much the better.

Ten minutes in, Bella couldn't feel any *less* relaxed though. The warming cups of mint-infused hot chocolate Stuart and Marie handed out before the session seemed like a good idea at the time but hers isn't sitting happily with her now. She couldn't feel any less healed, either, as she lies there on the hard ground, with her head pounding to the vibrations of the largest gong – *bong* – and a horrible tickling sensation along the backs of her legs . . . like a spider – a *pair* of spiders – crawling up the inside of her jeans.

Bong . . .

The longer Bella lies there, the harder it is to stay still. But when she sits up and tries to brush the spiders away, there's nothing there.

'What are you doing?' whispers Krista. 'What's wrong?'

'Shhh,' says Stuart. 'Lie back and close your eyes, and let the vibrations work their way through your body.'

Bong . . .

But when Bella closes her eyes, she finds Asher waiting there, his face screwed up in fury, just like in her dream last night.

Bong . . .

'You kept my dad from me,' he screams. 'I hate you.'

Bong . . .

His face is wet with hot, angry tears. 'I hate you, I hate you.'

'Shhh,' Stuart's voice says again.

Who's he talking to? Maybe that funny whimpering noise Bella can hear is *her*.

'Feel the energy resonating inside you . . .'

Bong . . .

It's no good, she can't bear it any longer. Bella opens her eyes, blinking away the image of her son's face to see the beat of the gong exploding around her pulsing head like a dark firework of colour. The energy isn't resonating *inside* her, it's right there in front of her.

Bong . . .

Woah.

The sound brings another dizzying flash and ripple of colour. Bella doesn't know how Stuart's doing it but it's pretty incredible. If this is what a real meditative state feels like, then she's clearly been doing something very wrong with those focus-on-your-breath-and-imagine-a-healing-colour-filling-your-body phone apps she's tried in the past. She's been missing out on something truly amazing. Something mind-changingly wonderful and strange.

Bong . . .

Bella doesn't need to imagine any healing colours – they're

right there in front of her. Incredible. At least it is for the next five minutes or so. *Bong . . . bong . . . bong . . .* But after a while the lights and colours become too much. Too intense. Dizzying to the point of nausea. It's not energy Bella can feel resonating inside her now, as the smaller gong sends out rippling red flower shapes, so much as breakfast. Breakfast and hot chocolate, swirling queasily inside her stomach as the spiders return – a long line of them wriggling up her left leg.

'Stop it,' she says, trying to kick them away with her right foot, the heavy textured sole of her walking boot scraping at her jeans. 'Get off!' Her voice flickers in blue shards in front of her face.

Bong . . .

'Are you all right?' someone asks in a low voice, the colour of burnt toffee. Somewhere in the inner reaches of Bella's mind she knows that's not right, that voices aren't usually colours, but that's exactly what it sounds like . . . what it looks like . . .

And now another voice joins in, a brighter, orangey-pink tinted voice asking whether she's taken anything. 'Look at her eyes . . . her pupils . . . She seems pretty spaced out.'

'Bella? Can you hear me?' The burnt-toffee voice is a ribbon of dark caramel twisting and swirling round her head.

A gurgle of laughter comes bubbling up from Bella's stomach, bringing something sour and acrid with it.

Bong, she thinks, anticipating the next dark firework. But the bongs – the gongs – have stopped now.

Or maybe it's not laughter bubbling up inside her body after all. Maybe it's her half-digested food coming back for a repeat performance. Maybe it's rye bread with cheese, mixed with coffee and . . .

'I'm going to be sick,' she cries, sending another round of blue shards flickering into the air as she lunges sideways off her mat onto the pine-needled ground.

Chapter 24

'Honestly, some people will do anything to get out of my aromatherapy tapping session,' jokes Stuart, as Bella sits in the lounge area sipping a cup of ginger tea. The sound-colours have retreated again now, along with the invisible spiders, leaving her with nothing more than a thick head and a puzzled sense of guilt and embarrassment. So much for being there to support Krista today.

'I'm sorry,' she says with a weak smile. 'I really don't know what happened. It felt like I was . . .' *Like I was drugged*, she thinks. At least, that's what she imagines being drugged – being *on* drugs, rather – would feel like. Aside from a few puffs on a feeble spliff at a university party, and gas and air during labour, Bella's never taken anything stronger than paracetamol . . . and alcohol, obviously. But isn't that what Ludwell said about Julia at dinner the night before? That *she* felt like she'd been drugged too? From Bella's slightly hazy memory of the conversation, that had more to do with Julia feeling washed out and spacey rather than a full-on hallucinatory episode though. She's sure she'd have remembered if he'd mentioned anything about synaesthesia or spiders.

'Do you think someone could have slipped something into my

drink at breakfast?' she asks, thinking out loud. 'Or my hot chocolate?' She's got no idea what that 'something' might be though. Would the effects have been as quick as that? As short-lived?

Stuart's face falls, the colour leaching out of his suntanned cheeks. 'I . . . I suppose it's possible,' he admits. 'But I sincerely hope not. That would be . . .' He pauses, biting his lip. 'It would be a very serious matter indeed. A police matter. What makes you think they might have done? Did you see something?'

'Yes, colours floating in the air,' says Bella. 'Oh wait, you mean did I see something suspicious?' She thinks for a moment. 'No.' It's true. She didn't see anyone acting strangely at breakfast and she can't recall leaving her coffee unattended to go back to the buffet table. And Krista was right there beside her the whole time. If someone had slipped something dodgy into Bella's mug it would have been a pretty brazen way to go about it. And the same was true for her hot chocolate. Maybe she's being paranoid again. Maybe it's that article she read about students having their drinks spiked in nightclubs, putting scary ideas in her head. As if there weren't enough scary ideas in there already.

'Perhaps I just had an odd reaction to something,' she says, at the sight of Stuart's wide eyes and pale face. At the small bead of sweat glistening in the middle of his softly lined forehead. He's probably imagining his business disappearing down the toilet in a cloud of scandal. 'It could be too much coffee, even,' she adds. Two cups per day is usually her absolute maximum. 'It could have been anything.' But it's not *anything*, is it? It's more than articles on student life playing on her mind. It's this place. It's notes under her door and strange sounds in the middle of the night. It's being cooped up with Ludwell and Julia for days on end. *That's* what's making her paranoid.

'Yes, tests have shown that something as simple as too much caffeine can cause mild hallucinations,' says Stuart, the relief evident in his eyes. 'Or perhaps it was the rye bread . . . ergot poisoning can be pretty serious by all accounts. Oh gosh, I do hope it wasn't that.'

Bella doesn't know what ergot poisoning is, but it doesn't sound good. Perhaps she should stick to the white bread tomorrow.

'Do you want me to call you a doctor?'

Bella forces a smile and shakes her head. How would a doctor (or the police come to that) even get out here if the road's still blocked? Not that she needs medical attention anyway. She's feeling better already. Still embarrassed, still worried, but physically pretty much back to normal now. All she wants is to retreat to her room, away from judging eyes, and see if there's been any further word from Lena. 'No, really, I'm fine,' she assures him. 'Or at least I will be after a quiet sit-down. You get off to your aromatherapy session and I'll catch up with you all at lunch.' The mysteries of aromatherapy tapping will have to remain a mystery as far as Bella's concerned.

'At least let Marie take a look at you once she's finished on the phone with the supplier. She doesn't practise medicine any more but she's fully qualified . . .'

'No, really,' Bella insists. 'I'll be fine.'

There's no note waiting for her when she gets back to her room though. No explanation from Lena. *What's she playing at? Where is she?* Bella splashes cold water on her face and stares at herself in the bathroom mirror, trying to think what to do next.

'I've got this,' she tells her reflection.

'I am brave and resourceful.

'I feel confident and in control.' But her reflection isn't so easily fooled as all that.

'I feel . . .' She stares at the circles under her eyes, at her puffy cheeks and dry skin. Too much alcohol and too little sleep are playing havoc with her appearance. And the stress can't be helping either. She was stressed enough before she arrived, let alone now. So much for Marie's 'wellderness retreat', Bella thinks. Why couldn't Rachel have sent her a plane ticket to California for her birthday instead?

'I feel like shit,' Bella admits.

'I am tired.

'I am scared.

'I am lonely . . .'

Yes, she thinks with a jolt of recognition. *I'm lonely.* She's got friends, of course she has. Friends from her old job. Mum-friends she got to know from playgroup pick-ups and all those mornings and afternoons at the school gate when Asher was young. But she misses her family, her support network. She misses her sister. It's been three years since they moved to America now. Video chats are great but they're not the same. There's no popping over to San Francisco for a chat after work. There's no cosying up on the sofa together for some trashy TV with a bottle of wine and an oversized bag of prawn cocktail crisps. And now Asher's gone too. It's not just the end of an era, it's the end of everything she's known for the last two decades. She was only a kid herself before Asher came along and now . . . well, Bella's not sure she knows *what* she is now. A frazzled-looking, lonely thirty-eight-year-old who needs to get a grip. Who needs to get a life.

Things will be different when I get back, she promises herself. *It's time to focus on me now. On my career. On my relationships.* Bella's been treading water these last few years and she knows it. She needs to get out more – to *force* herself to get out more. She needs to try new things, meet new people . . . which is exactly what she's been doing this week. *And look how that's turned out*, she thinks, wryly. But then she thinks of that Kelly Clarkson song Asher used to play at top volume after his first girlfriend ended things with him, 'Stronger (What Doesn't Kill You)', and she almost smiles. *Almost.* Maybe a miserable week here, being forced to face her fears about Ludwell, really *will* make her stronger in the long run. Always assuming it doesn't kill her in the meantime . . . which brings her thoughts circling right back to Lena, and the notes. To the maggot-infested apple and the weird experience at the gong bathing session . . . It's all very well promising herself things will be better when she gets back, but that's still three long days away, and no matter how hard Bella tries to ignore that paranoid little voice inside her head, she can still hear it: *If you get back.*

'I *will* get back,' Bella tells her reflection, firmly. *Of course I will.*

'I'm going home.

'I'm going to find Lena.

'It's going to be all right.'

She's still telling herself it's going to be all right as she heads back to the studio. Not that she's actually expecting Lena to be there, but it's as good a place to start her search as any.

'Hello?' she calls, her voice echoing round the empty room. 'Lena?' Bella adds, pointlessly, as if the woman might be hiding out of sight or locked in one of the tall cupboards at the far end of the room. But then an image of Lena's *body*, stuffed inside a cupboard like one of Oscar's imaginary corpses, forces its way, uninvited, into Bella's mind and she shivers. She's being ridiculous now, she knows that, and yet . . .

Bella crosses over to the first cupboard, just to make doubly sure. Just to put her mind at ease. *There's not going to be a body in there. This is stupid.* Her heart is beating double time all the same, as she tugs open the door and peers inside.

No corpses. Only chairs. Spare fold-up chairs and what looks like a rolled projector screen peeking out from behind them. And as for the second cupboard . . .

The second cupboard is locked. Now what? Bella works her way back through the lodge, searching every public space in turn, from the sauna down in the basement to the dining room and the kitchen, where Rosel is busy with lunch preparations, a sharp paring knife in her hand.

'Lena?' she says, looking hot and flustered. 'No, I haven't seen her.'

'What about earlier? Have you seen her since last night?'

'No,' Rosel repeats, an edge of annoyance creeping into her voice. 'I told you, I don't know *where* she is.'

'Okay,' says Bella, not wanting to make a nuisance of herself two days in a row. 'Thanks anyway. Maybe I'll try her room. Which one is hers? Are you allowed to tell me that?' Perhaps Lena's unwell. Perhaps *that's* why she didn't show up.

Rosel stiffens visibly. 'No, I er . . . I already cleaned her room today and she wasn't there. Perhaps she's . . . perhaps she's off doing more research for her magazine piece, or writing up her interview notes from yesterday, somewhere quiet.'

Somewhere quieter than her own room? 'Yes, I guess so,' says Bella, 'it's just . . . well, we'd sort of arranged to meet this morning, and she didn't show up. It seemed a bit odd, that's all,' she says with a practised casualness she doesn't feel. The more time she spends looking for Lena, the more unsettled – the more unnerved – Bella's becoming.

'Maybe she forgot.' Rosel reaches across the counter, sending a jug of what looks like vegetable stock flying. *'Fan också!'* she cries as it smashes on the tiled floor. The oven timer starts to beep.

'Here, let me help you,' says Bella. 'You look like you could do with a hand. Where's Saga today?'

'No!' Rosel almost shouts the word at her. 'I mean no, it's fine, thank you, I can manage,' she adds over the *beep, beep, beep* from the oven.

Bella takes a step back. 'Okay, I'll just keep out your way, shall I?'

'Thank you, yes. I'm sorry, I didn't mean to be rude.' Rosel sounds like she's on the edge of tears as she picks her way past the mess on the floor towards the oven and turns off the timer.

'No need to apologise,' Bella says into the sudden quiet, forgetting about Lena for a moment. She's thinking about Hamar now. She's not the only one who's noticed the strange vibe between him and Rosel. 'Is everything okay? You're not having any trouble with the other guests? With Hamar?'

There's a sharp intake of breath as Rosel turns away, reaching for the silicone oven glove on the side.

'No,' she says. 'Of course not. Hamar's fine. Everything's fine.'

But it's clearly *not* fine. Bella can see there's something upsetting her. 'Is it about the missing keys? Did Stuart and Marie find out? I hope you didn't get into any trouble. At least they're found now – that's the important bit.'

Rosel doesn't answer. She bends down, a thick cloud of steam enveloping her as she opens the oven door.

'Where were they in the end?' Bella realises she never did find out.

'Please,' says Rosel, re-emerging with a sizzling dish of something spiced and meaty-smelling. 'I really don't have time to chat today.'

'Of course, I'm sorry,' Bella says, wondering again where Saga is. Is she missing too? And what's up with Rosel? Why's she so on edge? 'I can see you're busy. I'll leave you to it.'

She cuts back through the dining room and heads for the other guest wing, to try and find Lena's room. Just because she wasn't there when Rosel cleaned it, doesn't mean she won't have returned by now. Maybe she popped out for some fresh air if she's feeling poorly, and now she's gone back to bed. It seems like a long shot but Bella's rapidly running out of other ideas. Rapidly running out of straws to clutch at. The door to the corridor swings open as she's reaching for the handle and she leaps back in shock.

'Saga! You made me jump. I've just come from the kitchen now.'

Saga's eyes widen, her cheeks flushed. She looks every bit as surprised to see Bella. 'The kitchen? I thought you were supposed to be in a workshop.'

'I am . . . I mean I should be . . . I was just . . .' Bella feels heat rushing to her own cheeks, as if she's been caught doing something she shouldn't. Playing truant. 'I wasn't feeling very well and then . . . I'm looking for Lena,' she explains. 'Is that where *you've* just come from?'

'Sorry?'

'Lena's room,' Bella says, a little louder. 'No one's seen her today. I . . .' *I need her to tell me what's going on.* 'I wanted to make sure she was okay. I thought you might have had the same idea.' She's still trying to make sense of it all. It should be Saga in the kitchen and Rosel here, surely? But Rosel said she'd already done the rooms, and Saga's not carrying any dirty laundry or cleaning equipment.

'Ah, right, *Lena*. Yes, of course,' says Saga. 'Sorry, I haven't seen her. I was just dropping off some spare towels to one of the other guest rooms.' She rubs at the back of her neck. 'Perhaps she went for a walk. Some people prefer to skip the organised activities and make the most of the tranquillity. Or perhaps she's somewhere quiet working on her travel article.'

Bella bites back her frustration. 'Yes, that's what Rosel said.' They're reasonable enough suggestions on the face of it. But what about the note? Why didn't Lena show up for their appointment this morning? That's the bit that doesn't make any sense.

'If you'll excuse me,' says Saga, 'I should be getting back to the kitchen.'

'Sure. Maybe I'll try outside then.' Bella turns on her heel and heads back towards the front door, conscious of the other woman's gaze following her as she leaves. But when she turns round to check, Saga's already gone.

Maybe they're right, Bella tells herself as she perches on the built-in shoe bench and laces up her walking boots. Maybe Lena fancied some fresh air and decided to take her work outside with her. Maybe she's feeling trapped too, stuck in the same lodge as her lover's wife. And as for this morning . . . well, perhaps something came up, or she overslept and she's planning on catching up with Bella later instead . . . Except Bella can't wait for later. There's too much spinning round her head for that. She needs to know what it is Lena's discovered. She needs answers.

She finds herself retracing her steps from yesterday, back to the bird hide where she'd finally unburdened herself of her Ludwell secret after all these years. *Somewhere quiet*, she thinks. *Maybe that's it.*

But there's no sign of Lena there, either. Bella crosses over to the viewing window and stares out through the trees, as if the answer to the puzzle might be lurking between the branches. She can't just have vanished. They're *all* stuck here whether they like it or not, until the road's cleared. But why leave that note and then disappear off for the day without revealing what it was she'd found? That's what Bella keeps coming back to.

New, darker possibilities start to raise their heads as the chilled, eerie silence of the forest seeps into Bella's bones. What if something happened to Lena between writing the note and their appointed meeting time? Something bad? Perhaps she had a fall when she was out for a walk, first thing this morning. Perhaps she's out there somewhere now, nursing a twisted ankle, trying to limp her way back to the lodge. Or worse . . . Maybe someone here in Dödmansskogen had a vested interest in making sure Lena's uncovered secrets stayed secret . . .

Bella finds herself thinking, yet again, about the dinner conversation that first night. About where the best place to hide a body would be: weighted down with stones at the bottom of the lake, a shallow grave in the woods or . . .

What was that? She jumps at a sound from outside, her heart somewhere up by her throat. Her pulse is already racing as she gets to her feet, shrinking away from the viewing window, pressing her back against the rough wooden wall of the hut. That's definitely not a bird she can hear, rustling in the undergrowth, it's the sound of someone breathing hard. It's the sound of heavy shoes crunching across fallen pine cones. Someone's coming.

Lena's killer, she thinks, her mind still deep in buried bodies. *They've finished her off and now they've come for me.*

Chapter 25

The walls feel like they're pressing in on her as Bella stares around wildly, looking for something she can use to defend herself. A rock . . . A sharp stone . . . but there's nothing. Of course there isn't. It's a bird hide. She's not thinking clearly though. She's too busy thinking like a victim in a thriller – one of the countless thrillers she's been watching as inspiration for her symphony – trapped in the wrong place at the wrong time, with the killer closing in . . . She's thinking about heavy rasping breaths in her ear. About strong, gloved hands tightening round her throat . . .

'Found you!'

'No! Get away from me!' She's already screaming the words by the time she sees who it is. It's not a killer after all. It's Marie.

'Shh, Bella, relax, it's only me. I didn't mean to startle you.'

'I know,' Bella gasps, her legs turning wobbly beneath her. 'I'm sorry, I thought . . .' But how can she explain what she was thinking? *I thought you were a murderer. I thought you'd bumped off Lena and come back for me.* No, she can't admit to that. It sounds ridiculous even to her, now that the danger's passed. The danger that was never there in the first place. 'I thought you were someone else,' she stammers.

'Clearly not someone you wanted to see.' Marie shoots her a

worried look. 'Is everything all right? Are you having problems with one of the other guests?' she asks, echoing Bella's questions to Rosel in the kitchen just now. Marie pauses, as if she's choosing her words carefully. 'Has something happened?'

Bella shakes her head. 'No. I'm just a bit jumpy at the moment.' But something *has* happened. The note. The apple. The lake. The scratching in the wall. Things *keep* happening. And now *Lena's* note, followed by her apparent vanishing.

'I'm sorry if I gave you a fright,' says Marie. 'Do you want to sit down? You're looking awfully pale.'

Bella *feels* pale. She feels washed out, *hollowed* out, and shaky. She does as she's told, sinking down onto the bench with her back to the viewing hatch.

'I've been looking everywhere for you,' Marie continues, taking a seat beside her. 'I heard about the gong bathing episode and I wanted to check in . . . make sure you were okay.'

An episode. That's what we're calling it now, is it? As in a psychotic episode? 'Thank you,' Bella says. 'I'm fine. I still don't know what happened but I'm okay now.'

'Really?' Marie raises her eyebrows. 'Because from where I'm sitting you don't seem very okay to me. You seem troubled.'

No shit, Sherlock, Bella thinks. It's one of Asher's sayings, copied from his uncle. 'I take it the road's still blocked?' she says.

'I'm afraid so. I've been ringing them twice a day, trying to chivvy them up, but these storms have really taken their toll across the entire area. They've assured me that the road will be clear by Friday night though, so there'll be no problem with your flight home on Saturday.'

'Saturday,' Bella repeats with a sigh. It still seems a long way off. 'I'm sorry. I know I'm lucky to be here. It was such a thoughtful present . . . and it's a great retreat, really. I just want to go home though. I miss my son,' she says, regretting it the moment the words are out of her mouth. Missing Asher after half a week apart is nothing compared to what Marie must go through every single day of her life. 'I'm sorry, I didn't mean . . . I'm all over the place at the moment. I don't feel safe here.' And there it is. That's the truth of the matter.

'You don't feel *safe*?' Marie looks horrified. 'Wait, is this something to do with that apple you thought you saw the other night?'

Bella nods. '*And* the threatening note.'

'Ah yes. The note you couldn't find afterwards. I heard about that.' Marie's voice is soft and tentative, as if she's skirting round the real issue. As if she's too polite to come out and say what she really feels.

You think I imagined that too, don't you?

'I still don't know what happened to it afterwards,' Bella says out loud. 'I guess I never will. But the note was real, I swear. As real as the one Ludwell found in his bag yesterday afternoon. And the more I think about it now, the more it freaks me out. Then there was the thing at the lake, with Hamar, and a weird scratching sound coming from the wall . . .'

'A scratching noise? Like mice, do you mean?'

Like fingernails. Bella shakes her head. 'No, not really. I don't know. It's probably nothing.' It doesn't feel like nothing though, in the quiet of the night. Far from it.

'I'll get Stuart to come and take a look if you'd like,' says Marie. 'As for everything else . . . well, I sense that you're in a difficult place right now, emotionally speaking, with your son . . . and perhaps with Ludwell too?'

'Ludwell? What's this got to do with him? Has he said something? Or was it Krista? I told her that in confidence.'

'No one's said anything,' Marie assures her. 'I've noticed a certain tension between you, that's all. I even wondered if that was behind your upset the other night, with the er . . . with the food poisoning.'

Wow. She's hit the nail right on the head. Bella didn't realise she'd been so obvious.

'I . . . I . . .'

'If it would help to talk about it, I'm in no rush to get back,' says Marie. 'You know what they say, "The truth will set you free".'

Bella certainly does know that. *John chapter eight, verse thirty-two.* She can still see the verse picked out in dark green thread in her mother's framed embroidery above the fireplace. It's still burnt into her brain all these years later, forever welded to the day she came back from university. The day she came clean about the baby. But it wasn't the truth that set Bella free that day; it was her mother, throwing her out of her own house.

'Thank you,' she says, forcing her mind back to the present. 'I appreciate the offer, but I'll be fine. I'd rather talk about Lena. Have you seen her? I was supposed to meet her this morning, before breakfast . . . for a walk,' Bella lies, not wanting to say anything about the note. Not until she knows what it is Lena's found. 'But she didn't turn up. She wasn't in this morning's sessions either, and Rosel said her room was empty when she went to clean it.'

Marie's usual calm expression falters a second time, her brow furrowing. 'Really? That's strange. She was just coming back from a swim when Stuart saw her this morning. But now I come to think about it, you're right. She wasn't at breakfast today, was she? And you haven't seen her since?'

Bella shakes her head. 'What time did Stuart see her?'

Marie thinks for a moment. 'Quarter past seven, maybe? Possibly a bit later. He said he had words with her. He told her she shouldn't really be swimming on her own, just in case she got into difficulties. I think he was a bit worried he'd upset her. It rather sounds like he did.'

What was she doing swimming at that time anyway? thinks Bella. *She was supposed to be meeting me.* None of this makes any sense.

'I'm sure it's nothing to worry about,' says Marie, although her cheerfulness sounds forced to Bella's ears. 'She can't have gone very far. I'm more concerned about *you*. It's a shame you weren't feeling up to Stuart's aromatherapy tapping workshop. Tapping can help with all sorts of issues and anxieties and it's usually very popular with our guests. Still, perhaps you'll be able to join us for some guilt-purging this afternoon? We can't rewrite the past, but we can try and find a way of making peace with it in the present.'

'Perhaps,' agrees Bella, but it's answers she wants, not purging. Why did Lena stand her up this morning and where is she now? What's going on?

Chapter 26

Bella feels oddly jittery as she heads into the dining room, alone, to face the others. The head-clearing walk she embarked on after her talk with Marie has had quite the opposite effect. Her head's more full of worries than ever: about Lena's secret discovery and strange disappearance, about her and Ludwell's matching notes, about what the others will think of her after the disastrous gong bathing session, and about everything else, all tangled up together.

The other guests are already there, apart from Lena and Julia, talking round the lunch table in low voices. But the conversation stops as soon as they see her, and Krista's refusal to meet Bella's eyes as she joins them does little to reassure her.

'What's happening? What have I missed?' Bella asks, trying to keep her voice bright and ignore the queasy fluttering in her stomach. She already knows the answer to that one of course. It doesn't take a genius to work out that they've been talking about her gong bathing performance.

No one answers.

'Let me guess. You're doing a sweepstake on how many more times I'm going to throw up between now and our flight home on Saturday. I'm right, aren't I?' The joke sounds flat and false, even to Bella, but she ploughs on all the same, resisting the urge to turn tail and run back to her room. 'Put me down for six, or has that already gone?'

Still no one says anything. No smart remarks from Hamar, which makes a change. Not so much as a flicker of a smile.

'Come on,' says Bella. 'What's wrong with you all? Anyone would think someone had . . .' She's about to say 'died' but stops herself in time, catching sight of Marie and Stuart through the open kitchen door. That really wouldn't be funny, given what Bella knows about Marie's son. And a doubly unfunny joke to make on the anniversary of Krista's husband's death. But then she hears Rosel talking in an emotional rush of Swedish and starts to wonder if something terrible really *has* happened. Maybe Julia's taken a turn for the worse. Maybe they're waiting for the ambulance to arrive. No, that can't be right. Ludwell wouldn't be sitting around waiting for his lunch if his wife was at death's door. Perhaps it's Saga, then . . . or Lena. Maybe it wasn't a migraine after all . . .

'Sorry,' says Krista, finally breaking the silence in response to Bella's half-finished question. 'We're a little surprised, that's all. We didn't have you down as a user.'

'A user?' As in someone who exploits other people? Bella's chest tightens. 'What do you mean?' But then the penny drops. *You mean someone who takes drugs.* 'No,' she says. 'I don't know what happened with the gongs. It was seriously weird. But I hadn't taken anything, I swear. I wouldn't. I don't.'

Krista shakes her head, still refusing to meet her eye.

'It must have been a reaction to something I ate or drank. Too much coffee, maybe. Stuart said that can sometimes affect people strangely.' Bella's babbling now, but she can't stop. 'He even thought it might be the rye bread. Something toxic . . . ergon . . . erlon . . .? I can't remember the name now. Oscar, you're our resident poison expert. You must know what I'm talking about.'

Oscar nods. 'Ergot,' he says. 'It's a fungal disease associated with rye, which is where LSD comes from. Some people think that it was ergot poisoning that led to the accusations of witchcraft in Salem . . .'

'Exactly,' Bella says. She remembers the invisible spiders and sound-colours in the Salem witch trials from studying *The Crucible* at school. 'I mean, I'm not saying it *was* ergot poisoning, because everyone else seems fine, but it could have been. It could have been anything. Nothing illegal though, I swear,' she adds.

'This isn't about the gongs,' says Krista, looking pained. 'It's about the used needle Rosel found.'

'A used needle? Well, it's nothing do with me. Where was it?' Bella feels cold suddenly, as a horrible thought strikes her. Perhaps it *is* to do with her after all. That might explain a lot. 'Someone must have spiked me,' she says, remembering that article about the dangers of freshers' week. It wasn't only students' drinks that were getting spiked, it was the students themselves. *Someone* here *must have spiked me*, she corrects herself, with a shiver. No wonder she was off her head during the gong bathing. It all makes sense now. Her gaze flicks round the table, eyeing each guest in turn, and then over to the kitchen door. *It was one of you*, she thinks. 'It must have been while we were down at the lake,' she says. 'During the visualisation bit we did at the end. I wouldn't have seen because I had my eyes shut.' But surely she'd have felt it?

'The needle was found in your room,' says Krista, treating Bella to a cold, appraising stare.

Bella shivers again, picturing a dark, shadowy figure leaning over her bed during the night, injecting her as she slept. A dark shadowy figure in possession of Rosel's missing keys, perhaps . . . No, that can't be right. The keys had been found by then. But Krista's not finished yet:

'Right there on your bedside table,' she says.

'What?' Bella shakes her head. 'No, that doesn't make any sense. I'd have seen it when I woke up this morning.' She'd have seen it when she was pacing up and down her room, waiting to go and meet Lena. 'And I saw Rosel earlier – I was talking to her in the kitchen. That was *after* she cleaned the rooms. She didn't say anything about a needle.' *Although she did seem very on edge,* Bella thinks.

Krista's voice is almost as cold as her stare. 'This was just now, when she went back with the sleep tea she was supposed to leave out for you. *That's* when she found the needle. Hamar overheard her telling Stuart. She was pretty upset – apparently Swedish drug laws are *very* strict.'

Bella can already guess the rest of the story. *And then Hamar told you lot and you've been sitting here gossiping about it ever since.* 'Why would she assume I was shooting up though? Why would *any* of you assume that? I could be . . . I don't know. I could be diabetic,' Bella says. 'Or on IVF.'

'Are you?' asks Krista.

Bella shakes her head.

'I guess she heard what happened at the gong bathing and put two and two together,' pipes up Oscar, who looks like he's enjoying himself. It's all story fodder for him, isn't it?

'You were clearly on *something* this morning,' says Krista. 'Your pupils had gone all weird.' She pauses, her eyes fixed on Bella as if she's waiting for a response. The *right* response. Not that Bella knows what that is. She's still trying to get her head round it all. Someone here injected her with something and now everyone thinks she's some kind of junkie.

'It wasn't *my* needle,' Bella insists. She's the victim here, not the bad guy. She can hear her voice getting louder and shriller as she tries to convince them. 'Maybe someone injected me while we were down at the lake and then left the needle by my bed to frame me. Did you ever stop to consider that?' Of course they didn't, because it's a ridiculous idea, but Bella ploughs on all the same, desperate to make them understand, to prove that someone here – one of the gawping, judging people round the table – is out to get her. Why would Krista automatically assume the worst of her? *I thought you were my friend.* 'You don't know me,' she says. 'None of you do. So what gives you the right to judge me?'

'Bella,' says Marie, coming back from the kitchen. 'I need you to calm down for a moment and . . .'

But Bella's gone beyond that now. The words are spilling out of her mouth of their own accord. 'Do you want to know the truth?' she asks, spitting the question across the table at top volume. 'I wish there *was* some kind of drug I could take to make this all go away. I'd have a double dose of it right now. I hate it here.' She sounds like a stroppy teenager in a temper. Like Asher in one of their rare rows over the state of his room or some other trivial disagreement that had somehow spiralled out of control. Bella's the one out of control now though, getting more hysterical with every passing moment. 'There's something weird going on – something *bad* – and none of you can see it. Anonymous notes under people's doors. Maggot-infested apples. Lost keys. Weird noises from rooms that are supposed to be empty. Someone here is messing with us – messing with *me* – and I don't know why. I don't know *who*. But I'm going to find out. Do you hear me? I'm not just going to sit in my room feeling scared, I'm going to get to the bottom of it . . .'

She stares round the table, trying to gauge their reactions. Trying to see beyond their surface expressions of shock and distaste to the real emotion underneath. Whoever the culprit is, they must be feeling pretty pleased with themselves right now. They must be lapping it all up, laughing at her behind their fake look of horror. *Which one of you is it?* But no one's giving anything away. No one speaks. No one moves, except for Oscar, automatically reaching for the notebook and pen beside his water glass.

'Don't even *think* about it. This isn't fucking research for your book,' Bella snarls, surprising herself with the language coming out of her mouth. She can probably count the number of times she's used the F word on the fingers of one hand, and that includes finding out she was pregnant with her lecturer's baby and actually

212

giving birth. But there's no stopping her now. 'I'm not a fucking character study. This is real life. *My* life.'

Oscar pulls his hand back again. 'I know that. I was just going to . . .'

'Oh yes, I know exactly what you were going to do. You've been watching me all week, haven't you? Jotting down every little reaction while you plan out the next stage of your game. It *was* you who put that note under my door, wasn't it? You must have got another notebook somewhere in your room. And the apple with the maggots, I bet that was you too . . . You're sick, do you know that?'

Oscar stares at her, open-mouthed.

'Or was it you?' Bella says, turning to Hamar. 'No lies this time. Do you get off on scaring people, is that it? Do you get a thrill from watching them suffer? Or is it all just a game to you?'

Hamar shakes his head. 'I already told you, it wasn't – I . . .'

'Unless it's *not* a game,' says Bella before he can finish speaking. 'Maybe I really am in danger. Maybe we're *all* in danger.'

'Bella!' Marie's voice is sharper now. More urgent. 'That's enough. Nobody's in any danger.'

'Or is it you?' Bella swings back round towards Krista. 'Is this some kind of twisted payback for what happened to your husband? Is that why you're really here? Do I match the description of the woman your crackpot medium told you was driving the car that day, is that it? What did she say exactly, single mother with a Scandinavian connection? Sounds pretty conclusive to me. And you've been playing me this whole time, have you, offering to help me back to my room the other night so that you could plant the apple? Pretending to be my friend . . . letting me spill out my deepest, darkest secrets so that you can use them against me?' The accusations are coming too fast for Bella to stop. 'Have you told him yet then? Ludwell, I mean. Have you told him about Asher?'

'Bella!'

Strong hands take hold of Bella's shoulders from behind,

213

pulling her back down into her chair. Not that she remembers standing up in the first place. 'Come on now,' says Stuart. 'That's enough. You need to take a deep breath. Can you do that for me? Deep breath in through your nose and out through your mouth.'

Bella doesn't want to breathe. She doesn't want to be patronised by some would-be guru telling her to settle down like a good girl. But the wild anger is draining out of her all the same.

'Deep breath now, come on, Bella, it'll help, I promise.'

Bella breathes in.

'And out again. That's it. You're okay, Bella. It's all going to be fine. Slow, steady breaths now, that's the ticket.'

But it's *not* all going to be fine, is it? Bella can hear Ludwell from the other end of the table. 'What does she mean?' he asks. 'Who's Asher?'

Chapter 27

Bella doesn't remember much after that. She doesn't remember what was said. She doesn't remember how she got back to her room – did someone have to help her again, like before? – and she doesn't remember getting into bed once she was there. But bed's where Bella finds herself now, at half past three in the afternoon according to her bedside clock, tucked up under her duvet, fully dressed, with a weird, fuzzy feeling in her head and a heavy sensation in her limbs. When she lifts her head off the pillow, she can see a wooden tray on her desk with what looks like a plate of open sandwiches, an apple and a glass of water. She ought to be hungry by now – it seems safe to assume she missed the actual eating part of lunch after her outburst – but her appetite is as drowsy as the rest of her. In fact, drowsiness is putting it lightly. The mere effort of holding up her head requires more strength and energy than Bella can muster right now. She drops back onto her pillow and closes her eyes again.

It's quarter past four when she peels them open a second time. The tray is still there, the food still untouched. Bella wonders, dopily, if she managed to get through to the others with her warning: *There's something weird going on – something bad – and none of you can see it . . . Someone here is messing with us.* Or did they write it off along with her absurd theories and wild accusations and finish their lunch without her? Yes, 'absurd' and 'wild' pretty much sum up her performance in general. Bella still can't remember what happened after Stuart sat her back down on her chair – did she pass out? Did they give her something to knock her out? – but she can remember everything that happened up until that point. Even in her strange, woozy state she can still recall every toe-curling detail.

Poor Krista, Bella thinks, her chest clenching at the memory of the dreadful things she'd said to her. How could she have thrown her husband's death in her face like that? Today of all days. What was she thinking, belittling a grieving woman's need for justice and closure by pouring scorn on her for consulting a medium? Betraying her confidence by publicly ridiculing her? And then accusing Krista of betraying *her* confidence by talking to Ludwell behind her back . . . Bella can still hear herself now: *Have you told him yet then? Ludwell, I mean. Have you told him about Asher?* And she can still hear the confusion in *his* voice afterwards:

What does she mean? Who's Asher?

Pretty much everyone round the table could tell him the answer to that. Bella might as well have stood up and confessed there and then. *Asher's my son . . . and your son too. The one I tried to tell you about all those years ago but you refused to listen. Refused to let me finish. The son I've been keeping from you ever since.*

Julia probably knows as well by now. However ill the poor woman was feeling before, she'll be feeling twice as bad after that bombshell. *What a mess*, Bella thinks, as a double line of tears trickles down her face into her pillow. *What a stupid, crazy mess.* And she's *still* no closer to finding out who's behind that blasted note – *I know what you did* – or who drugged her and planted the needle in her room for Rosel to find. Ludwell aside, she's only known these people for a few days. What can she possibly have done to upset them in that time? Unless . . . unless they spotted her name on that group email Stuart and Marie mistakenly sent

216

out with everyone's addresses included. Unless they've been plotting against her since before she even arrived.

Bella runs through the list of suspects again in her head as she lies there, weeping silently to herself – a list which covers every single person at the retreat – trying to work out what possible motivation they might have for targeting her. Did she accidently sleep with one of *their* partners too? Did she steal the film-music job out from under the nose of someone they care about? Or could it be something to do with Lena and the mysterious discovery she thought Bella should see? If only she knew what that was. Why didn't Lena turn up when she said she would? Why did she choose to go swimming instead?

But maybe Stuart was mistaken about what time he saw her this morning. Or maybe Marie misremembered. And maybe . . . maybe something happened between Lena coming back from her swim and coming to meet Bella. Maybe she bumped into someone else afterwards. Someone who didn't *want* her to share what she'd found. The same someone who's behind all the other strange goings-on at the retreat. Perhaps they drugged Lena as well, or worse . . . And, just like that, based on nothing but maybes, Bella's back to corpses in the woods, back to imagining Lena's lifeless body buried under a blanket of soil and pine needles.

They'll be coming for me next, she thinks. *Perhaps they're watching me, even now . . . watching and waiting.*

Bella stares at the wall between her room and number twelve, as if there might be secret eyes concealed behind the smooth white plaster, monitoring her every move. But then common sense prevails. *Stop it*, she tells herself. *Get a grip.* There's enough weird, creepy stuff going on without her dreaming up even more to torture herself with.

It's this place: Dödmansskogen. It's not merely getting under her skin, it's starting to eat away at her sanity. And it's *still* only Wednesday afternoon. That leaves two entire days to get through.

Three long, lonely nights. A lot can happen in that time. None of it good though, Bella's quite sure of that.

She stiffens at a soft rustling sound coming from the other side of the room. A rustling sound that grows louder and more insistent the longer she listens. It's growing more rhythmic too, like . . . like sharpened fingernails scratching the wall again.

'Stop it,' she whispers, pressing her hands over her ears. 'You don't scare me.'

Scrraaaaatch. Scrraaaaatch.

'I'm not scared,' she insists. 'I'm not.' But it's a lie and Bella knows it.

She thinks of Asher and his recurrent nightmare about the faceless man hiding in his wardrobe, after they first moved into their own house. He must have been about four and a half at the time. She remembers his own pale, tear-stained face appearing in the doorway night after night. *He's back again, Mummy – the man with no face. I heard him in my clothes cupboard.* Remembers how he'd hide under the covers while she and Lulu, his stuffed armadillo, checked the wardrobe for him, reassuring him that there was nothing there. Nothing but clothes and a pile of puzzles.

'Come and see for yourself,' she'd tell him. 'There's nothing here to be scared of, is there, Lulu?'

'No,' she'd say in her best squeaky Lulu voice. 'Nothing at all. I pwomise you. Come and have a look, Asher.'

Night after night he'd refuse, insisting that Bella stay with him and stroke his hair until he got back to sleep. Until one day Lulu told him that there *was* something in the wardrobe – something exciting. Something wrapped up in shiny blue wrapping paper with a big gold bow. That was the night he got out of bed and took Bella's outstretched hand, creeping over to join her by the open wardrobe.

'A present,' he'd whispered, wide-eyed.

'I wonder who it's for,' Bella said.

Asher reached into the wardrobe and took it, without thinking, ripping open the paper to find a knitted owl inside. It was wonky and misshapen, with one wing longer than the other – Bella never was much good at knitting – but he clutched it tightly to his chest and beamed.

'You know what's special about owls, don't you?' Bella had asked him.

He nodded. 'They're very clever. Like in my *Goodnight Mr Hoot* book.'

'That's right. And what else makes them special?'

'They stay awake all night and go to bed in the day.'

'Exactly,' Bella had said. 'Maybe this owl would like to stay here in your bedroom where he can keep an eye on Lulu for you and make sure she doesn't get scared.'

Asher had nodded in solemn agreement. 'Yes, Owl said he'd like that. And so would Lulu.'

There was no begging Bella to stay after that. No more faceless man haunting his dreams. She was never quite sure if it was the owl itself that did the trick, or if it was Asher finally facing his fears and looking inside the wardrobe. But maybe that's what *she* should be doing now – facing her own fears – instead of cowering in bed like a frightened child. If it is just mice or rats, or noisy insects, that's hardly anything to be scared of. And if it's not . . .

Scrraaaaatch.

Bella's head spins as she hauls herself out of bed. Something's not right. She feels . . . she feels drugged. And there it is again – the same phrase Ludwell used to describe Julia. Not that he'd mentioned anything about hallucinations or used needles. Not that he was seriously claiming it was anything more than a bug. Bella does a quick inventory of her own symptoms, trying to decide if she might be coming down with the same thing: dizziness, lethargy, loss of appetite, feeling cold and shivery, hearing things . . .

Scrraaaaatch.

Scrraaaaatch.

Her limbs feel heavy and stiff as she shuffles towards the door.

Perhaps she really is sick. But she pushes on, picking up her key and stepping out into the corridor, determined to find out what – or who? – is making the noise.

Her fingers curl into fists as she stands outside the door to number twelve, the empty room between her and the Storms. What if it's not empty after all? There could be someone in there right now, watching her through some carefully concealed peephole, or a hidden camera, scratching at the shared wall to mess with her mind. And what if her tormentor *isn't* one of the others after all? What if there's someone else here at the retreat too? An extra guest who isn't here for the wilderness, *or* the 'wellderness'? Someone with a different agenda altogether . . . The image that flashes into her mind, of a cold, blue eye staring unblinking through a drilled hole in the plasterwork, just like the killer in *The Screaming Hours*, is so disturbing that Bella doesn't stop to think. She doesn't stop to wonder why Stuart and Marie would be harbouring a secret ninth guest. She doesn't think to question how he's been getting his meals delivered without anyone noticing, or how he got to the lodge in the first place. She doesn't think at all, she's too busy hammering on the door to number twelve with both hands, pounding her knuckles against the wood until they're raw and throbbing.

Nothing happens.

No one comes.

The door stays firmly shut.

Bella's not giving up yet though. 'I know you're in there,' she yells, letting rip with a fresh volley of knocks. 'I know what you're doing but it won't work. You don't scare me.' If only that was true. 'Do you hear me? You. Don't. Scare. Me.' And with that she slumps her body against the door and collapses in a frightened, sobbing heap on the floor.

She's still sobbing, still shaking, when she hears the creak and grind of a door handle turning . . . Bella shrinks back, crunching her body up into a tight defensive ball as the door to the next room opens. As a pale, ghostly face looks down at her.

Chapter 28

'What's going on?'

Bella opens her mouth to explain, but her tongue doesn't seem to be working properly. She's as shocked and confused by her own outburst as Julia, who's standing in the open doorway of number eleven in an expensive-looking, peacock-patterned kimono, gazing down at her with a furrowed brow.

'Who's in there? Who are you talking to?'

Bella hauls herself clumsily back onto her feet, shocked by Julia's appearance. Her face is bleached and puffy, framed by lank, unwashed hair. She doesn't look well at all. She doesn't smell great either, giving off an unpleasant scent of sour breath and dried sweat as she draws closer. 'Are you all right?'

Bella nods. 'I'm sorry,' she says, finally finding her voice. 'Did I wake you?'

'I'm not sure *what* woke me. I heard banging,' Julia tells her. 'Was that you?'

Bella nods again. 'Yes. I thought . . .' *I thought there was someone hiding in the room nextdoor. I thought they were spying on me.* How can she admit to that? 'I thought I heard a noise,' she says instead. 'A sort of scratching noise. Could you hear it too?'

'I was asleep,' says Julia, rubbing at her eye. 'And I don't think there *is* anyone nextdoor. Marie said it was only you and us in this bit of the lodge.'

'Yes,' Bella agrees. 'You're right. It's empty. I just . . .' She racks her brain for some kind of explanation. For something that might make sense of her strange behaviour. But there's nothing. 'I'm sorry,' she says. 'I'm not quite myself at the moment. I've got a lot going on . . .'

'With your son, you mean?' Julia's voice is flat and expressionless, but Bella's not fooled. She must have given the game away to Ludwell at lunchtime, like she feared, and now Julia knows too.

Me and my stupid big mouth! 'My son?' she repeats, playing dumb. My *son. Not yours. Ludwell had his chance and he blew it.*

Julia nods. 'When you were ill the other night – the night we arrived – someone said you were missing your son. They said that's why you were a little worse for wear. I assumed that's what you meant.'

'Yes!' A cool flood of relief sweeps through Bella's body. 'Yes, that's right. He's just started at university and I'm missing him like . . .' She breaks off at the arrival of Rosel, who seems surprised to see them out of their rooms.

'Hi. Stuart sent me to check on you both. To see if there's anything I can get you.'

'I'm glad *someone* cares how I'm doing,' says Julia. Is that a dig at Ludwell? Are things still bad between them? 'Tell him I'm feeling much better, thank you,' she adds. 'I think I'm over the worst of it now. I might even manage to join you for dinner tonight . . .'

'I'm glad to hear it,' says Rosel. 'You're certainly looking better.'

Really? Bella hates to think what she was looking like before, in that case.

'And how about you, Bella? How are you feeling now?'

Tired. Achy. Scared. Miserable.

'I'm not sure, to be honest,' Bella says. 'I don't even remember getting back to my room. Did I black out or something?'

Rosel looks nervous. 'I don't know. I didn't see. The others

222

seemed to think you'd taken something. They thought it was something to do with that needle I found in your room.'

Bella shakes her head, her cheeks flushing under the scrutiny of Rosel's gaze. She can feel Julia looking at her too. Judging her. 'No, the needle wasn't mine. Someone must have left it there to frame me – to make me look bad. Someone who's got it in for me. I don't know why but . . .' It still sounds crazy when she says it out loud. *She* sounds crazy, but she presses on, regardless. 'I think it's connected with that note under my door. The one we were talking about yesterday.' Bella turns briefly back to Julia. 'It was just like the one they put in Ludwell's bag. It's the same person. It's got to be. And the apple . . . I suppose you know about the apple with the maggots in it?'

'Maggots?' The look of shocked disgust on Rosel's face suggests that this is the first she's heard about it. Perhaps she was still in the kitchen at lunchtime, when Bella was accusing Oscar of planting it. Or perhaps she's just playing dumb. 'I didn't imagine it,' Bella says, turning back to Julia. 'At least I don't *think* I did.' Surely the business with the needle *proves* that someone's out to get her? That they've been playing her all along? 'Or the creepy scratching noise,' she adds. 'I didn't imagine *any* of it. Apart from the spyhole in the wall . . .' *Wait, did I say that out loud?*

'A hole in the wall? Which wall?'

And just like that, Bella's credibility – if she still had any – is gone. Who's going to believe her now? 'No, nothing, forget I mentioned it. I think I must be coming down with something. Perhaps another lie-down will help . . .' Bella says, already backing away along the corridor towards her own room. 'But tell Stuart I'm fine,' she calls back to Rosel. 'Tell him it's nothing that a bit of peace and quiet won't take care of.'

What she really needs, of course, is to get out of here. She needs to be back home in the safe sanctuary of her own house, away from all of *this*. If it wasn't for those stupid fallen trees, Bella could be there already, working on her new project in peace and safety, pestering her poor son with casual, thinly veiled attempts to drill him for information until he asked her to stop.

Two more days, she tells herself as she slinks back into her bedroom and shuts the door behind her. That's assuming she's fit enough to travel . . .

Two more days, she tells herself again as she sits at her desk and forces down one of the sandwiches, as if to prove to herself that she's fine. She can't bring herself to touch the apple though. She can't even bring herself to *look* at it, putting it straight into the bin under her desk.

'Two more days,' she mouths at her reflection as she refills her water glass in the en suite bathroom. As the drawn, pale face in the mirror stares back at her in despair.

*

Bella hardly knows what to do with herself the rest of that afternoon. She doesn't know what to think any more, who to trust. She can't stay in her room listening out for strange sounds that no one else can hear, but she can't face the others. Not after her humiliating outburst at lunch. And not knowing which one of them is behind it all. There are no signs of any needle marks on her arms though, thank goodness. The idea that someone at the retreat really *might* have spiked her with some weird hallucinogenic drug is downright terrifying. That's proper call-the-police territory. But there's no bruising. No puncture marks. Nothing, in short, to suggest an injection of any kind. Nothing but an empty hypodermic needle and her own overwrought imagination. *This isn't a scene from your film, Mum.*

A small part of her almost wishes it *were.* If this were a film, she'd be able to tell by the music playing in the background whether she was in danger. Whether she should be pounding on Stuart's door right now, demanding he call the police, before things get even more out of hand. Always assuming that Stuart himself can be trusted . . . and assuming she wouldn't get herself arrested in the process, given that the needle was found in her room.

Bella doesn't know *whom* she can trust any more, that's the problem. She's not even sure she can trust herself. One moment she's so sure it's real – all the weird stuff that keeps happening to her – and then the next moment she's full of doubts again. Maybe that's exactly how they *want* her to feel. Maybe that's all part of the twisted game they're playing with her, whoever 'they' are. If only Bella knew *that* then she'd know what she was up against.

Lena, she thinks. If anyone can shed some light on all of this, it's her. Bella needs to find out what she's discovered. She needs to make sure she's okay.

The others should still be in their afternoon workshop. Guilt-purging – that's what Marie said, wasn't it? Bella doesn't stop to check the timetable though. She slips on her trainers and throws some more cold water on her face in an effort to clear her mind – to fight the wooziness in her skull – then creeps back through the lodge towards the other guest wing. There's no Saga blocking her way this time. No sign of anyone at all.

Bella still doesn't know which room is Lena's, but that doesn't matter if everyone else is out. It's not going to be a problem if she knocks on the wrong door by mistake. She rules out Oscar's room and tries the next door along – 'Lena? It's me, Bella' – listening with her ear pressed against the wood for an answer which never comes. There's no answer at the next door, either, or the next, her frustration and unease growing with each silent response. That just leaves one last door.

'Hello? Are you there? Can you hear me? It's Bella.'

But this time she *does* hear something. She hears the jangling clank of metal and the splintering smash of glass. She hears muffled swearing. And then the sound of someone at the door . . . someone twisting back the catch . . .

Chapter 29

'Bella? What are you doing here?' A dishevelled, bleary-eyed T stares back at her, a stale waft of Asher's deodorant seeping out through the open doorway.

'Oh, it's you! Sorry,' says Bella. 'I was looking for Lena.'

'Lena?' T seems half-asleep. Perhaps he *was* asleep.

'Sorry, did I wake you? I thought everyone would be in the guilt-purging session.'

He shakes his head. 'Didn't really fancy that one. I'd rather keep my guilt to myself, thank you very much. I thought I'd catch up on some sleep instead – had a bit of a disturbed night last night.'

Bella apologises again. 'As I said, it was Lena I was looking for. I haven't seen her since yesterday.'

T scratches his nose. 'Oh right, yeah. Turns out she's been off her feet with a bad migraine. That's why she wasn't at breakfast this morning. She's been in bed all day.'

No, that's not right, Bella thinks. *She went swimming this morning.* 'Really? Are you sure?'

He shrugs. 'I certainly haven't seen her.'

'How do you know?'

'How do I know I haven't seen her? I think I'd have remembered.'

'No, I mean how do you know it's a migraine?'

T sighs – the same petulant tone of sigh that Asher excels in.

Same smell, same grunts, same sighs, Bella thinks. She can always tell when Asher's losing patience with something – or someone – by the amount of sighing that goes on.

'What is this,' T asks, 'twenty questions? Someone told me, okay? I don't remember who it was, now. But I haven't seen her.'

Why's he being so defensive? Is it something to do with his row with Lena yesterday? *And he was acting all cagey last night,* Bella recalls, when Krista mentioned her name.

'She's definitely not here,' T says sarcastically, turning sideways and gesturing with his arm as if to prove it.

Bella catches a brief glimpse of a broken glass on the floor behind him, illuminated by the thin shaft of light coming from the gap under the blind. A broken glass and a bunch of keys lying in a wet puddle beside it. 'Wait, what's that?'

T turns back to see. 'That's the glass of water I knocked over when I got up to answer the door. At least it *was* a glass of water.'

'No, the keys, I mean.' Bella points. 'Those ones there.' She's thinking of Rosel's missing keys – the keys she said she'd found, but then wouldn't say *where* she'd found them.

'Oh right, yeah. I must have caught them with my elbow too.'

No, wait, she didn't say she'd found them, Bella realises. She just implied it. '*Everything's fine.*' That's what she *actually* said. Perhaps she was being deliberately evasive. 'Are they yours?' she asks T.

'No, I found them outside when I popped out for a cheeky smoke. I assumed Stuart or Marie must have dropped them. But there was nobody in the office when I went to take them back.'

'Or Rosel's,' says Bella. 'I bet they're the ones she lost at the weekend.' *She was fobbing me off last night, wasn't she?* she thinks. *To stop me telling Stuart and Marie. But then why mention that she'd lost them in the first place? It doesn't make sense. Nothing about this place makes sense.*

'Oh okay, I'll try her now then,' he says. 'Thanks.'

'Or I can take them if you want,' Bella offers before he can close the door again. She wants to know why Rosel lied to her by omission. Was she genuinely so scared about losing her job that she'd risk the security of every guest there?

T frowns. 'It's fine,' he says. 'I need to see if she's got some old newspaper or something I can use to wrap the broken glass in. I'll see you later.' He shuts the door, leaving Bella standing alone in the corridor, trying to collect her thoughts. Trying to make sense of it all. She's still standing there when he opens the door again, clutching the keys in his hand.

'Still here?' he teases. 'What's wrong, don't you trust me?'

Bella forces a smile. *No*, she thinks. *I don't. I don't trust anyone.*

She follows him as far as the first door, then hurries outside, skirting round the outside of the building in the hope of finding Lena's window before T gets back with the newspaper. Hopefully he'll stop in the kitchen for a chat. If he's right and Lena really *is* sleeping off her migraine then there won't be much to see. The blind will almost certainly be down. But if he's *not* then . . . Bella doesn't know what to think (other than the worst) if he's lying. All she knows is it's better to be doing something than sitting in her room, stewing in her own fear. And maybe a sly peek in some of the other guests' windows while she's there wouldn't go amiss either. *Let's see what they're hiding.*

She doesn't linger outside T's room in case he comes back. The blind's still down anyway after his afternoon sleep and the gap left at the bottom is too small to see anything through. Even if Lena *was* lying bound and gagged on the sofa Bella wouldn't be able to tell. She moves on, her pulse quickening with antici-pation as she peers into the next room, although she's not sure what she's hoping to find exactly. A box of hypodermic needles waiting there in the window for anyone to see? A bluffers' guide to anonymous letter-writing? It's just a regular-looking room, with a couple of books on the desk, a half-unpacked suitcase in the corner and what looks like a framed photograph by the bed. It could be anyone's. There's nothing of interest in the next room,

228

which is even barer than the first, and the blinds are firmly down in the fourth window she comes to. No amount of listening at the glass can tell Bella whether there's anyone asleep inside though, which just leaves Oscar's room at the end, and there's nothing more incriminating to see in there from the outside than there was from the inside yesterday. So much for *that* plan then. But as Bella retraces her steps back along the row, something in the second window – the one belonging to T's neighbour – catches her eye . . . something she missed before: a bottle of pills nestling behind the books on the desk.

They could be anything of course. She can't see the label on the front from here, can't see what they are or who they belong to. But she keeps coming back to that same word: *drugged.* What if she was right the first time? What if someone slipped something into her drink before the gong bathing session, and the used needle in her room was just a red herring to throw everyone off the scent? The idea makes her feel hot and panicky inside, despite the cold air biting at her cheeks. If only she knew whose room it was, then she could . . . could what, exactly? Report them to Stuart and Marie? Admit that she's been spying and demand a search of their room? Confront them directly and accuse them of poisoning her? How's that going to go down after her last crazy outburst? Besides, the pills could be perfectly harmless: prescription antibiotics, vitamin C lozenges, a herbal cold remedy, homeopathic headache tablets . . . They could be anything at all.

As surreptitious investigations go, it's not very conclusive, or helpful. All she's done is scare herself even more. There's no peeking into the staff quarters at the rear of the lodge – not without a ladder, anyway – but Bella's not ready to give up yet, carrying on round the outside of the building towards her own room. It's time to check out the empty room again – room twelve – on the off-chance that she might actually be able to see in today.

No such luck. The blind's pulled down again, just like before, and no amount of pressing her face up against the glass can make it any more transparent. There's nothing to hear from outside either. No rustling. No scratching. Nothing but the sound of her own shallow breathing, broken by a loud expletive issuing from the half-open window nextdoor. *Julia.*

'Sorry, darling,' comes Ludwell's voice. 'I didn't mean to make you jump. I thought you'd still be in bed.'

'Thought or hoped?' asks Julia. It doesn't sound like a come-on though, judging by her tone of voice. Quite the opposite.

Bella steps quietly back into the shadows, pressing her spine tight into the wall.

'Don't be like that,' says Ludwell. 'It's good to see you up and about again. How was your shower?'

'Fine,' snaps Julia. 'How was Lena?'

Bella's ears tingle. *Lena?*

'I wouldn't know,' says Ludwell. 'She wasn't there.'

Wasn't where? He can't be referring to Lena's room or Bella would've seen him. Perhaps there'd been a note from Lena under his and Julia's door too, asking Ludwell to meet her somewhere this afternoon. *I found something I think you should see.* And then what, she'd stood him up too? She must have done.

'Which was just as well,' Ludwell adds quickly. 'I'm not sure I'd have been able to join in the workshop with her there. But nobody's seen her all day. She's not very well apparently.'

Oh, thinks Bella. They're talking about Stuart's guilt-purging session, aren't they? *Of course.* It must have finished already.

'My heart bleeds for her,' says Julia. The venom in her voice is tangible.

Bella's mind races. Does that mean she was right? That Lena's the 'certain someone' Ludwell was talking about at breakfast? The other party in his 'long, sordid story'? She feels a stab of sympathy for Julia, imagining what it must be like finding herself trapped in the middle of nowhere with the woman her husband cheated on her with. If it's true – if Lena and Ludwell really *do* have romantic history – then no wonder Julia's been feeling ill. *Imagine if she knew about me too*, she thinks. But even if Ludwell *has* put two and two together after what happened at lunch – even if he knows who Bella is now, knows who *Asher* is – it doesn't sound like he's shared his discovery with his wife. Not given how nice Julia was to Bella earlier, checking she was all right and asking about her son. No, Ludwell can't have told her yet. Mind you, they barely sound like they're on speaking terms at the moment.

'Julia, please, don't be like this,' he begs. 'It's hard for me too, you know.'

'Poor Ludwell,' she says sarcastically. 'I forgot that you're the one who's been in bed all week, feeling like death warmed up. That you're the one Little Miss Crazy threw up on as soon as you arrived. I forgot that *you're* the real victim here . . . the one who gets to be humiliated all over again.'

Little Miss Crazy? Bella can feel her sympathy slipping away again. Why would Julia call her that? She knows the answer, of course. Hammering on the doors of empty rooms and rambling about strange noises and spyholes in walls would be enough to put anyone's sanity in question. But there's something about the way Julia says it that makes it sound like a shared nickname. As if Ludwell thinks of Bella as unhinged too. Is that how everyone here sees her? And what if they're right? What if the stress of leaving Asher – of seeing Ludwell again after all these years – has done something to her brain, making her see and hear things that aren't there?

No, she tells herself, blinking back frightened tears. That's exactly what someone here *wants* her to think. It's all part of their game, isn't it? A game with Bella as the helpless pawn, stuck in the middle.

Chapter 30

Bella forces herself to join the others for dinner, even though her appetite is still non-existent. Even though she knows that one of the laughing faces round the table is behind every horrible thing that's happened since she arrived. But there's safety in numbers and that's what sways it for her. That and the need to prove to the others that she's not some paranoid junkie, shooting up in her room while they're busy communing with their inner gurus. She's desperately hoping Lena will be there too, to finally explain what she meant by her message – the message that's been going round and round Bella's head all day: *I found something I think you should see.* It's been torture knowing Lena could have the answers she needs and not being able to find her. Even if her note *does* turn out to be some kind of blackmail attempt – even if *Lena's* the one who's been taunting Bella this whole time – it would be better to know. Better than jumping at shadows and fearing the worst.

Lena's still not there though, and Bella regrets her decision the minute she walks into the dining room. The minute everyone stops talking and turns to look at her. It's like lunchtime all over again. But she ignores the urge to turn tail and hide in her room, pulling her head up and her shoulders back, with a fake smile plastered across her face. She takes her usual place at the table, apologising to Krista and the others for her earlier outburst and sipping demurely at her water, keeping her inner turmoil to herself. No wine for her tonight. She picks at her food without tasting it and tries her best to look sane and sober.

Conversation ebbs and flows around her, but Bella barely hears any of it. She's too deep in her own thoughts. Thoughts about the needle in her room, the unidentified tablets she saw in the bedroom earlier, and the possibility of something romantic between Ludwell and Lena. Could that explain the note under T's door about meeting at the lake? Was it intended for Lena? Do the timings add up or would that have been before Ludwell got here? Bella's starting to lose all sense of time – it feels like she's been here for ever.

No one would guess the Storms were having marital problems to look at them now, laughing together at the other end of the table. Julia looks considerably healthier for a shower and a spot of make-up, too. But it's all a lie, Bella thinks. It's beginning to feel like nobody here is quite who they say they are.

She excuses herself as soon as dinner's over, retreating back to her own room and shutting the door behind her, then checking it again to make sure she closed it properly. At least she knows the missing keys have been found now – for *real*, this time – although Bella didn't actually see T hand them back. He could have been bluffing. Perhaps she should have checked with Rosel over dinner, although that didn't get her very far last time, did it? Bella's not sure she can trust either one of them. She's not sure she can trust Marie, either, who said Lena was still sleeping when she went to check on her before dinner. Or Krista, who broke down in tears – ugly, angry tears – over her husband's death, halfway through dessert. Or Oscar, who left the table at the same time as Bella, loudly announcing that he was planning an all-nighter on his novel and would be firmly glued to his desk until morning. She's not sure she can trust anyone.

Bella pulls the blind and makes herself a calming cup of camomile, not trusting Stuart's sleep tea any more either, fiddling with the yellow label on the string until it comes off in her fingers. Then she settles herself down at the desk and gets out her composition, hoping work might provide some small respite from the troubling thoughts barrelling round her brain. But the soaring oboe line that was so clear in her mind when she broke off yesterday is steadfastly refusing to soar now, and the few pencilled notes she manages to get down are soon rubbed out. She picks up the pamphlet of local myths and legends that Oscar gave her, only to put it down again. One creepy local story was more than enough, on reflection. Finally, she settles on the novel she bought at the airport, changing into her nightclothes and curling up with it in bed. And even though she barely takes in a single word, even though she finds herself reading the same paragraph over and over again, the association in her brain, with bedtime – and the accumulated tiredness of so many broken nights in a row – has her eyelids drooping before she's more than a few chapters in.

No sooner has Bella switched off the light and shut her eyes than her brain goes back into overdrive though, still trying to puzzle out which one of the other guests is behind it all. And the longer she tosses and turns in the dark – one hour . . . two hours . . . three hours and counting – her jaw clenched tight and her heart racing, the more her imagination takes over. Before long she's hearing scratching noises coming through the wall again, soft and slow at first, growing louder and more insistent – *scrrrrraaaatch* . . . *scrrrrraaaatch* . . . *scrrrrraaaatch* – as she thinks about the story of the bandit in the forest. About bloodied finger stumps that carried on scratching away at the lid of the coffin even after the man had died – still scraping away at the wood. She thinks about the eerie tapping noise of gloved knuckles against the wall in *The Screaming Hours*, as the killer closes in on his next victim. She thinks about someone right there in the next room, watching and waiting . . .

It's no good. Even if the keys are back in the office where they should be, that still leaves four people with sets of their own: Stuart, Marie, Rosel and Saga. Any one of them could let themselves into Bella's room during the night. And what about the window? Even though it's locked, someone could still get in that way if they knew what they were doing. Bella can't just lie there, waiting for whoever's been targeting her to strike again. Because this time it might be something more than mind games.

Breathing hard at the thought of what she's about to do, she switches on the bedside light, pulls her cardigan on over her pyjama top and picks up the torch. There's a strong sense of déjà vu as she heads out into the darkened hush of the corridor, hoping that everyone's in bed by now. It feels like her first morning here all over again, creeping round in search of food, only it's not food she's after this time. Or maybe, with the torch gripped tight in her hand, it feels more like Monday night, when she was skulking through the lodge again in search of bug spray. Bella's had more practice at sneaking around while everyone else is asleep than she cares for, but that doesn't make it any less creepy now. It doesn't make the whining creak of the polished oak floorboards under her feet any less eerie, or the shadows at the outer edges of her torch beam any less menacing.

Bella shivers at the memory of the writhing apple sitting on her desk as she crosses towards the dining room. It still feels every bit as real to her now as it did then, regardless of what Marie says. In her mind's eye she can still see the pale wriggling bodies squirming over each other inside the hollowed-out fruit as clear as anything. It's like a film, playing on a loop inside her head, like a scene from one of the creepy thrillers she's been watching as research. But Bella's the one in the film this time – that's what it feels like, stealing through the torch-lit dark in her socked feet, her breath catching in her throat at every imagined movement behind her. She feels like the victim-in-waiting, following the thin beam of light through the house, straining her ears for the sound of footsteps tracking her through the sleeping lodge.

The sense of being followed – of being watched – is stronger than ever as Bella tiptoes towards the kitchen, but when she turns to look over her shoulder there's no one there. There never is.

'I know you're here,' she whispers into the stillness.

The lodge breathes back its eerie silence.

'You don't scare me,' she lies, the hairs on the back of her neck prickling. In truth she's terrified. Terrified of what she's about to do. Of what it signifies. Terrified that it's come to this.

Bella can smell the stale, sour-sweat scent of her own body as she stops to listen at the closed door, resting her ear briefly against the smooth waxed wood – all clear – before pressing on into the quiet chill of the kitchen.

Once inside, she scans the oak worktops like a thief, the circle of torchlight skimming across the polished surfaces. But it's not an apple she's come to steal this time. It's not bug spray she's after . . .

There! The knife rack is a fancy magnetic affair with an impressive selection of blades, from tiny paring knives to an enormous, jagged bread knife. Bella's heart is beating double time as she swaps her torch into her left hand, her right hand reaching towards the rack of waiting blades. She checks over her shoulder one last time – still no one there – before selecting a small-to-medium-sized knife, wrapping her fingers around the weighted black handle and trying it for size. It seems about right. Not that Bella can actually imagine using it on someone . . . the mere thought of the sharpened metal slicing through living flesh makes her feel physically sick. But the idea of someone breaking into her room in the middle of the night while she's completely defenceless is even more sickening. She rearranges the other knives on the block to disguise the gap left behind and smuggles her stolen weapon back to her room inside her sleeve, her heart still thumping at her own audacity. *I did it.*

No sooner has Bella locked the bedroom door behind her again and pulled out the knife than the full weight of the situation overwhelms her. This isn't a film, this is real life . . . Not a life she recognises though. It's not *her* life. She's a thirty-eight-year-old single mother, for crying out loud, with frizzy hair and a coffee stain on her pyjama top. Why would a potential killer be stalking her? She looks down at the real-life kitchen knife clutched in her sweating hand and shudders.

A violent shaking takes hold of her body as she drops the knife onto the bed – a gash of black and metal against the stark whiteness of her rumpled duvet cover. *What am I doing? This is crazy.* Bella sinks down onto the bed beside it, cradling her head in her hands. How has it come to this? It's supposed to be a holiday. It's supposed to be a restful break from the stresses of the last few weeks; a chance to reset. But Dödmansskogen is none of those things. It's a nightmare – a living nightmare she can't wake up from, and Bella's seriously out of her depth.

'This can't be happening,' she whispers into the quiet of her room. But it is. She's here, trapped in the middle of nowhere, alone and shaking, feeling scared and paranoid. A sudden wave of loneliness sweeps through her as she picks up the knife again and tucks it under the bed – out of sight but not out of reach.

Oh Asher. Bella wraps her arms around herself, rocking gently backwards and forward on the bed. If she'd known what was lying in wait for her here, she'd have held him so much tighter when they said goodbye. She'd have put aside her worries about embarrassing him and shouted after him as he walked away: 'I love you. I'll always love you.' What if that was her last chance to tell him? Her last chance to hold him?

Fear pressing down on her bladder, Bella pads across to the bathroom, checking her reflection in the mirror.

I'm not a victim, she tells the pale face staring back at her.

I'm not Izzy. It's true. She's not a frightened teenager any more.

'I am strong,' she says out loud, trying to convince herself.

'I rise above silly jokes and mind games.

'I am brave.

'I am determined.

'I have a son who needs me.'

Mothers *have* to keep going. It comes with the job description.

'I'm going to get through this,' Bella tells her reflection. Whatever *this* is, exactly. In two-and-a-half days she'll be back home again. And in eleven weeks Asher will be home too, with his dirty washing and his uncut hair and his beautiful, lopsided grin. *My boy.* The thought gives her strength – a calming strength that stills the trembling in her limbs and eases the painful thump of her heart inside her ribs.

'My boy,' she says, whispering it out loud into the stillness of the bathroom as she washes her hands afterwards, holding his image in her head like a talisman against her own dread. Against whatever – or *whoever* – might be coming for her in the night. 'I am brave for my boy.' And then, as if to prove it, she slips off her cardigan and hangs it on the back of her desk chair before pulling up the blind and peering out towards the eerie moonlit forest beyond. *Dead Man's Forest.*

'I rise above silly mind games and jokes,' Bella tells the dark, looming trees.

'I am determined,' she tells the stars that pinprick the inky sky with flecks of gold.

'I am . . .' *Wait, what was that?* Bella stiffens at the sound of movement outside. Of footsteps crunching across the gravel. She presses her face to the cold glass, staring into the darkness. There! Her throat tightens as a telltale beam of torchlight comes bobbing into her line of sight. The person carrying the torch is harder to spot but she can just about make them out now, a tall, shadowy shape moving in the darkness. She didn't imagine it. There really is someone out there.

Her first thought – her first *rational* thought after the initial shock – is that it might be Marie or Stuart, doing a final late-night check of the premises before they lock up and turn in for the night. But the torchlight keeps on moving away from the lodge, heading off towards the lake path.

Her second thought is that it's an insomniac fellow guest in search of some fresh air – Lena, maybe, finally recovered from her migraine – or a smoker craving a night-time cigarette. *T*, she thinks. The air's just as fresh close to the lodge though. Why would he choose to head off into the forest all alone in the middle of the night? But that's when rational thought abandons Bella altogether. That's when her overwrought emotions and imagination take over again, her thoughts spiralling out of control. Suddenly she's back to Lena and her migraine. Back to wondering if there's any truth to the story. How did Marie know Lena was still sleeping? Did she check inside her room, or did she just assume that was the case when she didn't get an answer? And what about T? Where did he get his information from? Has anyone, apart from Stuart, actually seen Lena in the last twenty-four hours? And how does Bella know that *Stuart* was telling the truth, given that Lena was supposed to be in the studio with her at the time? What if her earlier wild imaginings weren't so wild after all? What if the real reason Lena never showed up for their meeting this morning is nothing to do with a migraine and everything to do with someone else getting to her first? Someone with an axe to grind . . .

Julia, she thinks. Maybe Julia attacked Lena in a fit of jealousy last night and Stuart and Marie are helping with the cover-up to avoid a scandal . . . pretending she was out and about this morning, then conveniently confined to bed for the rest of the day. Maybe all that business with Ludwell this afternoon, when Julia was asking after Lena, was to cover her tracks with him, too. To make sure *he* didn't suspect anything . . . Or maybe Ludwell's in on it as well . . . maybe he'd do anything to save his marriage. Maybe they knew someone was listening in at the window and the whole fake row was for *Bella's* benefit. *That's* why Ludwell and Julia were back round the dinner table this evening, laughing together as if nothing's happened. And now . . . and now Julia just needs to dispose of the murder weapon down at the lake, and she's home free.

This isn't a scene from your film, Mum, warns the Asher voice in Bella's head. But there's a louder, more urgent voice telling her that Julia's getting away. A sudden charge, somewhere between fear and excitement, shoots through Bella's body as she pictures Julia disappearing off into the darkness to dispose of the evidence.

She's getting away.

Bella's watched enough thrillers lately to know what happens to people who investigate suspicious noises in the middle of the night. Who go chasing after suspected murderers. It never ends well. But she's not thinking about that now. She's barely thinking at all as she slips on her shoes and coat, scooping up her torch and key from the bedside table. Her breath is coming short and fast as she reaches under the bed for the knife, tucking it blade down into her padded coat pocket . . . as she opens the bedroom door and closes it softly behind her. There's no time for second thoughts. No time to stop and realise what a crazy, dangerous plan this is. Bella's already sneaking back through the shadowy silence of the lodge and out through the unlocked front door. She's already creeping off into the biting cold of the night in search of answers. In search of proof.

Chapter 31

The wind has picked up again during the night, howling round the lodge and shaking the trees. It feels like there's another storm coming. Or maybe it's danger Bella can sense prickling the air as she crunches across the gravel, following the beam of light, her feet crazy-loud against the stones. But she's too intent on keeping her target in her sights, without drawing attention to herself in the process, to question the wisdom of her plan. Even when she realises it can't be Julia – the height of the torch and the speed with which they're covering the ground makes her think it must be a man – she still doesn't stop. She doesn't pause to think what she'll do when she catches up with him. She simply hurries on into the darkness, the wild thump of her heart almost as loud as the gravel beneath her feet, praying that he won't hear her coming.

It's a relief when she hits the needle-muffled quiet of the lake path, the sweet scent of pine filling her nostrils. There are other dangers underfoot here though, like stray tree roots and loose rocks. Bella remembers that much from her daylight walks, but she can't risk using her own torch to guide her in case he notices the light behind him. She needs to find out what he's up to – she needs to know if it's connected to Lena, and to all the strange, disturbing things that have been going on since she arrived – but even in her crazy, reckless state of mind, she knows that she shouldn't let him see *her*.

A loud, ghostly hoot bursts from the dark flank of trees on Bella's right and the man turns, his torch swinging back round towards her. Bella freezes, her breath catching in her throat as she waits for the light to pick her out. But the beam loops up and away from her at the last minute, sweeping across the tops of the trees like a searchlight, and then back down to the path as before.

That was close. Close enough to have turned Bella's legs soft and wobbly beneath her. Close enough to make her think twice about what she's doing creeping through Dead Man's Forest in the middle of the night. But the need to see what he's up to – to find out how the man striding on into the blackness is connected to all the dark goings-on at the lodge – keeps her from turning round and heading back inside. The need to find out *who* he is makes her push on through her fear, sneaking soundlessly after him.

His pace is beginning to slow now though. Bella squints through the darkness, trying to get her bearings, her heart beating faster than ever. Surely they're not at the lake already? He's casting his torch around, as if he's trying to find something he's dropped on the ground. But then he veers sharply off to the left and Bella realises it was a turning on the path he was looking for. The turning for the bird hide.

The idea of following him along that narrow, winding path, with its sharp, scratchy plants and slippery rocks, is what finally brings Bella to her senses. What on earth is she playing at, trailing a dangerous man through the night on her own? And with a kitchen knife, for crying out loud. All those lectures she gave Asher about thinking before he acts and not getting caught up in other people's silly behaviour, and look at her. If the man really *is* behind all the horrible things that have been happening, then he's definitely not the sort of person she should be following to a deserted bird hide. And if he's behind the needle in Bella's room then he could be on his way to meet someone equally dangerous. Some dodgy drugs dealer with a motorbike, for whom the blocked road is no issue.

She runs through the possible suspects in her head. T? Oscar? Hamar? Ludwell? It could be any one of them. Or Stuart . . . Yes, Stuart seems much more likely. He's the one with the local contacts after all, and the only one of the men with easy access to a phone. *And* easy access to her room in order to plant the needle. *He* wouldn't have to worry about getting his hands on the spare keys. And if someone really did slip something into Bella's hot chocolate before the gong bathing session, who'd have had a better opportunity than him? Stuart's the one who makes his own 'special sleep tea' too, *and* the one who told everyone the story about the man in the coffin haunting the forest. Was that to try and scare them off any nocturnal wanderings of their own? But no sooner has Bella worked it all out, jumping to an entirely new set of conclusions, than a second figure appears on the lake path from the other direction – coming from the lake itself – heading straight towards her.

No, no, no. She flings herself sideways into the cover of the trees, pressing herself into the branches. Beads of sweat collect on her upper lip, despite the cold, as she wills herself invisible. *Please don't let them see me.* Bella can see *them* though, whoever they are. She can see the bright halo of the figure's hair catching briefly in the beam of their torch. Blonde hair.

'Hamar!' A woman's voice rings out through the night. 'Wait. Come back.'

It's not Stuart after all then, Bella thinks, reassessing her theory. Does that mean she's wrong about the drugs too, or does Hamar have his own dodgy contacts from previous visits to Sweden? Could *that* explain the note T found under his door? *Sorry about yesterday. I'll explain everything. Meet me by the lake at midnight.* Yes, if Hamar was the intended recipient, it could have been about a drugs drop rather than a romantic rendezvous. Unless Bella's right about him and Rosel, of course. Unless there's more to his flirtatious ribbing than mere banter.

'Saga?' comes Hamar's surprised reply, as his torch carves out a fresh line through the darkness to find her. 'I thought we were meeting at the hide again.' He turns round and starts walking back towards the main path.

Bella blinks in surprise.

'No,' Saga says. 'I've changed my mind. I can't do this any more. It's not fair on Lisbeth. Just because things are difficult between us at the moment, doesn't mean I get to take up with my ex-boyfriend behind her back.'

Woah, Bella thinks. Of all the crazy thoughts and theories swirling round her head, she didn't see that one coming.

'But you said you still had feelings for me . . .' Hamar sounds less sure of himself than usual. Less cocky.

'I know what I said, but I'm telling you, I can't do it any more. It's wrong. I'm married. You made your choice three years ago and now I'm making mine.'

'I made a mistake,' Hamar says. 'A big mistake. But I'm here to fix it. This isn't just a holiday fling for me, you know. That's not what I'm here for . . . These last few nights . . . you felt it too, I know you did.'

'No,' Saga says softly. 'I can't. It's not fair on Lisbeth. And it's not fair on Rosel, expecting her to cover for us while we sneak around behind everyone's backs. To lie for us.'

'We don't have to sneak around,' Hamar begs. 'We could come clean. To *everyone*. I can look for work locally . . . maybe even right here at the retreat. I can talk to Stuart . . . or you can come back to the UK with me . . .'

'No,' Saga says again. More firmly this time. 'It's over, Hamar. We were over a long time ago, I shouldn't have let myself get caught up in old feelings . . . I've moved on. I'm happy now.'

'But you're not,' Hamar insists. 'You told me you spend half your time rowing.'

'It's a rough patch, that's all. We'll get through it. I love my wife. I do. And if you have any real feelings for me, you'll respect that. You'll leave me to fix my marriage in peace.'

'But . . .'

'I mean it. Please, Hamar. I only came to say goodbye.'

'At least let me . . .'

'*Låt bli mig!*' she calls, switching into Swedish as her voice cracks and emotion gets the better of her. 'Leave me alone!'

A low, strangled sob breaks through the quiet that follows. And then another. But Saga is already heading back towards the lake, alone – towards her house, somewhere on the far side of the water, her torch drooping low in front of her.

Bella feels heartless standing there, listening to Hamar cry. She feels guilty for having been party to such a private conversation in the first place. But what else can she do? She hugs herself tighter into the tree as he picks his sorry way past her, still sobbing to himself. And then, when the coast is finally clear, Bella follows after him, reeling from everything she's heard. Hamar and Saga? Who'd have thought it? And poor Rosel caught up in the middle of it all. That explains the figure Oscar saw heading down to the lake before, and finally solves the mystery of T's note. It *was* intended for Hamar then, and it *was* about a secret rendezvous. A romantic one. Saga, or Rosel, must have got the two men's room numbers muddled up and slipped it under the wrong door. Does that mean Saga was behind *Bella's* note too? And Ludwell's? If only she'd thought to question T more closely at the time and find out if his note was written on the same paper. Bella switches on her torch as her own dark thoughts return, crowding in on her from all sides again, like the forest itself.

Chapter 32

Bella's glad to get back to the warmth of her room. Shivering from the sudden change in temperature, she puts the kettle on for another drink, tucks the knife under her bed again, out of sight, and double-checks the door and windows are firmly locked.

Her thoughts and feelings are all over the place after the adrenaline rush of her night-time pursuit. Even the camomile tea tastes different, somehow – sweeter and stronger. Ah wait, maybe it's a different brand to the one she was drinking earlier. Yes, this one comes with a plain blue label attached to the end of the dunking string, and Bella's pretty sure the other one was yellow with a flower logo on it. She remembers looking at it and wondering what the difference was between a camomile flower – if that's what it was – and a regular daisy. Remembers playing with it until it came off in her hand. Hopefully *this* brand will do a better job of calming her nerves and helping her off to sleep.

She drains the last of the cup and climbs back into bed with a yawn, closing her eyes (again) on what's been a very strange, troubling day. But sleep, when it finally arrives, brings little relief from her waking worries. Bella finds herself back at The Black Swan, only the inside looks more like her mother's sitting room than a proper pub, with a piano and music stand in the corner and framed music certificates adorning the walls. Ludwell's there too, his violin resting on the sofa beside him, offering Bella a drink 'to wet the baby's head'. None of the beer taps along the piano lid seem to be working though, and the one sticking out of the bookcase is too stiff to move. He carries on trying, pulling harder and harder, until the entire handle comes off, flying across the room. Bella bends down to pick it up and realises that Ludwell's amputated fingers are still attached to it, slick with fresh blood.

She drops the handle in horror and runs for the front door – slow, heavy-limbed dream running – with Ludwell chasing after her, shouting that it's all her fault, that she'll pay for what she's done. But the door handle's jammed as tightly as the beer tap. There's no way out. And now Bella can see a dark shape moving through the textured glass ahead of her, as Ludwell seizes her from behind. The shape of someone trying to get in from the other side – the man with no face! – and then the handle turns . . .

Thump! Something – or some*one* hits the ground. Hard.

'NO!'

Bella wakes to the sound of her own scream, blood pounding in her ears and a cold slick of sweat along her back. *He's coming*, Bella thinks, fighting against the tight cradle of Ludwell's arms to free herself. She needs to escape before the faceless man on the other side of the glass reaches her. *Let me go!* But then her brain catches up with her altered state of consciousness, and the tight press of Ludwell's arms becomes a damp tangle of duvet around her shoulders, the Black Swan shrinking back to a bedroom in a Swedish lodge. It was only a dream. There *is* no sinister, shadowy shape trying to get in through the locked front door. And there are no severed fingers on the floor, Bella's relieved to see, now that her eyes have adjusted to the darkness – only the fallen torch. It must have rolled off the bedside table while she was asleep. *That's* what the thump was, she realises, her pulse slowing and her breathing beginning to settle again. Only a torch. Only a dream. *Thank goodness.*

She thinks, briefly, of the knife waiting under her bed, but there's no need for that now. In fact, now that the shock is over, now that the brief rush of adrenaline has passed, Bella finds her eyelids drooping again. She finds herself drifting back into the warm pull of sleep, slipping seamlessly into a new dream – about Asher this time. He's a toddler again, chasing after his aunt's new puppy, laughing his throaty little chuckle. And then Ludwell is there, scooping up the puppy in one arm and Asher in the other and swinging them round together as Asher squeals with delight.

'Again, Daddy, again!' he cries, his chubby face shining with excitement.

'He's not your daddy,' says Bella as she snatches him out of Ludwell's arms and presses him tight against her chest. 'You don't *need* a daddy. You've got me. I love you three times as much as any other boy.'

'No!' Asher screams, his little feet kicking at her stomach. 'Put me down. I want my daddy.'

Bella drifts back to wakefulness a second time, to a rustling noise somewhere in her room, and then a soft clicking sound. Like a door opening . . . Or closing . . . The thought should be enough to frighten her into consciousness, but somehow the fear isn't there this time. That second cup of camomile really *must* have been a stronger blend. She can barely keep her eyes open.

'Hello?' she calls out, thinking of missing keys and wriggling apples on waiting desks. But the thoughts are distant and muted, like they belong to somebody else. 'Is someone there?' Her voice sounds odd and croaky, echoing in her ears as she listens for the noise again. Was she awake when she heard it or still dreaming? Lying there, heavy-skulled against the soft comfort of her pillow, it's hard to tell the two states apart.

Long seconds tick by on her watch. Bella can hear them as she waits in the darkness, ears straining for any other sounds of life. *Tick. Tick. Tick.* But other than the gentle nudge of the second

248

hand round the darkened face, the room's quiet. Silent. She must have imagined it.

It feels later – much later – when Bella wakes again to a thick head and a sour taste in her mouth. There are no imagined noises this time though, just a light cramping ache in her stomach. She could do with the toilet again, too. She twists round under the duvet, craning her neck to check the red glowing numbers on the alarm clock. 07:15. Still only Thursday, she thinks with a sigh. How can it only be Thursday?

If she gets up now, there'll be no going back to sleep again. But her bladder's too full to ignore. Bella switches on the bedside lamp with a sigh, screwing up her eyes against the sudden glare, and drags her legs out of bed.

The room feels different somehow, now that's she's vertical. The *air* feels different. Her stomach tightens as she recalls the *click* she heard in the night, like a door opening or closing, coming back to her like a half-remembered dream. How could she have gone back to sleep without checking it out? What if it *was* someone in her room? *What if . . . what if he's still there now?* she thinks, glancing over at the closed bathroom door.

Bella reaches under her bed for the kitchen knife, imagining him holed up in her shower, waiting for her.

'Hello?' she calls, her fingers gripping the handle tight. 'Who's there?'

Stupid question. Since when did sinister intruders pop out of their hiding places to introduce themselves to their victims?

Bella pauses at the bathroom door, flicking on the main light instead. She turns round on a whim, to inspect the rest of the room. No, not a whim exactly. It's that feeling again. That skin-prickling sense of being watched. But there's no one there. Of course there isn't. She's being ridiculous. She shakes her head at her own jumpiness and opens the bathroom door.

What the . . .?

Bella reels back in shock, the knife slipping out of her fingers and bouncing off the white tiled floor. For a moment she thinks it's blood, but it's lipstick. A single lipsticked word scrawled across the side of the shower cubicle in thick red capitals: SLUT.

The letters swim and blur as a sudden dizziness takes hold of her. She clings onto the heated towel rail to keep from falling, only dimly aware of the hot metal burning her clenched hands.

Someone was in my room.

Someone was right here, watching me while I slept.

The word echoes in her head, over and over, burning its way into her brain. *Slut, slut, slut.* Such a nasty, poisonous word, full of hate and anger. Full of rage.

It must have been Julia . . . She must have finally found out the truth and got hold of the spare keys somehow. And Asher? Does she know about him too?

Oh Asher. What if he resents her for keeping his paternity a secret all these years? What if he chooses *them* over her?

Bella examines the message more closely, staring at the ugly crimson letters, thinking about the pent-up resentment that must have gone into writing them. That's when she notices the short, curved line underneath, like the start of another letter – like the top of an S. *That must have been when I knocked the torch on the floor. I must have disturbed her.* For some reason this scares Bella even more. What was supposed to come next? Another SLUT? SKANK? SEE YOU IN HELL? Or maybe it was the start of a B . . . B for BITCH. D for DIE. Or the top of a G, an O, an R . . . It could be anything.

It feels like someone's sucked all the oxygen out of the room, making it hard to breathe. Bella's legs are shaking as she heads back into the main room to open the window. Fresh air, that's what she needs. Fresh air and daylight. She pulls up the blind and lets out a strangled cry at the sight of another message, smeared across the outside of her window in the same blood-red lipstick as before:

SON STƎALƎR

It takes a moment or two for her shocked brain to work out what it says, foiled by the back-to-front Es. Julia must have got confused trying to write in reverse. And then it clicks: SON STEALER.

She knows. She knows about Asher . . .

Fear turns to bewilderment though as Bella stares past the crimson letters to the misty morning beyond, as if her graffitiing neighbour might still be out there, clutching the incriminating lipstick in her hand. 'Slut' she can understand, but 'son stealer'? For all Bella's worrying over the years about the childless Storms seeking custody of Asher – for all her fears that they'd be able to offer him a better start in life than her – she never once thought of herself as having *stolen* him. Ludwell had his chance to know he was a father and he blew it. Not just once but twice. *He's* the one Julia should be punishing, Bella thinks, and she's got a good mind to tell her just that. Where does the woman get off creeping round Bella's room in the middle of the night, leaving offensive messages to scare and humiliate her? Whatever guilt and pity she may have felt towards Ludwell's wife are long gone now.

Bella's already hammering on the Storms' bedroom door before she knows what she's doing. Before she has a chance to change her mind.

'Julia,' she calls, her voice amplified by anger. 'I need to talk to you.'

There's no answer. Bella knocks again, even harder, beating both fists against the wood and shouting: 'JULIA!'

But when the door finally opens it's Ludwell who's standing there, pale-cheeked, blue eyes wide with concern. Bella's surprised to see how rough he looks – unshaven and tousle-haired, boxer shorts and T-shirt clearly visible through his gaping dressing gown – but he seems every bit as surprised by *her* appearance.

'Bella? What are you doing here?'

'I need to talk to your wife. She knows what it's about.' *Oh yes. She knows all right.*

251

'Now's not a good time,' says Ludwell. 'We've had a bit of a shock.'

'Me too,' Bella tells him, standing her ground. 'Which is why I'm here.' She's about to say more but Ludwell cuts her off:

'Someone graffitied on our window during the night,' he says, and then lowers his voice. 'It's rather shaken Julia up.'

'What?' Bella stares at him in confusion. 'But I thought . . . What did it say?'

'Nothing nice,' says Ludwell evasively, his gaze dropping to the floor.

'Show me,' Bella orders. 'Please, it's important.' *If it wasn't Julia, then who on earth . . .?*

Ludwell stands aside and Bella barges past him to find Julia standing by the window, already fully dressed, staring out at another set of red letters smeared across the glass:

ADULTERER.

The Es are the right way round this time. Whoever wrote it must have learned from their previous mistakes.

'Lipstick,' Bella murmurs. 'Just like in my room.' She turns back to Ludwell. 'What about your shower? Did they leave a message on the shower screen too?'

'No, only the window.'

'Do you have any idea who it was?'

'Lena,' says Julia, before Ludwell can answer. 'As if the bitch hasn't done enough damage already with her stupid story. As if it wasn't enough to smear my husband's infidelity across her tacky magazine, she has to follow us here and rub my nose in it all over again. It's not my fault she lost her job. She should have checked her sources more carefully.'

Bella's even *more* confused now. 'So Lena wasn't the one you had the affair with?' she asks Ludwell, trying to make sense of this new information. 'I thought you said . . .' She pauses, trying to recall his exact words. *I wouldn't have come if I'd known a certain someone was going to be here too . . . and I definitely wouldn't have persuaded Marie to let Julia join me . . . It's a long, sordid story, I'm afraid. Certainly not my finest hour.*

'No,' Julia snaps. 'It was a local politician. Lena's just the journalist who decided to share it with the rest of the world, along with some made-up nonsense about Ludwell fraternising with students while he was teaching at the university. The journalist who lost her job after we threatened legal action and clearly hasn't forgiven us.'

'I had no idea,' Bella tells her. Of course she didn't. She's gone out of her way to *avoid* reading anything about Ludwell Storm and his wife. 'But that doesn't explain why Lena would write SON STEALER on *my* window and SLUT across my shower screen. Even if she knew about us,' she says without thinking, turning to Ludwell, 'why would she care? It was years ago.'

'Knew about us?' Ludwell repeats, slowly. 'What do you mean? There *is* no us.'

Shit. If he hasn't already worked out the connection between them, he will now, Bella realises. But maybe that's a good thing. Maybe she's through with pretending, with secrets and hiding and lies, if this is where they've got her. And she's through with being scared of Ludwell and Julia, with so many other things jostling for her fear. She's not that terrified girl who stood outside their door any more and they can't take Asher away from her now even if they want to.

'Yes, what do you mean?' echoes Julia, her eyes narrowing.

'I *mean*, why would Lena care about a one-night stand from nineteen years ago . . . unless . . . unless she's after evidence that she was right all along? That Ludwell *was* fraternising with his students? Maybe she's trying to force out the truth about Asher.'

'What one-night stand and who's Asher?' says Ludwell, looking paler by the second. 'You mean your son?'

'*Our* son,' Bella corrects him.

And there it is.

'What the fuck is she talking about, Ludwell?' says Julia, looking from one to the other of them. 'What did you do?'

'I'm talking about our son,' Bella replies, holding her nerve. Lifting her chin and pushing her shoulders back. Ignoring the frightened little voice inside telling her to shut up and get out of there. 'Mine and Ludwell's,' she adds. 'But only biologically speaking. Not in any way that matters. As far as Asher's concerned, he never had a father. Never needed one.'

'No.' Ludwell shakes his head. 'That's impossible, you know it is. I've no idea what she's on about, I swear,' he tells Julia. His voice is calm and level, but Bella can see the panic in his eyes as he turns back to face her. 'Why would you say that?'

'Because it's true.' It's Bella's voice that sounds shaky. Her bottom lip's starting to wobble as she takes a deep breath and forces herself to keep going. 'It's me, Isabella – Izzy – the student you took back to your house after we'd been drinking in The Black Swan nineteen years ago. The same student you threw out the next morning because your wife was coming home. I came to tell you I was pregnant – *twice* I tried to tell you – but you refused to listen. You wouldn't even let me get the words out. You were too busy denying anything had happened in the first place. Too busy threatening me. And it worked. I dropped out of uni and never told anyone who the father was. But Asher's the best thing that ever happened to me and I'm glad I didn't have to share him with you. I loved him enough for both of us.'

Ludwell's still shaking his head. All these years Bella's spent worrying that the truth will somehow find its way out and now the moment's finally come, no one believes her.

'No,' he insists. 'She's wrong,' he tells Julia. 'I *do* remember her now. But I never slept with her. You have to believe me, darling.'

Something twists inside Bella's chest. He can deny *her* all he wants but not Asher. 'He took me back to your house while you were away,' she insists, locking eyes with Julia. 'To your bedroom. With a clock shaped like a violin next to the bed, and a fancy en suite with a walk-in shower. With gold-coloured tiles behind the sink . . .'

Julia's nostrils flare. Her lips tighten into a narrow funnel of anger.

'I'm sorry,' Bella tells her. 'It was only the one night and it clearly didn't mean anything to your husband. But it changed my life forever. I'm sorry for *you* but not for what happened. Asher's my world. My whole world. And any man would be lucky to call himself his father.'

'No,' Ludwell insists. 'It's not what you think. Please, darling . . .'

'Don't you "darling" me, you lying bastard!' Julia roars, her face twisted with rage. She storms over to the wardrobe, yanks out a blue suitcase and throws it onto the bed.

'What are you doing?'

'What do you think?' she hisses, flinging in clothes – hangers and all – along with the books from the bedside table and the shoes from under the bed. 'I knew taking you back was a mistake, but you promised me the affair was a one-off. You swore blind to me. Once a cheating liar always a cheating liar, I guess.'

'I'm not lying. Please, you can't leave me,' says Ludwell. 'Not again.'

'Just watch me.'

'But the road's closed,' Bella points out. 'Nothing can get in or out until they've cleared away the trees that came down.'

'Then I'll find somewhere else to stay. There's a spare room nextdoor, isn't there? I'll sleep in the kitchen if I have to. Anywhere's better than here.'

Bella's never seen anybody pack a case with such speed or fury. And now Julia's zipping it back up again and wheeling it to the door.

'No,' Ludwell begs. 'This is crazy. Nothing happened, I swear.'

Julia doesn't answer. Her fingers are already reaching for the door handle.

'Please. You're my wife . . . for better or worse,' Ludwell cries, his voice growing higher with desperation. 'I love you.' And for a moment it looks like his plea's worked. Julia stops in her tracks, her hand dropping away from the door again. But now she's tugging at the rings on her finger – wedding, engagement and eternity – tears streaming down her face as she twists them free.

'No,' she says, flinging them back to land at Ludwell's feet. 'I *was* your wife. You know what?' she hisses, turning to Bella. 'You're welcome to him. *Slut.* Our lipstick friend got that bit right, didn't they?'

'You're being ridiculous,' Ludwell tells Julia, picking up the fallen rings and chasing after her as she yanks open the door and manoeuvres her case out into the corridor. 'Please Julia, I love you. I *need* you.'

'Ridiculous? *Ridiculous? You're* the ridiculous one,' Julia screeches. 'Get off me,' she says as he reaches for her. 'You're the one that needs *therapy,* and I don't mean music therapy.' She shoves him, hard, sending him sprawling backwards, twisting through the air as he falls. There's a shriek of pain as his face makes contact with the bathroom door handle, and a sickening crash as the side of his head bounces back into the doorframe. But Julia's already gone, the door slamming behind her. Or maybe it's the noise of Ludwell's skull slamming against the floor as he lands that Bella can hear. It all happens so quickly: the blur of his body as he falls, the spurt of blood running down his face, and his strangled cry of 'Julia' before he passes out altogether.

Shit, Bella thinks, frozen with shock. Her brain doesn't seem capable of proper thought, or action. Only expletives. All she can do is stand there, staring like an idiot, a string of swear words scrolling through her head. But then Ludwell lets out a low groan, blood trickling down over his mouth and dripping off the end of his chin, and the spell is broken.

'Julia,' he gasps. 'Where's Julia?'

'It's okay,' Bella tells him, trying to stay calm. Trying to ignore the queasy panic inside. 'Don't try and move.' That's what they say to people after an accident, isn't it? *Don't move. Stay still. Help's on its way.* She seems to remember something about keeping them warm, too. She pulls the duvet off the bed and drapes it over him, wincing at the sight of his closed-up left eye and the angry red swelling spreading across his face. 'I'm going to get Marie . . . or Stuart.' Someone with some first-aid experience who actually knows what to do with a barely conscious man still bleeding from the nose. Someone with access to a phone to call for an ambulance. 'Stay there,' she says, as if he's capable of doing anything else. 'I'll be back soon.'

Chapter 33

Bella doesn't have to go far to look for help. Marie's already on her way, her usually calm face a picture of concern.

'Is everything all right?' she asks. 'I just saw Julia. She seemed pretty upset.'

'Oh thank goodness,' Bella breathes. 'It's Ludwell. There's been an accident. He's in his room,' she adds. 'He's conscious now but he's still bleeding.'

'Okay,' says Marie, pulling a bunch of keys out of her pocket. 'I need you to stay calm for me, Bella. Can you do that?'

Bella nods, feeling anything *but* calm as she follows Marie back to the Storms' room.

'Is he going to be okay?' she asks, shaking now as Marie bends down to examine him, her long silvery hair falling like a curtain around his face. 'One minute he was just . . . and the next . . .' Her voice sounds strange and far away as if it belongs to someone else, and the thought of Ludwell's blood trickling into Marie's hair is making her feel quite peculiar. Their bedroom is suddenly the last place she wants to be. 'Sorry, I've come over a bit funny,' she says. 'I . . . I need to get out of here. Back to my room . . . I need to sit down.'

Marie turns briefly to face her. 'Hmm, yes, you do look very pale. Maybe you *would* be better off out of the way. Sit down and put your head between your knees once you're back in your room and take nice deep breaths. And try not to panic. He's going to be all right. It's really not as bad as it looks.'

'Are you sure?'

'I was a doctor for twenty years,' Marie tells her. 'I know what I'm doing. And once I've taken care of Ludwell, I'll come and check on you, okay?'

'Thank you,' Bella says gratefully, taking herself back to her own room as instructed and sitting down on the bed. She closes her eyes against the scarlet lipsticked message on her window and leans her head down over her legs as far as it will go.

What a mess, she thinks, as the guilt hits her. *It's all my fault.* Her need to tell the Storms everything, to make them understand, make them *believe*, has faded away again as quickly as it arrived. All she's done is make everything ten times worse. What if Marie's wrong? What if Ludwell *isn't* going to be fine? What if he loses his eye altogether, or ends up brain damaged? He might be a cheat and a liar – Bella's in full agreement with Julia there – but no one deserves that. He's Asher's dad, whether he's willing to admit it or not, and the two of them deserve the chance to get to know each other. If that's what Asher wants. Yes, Bella sees that now. But what if it's too little too late? What if she's already stolen that chance away from them? *Son stealer. Father stealer.*

'I'm sorry,' she whispers into the stillness of the room, gently rocking backwards and forward on the bed. That wasn't part of Marie's instructions but somehow the soothing rhythm and motion help. 'I'm sorry. I'm sorry. I'm sorry.' The words become a mantra as Bella sits there, rocking, blocking out the cacophony of conflicting thoughts battling for her attention. Blocking out the writing on the window and the knife under the bed. 'I'm sorry. I'm sorry.' She's still rocking, still chanting her whispered apologies however many minutes later – five, ten, fifteen? – when a sharp knock at the door rouses her from her hypnotic stupor.

Bella jumps, the rocking spell broken as she shifts back into high alert. 'Who's there?'

'It's Stuart. Can I come in?' But he's already letting himself in as he says it, the key already turning in the lock. 'I hear you've had a bit of a shock,' he says, as the door falls shut behind him, 'so I made you some sweet coffee.'

'Thank you.' Bella frowns. 'I thought it was tea you were supposed to drink after a shock.' That's what her mother always used to say, although the shock of her death had Bella reaching for the gin rather than the teabags.

'Coffee works just as well. It's the sugar that's the important bit. I'll leave it here for you,' he says, putting it down on the bedside table. 'Nice steady sips, that's the ticket. And I'll be back to check on you later, okay?'

'Wait, what about Ludwell? How is he?' Bella asks. Or maybe she only *thinks* it, because Stuart's already leaving, the door closing behind him again, leaving Bella alone with her coffee and a head full of guilt and worry.

She picks up the mug, steeling herself for the unpleasant sweetness, her mouth already puckering in anticipation as she brings it to her lips. *Yuck.* It's every bit as disgusting as she imagined but more palatable than the sweet milky tea after her plunge into the lake on Tuesday. She takes another sip to show willing. And then another. By the time Marie knocks on her door, it's almost all gone. Stuart was right, she does feel better for it. Calmer.

'How are you feeling now?' asks Marie.

'I'm okay,' says Bella. 'What about Ludwell? Will he need to go to hospital? How will he get there if the road's still blocked?' She imagines an air ambulance trying to land in the gravel parking area outside.

Marie shakes her head. 'He's going to be fine. I've given him a good check over and got him all cleaned up and there's nothing to worry about. Just a few cuts and bruises.'

Thank goodness.

'And the trees should be cleared by lunchtime.'

Even better. 'And Julia?'

Marie smiles. 'She's fine too. It's all taken care of. Everything's under control.' Her voice sounds different somehow though. Lower . . . and slower.

'And what about flights?' Bella asks. Her own voice sounds slower too. 'Is there . . .? Does that mean . . .?' She reaches for the right words. 'Can I go home?'

'I'm not sure you're fit to go anywhere right now, I'm afraid' says Marie. 'Not in your condition. You just stay there and finish your coffee. Drink up, that's it.'

No, Bella thinks. *I need to go home. I need to get out of here.* 'My phone . . . I need my phone back,' she says, the words slurring at the edges.

Marie shakes her head. '*Rest* is what *you* need.'

'No . . .' Bella says, blinking hard. It looks like there are two Maries now, both shaking their heads at her. 'I need . . . I need . . .' What *does* she need? She scans the room, trying to remember. There are two desks now as well . . . two windows filled with blood-red writing . . . what does the writing say again? Something about Asher . . . or Ludwell . . . She can't remember the words but she can remember the feeling. The fear.

I need to get out of here . . . Yes, that's it. I need to find a flight and get out of here. 'I need my phone,' Bella says again. 'Stuart said I could have it back if I needed it.'

The matching Maries smile as they take the double coffee cups from Bella's drooping hands. 'Did he? I guess we all say things we don't mean sometimes, don't we?'

What? I don't understand, Bella tries to answer. But her mouth doesn't seem to be working properly. Her lips are the wrong shape and her tongue . . . her tongue . . .

'Yes, we all say things we don't mean,' Marie repeats, guiding Bella's head down onto the pillow and pulling her legs up after

261

her, tucking her back into bed like a child. 'Like "I love you". Like "I've never felt this way about anyone else before".'

Bella's head swims as she tries to make sense of what Marie's saying. *What?* But she can't think straight. She can barely keep her eyes open. *Too tired. Something's wrong. Something's very wrong.*

*

Something's wrong. Izzy senses it even before she sees the blood on the sheet.

She screams for her sister, tears already coursing down her cheeks. What if it's all her fault? What if the baby knew he wasn't part of the plan? What if this is karma for those first terrified weeks when she wished him away?

'I didn't mean it. I love you,' she sobs, hands clasped round the curve of her belly. 'Please be all right.'

And then Rachel's there, wild-haired and breathless, telling her everything's going to be okay. 'We'll take you down to the hospital and get you checked out. Try not to panic. It's probably nothing.'

Please, please be nothing. Please let it be okay. Izzy's not even sure who she's appealing to. God? The universe? The baby? But she begs all the same. I'll do anything . . . whatever it takes to be a good mum. Just give me a chance. Give *us* a chance.

*

Head, body, arms, legs. Heart.

Please tell me it's still beating. 'Is he okay?' Izzy can barely get the words out for sobbing.

The pause before the sonographer replies is the longest pause of Izzy's life. 'Baby's doing fine,' he says at last. 'I can't see any cause for concern.'

'Are you sure?'

The sonographer's taut face relaxes into a smile. 'You've got yourself a nice, healthy boy there, Izzy.' But the slight lisp when he says her name reminds her of Ludwell . . . of his hands cupping her face . . . It reminds her of that article she read about the children's orchestra . . . about how much Ludwell and his wife would have liked a family of their own. The thought of losing her baby to him now – to them – is almost as scary as thinking she'd lost him altogether.

Izzy stares at the black-and-white image of her baby on the screen, a new determination taking hold of her. 'Bella,' she whispers, trying the name out for size. Bella Burnstone.

Maybe it's time she left Izzy behind – silly, dizzy Izzy who slept with her lecturer. Who stood in that office and let Ludwell Storm tell her nothing happened between them.

'Sorry?' says the sonographer. 'What was that?'

A proper grown-up name for a proper grown-up mother, *Izzy thinks.* Someone who thinks before she acts. Who puts her child first.

'My name's Bella,' she says.

Chapter 34

The air smells of chicken and warm cinnamon. Bella opens her eyes and stares at the red numbers on the bedside alarm clock, waiting for them to come into focus. 22:55. *No, that can't be right.* But no matter how hard she squints, screwing her eyes up against the heavy throbbing in her head, the numbers stay the same. But that means she's been asleep all day. That means it's Thursday night already.

'It's good to see you awake at last,' says a voice. 'I was starting to get worried.'

Krista, Bella thinks groggily. *How did she get in here?* She swallows, wincing at the soreness in her throat. It's hard to know what hurts more – her throat or her head.

But it's not Krista, it's Marie. 'I brought you a couple of paracetamols and some hot soup,' she says, her face looming suddenly into Bella's line of vision. 'You need to try and eat something. Can you sit up on your own, or do you need a hand?'

Something nags at the back of Bella's mind. Something about Marie . . .

'I . . . I don't know.' Bella's body feels like it belongs to someone else, her limbs somehow both heavy and floating at the same time. She pushes herself up on her hands, shuffling her bottom up the bed towards her pillow.

'That's it. Well done.' Marie places a bird-patterned melamine tray on Bella's lap, laden with food: a pale brown chicken broth with a light sheen of oil clinging to the surface, a buttered roll, a cinnamon bun, two white tablets nesting in a china dessert pot and a glass of water.

Bella gazes at the spread for a moment, trying to decide if she feels hungry or sick. Or both. But then she picks up the spoon and takes a long, slurping mouthful of soup, the hot liquid soothing her throat as she swallows it. *Mmm*, maybe she *is* hungry after all. And thirsty . . . She feels ferociously thirsty suddenly, in fact, as if she hasn't drunk in days, picking up the glass and draining it in one go.

'Steady now,' Marie warns her. 'You haven't been well. You're still very weak.'

'Not well?' Bella says, trying to remember. The gong bathing, she remembers that, and the needle . . . and . . . 'The writing!' she gasps, soup spilling over the top of the bowl as she recalls the hate-filled scarlet scrawl across her shower screen and window. 'Did you see it? It was right there,' she says, pointing to the pulled-down blind. 'And another one in the bathroom. There was someone here in my room.'

'Shhh,' says Marie, placing a steadying hand on top of the duvet. 'It's okay. Take it easy. I'll get you some more water. And don't forget your tablets. You'll feel better once they kick in.'

'But we need to find out who it was,' Bella stammers. 'They might be dangerous.'

She can hear Marie laughing from the bathroom as she refills the water glass. 'I think you must have dreamt it,' she calls back. 'There's nothing in here and if there's anything on the window, I'll be having words with Rosel. She was supposed to have cleaned them yesterday.'

'It's there on the window. I saw it,' Bella insists, 'written in bright red lipstick.'

Marie hands her the water glass and crosses over to the window, pulling up the blind with a theatrical flourish. 'Nothing there. See? You must have dreamt it,' she says again. 'You did seem a bit feverish earlier.'

A dream. Is that all? Bella downs the second glass just as quickly as the first but remembers to swallow the tablets this time.

'And Ludwell?' she asks. 'Did he hurt his face when Julia pushed him into the door or did I dream that bit too?'

'I think you must have done.' Marie laughs again. 'This dream of yours sounds very dark, I must say!'

Yes, Bella thinks, remembering the sickening crunch as his head hit the floor after Julia pushed him. *Because of what I told her*. That's right. In the dream she told Julia everything about that night with Ludwell. About Asher.

'I'm sure he'd be flattered to know that you're still pining for him after all these years,' Marie says, as Bella takes another spoonful of soup. 'Pathetic little bitch that you are.'

'Sorry, what?' Bella almost spits the soup straight back out again.

'I said I hope it's not too spicy. Saga can be a bit heavy-handed with the pepper sometimes.'

Bella stares at her in confusion. 'No, you didn't, you said . . .' But what she *thinks* she heard Marie say is too preposterous to repeat. Too awful. She must have misheard. Her heart is racing all the same though. 'I . . . I think I'm still a bit out of it,' she says, as the room starts to spin around her. 'Perhaps I'll leave the rest until later.'

What if it's her? What if Marie's the one who wrote the message. The very idea makes Bella's blood run cold.

'All right,' Marie agrees cheerfully, picking up the tray as if nothing's happened. 'I'll pop it on your desk for you, shall I?'

Bella forces a nod, resting her head back down on her pillow in an effort to stop the room from turning. Maybe she's still feverish. 'Thank you.'

'No problem.' Marie deposits the tray and comes back to the

bed, smiling. She leans in close, smoothing the duvet down over Bella's shoulders, the silver heart on her charm bracelet glinting in the overhead light. 'Nothing's too much trouble for a son-stealing slut like you,' she hisses.

There's no mistaking it this time.

'It was you,' Bella gasps, trying to claw her way out of the bedcovers as a dark wooziness spreads through her limbs. She doesn't understand what's happening. She doesn't know why Marie would say those things . . . would *write* those things. All she knows is she has to get out of here before . . . before . . . But her body seems to have glued itself to the bed and her head is too heavy to lift. And her eyes . . . her eyes are even heavier . . .

*

The dreams – the nightmares – are relentless. Oscar's chasing Bella through the lodge with the kitchen knife, telling her it's for research. Telling her she needs to die so that his book can live . . . and now Bella's hammering at the door, clawing at it with her nails – *let me out, let me out, I have to save Asher* – but it's sealed shut, and now . . . and now somehow it's not Oscar any more, it's Marie, scarlet lipstick painted round her mouth like a clown, with maggots crawling over her hair.

Let me out!

01:26. Someone else is hammering at the door now, from the outside, calling her name. Bella forces her eyes open, her heart racing. Something's wrong, she knows that. Something happened – something bad – but she can't remember what.

'Bella, please, wake up! It's Julia! She's gone.'

Ludwell.

'You have to help me find her. You have to tell her it's not true.' His words sound slurred at the edges. 'I never slept with you.'

But you did, Bella thinks. *Why would I tell her that?* It's taken nineteen years after her first attempt to finally get the words out – to tell them about Asher – and she's not taking them back again now. Except that was only in her dream, wasn't it? Marie said she only *dreamt* that Julia pushed Ludwell into the door . . . But that was before . . . yes, she remembers now, before Marie called her a son-stealing slut. *The writing on the window. It was Marie.* Unless . . . Was that a dream too? Is this?

'Please,' Ludwell begs. 'He's not my son. He can't be.'

Bella doesn't *feel* like she's dreaming. She feels sluggish and nauseous but awake. Just about. Awake enough to notice the sweat pooling under her back. To hear her blood pounding in her ears. Awake enough to experience a muted rush of anger mixed in with her fear and confusion. Even as she's struggling to keep from slipping under again, back into the dizzy darkness waiting behind her eyelids to claim her, she knows what Ludwell's saying is wrong. *You don't get to decide if he's your son or not,* she thinks. *That's up to Asher.*

She opens her mouth to tell him exactly that, but it must be a dream after all because the muscles in her mouth don't seem to work and she can't get the words to come out.

'That's enough,' comes a second voice from outside. Bella holds her breath, listening hard. It's Marie again. But which Marie? The kind, Zen-like retreat host, or the nightmare version who breaks into guests' rooms and writes poisonous messages over their windows? Bella's head feels like it's swimming trying to work it out. Swimming, spinning, splitting. Did Marie really call her a son-stealing slut?

'Julia's perfectly safe,' Marie's saying. 'She's back in the UK now. Stuart took her to the airport this morning.' But that's wrong too. The road was still blocked. Marie said it wouldn't be clear until lunchtime. Or was that yesterday?

'No,' Ludwell says. 'No, she can't be. I have to talk to her. I have to make her see. It's not true – none of it's true.'

Bella clings to his words as the darkness comes for her – *it's not true. None of it's true* – praying that this time he's right.

*

04:38. It's Bella's bladder that rouses her this time. But not for long. Not long enough. By the time her brain can make sense of the wet warmth running down her thighs, seeping into the sweat-damp sheet beneath her, she's already gone again.

*

05:56. Something's not right. The bed feels cold and wet. And the smell . . . Bella sniffs. It smells like sodden reusable nappies waiting to be disinfected. It's a long time since she's smelt that. There are no nappies here though. Just her and the wet bed and her wet jeans and knickers . . . and the back of her T-shirt . . . *No. She hasn't. She can't have done.* But she has.

Shocked, finally, into proper wakefulness, Bella drags herself out of bed and rips off the offending sheet. The smell and the shame prick tears from her eyes as she bundles it up into a ball and stuffs it into the shower, climbing in after it. She turns the tap on full blast and lets the water cascade down on her head like a punishment, gasping for breath at the cold hits, soaking into the thick denim of her jeans. How has it come to this? How did she end up here?

The water begins to warm after a while but Bella still feels cold inside. Cold, scared and out of control. And dirty.

I'm not well, she tells herself. *That's why I didn't wake up in time. Because I'm sick.* It's true. Her head is pounding and muddled, her muscles ache, and her heartbeat's all over the place. What if she's not fit enough to travel by Saturday? By *tomorrow,* she realises with a jolt. It's Saturday tomorrow. Is that right? But that would mean she's slept through an entire day . . .

I have to get out of here, she thinks, staring at the shower screen – the perfectly clear shower screen. Bella runs her fingers across the glass searching for a trace of lipstick letters. For a sign that she didn't dream the entire thing. But the glass is smooth and clean to the touch. The lipsticked message seems to have slipped away as she slept, like her own weakening grip on reality.

Chapter 35

Bella abandons her wet sheet and clothes in the shower and pulls on fresh jeans and a clean T-shirt and jumper. She needs to get out of here. She needs to find out if the road really is open again and work out her escape. But she can't ask Marie, not after last night. Or Stuart. What if it's not a bug making her sick and confused? What if she was drugged? It could have been something in the coffee Stuart brought her. Or Marie's soup. Or the paracetamols she swallowed like an idiot, without thinking . . .

Rosel, she thinks. *Rosel must have her own phone – she'll be able to find out for me. I'll ask her to call me a taxi.* And Rosel must have keys to the office too. Maybe she can be persuaded to retrieve Bella's phone from Marie's black box.

It doesn't take her long to throw the rest of her clothes into her suitcase, even in her woozy state, along with her manuscript paper and toiletries. She weighs up packing the kitchen knife too, sticking it into her rucksack pocket for ease of access, just in case, but then dismisses the idea. She'll be safe enough once she's out of here. And besides, what if she forgets about it? What if she turns up at airport security with a four-inch blade tucked into her bag? That would take some explaining. She hides it away in the desk drawer instead, too embarrassed to take it back to

270

the kitchen in case someone spots her, tucking it out of sight underneath the pamphlet of local legends.

That's everything, Bella thinks, casting a quick eye around the room. *Wait, no it's not – Asher's jumper!* She can't leave without that – it feels like leaving a part of *him* behind. It's not just the thought of all those early mornings he put in to pay for it, struggling up the hill with the heavy bag of papers, *or* the idea of him trawling round the clothes shops on his own in search of the perfect shade of blue. It's the memory of his face when he gave it to her, the curious mixture of excitement, pride and worry in his eyes as she peeled open the wrapping paper. 'You do like it, don't you?' he'd asked, in that new low voice of his, before she'd even finished unwrapping it.

'I love it,' she told him.

No, Bella can't leave without at least *looking* for the jumper, no matter how desperate she is to get away. What if she really is in danger? What if she doesn't make it home? How can she turn her back on what might be her last remaining link with her son? Krista said she left it soaking in the laundry room, didn't she? Maybe it's still there. She can check on the way.

Bella leaves her bags by her bed, all ready to go, picks up her key and creeps across the corridor to the laundry room. She opens the door and switches on the light, expecting to find a glorified airing cupboard with a washing machine and tumble dryer. The room's considerably bigger than that though, with two enormous washing machines side by side and a matching pair of dryers. It's got double-fitted cupboards, a gleaming white worktop with a full Belfast sink, a pull-down ironing board *and* a free-standing steam ironing press by the far wall. There's no sign of her jumper though. It's not soaking in the sink and it's not waiting, forgotten, in either of the machines. She'll have to add that to the list of things to ask Rosel.

Something on the floor catches Bella's eye as she turns to leave, something silver and shiny sticking out from under one of

271

the cupboards. It looks like . . . yes, it looks like a lizard – half of one anyway. Part of an earring, maybe, or a charm from a bracelet? She bends down to investigate, too fast, shutting her eyes against the sudden wave of dizziness that engulfs her. *Woah. Bad idea.* But then the dizziness passes and she opens her eyes again, reaching for it with her fingers. It's stuck fast though, the other half jammed tight underneath the kickboard. Bella thinks of Marie's silver charm bracelet, the one she fiddles with whenever she talks about her son. Maybe it's one of hers.

Her initial instinct is to leave well alone and get out of there. The memory – real or dreamt – of Marie leaning over her as she lay in bed, hissing those horrible words into her ear, still gives her the shivers. But then curiosity gets the better of her. It reminds her of something – something she can't quite put her finger on . . .

She pushes at one end of the cupboard plinth, a forgotten memory bubbling up out of nowhere as the wooden board springs free from its fixings. It's nothing to do with charms or bracelets though. She's thinking of Asher, of the time he 'broke the kitchen' practising his skids on Rachel's freshly polished floor. She's remembering how hard he cried when he came to tell her. '*I'm sorry, Mummy. I didn't mean to break it. Please don't tell Aunty Rachel.*' Remembering how tightly he'd hugged her after she 'mended' it, promising through his broken sobs that he'd never do it again.

Bella's on all fours now as she picks up the freed silver lizard. She was right. It's a charm from a bracelet. It *must* be Marie's. How did it get down there though, trapped so tightly underneath the plinth? She bends down even further, peering into the dark gap underneath the cupboard with a prickling sense of foreboding. There's something else there too . . .

A notebook. A *hidden* notebook. Presumably that's Marie's too. She must have caught the charm on her bracelet when she was down there on her hands and knees, tucking the notebook out of sight under the cupboard. But why would she do that?

Bella breathes through another wave of dizziness as she leans in to fetch it. She's thinking of the anonymous note under her door, written on lined paper torn from a notebook. Was it from *this* one?

Her hands are trembling as she pulls it out and examines it more closely. It's expensive-looking, with a hard yellow cover and an elasticated loop to hold it shut. It's also surprisingly clean and dust-free for something that's been hidden away underneath a cupboard, out of reach of any passing vacuum cleaners. Except somehow Bella's not surprised at all.

Marie must have sent the note, she thinks, unlooping the matching yellow elastic. *She must have known about me and Ludwell all along.*

The tremor in her hands is a full-on shake as she opens the cover and turns to the first page.

What the . . .?

Bella stares in disbelief at the pasted-in photograph. It's her. It's her profile picture from her Facebook page, with her name written underneath in black ink, followed by two dates: the date of her birth and then a dash and then . . . and then tomorrow's date.

No, no, no. Her brain might still be a little fuzzy but Bella's cognisant enough to realise what it is she's looking at. Two dates together like that can only mean one thing . . .

She lets out a low moan of fear as she turns over to the next page. More writing – a bullet-pointed biography of some kind. *Her* biography, starting with the names of her parents and her school, her university . . . and Ludwell. His name's there too, underlined twice in red ink, and Asher, of course. Even Nat gets a mention. What *is* this?

Bella flicks through the pages – forward and back – in a blind panic. There's a picture of her and Asher on holiday in Crete a few years earlier, also taken from her Facebook page . . . a grainy black-and-white picture from the local newspaper of her, Nat and the Peters twins, holding up their A-level results . . . a carefully folded copy of her interview about *The Screaming Hours* in

Culture Vulture, with her comment about the killer's signature tapping sound – about weaving it through the score to increase the viewers' sense of unease and tension – highlighted in yellow.

The scratching noise, she thinks. Maybe there's a connection. Maybe Marie's been using Bella's own musical tactics against her, hiding out in the empty room and scratching her nails through the thinness of the wall to try and freak her out. And was it Marie who invited Ludwell here as the special guest? Is it *all* Marie? Why would a retreat host in Sweden – a complete stranger – be so obsessed with Bella's life? With making her life such a misery? She flicks on through the notebook, her heart thumping in her chest as she searches for clues. For something to make sense of it all.

There's a copy of Lena's article about Ludwell's affair with the politician . . . another newspaper cutting of sixth-formers holding up their exam results, only this time it's Asher and *his* friends stood outside the school. More photos taken from her Facebook page . . . The more Bella sees, the sicker she feels. The entire notebook is about her. Her and Asher. And Ludwell.

No, actually that's not quite right. Not *all* the pages are filled. There must be twenty or so blank pages right at the end, and two shorn stubs where the pages have been torn out . . .

Bella flinches at a noise from the far end of the room – a clanking sound from the pipes – shutting the notebook with a start. Marie could be coming back for it at any moment and Bella can't afford to be there when she does. And if she's right about the date under her photo on the first page, then she definitely can't afford to still be here – at the lodge – by tomorrow.

She wants me dead, Bella thinks, shaking all over as she levers the plinth back into position and hauls herself up onto her feet, clutching onto the cupboard handles for support. *Marie wants me dead*. This isn't somebody with a sick sense of humour pulling twisted pranks any more. It never was. The note, the apple, the needle, the lipsticked messages . . . they were merely the warm-up, weren't they? Warnings of what's to come.

Chapter 36

Bella takes the notebook back to her room to examine more closely, still shaking as she shuts the door behind her. She needs to be sure she's got this right – that it's Marie, and Marie alone, who's behind it all – before she goes charging off looking for help. Stuart could be in on it too – they might be working together. And what about Rosel? Could she be involved as well? She's certainly good at keeping secrets and covering for people – nobody guessed about Saga and Hamar, did they? What if she's been keeping Marie's secrets too? Maybe it *was* her who took the note out of Bella's bin that first morning, and then lied about it afterwards. And maybe . . . yes, maybe Rosel was *told* to find that hypodermic needle in her room. *Told* to make sure that everyone else got to hear about it, so that they'd all think Bella was some kind of junkie. Perhaps she does whatever she's told. Whatever she's paid to do.

Bella searches through the notebook more methodically this time, trying to make sense of it all. Why would Marie be so obsessed with a nobody like her? There are screenshot print-outs of her tweets . . . more pictures taken from her Facebook account . . . pictures from Asher's Instagram account . . . The thought of Marie snooping round *his* social media, of snooping into *his* life, makes her feel even shakier. *You leave him out of this,* she thinks – not that she knows what 'this' is – *or I'll . . . I'll . . .* Bella's not sure *what* she'll do, exactly. But she'd do anything to protect him, she knows that much.

She keeps on turning the pages. There's that Facebook photo of her and Asher in Crete again . . . and there, on the other side is another – her favourite one of all. Bella stares at the cheesy double-selfie taken on the harbourside in Chania, and her panic begins to crystallise into something harder and sharper. Into determination. She's not a nobody, she's a mother. And there's no way she's letting Sunday morning's goodbye to Asher be their final farewell. It doesn't matter *what* Marie's strange, twisted game is about, or who else is involved. Just so long as Bella gets out of there. As long as she gets back to her boy.

That's when she hears it – the soft tap of footsteps coming along the corridor. The sound of someone stopping outside her room. The sound of a door opening . . .

Not *her* door though. It must be the laundry room. She stiffens, holding her breath as she listens. *What if it's Marie, come back for her notebook? What will she do when she discovers it's gone?*

Bella doesn't wait to find out. She needs to *get* out. She can't risk going through the door though – not with the laundry room just across the corridor. Still clutching the notebook, she races over to the desk instead, scrambling on top of it and yanking the window open as wide as it will go.

There's another noise from behind . . . the sound of a key turning in the lock. But Bella's already halfway out the window, her elbow scraping against the handle as she squeezes her body through the gap. The pain barely registers. She's too busy leaping off the sill, setting off at a panting run the moment her socked feet touch the ground.

That's when she remembers the knife in the desk drawer. It's too late to go back for it now though. Too late to worry about a jumper or coat . . . or shoes. Yes, shoes would have been a good idea too. The gravel in the parking area is sharp and spiky through the thin fabric of her socks but she forces herself on, faster and faster.

'Bella!' A cry follows after her.

Marie.

She's coming.

'Wait! Come back!'

Bella's not waiting though. She's not going back. She'll run, stagger and crawl all the way back to the main road if she has to – to civilisation – clambering over any fallen trees on her hands and knees. But then she thinks about the minibus waiting there, ready to go. Ready to follow her up the track . . . Her escape will be over before it's begun.

She changes direction, heading for the lake path instead, the beginnings of a plan forming in her head as she runs. Saga and her wife live on the other side of the lake . . . hopefully their house won't be too hard to find. She'll head there and tell them what's been happening, hoping against hope that Saga's not in on it too. Hoping they believe her. She's got the notebook now, at least. That's proof of Marie's obsession. Proof of her true intentions towards Bella. She'll show them the first page with the dates under her picture and get them to call for help. For the police.

It's going to be okay, she tells herself as she hits the needle-strewn path, already gasping for breath.

I'm going to get help.

I'm going to get home.

Home to Asher.

It's Asher who gives her the strength to keep going as her lungs begin to burn, as the muscles in her legs begin to scream. It's been a long time since Bella's run anywhere and the harder she pushes herself, the more her body protests. But she forces herself on, thinking of her baby boy. She thinks about those raw, sleepless nights pacing the house while he screamed, and his first day at nursery when he went running off to join the other children before she could even say goodbye. She thinks about the school play where he forgot his lines and made up a different speech altogether. Another child might have lost their nerve and got upset, but not Asher. She thinks about his pale-faced smile as they stretchered him off the rugby pitch with a broken leg, and the way he buckled down harder than ever after his disappointing mock results.

It's going to be all right, she promises him as she runs, a blur of trees whipping past her. As another cry breaks the air behind her:

'Bella!'

It's louder this time. Angrier.

'Izzy!'

No, Bella thinks, as she passes the turning for the bird hide. *Izzy's gone.*

'This isn't part of the plan,' Marie shouts, a shrill edge of hysteria to her voice. 'You're doing it wrong.'

Bella doesn't have enough breath to answer. Her chest feels like it's going to explode. Not that there *is* an answer – only questions. *Why are you doing this? What have I ever done to you?* She's barely got enough breath to *think* any more. *Keep going,* is as much as she can manage now, the same two words pounding through her brain, over and over.

Keep going.

Keep going.

She's almost at the lake now. She can see the silvery surface of the water glimmering in the early morning light.

Keep going.

She can see the wooden landing stage up ahead. The circling birds swooping down towards the low bushes at the water's edge . . .

. . . towards the bloated body floating facedown in the shallows, legs tangled in the slimy weeds.

There's no keeping going after that.

Chapter 37

Bella stares in horror, bile rising in her throat.

A red striped blouse, she thinks, as a wild trembling takes hold of her entire body.

Lena's red striped blouse, she thinks, shutting her eyes against the gruesome sight. But she can still see it even through her closed eyelids. The image is already burnt into her brain. *That's what she was wearing on Tuesday night . . . the last time I saw her. The last time* anyone *saw her.*

'This can't be happening,' Bella whimpers. It's like a dream. It's like a scene from a thriller. From a horror film. But she knows she's awake this time. She knows this is real. She can feel the damp creeping through her socks. Can feel the cold morning air biting at her bare arms. She can hear Marie drawing closer and closer, the older woman's breath almost as ragged as her own. Bella knows she's in more danger than ever – *keep going, keep going* – but she can't move. *That* feels like a dream too, her legs rooted in place, refusing to co-operate.

'L-lena,' she stammers, opening her eyes and twisting round to face her pursuer. 'What did you do to her?'

But Marie doesn't answer. She's too busy swiping at Bella's head with a broken-off tree branch. That's what it looks like anyway in the millisecond before it makes contact with Bella's head, and then . . .

And then nothing.

*

Bella's back in Crete, with Asher, looking for their hotel. He's younger this time though – six or seven, maybe – and the streets of Chania are darker and more labyrinthine than she remembers. They seem to be walking round and round in circles.

'Stay with Mummy,' Bella tells him as she rubs at matching rows of insect bites around each wrist. 'We'll be there soon.' They *have* to be there soon. If they don't find the hotel by nightfall, they won't be allowed to check in. But Asher slips away into the gathering night as she stops to examine the map and no amount of running after him and screaming his name can bring him back. And then Bella's mother is there, shushing away her tears and telling her everything's going to be all right. Telling her Asher will be fine without her. Telling her to drink up her water like a good girl.

Bella drinks. She *is* a good girl. She doesn't mean to make her mother sad. She doesn't mean to make her cry. 'I'm sorry,' she whispers between sips. 'I'm sorry.'

'It's a little late for that,' her mother says in Marie's voice, laying her head back down on the pillow. 'Don't you think?'

*

It's dark when Bella wakes again, her head throbbing and a bruised feeling all along her spine. The blurred red numbers on the alarm clock tell her nothing. *The alarm clock? Wait, that's not right.* The last thing she remembers is running towards the lake with the notebook. That's when she saw it – saw *her. Lena.* And then . . . There's nothing after that. Nothing but scrambled dreams, strange aches and the thick throb of pain inside her skull.

Someone must have brought me back to the lodge, she realises, as her eyes adjust to the gloom.

For one crazy, hopeful moment she allows herself to picture a rescuer. Saga on her way to work, perhaps, stumbling across her fallen body. Or Krista out on an early morning walk. She imagines Krista running back to the lodge for help. Imagines Krista and Oscar carrying her prostrate body to safety between them while Hamar and T force their way into the office to tackle Marie and Stuart and call for backup. But the fantasy's over as soon as it's begun. As soon as she tries to move and feels the tight bands of rope against the cuffs of her jumper. As soon as she lifts her head and sees the shadowy figure waiting at the end of her bed with a hypodermic needle. There *was* no rescue, was there? Judging by the bruises on her back she was probably bundled back in a wheelbarrow while everyone else was asleep, or while they were all in a workshop, out of sight.

'No!' Bella shouts as the figure comes into focus. 'Get away from me.'

But it's no good. Here she comes . . .

'No,' she says again. It's more of a whimper this time though. 'Please,' Bella begs. 'Why are you doing this?'

'You really don't know, do you?' says Marie, her face twisted into a sneer. As she rests the tip of the needle against Bella's arm. 'But *I* know. I know what you did.'

*

'Bella! It's Krista. Stuart's taking us to the airport now. I just wanted to say goodbye. I hope you and Ludwell are feeling better soon. And I hope you get the help you need.'

Krista . . . The help I need, Bella thinks, turning the words over in her head, trying to make sense of them. *Krista . . .* She knows that name from somewhere. Krista, yes, that's right. The lady from the retreat.

The retreat . . .

Dead Man's Forest . . .

Lena! Bella's eyes flick open as it comes flooding back to her in a giddy rush of fear and nausea, of breathless panic. But she can't open her mouth. There's something stuck tight over her lips, gluing them together. Her hands and feet are bound too.

'No, don't go!' she screams. *Tries* to scream. But what comes out is nothing more than a garbled hum.

How can Krista and the others be leaving? How can it be Saturday already? A wild trembling takes hold of Bella as she remembers the dates in the front of the notebook. *Today's the day. The day Marie . . . the day I . . .*

'Please,' she tries to say, struggling in vain against the tape across her mouth, straining against her bindings. *You need to fetch help*, she thinks. *You need to call the police.* But it's no good. Krista's already gone.

Despair kicks in as she hears the minibus reversing on the gravel. As she hears it driving off without her. That's it. They've gone without her. No fallen trees to keep them here any more – if indeed there ever *were* any. It's all over.

Tears course down Bella's cheeks as she thinks of Asher, waiting for a message to tell him she's home safely. How long until he guesses something's wrong? What if it's too late by then? What if she never gets to see him again? Never gets to hear his voice, his laugh? Never gets to wrap him, embarrassed and protesting, in another hug? What if she never gets to tell him how much she loves him? How she wouldn't swap a single second of their life together. Not the late-night taxi service. Not the rows. Not the dirty nappies or the smelly football kit . . .

I love you, she shouts inside her head, picturing him propped up at his kitchen table, bleary-eyed and half-asleep, scrolling through his phone as he spoons chocolate-flavoured cereal into his mouth.

I love you, she tells him, over and over again, as if she can reach across an entire sea through the sheer strength of her feelings. *I love you. I love you. I'll never stop loving you, no matter what . . .*

No matter what she does to me. Bella doesn't want to think about what that means. She *can't* let herself think about that. But

282

it's too late. Something warm and wet trickles down the tops of her thighs as she remembers Lena's body floating in the shallows of the lake. Was that Marie too? Did she kill Lena? *And now she's coming back for me . . .*

She's coming.

Oh Asher. I'm sorry. I'm sorry I won't be there for you. She thinks of the rest of his life stretching out long and lonely without her. No mother to pick him up at the end of term – that's if he even makes it through university after this. No smiling parent taking photos at his graduation. No one except his aunty and uncle to pose for family portraits at his wedding. No proud grandma to help with babysitting.

No. She can't do that to him. Asher needs her. Yes, he's an adult now, but he's still her baby boy. A fresh rush of adrenaline and determination floods through Bella's body as she struggles against her bindings. Ludwell's still here too, that's what Krista said. Maybe the two of them together still have a chance. If Stuart's taking the others back to the airport that means Marie's on her own. That means there's two of them and only one of her.

Bella thinks of the knife inside her desk drawer as she grinds her right wrist against the edge of the headboard, trying to saw through the rope. It's futile, she knows that, but it's better than lying there in a pool of her own urine, waiting for the end. For as long as she can still fight, she can still hope. Maybe she can talk Marie round, mother to mother, make her see what it will do to Asher if he loses her now. Whatever her issue with Bella is, whatever's behind Marie's twisted obsession with her life – with her and Ludwell's one-night affair – surely she wouldn't want to destroy *his* life too? Whatever Bella did or didn't do, none of it's his fault.

Now's her chance to find out. Bella swallows down a muted cry of terror at the sound of a key turning in the lock. The door opens and there she is.

Marie sniffs the air, wrinkling up her nose in distaste. 'Oh dear,' she says, crouching down next to the bed and breathing warm, herb-scented breath into Bella's face. 'Did someone have a little accident?'

'You're crazy,' Bella shouts behind her tape gag. 'Get away from me.'

'Sorry, what was that?' asks Marie. She reaches a hand to Bella's cheek, peeling up an edge of the tape with a short-cut fingernail. And then, without warning, she wrenches it clean off, tearing at the skin round Bella's mouth. 'Shhh,' she says softly in response to her howl of pain. 'There's no need to upset yourself. No need to be embarrassed. That's what the mattress protector's for. I can always change the sheets again. Afterwards.'

Bella lets out a whimper of fear. 'Afterwards? What do you mean, "afterwards"? After what?'

But Marie carries on as if she hasn't heard. 'Nat was just the same towards the end. No longer in control of his own body. Or his mind,' she adds. 'Imagining things – such dreadful things – that weren't there . . . things that no one else could see. But they were real to him. They were real and scary and it broke my heart to see him suffering like that.'

Bella's breath comes fast and shallow as she stares at Marie in confusion. *Nat? As in my old boyfriend, Nat?* Has she been stalking him too? And what does she mean by 'towards the end'? None of this makes any sense . . . unless . . . unless . . . 'The son you lost,' Bella murmurs, the pieces finally clicking into place. 'It was Nat, wasn't it? *My* Nat.' *You're his mother.* The thin-faced, silver-haired woman in front of her now bears no relation to the woman in her memory – the woman in the framed photograph on Nat's desk. Time and grief have worn away any remembered family likeness. But she's right, isn't she? Bella can see it in the older woman's eyes. Can see the pain when she mentions his name.

Marie shakes her head. 'No,' she says. 'That's just it. He *wasn't* yours, was he? You made that quite clear. *Crystal* clear. I read his diary and the letters – your letter to him and all the ones that he wrote to you, half of them sent back unread. You broke my boy's heart and you killed him.'

Bella blinks. 'What? No! I didn't kill *anyone*. I don't know what happened to him. We lost touch after we split up. I went to live with my sister when my mum threw me out and I never saw him again . . .'

'You killed him,' Marie repeats, her voice cold and hard. 'All those years of drink and drugs . . . the depression. The overdose. It all started with you. You and Ludwell. He dropped out of college four weeks after you dumped him, did you know that? Never took his A levels. Stopped turning up for his job. You're the ones who knocked him off course. You're the ones who started his spiral into addiction. It was all you.'

No, not Nat. Not poor, sweet Nat. 'I'm so sorry,' Bella says. 'I . . . I didn't know. I didn't realise.'

'Of course you didn't. You never gave him a second thought, did you? You were too busy slutting around with your university lecturer.'

'No.' Bella's bottom lip trembles. 'I wasn't. I didn't.' But she's thinking of the red lipsticked SLUT on her shower screen and the matching ADULTERER on Ludwell's window. Marie already knows what happened between them. She must do. And about Asher . . . *SON STEALER*. Except maybe Asher wasn't the stolen son after all, she realises with a jolt. Maybe it wasn't about Bella keeping Asher from his father. It was about her stealing Nat away from Marie.

'I read your letter,' Marie says again, with a snarl. 'You said you'd moved on and he'd be better off without you. Moved on to your teacher. That's what you meant, wasn't it?'

Bella's voice is high and squeaky with fear. 'No, it wasn't like that. I wrote that letter before anything happened, I swear. And it was only ever one night . . .'

'I read his diary,' Marie repeats, talking across her. 'He *knew*. He knew how obsessed you were with him. He knew that's why

285

you'd chosen to study there. With *Ludwell Storm*. He knew that's why you'd ended it. Why you wouldn't even read his letters any more, sending them back, unopened.'

'It wasn't Ludwell,' Bella insists. 'That was afterwards. And it didn't mean anything. I can't even remember it. And neither can he.' *He's still denying it, even now.* 'It was just one night,' she whimpers as a double rush of guilt sweeps through her. Guilt over Nat, and guilt for having dragged Ludwell into this crazy, twisted mess. Where is he now? What's Marie done to him? 'It was a mistake. If I could go back and change things I would.'

Except she wouldn't. Of course she wouldn't. Without that night nineteen years ago there'd be no Asher. And without Asher there'd be no *her*.

'None of this has anything to do with Ludwell,' she says. 'He's not responsible for what happened to Nat, and nor am I. It was an overdose – you said so – and that's terrible. A terrible thing to happen and a tragic waste of a life. But it was an accident. You have to stop this. You have to let us go.'

'It wasn't an accident,' says Marie slowly. 'He left a note.'

Nausea rises in Bella's throat. But she's not thinking of Nat. In her head it's Asher lying pale and lifeless on the bed. It's *his* empty needle rolling away across the floor. His note waiting on the pillow beside him. 'I'm sorry,' she says, shaking her head. Trying to shake away the image. 'I'm sorry for him and I'm sorry for you. I can't even begin to imagine what that must feel like. But you can't blame me.'

'No,' Marie agrees. 'I blame myself. I blame myself for letting him live with his dad in the first place. Maybe if I'd been more than a weekend mother, I'd have spotted the signs sooner. I wasn't there for him when he needed me most, but I'm here now. I'm here to put things right.'

'And that's what this has all been about? Every horrible, creepy thing that's happened this week . . . it was you. And Ludwell . . . and Lena . . . you arranged for them to be here too.' *So much*

286

twisted thought and planning, Bella thinks, with a shudder. 'What happened to Lena?'

'Lena was a mistake,' Marie admits. 'I invited her here as a way of punishing Ludwell – of rubbing his face in his own disgrace and humiliation. The fact that his wife was here as well was a bonus. But she wasn't supposed to start poking around in things that were nothing to do with her. Once she found out who T was, she was like a dog with a bone. Digging . . . always digging . . . Getting hold of the spare keys and breaking into the office . . . going through my records, looking for proof . . . rifling through my desk . . . That's how she found the notebook . . .'

The notebook! That's what Lena wanted to show me, Bella realises. But the part about T is a mystery.

'What do you mean? What's T got to do with this? What have you done to *him*?'

Marie laughs. 'I haven't done anything to T. He's on his way home with everyone else, taking his secrets with him . . . until someone else puts two and two together and realises that scruffy, unassuming T Helton is the same T Helton behind that high-end dating app that's all the rage in the States. *Was* all the rage. The one that guy in Vermont was using to source his victims.'

Bella doesn't know what app Marie's talking about, or what happened in Vermont, and right now she doesn't much care. 'But what happened to Lena down at the lake . . . that wasn't anything to do with T, was it?' For a moment she wonders, thinking of the argument she saw between them. Then she catches sight of the look on Marie's face and she knows. 'You killed her,' she says, fresh bile rising in her throat. *That's how the notebook ended up in the laundry room. You stole it back after you killed her and hid it somewhere safer.* 'You're the only killer here. Not me.'

'That wasn't part of the plan,' Marie admits. 'I had to improvise.'

'The plan?' Bella echoes. 'The note, the needle, the lipsticked messages . . . you had it all worked out before I even got here, didn't you? And the apple – that was you too, wasn't it? I didn't imagine it after all.'

'An apple for your teacher, just like in the Bing Crosby song,' says Marie. 'I thought it was rather apt.'

'And the scratching noise I kept hearing in the night. I'm guessing that was you too?'

Marie nods. '"The Coffin Filler" is one of Stuart's favourite stories. He's been sharing it with guests since *I* first started coming here. I thought it would be a nice touch to bring it alive for you, after I read your interview, seeing as you're such an expert on creepy sounds. A simple speaker sewn into the back of the sofa,' she adds proudly. 'I'm guessing it worked . . . although it was no match for that special "camomile tea" I put out for you, was it? You were spark out after that.'

Bella's still trying to put the pieces together. It wasn't just her tea that was drugged, was it? 'You're the one who slipped something into my drink before the gong bathing session, aren't you? Because you wanted me to suffer like Nat suffered, is that it? You wanted me to feel the same sense of paranoia? To lose *my* grip on reality, just like he did?'

'I wanted you to *share* what he went through,' Marie says. 'I wanted the rest of the world to judge you, like they judged him.'

It worked, Bella thinks, remembering the look on Krista's face when she asked her about the needle at lunch on Wednesday. She thinks how crazy her own wild accusations sounded – even to herself – as she tried to explain. As she tried to make sense of all the strange things that had been happening to her. 'And now?' she asks, dreading the answer, a cold trickle of sweat already snaking down her back. 'Now that you've done all that. What happens next?'

'You finish it,' says Marie. 'You and Nat together again, like he always wanted.'

288

Chapter 38

'No!' The word comes tearing out of Bella with surprising force. 'That's crazy. *You're* crazy.'

Marie laughs. 'Me? You're the one who's been flinging round ridiculous accusations all week. The one who's been seeing things that aren't there. *You're* the one with the problem. That's what everyone thinks. Even Asher. And that's what they'll tell the police after I find you . . . too late to save you from yourself, sadly.'

A bolt of pure panic shoots through Bella's body. 'Asher?' she echoes. 'What do you mean?'

'Don't worry. I've been keeping him fully updated on your progress – your decline, rather. He's been ever so worried about you, bless him. Such a sweet, caring lad, isn't he? Just like my Nat.'

'What do you mean?' Bella says again, her voice cracking. 'When? How?'

Marie pulls Bella's phone out of her pocket by way of an answer and opens up WhatsApp in front of her, to reveal a long chain of messages between her and Asher. 'You really should be more careful when it comes to choosing a password for your phone you know. Your son's birthday, honestly – it was too easy! Let's see . . . He says he's settling in well and he hopes you had a good flight . . . that's because I deleted your last message before

I put your phone onto our Wi-Fi,' Marie explains. 'Oh dear, bit of a hangover on Monday morning – that's right, I remember that now – and would you be free for a quick ring sometime? *Sorry*, you reply. *Bit busy at the moment. Maybe we can catch up later in the week.*'

'No,' Bella says, jerking her head up. 'I'd never say that. He knows I wouldn't.'

'Yes, he did think that was a bit strange.' Marie nods. 'Let me see . . . *Are you OK, Mum? You seem weird* . . . and then a bit later we've got *Please Mum, just give me a quick call. Let me know you're OK. That stuff you were spouting on Facebook last night kind of freaked me out* . . . Oh yes, and this is my favourite: *WTAF Mum? Have you been taking something?* He's perceptive, isn't he? Not so sure about the language though. I had to look that one up.' She scrolls down with her finger. '*Please Mum, I'm really starting to worry here. You won't answer my calls and that emergency number you gave me doesn't work. Who is this Nat you keep posting about? Where does he live? How come I've never heard of him?*' Marie's face hardens. '*Because I'm ashamed,*' she reads. 'That's what your reply says. *He was the nicest, sweetest boy in the whole world and I treated him like he was nothing. I destroyed him. I see that now. That's why I need to make amends. To put things right.*'

'He'll see through it,' says Bella, feeling sick. 'He'll know it wasn't me.'

'That's not what his voicemail messages suggest.'

'No,' Bella cries. 'What have you done? Please,' she begs, 'I'm all he's got. Let me talk to him. Let me explain. Let me hear his voice.'

Marie smiles. 'Of course. I thought you'd never ask.' She moves her finger over the screen, swiping and pressing and . . .

Asher!

'Please, Mum,' he says, his voice tight and pleading. 'I don't know what else to do. If I don't hear from you by tonight, I'm coming out there.'

'No,' Bella says as if he's still there on the other end of the phone. As if he can actually hear her. 'Don't do that. Promise me you won't do that. It's not safe. Call Aunty Rachel and tell her what's happened. Show her the messages on your phone. Ask her to call the police. But whatever you do, don't come here.' Her voice breaks as she pleads with him, gulping sobs catching in the rawness of her throat. 'Please, Asher . . . please, Marie,' she says. 'I'm begging you, mother to mother.'

Marie's smile is gone, her lip curling up in a vicious, angry sneer. 'How dare you?' she hisses. 'You don't *deserve* to be a mother.' She slips the phone back into her pocket and breathes into Bella's face. 'He could have picked anybody. Any girl would have been lucky to have him. He could have *been* anybody,' she says, flecks of spit escaping from her lips. 'He had his whole life ahead of him. Until he met *you*.'

'I'm sorry. I'm so sorry. I never meant to hurt him. I was young. I didn't know what I was doing. I didn't think . . .' Bella's gabbling now, the words tumbling out over each other. 'Please, Marie. You're right. He was too good for me. He was too good then and he's too good now. He deserves someone better.'

'Yes. But you're the one he wants,' Marie says as if Nat's still capable of wanting anything. 'And a mother will do anything for her child. You know that.'

'Not *anything*, no. Not that.'

'Don't worry,' Marie says. 'I'll make sure it's painless. It'll be like falling asleep. And when you wake up, you'll be together again. You and Nat, reunited at last . . . and on the anniversary of his death too. It's almost like the universe planned it.'

'But . . . but what about Stuart?' Bella's voice is growing higher and higher with panic. 'W-what about the retreat? No one will want to come and stay here after . . .' She can't even bring herself to finish the sentence.

'The retreat was a means to an end,' says Marie simply. 'Stuart too. He thinks grief is something you can meditate away. He thinks loss is a state of mind.'

Bella can hardly take in what she's hearing. Is Marie saying she only married Stuart for *this*? For the chance to torture her son's ex-girlfriend for a week and then . . .? How long has she been planning it for? How far back does this craziness go?

'I came here as a guest,' Marie continues, as if in answer to Bella's unspoken questions. 'That's how we first met. I was still trying to fill the hole inside me after Nat. Still hoping this New Age mumbo jumbo might help. Then when I met Stuart, I thought *he* might be the answer. I thought *this* – this place, this *life* – might be the answer. And for a while I genuinely believed it was. I really thought I'd moved on.' She laughs a bitter laugh. 'Moved on! As if I could ever move on from losing my boy. My baby. What kind of a mother would that make me? But then I received an email, out of the blue, from the young man who'd bought Nat's flat after his slum landlord sold up. A nice young man who managed to track me down through Facebook. He said he'd found a box of personal letters belonging to Nat that had fallen down inside the loft space, and did I want them sending on? Letters to one Isabella Burnstone, returned to sender, and a diary . . .'

Marie pauses for a moment, as if she's lost in her own memories, and then laughs that tight, bitter laugh again. 'It's amazing how easy it is to track someone down through social media these days, isn't it? What's even more impressive is how closely it allows you to target a particular market . . . It took a while to hook her in, but I got there in the end.'

A particular market? You mean, Rachel, don't you? thinks Bella.

I thought of you as soon as I saw it. That's what her sister had said when Bella rang to thank her for the birthday present. *I read all about it in this blog post someone had shared, by a writer whose daughter had just left home. She said it helped her get over her empty nest syndrome and free up her creativity . . . it's like the universe was telling me to book it for you!*

Marie knew her market all right, Bella thinks, as another piece

292

of the story falls into place. And she already knows how the *rest* of the story goes. How it's *supposed* to go. But it's not finished yet – there's still a chance to change the ending. She *has* to find a way. 'What about Lena?' she asks, desperately trying to prove to Marie how flawed her plan is. 'And Ludwell? You can't stick a needle in *him* and pretend it's an accidental overdose. Julia would see through that in a second. She knows her husband.' *Apart from the night he's kept secret all these years. The night he's still denying now.*

'Of course she would,' Marie agrees. 'But it won't *be* an overdose. It'll be an accident. You'll spike him by mistake as he tries to wrestle the needle from you, like a hero, trying to save you from yourself. And then when his heart gives out and you find yourself with the guilt of his death on your hands, there's only one way left. A final note to your beloved son, confessing everything, and then off you go . . . As for Lena, well, she drowned, didn't she? You already know that. A night-time walk to clear her migraine that went tragically wrong, and an equally tragic mix-up in communication that meant nobody realised she was missing. And if the police don't buy it, well . . . that's a price I'm willing to pay for bringing you and Nat back together at last.'

'No,' says Bella. 'I won't do it.'

'Oh but you will,' says Marie softly. 'You will if you want to keep your precious boy safe. You heard what he said – he's on his way here now. And it's up to you what kind of reception he gets when he arrives. If you're a good girl, I'll look after him properly. I'll make sure he's safe. But if you're not . . .'

The unspoken threat feels like a noose tightening round Bella's neck, squeezing the air out of her throat until she can barely breathe. *No. Not Asher. Please no.*

Chapter 39

Bella's out of ideas. She's tried begging. She's tried pleading. She's tried shouting for Rosel – for anyone – to help, receiving a sharp blow to the cheek and more veiled threats against Asher for her trouble. She's tried telling Marie that she'll never get away with it, that this isn't what Nat would have wanted. But it's no good. Marie's beyond reason. And Bella? Bella's beyond help now. Beyond hope. She can't run – Marie's made sure of that – and she can't fight. And she can't risk anything happening to Asher. He could be on his way here right now, with no idea what he's walking into . . .

Bella says nothing as Marie disappears again, returning shortly afterwards with a black lacquered box. What *can* she say? Her mind feels like it's shutting down already of its own accord, her thoughts retreating to a single point: Asher.

It's Asher she's thinking of as Marie unties the rope binding her feet to the bed. As she reties it around Bella's ankles, shackling them together to keep her from running. It's Asher she's holding on to as Marie frees her wrists and drags her over to the desk. As she pushes Bella down onto the chair with another warning not to try anything – not if she wants to keep her precious son safe – presenting her with a sheet of her own manuscript paper and a pen. As she tells her what to write. *Dear Asher . . .*

But the words Bella copies down in her shaky handwriting aren't the words in her head. The suicide note Marie dictates as she remakes the bed with the fresh sheet bears no relation to the outpouring of love in Bella's mind.

I love you so much I don't know where to begin. You're everything to me, Asher. You always were and you always will be. From the moment I felt you kicking inside me I knew you were special. I knew I'd do anything to protect you. To keep you safe. And I'm sorry if I've been too overprotective at times, if I've slowed you down with my worries and fears. I've only ever wanted what's best for you. You deserve the best, my sweet, funny, caring boy. You deserve a long, happy life filled with love in whatever form that takes. You deserve every drop of happiness going, which means no looking back. No sadness. No blame.

I couldn't be prouder of you if I tried, Bella thinks, tears rolling down her cheeks. At least she got to tell him that part in person. In amongst all her last-minute neuroticism over leaving him to fend for himself for twelve weeks, at least she managed to tell him that. And now she's leaving him to fend for himself forever . . .

This isn't a scene from your film, she can still hear him saying. *I'm not going to get poisoned, or stabbed, or clubbed over the head with a walking stick.*

'It's not a walking stick,' she whispers as if he's right there with her now. 'It's an orthopaedic cane.'

This isn't a scene from your film, she hears him say again, louder this time, his voice echoing inside her head. He's right. The film ends with the heroine forced to make a choice – save the baby in the car or save herself. But she refuses to play by the killer's rules. Refuses to make that choice. And it pays off. In the film she gets to save the baby *and* live.

Bella's heart is pounding as she thinks of the knife waiting in the drawer beside her. Is it still there or will Marie have searched the room while she was out cold? If it *is*, there's a chance she can get out of this alive, but if it's not . . . if Marie guesses what she's up to and makes good on her threat to hurt Asher then . . . no, Bella doesn't even want to *think* about that option. It's too much of a risk.

But the Asher voice in her head isn't giving up so easily. *Promise me you'll make the most of this holiday*, she hears him saying now. *No changing your mind and checking out halfway through.*

I'm not checking out. I don't have a choice.

But she does. There's always a choice.

Promise me, Asher repeats. *Swear on Aunty Rachel's bird tattoo.*

Bella misspells the next word on purpose – writes 'conscious' instead of 'conscience' and makes a show of scribbling it out. 'I'm so sorry,' she says. 'I'll start again. I've got some paper here somewhere . . .'

Please let the knife be there, she prays as she opens the drawer beside her. As she reaches underneath the pamphlet.

'No,' says Marie. '*I'll* get it.'

Too late. Bella's shaking fingers are already closing round the handle.

She whips the knife out of its hiding place with a wild, animal roar. The roar of a lioness protecting her cubs. And now she's up on her feet, swinging round, knife first, in a rush of adrenaline. 'You hurt my boy and you'll know about it,' she screams, thrusting blindly.

Another scream – a scream of pain – and Marie crumples in front of her.

*

Blood. So much blood.

Bella leans over the prostrate figure on the floor, her own body trembling with shock.

What have I done?

'Can you hear me?' she asks. 'Marie?'

There's no answer.

'I'm going to get help,' Bella says, cutting through the rope around her ankles with the bloodstained knife. 'It's going to be okay,' she says as she reaches into Marie's pocket to retrieve her phone, trying not to look at the gush of red pumping out of her. Trying not to faint or throw up as she dials 112. Hopefully there'll be enough connection on one of the networks to get through. Yes, it's ringing. It's ringing. But the call cuts out again before anyone answers. *Outside*, she thinks. *Outside might be better.*

'I'll be back,' she promises as she staggers to the door, the room spinning and twisting around her as she fumbles for the latch. But Bella pushes on through the dizziness. This is no time to faint.

The white walls of the corridor swim and bend as she lurches towards the door leading back into the main area of the lodge. *Almost there.*

The main reception room is deserted. The only sound is of Bella's own heart thumping in her chest, her ragged breath echoing in her skull. *Not much further.*

For a moment Bella thinks she sees him, outlined through the mottled glass panel beside the front door. *Nat.* Poor dead Nat, with his baby blonde hair, peering back through the glass at her. But it's not Nat. It's a man with a gun.

Chapter 40

'There's someone here to see you,' says the nurse on Monday afternoon.

'Asher!' Bella can't believe it. Even as she folds him into her arms and squeezes him tight, it still feels like a dream. 'Oh my goodness,' she breathes. 'When did you get here? *How* did you get here?'

'On a plane,' he says, pulling away and grinning back at her. 'How do you think?'

'But . . .'

'I'm eighteen years old, Mum. I know how to book a flight and pack my rucksack.'

'Of course you do, that's not what I meant. I just . . . Oh, I can't believe you're actually here.' The voicemail message Asher had left before – the message Marie had played Bella in an attempt to blackmail her into cooperating – hadn't been a real message at all. He'd already confirmed that much during their tearful phone call on Saturday. It was a fake – a clever piecing together of bits of other recordings to make it sound like he was coming out to Sweden to find her, heading straight into Marie's trap. And yet here he is. There's no trap this time though. No danger. Just too-tight hugs and more embarrassing mum tears. Yes, Bella's crying already.

'Someone's got to look after you,' Asher jokes, but Bella can hear the fear behind his laugh. Can see the tears gathering in his eyes too. 'All that talk you gave me about keeping out of trouble,' he says, 'and look at you. One week on your own, without me to keep you in check, and you end up in hospital.' His voice breaks and he wipes at his cheek with the flat of his hand.

'Shh,' she says, folding him back into her arms. 'It's all right. I'm fine now. I'm safe. It's over.'

It was all over from the moment Bella stepped – fell, rather – through the front doorway of the lodge. It had felt like a miracle at the time, to find the policeman waiting there before she'd even managed to call for help. But it wasn't a miracle, it was Asher. It was Asher's call to his Aunty Rachel in California to tell her about the weird, worrying messages he'd been getting. It was Rachel's panicked call to the Swedish police, throwing in words like 'drugs' and 'suicidal' to get their attention, begging them to send someone down to Dödmansskogen and find out what was happening. And what they found, once they went in, was a woman in her early sixties with a non-fatal stab wound to the chest, a man in his mid-fifties with trauma to the head and eye in a narcotic stupor, and a black lacquered box of Schedule 1 class drugs. And Bella, of course. But they'd already found her.

'Seriously, Mum,' says Asher. 'What were you thinking? Drugs? A knife attack? This isn't your film, you know. What next? A walking stick to the head?'

Bella laughs. 'I told you,' she murmurs into his hair, squeezing him even tighter. 'It's not a walking stick, it's an orthopaedic cane.'

*

Asher waits outside while Bella pops in to say goodbye to Ludwell. She still hasn't plucked up the courage to tell her son the truth – to tell him who his father is and why she's kept them apart all this time – but she will. She's told him everything else. She's told him about Nat and Marie. About the retreat . . . the whole sorry mess. And when they get back, she'll tell him about Ludwell too. No more secrets.

'Hi,' she says, nodding to Julia who'd flown straight back out to be with her husband when she heard what had happened. 'How are you feeling?'

Ludwell attempts a smile. The bruising round his eye and across his face is still pretty shocking, but it's a relief to see him sitting up and talking. He's going to be okay – no lasting damage – that's what they told Bella.

'All the better for getting out of that place,' he says. 'Thank you.'

'Me?' Bella smiles back at him. 'I didn't do anything. I just collapsed on the front doorstep and let the police take care of everything else.'

'No,' says Ludwell. 'They told me what you did. Thank you,' he says again, as if stabbing someone in the chest with a kitchen knife is a *good* thing.

'I just want to try and forget it now. Put the whole crazy mess behind me and move on.'

It's true. After everything that's happened, the next chapter of Bella's life feels like child's play. Twelve weeks without Asher – less than that now by the time he gets back to uni – feels like nothing compared to what she's been through. He's an adult, he's ready to move on, and it's Bella's time to move on too. It's time to focus on her career – on finishing that symphony and making the most of the growing buzz around *The Screaming Hours*. It's time to focus on herself. That doesn't mean she has to stop being a mother. It doesn't mean she has to stop caring or worrying. That comes with the territory, along with loving your children unconditionally and teaching them how to cook a proper omelette. It's a shift in their relationship, that's all. Not a full stop.

'And how's your son?' Ludwell asks her. *Your* son, Bella notes sadly. Not *our* son. 'He must have been worried when he heard what had happened.'

'He's okay, I think,' Bella says. 'I hope. He's outside now if you wanted to meet him . . . no pressure . . . I haven't told him anything yet. About you, I mean.'

Ludwell shakes his head. 'There's nothing to tell. I'm sorry, Bella. He's not my son. He can't be. And nothing happened that night, I swear. Not because I didn't want it to,' he says, with an apologetic glance towards Julia, 'but you practically passed out after I kissed you in the hall. You could barely make it up the stairs. I was a cheating shit back then, there's no denying that – and not for the last time either, I'm ashamed to admit – but I wasn't a monster. I let you sleep it off in our bed while I spent the night downstairs on the sofa. I don't know who Asher's father is, but it's not me. Even if we had . . . you know . . . it still wouldn't be me. *I'm* the reason Julia and I couldn't have children of our own.'

Bella blinks. *No, that can't be right. It* has *to be you, otherwise* . . .

'I know I should have handled things better when you came to see me afterwards,' Ludwell goes on, 'at the house, and then again in my office. I should have explained there and then instead of threatening you. But I was scared. It's no excuse, I know that, but it's the truth. I was scared of what would happen if the university got wind of it – scared of *Julia* finding out. I just wanted it all to go away – I wanted *you* to go away. And you did. Until this week . . . *That's* why you looked so familiar. I don't know why I didn't make the connection before. I'm guessing you remembered me from the off though?'

Bella's too busy wrestling with this new information to answer. Too busy trying to recalibrate the last nineteen years of her life. Is it true? The reason she can't remember what happened that night is because nothing *did* happen? But that means . . . it means . . . *Nat. Asher's father is Nat.* She sways on the spot as her legs turn to water beneath her. *How can she have got it so wrong?* She and Nat always used protection, but it must have failed. It must have been that night he came to see her at university . . . *It was him all along.*

'Are you okay?' Ludwell asks.

'Here, sit down,' says Julia, jumping up to help her into a chair. 'You look like you're going to faint.'

Bella lowers her head towards her lap, remembering Marie's advice. Not that she wants to think about Marie. She doesn't want to think about *any* of it any more. But Marie is Asher's grandmother. They share the same DNA. There's no escaping that. How different might their lives have been if the truth had come out nineteen years ago? Not just hers and Asher's, but Nat's too. Maybe he'd still be alive today . . . and Marie . . .

'Mum?'

Bella turns to see Asher in the doorway, his face creased with worry.

'I'm all right,' she tells him, forcing a smile. 'Just a bit dizzy, that's all. Could you get me a bar of chocolate from the vending machine downstairs?'

'Sure,' he says. 'I'll be as quick as I can.'

'Thank you. Oh and Asher?'

'Yes?'

'I love you,' she says.

'I know. That must be the seven-hundredth time you've told me that since I got here.' He rolls his eyes and grins. 'And I love you too.'

'You've got yourself a fine boy, there,' says Ludwell after Asher's gone. 'Any man would be proud to call himself his father, I'm sure.'

'Yes,' agrees Bella. 'But he doesn't need a father. He's got me.'

'I'd be happy to take a DNA test if you still don't believe me,' Ludwell adds.

Bella looks at his heavyset nose and narrow-set blue eyes. She looks at his squared chin and straight hair . . . at the face that bears no relation whatsoever to her son's. And then she thinks about Nat, forcing herself to remember. The hair's different of course, but the button nose is the same. The same low forehead and the barely there ear lobes. She's already got her answer. 'No, there's no need for that,' she says. 'I believe you.' She can almost see it now – can see Ludwell laying her down in the bed and pulling the duvet up around her neck. Can see him pausing in the doorway to look at her before he switches off the light. Can see herself waking up in the night, hot and dizzy, pulling off her dress and tossing it onto the floor before she slips back into a drunken sleep. Maybe they're real memories, finally resurfacing after all these years. Or maybe they're just her brain's way of making sense of it all. It hardly matters either way. It's too late to change the mistakes of the past. All she can do now is look to the future.

*

'Are you okay? Is the chocolate helping?' Asher asks as they head for the lift.

'Much better, thanks,' Bella tells him, through a mouthful of KitKat – her favourite. Asher knows her too well.

'And how's your friend doing?'

'He'll be fine,' says Bella. 'He's not really a friend as such. I met him a couple of times when I was younger but . . .' But nothing. 'Listen,' she tells him. Now isn't the time or the place, but maybe it never will be. 'I've been meaning to talk to you about your father. It's something I should have talked to you about a long time ago.'

'You did,' Asher reminds her. 'You said I didn't need a dad. You said you loved me enough for two parents put together. For *three* parents.'

'I know, and it's true. I couldn't love you any more if I tried. But you must want to know where you come from. Who you are.'

'I've waited this long, I can wait a bit longer,' he tells her, pressing the button for the ground floor. 'Until you're fully recovered. Besides, I know exactly who I am. The son of a drugged-up knife fiend who's weirdly obsessed with orthopaedic canes. Not to be confused with walking sticks,' he adds with a grin.

Bella grins back at him. Motherhood's all about smiles – she knows that as well as anyone. She's done the long, sleepless nights, listening for the sound of his key in the lock. She's served her time with mouldering food left on messy floors and grunting taxi-service pick-ups at two o'clock in the morning. She's dealt with sharp, thoughtless words and slammed doors, with embarrassed public brush-offs and bare-faced lies. With two broken wing-mirrors and three smashed phones. But it all fades away to nothing – every single time – in the wake of that cheeky, lopsided smile.

'I don't know what the difference is either,' she tells him. 'Maybe it's like hamsters and hamstrings.'

'I guess it must be,' he says.

Epilogue

Everyone's turned out for the book launch: Krista, Hamar, T, Ludwell and Julia. And Oscar, of course. Everyone's here except for Lena.

Bella wasn't sure whether to come at first – wasn't sure if it was a good idea to dredge up the nightmare of Dödmansskogen again – but Oscar had proved surprisingly persuasive.

'It's so good to see you,' says Krista.

'You too,' says Bella. 'Thank you again for your letter. How are you doing now?' It's been six months since the police arrested one of Krista's neighbours for drink driving. Six months since the same neighbour – a waitress at the local Danish café – broke down under questioning, confessing to a fatal hit-and-run in the same spot years before.

'Better,' Krista says. 'It's been good to finally get some closure. To get justice. But what about you? How are you doing now? I still feel terrible about what happened. About leaving you like that.'

'You weren't to know,' Bella tells her. 'No one could have guessed what Marie was planning. I feel sorry for her really.' It's true. Bella's still got her son and her life, while Marie *got* life – life imprisonment – for killing Lena, and nothing can ever bring *her* son back.

'It's Lena I still feel bad about,' says T, lowering his voice as a group of women pass by clutching books and wineglasses. 'If *I* hadn't been there she wouldn't have been poking around in the first place. She wouldn't have found Marie's notebook and then . . . Well, she'd still be here, wouldn't she?'

Bella lays a hand on his elbow. 'It wasn't your fault. You can't blame yourself. If *I* could go back and do it all differently, I would, of course I would, but the past is the past. Raking over it doesn't help anyone in the long run.'

'Except for Oscar,' says Hamar, grinning.

Bella smiles back at him. 'Well yes, apart from Oscar. And Stuart, from what I hear. Apparently bookings went through the roof after the trial, after he and Rosel were acquitted of any involvement. Any *conscious* involvement anyway – Stuart clearly didn't know what was in that coffee he brought me, or what Marie was planning.' She shakes her head in wonder. 'You'd think it would put people off, wouldn't you, knowing what had happened there? It would certainly put *me* off, but I guess it holds a kind of morbid fascination for true-crime fans. As I say, the retreat's never been more popular.'

'Or maybe word got out about Saga's incredible cooking,' says Hamar, who's clearly moved on, judging by the way he's been looking at his date all night.

'How's your son doing now, Bella?' Krista asks, changing the subject.

'Really well, thank you. He's halfway through his third year at university now. I can't believe how quickly it's gone. He's started applying for graduate jobs already. How about your family? How are the twins?'

Krista rolls her eyes. 'The terrible twins? They're hard work – *very* hard work. It takes me a full day to recover after I've been looking after them.' And then her face softens. 'But I wouldn't have it any other way.' She turns with a smile to Ludwell and Julia, who've finally extricated themselves from the gaggle of Ludwell's fans over by the door. 'Hi there. How are you two doing?'

'We're good,' says Julia, squeezing her ex-husband's hand. 'We're not together any more but we're in a good place, aren't we?'

Ludwell nods. 'Absolutely. Nothing like a bit of quality time out in the wilderness to put things in perspective.' He's about to say something more but Oscar's agent is tapping her pen against the side of her wineglass, calling them all to attention.

'Ladies and gentlemen,' she begins, 'it gives me great pleasure to introduce our star of the evening, Oscar Wildman. With a name like that I think he was always destined to become a writer, don't you?'

Everybody laughs.

'Oscar's going to be reading from his chilling debut novel, *Dead Man's Forest*, which was inspired, as I'm sure you know, by his time at a real-life retreat in Sweden. Rights to the book have been sold in over thirty territories across the globe, and rights for the film version were recently sold for a record figure. But that's enough from me, I'll let the star of the show take it from here . . .'

*

'Wow! I had no idea you were so good,' Krista confesses, when Oscar joins them afterwards. 'That was amazing.'

'Yes,' Bella agrees. 'Congratulations. And congratulations on the film deal too.'

'Thank you,' says Oscar. 'I'll be putting in a good word with the director, obviously, if it ever gets made. I'll tell him I know the perfect composer to do the score.'

Bella laughs. 'I'll have to see if I can fit it into my busy schedule.' The commissions are coming from all directions these days.

'Cheers to that,' says Hamar and everyone clinks their glasses together. 'To Oscar and his surprisingly good novel and to Bella and her creepy music career. And to absent friends,' he adds. 'To Lena.'

'To Lena,' everyone echoes. The mood turns serious and sad again. But not for long.

'To the sequel,' says Oscar with a wink, holding up his glass a second time. 'Who's for a return trip?'

For a moment Bella's back there again, back in the silent wilderness of Dead Man's Forest, staring down into the icy depths of the lake. But only for a moment.

'No chance,' she tells Oscar. 'You're on your own there.'

A Letter from Jennifer

Thank you so much for choosing to read *The Wilderness Retreat*. I hope you enjoyed it! If you did and would like to be the first to know about my new releases, you can follow me on Twitter/Facebook/Instagram/my website below.

I'd like to think it's purely coincidental that I started writing this book a few months after my youngest left for university, but who knows? While my own experience was very different to Bella's, the sudden switch to an 'empty nest' can be a pivotal moment of readjustment in much the same way as becoming a parent for the first time.

The subsequent events of the novel are *entirely* fictional, thankfully, but both the setting and Bella's musical background were partly influenced by my own experience. Like Bella, I played a lot of music when I was younger, taking part in various festivals, competitions and orchestra tours, although I attended the Royal Academy of Music on Saturdays rather than the Royal College. I don't miss the nerves associated with standing up on stage to perform a solo in front of a roomful of strangers, but it's turned out to be good practice for author readings!

Having lived in Norway as a young child, I'm a big fan of

all things Scandinavian (with the possible exception of salted liquorice!) and have always enjoyed my visits to Sweden. It seemed like the perfect setting for my retreat. I've never been as far north as the fictional Dödmansskogen but am looking forward to remedying that one day.

I hope you loved *The Wilderness Retreat* and if you did I would be so grateful if you would leave a review. I always love to hear what readers thought, and it helps new readers discover my books too.

Thanks,
Jennifer

https://twitter.com/JennyWriteMoore
https://www.facebook.com/JennyMooreWriter
https://www.instagram.com/jennymoorewrites/
http://jennifermoore.wordpress.com

The Woman Before

A perfect home

When Fern and Paul move into the large, old house on
Crenellation Lane, with beautiful high ceilings and a luscious
garden, they think they've found their dream home. After
the devastating loss of Fern's twin sister, it will be a fresh
start and somewhere to raise their first baby.

A destructive obsession

But as soon as they arrive, Fern starts having terrifying nightmares about the woman who lived there before. When the
woman showed Fern around, they bonded over their pregnancies.
Now, Fern can't let her go. Does she have something to do with
the strange things happening in the house? Paul fears his wife has
relapsed, obsessing in the same way she did with her twin.

A fatal secret

Fern questions the neighbours about the previous owner, but
nobody wants to talk. It's like the woman never even existed.
Refusing to give up, Fern uncovers a shocking secret and now
suddenly her whole family is in danger . . .

Acknowledgements

The Wilderness Retreat wouldn't be the book it is today without the expert guidance and enthusiasm of my amazing editors, Rebecca Jamieson and Abigail Fenton. Thank you for steering me through the various drafts and ensuring Bella's story stayed on track. And thank you to the rest of the HQ team for your book wizardry – the transformation from words on my computer screen to a finished book with a fantastic cover is pure magic.

Talking of magic brings me to my next big thank you: I'm enormously grateful to all the fabulous Write Magic Zoom sprinters who've kept me smiling throughout the writing process, from that first Nano-style dash to the final edits. Thank you for the fun, friendship and collective inspiration. It's been an excitingly hectic time, juggling a variety of writing projects, and it's been lovely to share the journey with you.

Tusen takk to my dad for all your help with the Swedish phrases (any remaining mistakes are entirely mine) and to all my family and friends for your ongoing support and encouragement.

Special thanks, too, to The Ivybridge Bookshop for everything you do to support local writers, and to all the fabulous book bloggers, book tweeters, and word-of-mouth book-sharers for your help in getting my books out there. I really appreciate it.

And last, but by no means least, I'd like to thank the three special people to whom this book is dedicated: Dafydd, Lucy and Dan. Thank you for everything.

Dear Reader,

We hope you enjoyed reading this book. If you did, we'd be so appreciative if you left a review. It really helps us and the author to bring more books like this to you.

Here at HQ Digital we are dedicated to publishing fiction that will keep you turning the pages into the early hours. Don't want to miss a thing? To find out more about our books, promotions, discover exclusive content and enter competitions you can keep in touch in the following ways:

JOIN OUR COMMUNITY:

Sign up to our new email newsletter:
http://smarturl.it/SignUpHQ

Read our new blog www.hqstories.co.uk

🐦 https://twitter.com/HQStories

📘 www.facebook.com/HQStories

BUDDING WRITER?

We're also looking for authors to join the HQ Digital family!
Find out more here:

https://www.hqstories.co.uk/want-to-write-for-us/

Thanks for reading, from the HQ Digital team